TRUTH
CURSED

TRUTH CURSED

ANGIE DICKINSON

To Liam, Elena, Evangeline, and Rosalie.
For truly bringing me more joy than I could ever express,
this book is for you.
Also, in the spirit of honoring the Truth . . .
I am the Tooth Fairy.

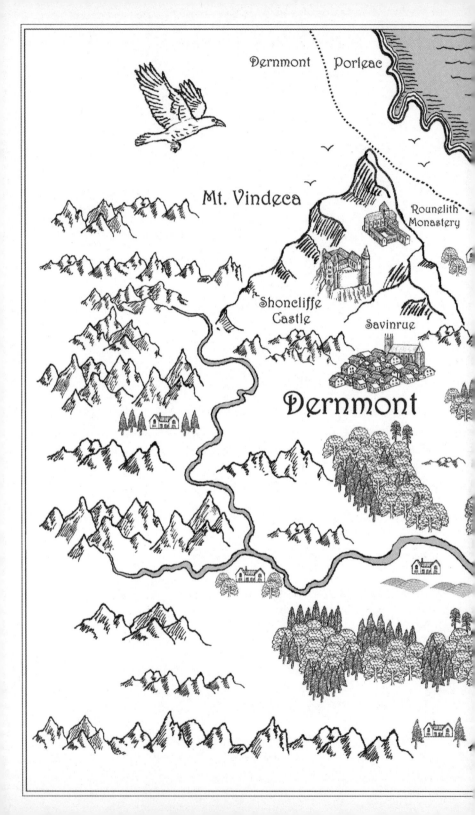

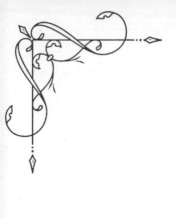

PART
ONE

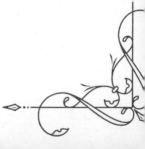

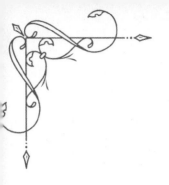
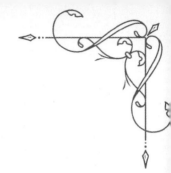

1

I WAS ONLY EIGHT YEARS OLD when my aunts cursed me. It was, in my opinion, an extreme punishment for cutting Aunt Fenella's corset stays and hiding biscuits in my room. Seven years later, standing on the doorstep of the worst place in the world for an oddity like me, I vehemently maintained that view. And I would tell the same to anyone who asked me, because I was physically incapable of telling a lie.

Perhaps cursed was a strong word, but it was the one I'd adopted in the beginning. Fighting against the affliction of forced honesty with every atom of my energetic little body, I'd called it what it was. A curse.

They meant well, I supposed. I glanced back at my aunts' retreating carriage as it trundled away from the finishing school where they'd deposited me. Moral zeal might account for any number of atrocities. Good intentions, and all that.

The conveyance swayed out of sight down the lamplit, rain-slicked street, like a lumbering, glistening spider. Good riddance.

Shifting in my too-tight boots, I looked nervously up at the neatly painted door in front of me. I pulled my hood over my head and made sure that no black strands had escaped my braid. The rain-streaked plaque beside the door gleamed in the light of the oil lamp that hung over it, heralding *Miss Tepsom's School for Gently Bred Young Ladies*. I shook my head at the doomed venture I was about to embark on, and pulled the bell.

The tones echoed inside, followed by a brisk click of heels. The door was opened by a petite blonde housemaid, a good three inches shorter than I. She stepped back without a word and held the door open for me. I entered and stood on a braided mat in a darkly paneled foyer. The maid closed the door behind me and looked up at me expectantly, still saying nothing. I did not know what to do. I stared back, feeling large and out of place. After a long moment, the maid twitched her pert nose, then turned on her heel and walked across the foyer and through a doorway directly ahead.

I could not stand in the foyer indefinitely, so I followed. The door led into a short, narrow hall with a closed door at the end of it. The maid rapped sharply on the door, then entered without waiting for an answer. She strode into the room, and I hovered in the doorway.

The room was an office. A small fire crackled in a grate, with two striped armchairs and a tea table before it. A woman sat at a desk by the window, and did not look up when we entered. The fire instantly made me feel a surge of relief; perhaps the headmistress would not be a chilly dragon like Aunt Fenella, whose hearth was always cold and swept. The lady behind the desk betrayed nothing dragonish in her appearance, anyway. Gently parted brown hair was pulled away from a thin face, and her eyes were narrowed at a sheet of paper that she inspected with the help of a quizzing glass on a chain.

The blonde maid cleared her throat rather ostentatiously, and I inched further into the room.

"Yes. Thank you, Iris," the woman said patiently, and the maid left without a word. The woman set the paper down on her desk, covered it with another sheet, and tapped the quizzing glass against her palm as she squinted over at me.

"Well, don't just lurk near the door, child, come here," she directed in the same patient tone. I approached her desk, happy to receive some instruction. "Which one are you?" she asked, inspecting me from head to toe.

"Cressida Hoth, ma'am." I bobbed an awkward curtsy in case it was the thing to do. I had never curtsied before, so a nervous laugh bubbled into my throat, but thankfully did not escape. I was anxious to make a better impression on this woman than I had made on the aunts when I'd first met them. I would prefer not to be cursed a second time.

"And are you pleased to be here, Cressida?" the woman asked, startling me with a question that seemed beyond formalities.

"Not really pleased yet, ma'am." The truth popped out immediately, as it always did. I suppressed a wince.

She contemplated me for a long moment without responding. Her pale blue eyes looked tired. "I am Miss Tepsom," she said finally. "I hope you will be pleased eventually." She still did not smile, and I thought her tone a little dry, but I felt relieved that she had not asked me anything else, yet.

My palms began sweating inside my secondhand gloves.

Miss Tepsom rose to her feet. "Do you have better-fitting clothes in that portmanteau?"

My cloak was too short and barely closed over a dress that stretched tightly across my chest. "No, ma'am." The curse didn't make me embellish, but nerves did. "Aunt Millicent says there is little point in buying me new clothes when I grow an inch every other day."

I took serious umbrage with Aunt Millicent's logic, and clearly, so did Miss Tepsom. She regarded me with undisguised disapproval. I chose not to add that my parents had left me very little money, as the aunts frequently reminded me, and most of it was now invested in my education, rather than a well-fitting wardrobe. Miss Tepsom's next words indicated that she had read between the lines.

"My school is an exclusive one," she said. "You will notice that its very name evokes the sort of young lady I welcome here.

Your guardians managed to convince me that you qualify. I confess I feel some reservations, but I believe in giving a person a chance. And you? Now that you're here, how do you feel?"

My breath caught in my chest, and I waited, hoping desperately that she would complete the question with *about being here*, or something specific. Questions were my bane, but personal, open-ended questions were my ruin. She said nothing more, only watched me expectantly as familiar symptoms slowly crawled over me.

My honest, undignified response floated to the forefront of my brain, trying to push its way past my lips. With the slightest resistance, my head began to pound, my windpipe closed, and spots danced at the corners of my vision as no oxygen was allowed to pass into my lungs. The truth would choke me if it wasn't set free.

Only once, I'd pushed past the initial, terrifying symptoms and refused to answer my aunts. I'd uncontrollably thrashed and seized, then blood oozed from my nose as I'd finally passed out from lack of oxygen. This resulted in a splitting headache and weakness for hours afterward, and I'd seen true fear in my aunts' eyes as they instructed me to never try to withhold the truth again, lest it cost me my life.

This wasn't worth such a risk. But I almost would have preferred to pass out than utter the words that burst forth in a mortified rush.

"I feel frightened, exhausted, and sad that the aunts have given me up, even if I do hate the sight of them." The words continued to spill out of my unwilling mouth. Apparently, I felt a lot. "I feel hot and itchy and achy, my backside hurts from the coach, I am hungry and thirsty, I have cramps from trapped wind, and I've a terrible need to use a privy. Ma'am."

The added formality at the end of my indecent speech only seemed to intensify the extreme impropriety of the rest of it. Miss Tepsom's mouth dropped slightly open, and I wondered if it was too late to run down the street and catch my aunts' carriage before it left the city. I was a fairly fast runner.

"Well," she finally said with a touch of severity. "I suppose I *did* ask. I can see immediately that you do not suit. But you are here to be finished properly, and I am not one to shirk a challenge. If you tend toward recalcitrance, I will not be giving any second chances, Cressida Hoth. Consider this your only warning."

I blinked away tears of shame. I'd embarrassed myself hundreds of times, but it never got any easier.

"Classes begin tomorrow, and you may take the rest of the evening to settle in. Your background is humble, but respectable. However, you have an air of a churlish country calf about you, and will have to work very hard to acquire the genteel sheen possessed by my other students. I have no qualms about sending you home if you do not adapt." Miss Tepsom looked directly at me. "Is that understood?"

"Yes, ma'am," I answered quickly.

"Iris will show you to your room."

I ducked my head to hide my burning cheeks and turned to scurry out the door.

"Oh, and Miss Hoth?"

I turned back miserably.

"The privy is down the hall and to the left."

⬦ ·· ———————— ·· ⬦

After a relieving visit to the tiny privy, I followed Iris back down the hallway and through another door to the right of the foyer. It led down another hallway, with a staircase at the end. The drafty house was all paneled in the same dark wood, and our heels echoed as we walked; I had yet to see a rug or carpet upon the floors. Nothing hung on the walls. I set my jaw and clutched my portmanteau as I followed, determined to pretend my first meeting with Miss Tepsom had not been a devastating humiliation. We ascended the stairs that led to a narrow corridor and passed six doors before we reached one at the end of the hall.

Iris pushed the door open without knocking and waved me inside. "This is your room," she said, speaking for the first time. Her voice was surprisingly rich and elegant. She clicked away as I stepped through the door.

I had a roommate. A girl sat listlessly on one of the beds and looked up when I walked in. She was slight, with a thin face and a single dark braid over her shoulder. She looked mournfully bored.

In between the two beds, there was a small window that overlooked the street. An oil lamp sat on a table below the window, and hooks and shelves jutted from the walls. The other girl had several dresses and a cloak hanging on the hooks on her side, as well as some assorted items shoved onto the shelves.

I took off my cloak and hung it, trying not to mind the steady observation of the girl on the bed. I unpacked my portmanteau, folded up my undergarments and nightdress, and hung my spare dress on a hook. I stowed the portmanteau under my bed. After that, there was nothing left to do to keep myself busy, so I sat on the bed and met the unswerving stare of the girl across from me.

"You must be my roommate," she said, after a pause. It seemed an unnecessary observation, but conversation had to start somewhere.

"Yes," I said. I tried to infuse some pleasantness into my voice, but it sounded somewhat hollow. "I'm Cressida."

"Rubia Feldingham," she said, eyeing me. "Feldingham Fields?" I shook my head in apologetic ignorance. "Feldingham Fields are the finest," she sighed in a bored monotone. She inspected my worn boots and took in my black dress with the tight sleeves, then stared into my face. It was unsettling.

"Did you like Miss Tepsom?" she asked after a moment.

"Um, I don't know. Not really," I said.

Rubia nodded, but her dark eyes narrowed slightly.

"Why not?" she asked. I'd hoped for agreement and commiseration in return for my honesty, not more questions. A prickling feeling of dread stole over me.

"She seems severe," I answered.

"I don't like her hair," she said. I didn't answer, not sure what one should say to that. "You've got rather long hair," she added. "Is it curly?"

"A bit," I said, resisting the urge to smooth my braid.

"Mine will have to be curled when I put it up," she said sourly.

"That will be lovely," I said, anxiously hoping she would prefer to speak about herself. "When will you put it up?"

"Mother says when I am sixteen," she said darkly. "A year away." She rolled her eyes, pulled her braid forward, and retied the cream ribbon at the end with more vigor than seemed necessary.

"We're the same age, then," I said.

"Are your people well-off?" she asked boldly, now folding her hands primly in her lap.

I stared at her for so long, my cheeks burning, that my symptoms began to set in: my answer mentally blotted out all other focus, vision blackened around the edges, throat and chest tightened. I coughed through my response. "No."

"Goodness, you look ill," she remarked, looking me over like a sow at the fair. "You're rather larger than me. Mother says I am delicate, which I suppose is preferable." Her eyes glinted. "Although my brothers often said, if she'd felt the wrath of my teeth as often as they had, she'd never call me that. Do you like having a woman's shape already?" she asked abruptly.

The personal nature of her prying, and my compulsion to respond, flooded me with a fresh dousing of humiliation. My aunts had asked embarrassing questions often. I'd fervently prayed those days were behind me.

"Um . . . no. I don't know. Not really," I answered in heated confusion. "I would much rather not discuss it."

Rubia's returning expression was mutinous. "Do you—"

I suddenly felt compelled to make myself clearer. "Don't ask me questions like that again," I interrupted, abandoning all attempts at cordiality and even allowing a note of danger to creep into my tone.

Rubia slumped sullenly and twitched aside the net curtains to peek out the window.

"It's going to be awful here, and now I have a horrid roommate." She sighed.

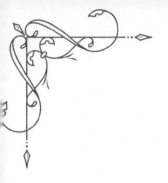
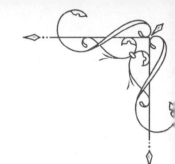

2

MY NEW SCHOOL WAS IN
the city of Savinrue, many miles to the west of the small hamlet
where I was raised by my father's sisters. The chilly autumn
morning when they had bundled me into the coach felt like days
ago, instead of mere hours. It had been easy to lose track of
time after the first hour of bone-jarring coach travel, but finally,
as the sun emerged, high and bright, the land to the north had
become level. My breath caught as the mountain was revealed.
I'd glimpsed the forbidding, impassible crags of the southern and
western ranges before, but they were nothing to Mt. Vindeca,
the emblem of Dernmont and majestic home of the royal family.

I'd barely taken in the sight of the forested slopes and
the sky-scraping, snow-capped peak before my coach was
swallowed by the city of Savinrue, nestled in a valley of Mt.
Vindeca's foothills. The city's unfamiliar closeness and activity
overwhelmed my senses. Even now, sitting in my new bedroom
past the dinner hour, the cacophonic clopping, creaking,
whirring, and shouting stacked atop each other, impossible to
distinguish. The noises bled through the chilly, thin glass of the
dormitory window.

I tried to pass the evening by taking in as much as I could see
from my window. However, as it became apparent that Rubia
could only be intimidated into silence for a short time, I left the
room to escape my roommate less than twenty minutes after
I met her.

Leaving Rubia to roll her hair in rags and keep her questions to herself, I wandered down the hall of bedrooms, counting eight doors in all, four on either side of the long hallway. I could hear the voices of young ladies through a couple of the doors, but was not ready to seek out more new acquaintances yet. I was now afraid that every person I met would bring her own special brand of torture to the conversation. Perhaps Rubia was simply trying to bypass social niceties and move on to being fast friends by asking personal questions. Maybe that's what girls our age did? I didn't know, as I hadn't had a friend in recent memory. But regardless of the secret workings of young ladies' friendships, the nature of my curse brought forth a passionate antipathy to the idea that I would have to confess intimate details about myself at the whim of another.

I quietly passed my room on my listless journey back down the bare hallway. My door was farthest from the stairs I had originally come up, but near a second staircase going down the opposite way. Hoping that this staircase would lead to a currently unoccupied part of the house, I quietly descended, lightly gliding my hand over the polished surface of the banister.

The staircase curved out into a silent hall, with a door directly opposite. I pushed the door open and stepped quietly into a large, bare room. It looked how I imagined a smallish ballroom might, with polished floors, a fireplace, and some chairs lining the walls. A piano and a harp stood at one end, with a cabinet in the corner behind them.

I walked across the room, my heels clacking against the wooden floor. I brushed past the harp and piano, which smelled of dusty wood, oil, and paper, and inspected the cabinet. It was rather like a wide wardrobe, and I wondered if it stored music books. There was a lock, so I doubted its doors would open, but I gave the brass handles at the center a tug anyway. I was surprised when they pulled open easily. It did not contain books.

It was packed full of swords.

I froze, then threw a quick glance over my shoulder. Careful not to touch any of the swords, I peered inside as closely as I could. There were three rows of them, hanging from wooden slats with holes for the blades to drop through, the slats affixed at staggered heights so that the large, round cups at the handles would not bump each other. The swords seemed to be well used, and not at all decorative. The blades shone, but the leather strips wrapped around the grips were worn, and the cups showed black spots. My knowledge of weaponry was slender, but I thought they looked like fencing swords. At eight swords to a row, there were twenty-four in all.

Blinking, I shook my head in confusion, wondering why they could possibly be needed at a school for gently bred young ladies to learn ladylike accomplishments. As I finally shut the doors and turned away from the sword case, I realized just how heavy I had been feeling since I'd arrived. Now, a lightness began to fill me, and the ghost of a smile touched my lips. Perhaps my education at Miss Tepsom's would not be completely dull, after all.

By the next morning, it seemed that most of the students had arrived. I managed to stay out of everyone's way and engaged in only minimal conversation with my sulking roommate. The school hummed with the activity of girls settling into their rooms, bidding family farewell, and making friends. I sat on my bed reading a book I had swiped from the library (which I'd found opposite the music room), when a bright, clanging bell rang up and down the hallway. I pushed *The Ancients of the White Mountain* underneath my pillow and opened the door to see heads popping out of rooms all throughout the dormitory.

Miss Tepsom was gliding down the hall, solemnly ringing a

large, brass bell. She stopped in the middle of the hall and spoke in a voice that I had to strain to hear, as she did not bother to raise it. "You have all had ample time to get settled and are required in the dining room for luncheon in ten minutes' time. Please be tidy and punctual."

I took a moment to smooth my hair and dress, then followed the other girls to the dining room. We took our seats at the single, long table, which barely fit in the narrow room. There were eight students on either side of the table, Miss Tepsom at the head, and at the other end sat a short, plump woman with golden-brown skin, a young, pretty face, and artfully arranged dark hair. The room would have been cheerful if the curtains had been open; as it was, the heavy pink drapes cut out all daylight, and the lamps set along the table cast a sickly sheen over the yellow walls. I tried not to look like I was staring at all my classmates, but I was vastly curious.

I was unsurprised at the cultural variance of the girls present. Even in Ramshire there was a clear spectrum of ethnic backgrounds. My limited experience indicated that Dernmont was a diverse kingdom, with native heritages blended for generations with the kingdoms from the southeast, west, and even from lands across the northern Wulfestar Sea. I had inherited my mother's lightly freckled skin, generally considered an ancestral feature from beyond the sea, but little of her delicate bone structure. From my father I'd received my strong shoulders, brown eyes, and dark, unruly hair—striking traits he had not shared with my aunts, his two sisters.

What surprised me more among the assembled girls was the discrepancy in dress. The girl directly across from me wore a vivid fuchsia dress with luxuriously puffed sleeves and a snowy white pinafore frothing with lacy ruffles. Her dark brown, beribboned hair was carefully set in fat curls. The tall, blonde girl to her left was dressed more like I was, in a plain, dark grey dress of clean lines, and no pinafore. Her dress seemed to fit, however, while my sleeves strained uncomfortably where my arm had shot past the cuffs in a recent growth spurt. I noticed that most of the young ladies seemed to be dressed finer than I was, but I was relieved by the few girls in plain clothes that made me feel less of a sore thumb.

Miss Tepsom rose and rang her bell briskly, effectively silencing the small pockets of whispered conversation around the table. "Quiet, now, quiet!" she proclaimed unnecessarily. "As you all know, I am your headmistress, Miss Tepsom. Do not call me Tepsom, or Miss T, or Mrs. Tepsom. I am no housekeeper; I am to be afforded your utmost respect." She straightened her spectacles and took in a deep breath through her nose.

"Welcome students, to the inaugural year of Miss Tepsom's School for Gently Bred Young Ladies. Based on our excellent credentials in private tutelage and the high demand for our services, we have chosen this year to begin training young women in this setting. Your families have seen fit to entrust your cultivation to our care, and it is a responsibility we do not take lightly. By the end of this three-year program, you will be well equipped to be the most sought-after socialites in Dernmont, sure to succeed in high society, or even at court. We have divided the classes according to our own criteria, but this may be subject to change." She gestured across the table elegantly. "At the opposite end of the table is Miss Selkirk, your music and deportment mistress."

The pretty, plump woman nodded to us with dignity, but said nothing.

Miss Tepsom continued, "As you are well aware, you are here to learn. To acquire the accomplishments necessary to flourish, not only socially, but in many other settings. We begin lessons immediately, and there are no breaks, as you will be putting everything you learn into practice at all times. As you partake of luncheon together, I encourage you to converse and greet one another . . . *with purpose.* The intention in any social relationship is to learn more about one another. Sometimes, we must learn specific information without seeming to pry. I want you to practice just that." She sat down serenely and immediately began conversation with the startled-looking girl to her left, while serving herself potatoes. A hesitant hum of chat arose. My skin seemed to freeze and then heat, then freeze again as I anticipated the conversations that I was expected to take part in.

On my left sat Rubia, pointedly ignoring me as she droned about her brothers to the girl to her left. On my right sat a dainty girl with sandy hair pulled back in a sophisticated chignon. She wore a striped blue silk gown with a neat linen pinafore. She glanced at me critically as she passed a basket of rolls. She seemed ready to begin Miss Tepsom's task, so I forestalled her.

"I am Cressida Hoth. What's your name?" I blurted before she could speak.

"What sort of a name is that?" she asked rudely, without answering my question.

"It's mine, obviously," I said, with pique.

"Oh, wait. I *have* heard your name somewhere. Is your family old? Is there a Hoth estate?"

"Oh—um, I suppose so . . . and yes, there is," I answered, flustered. I hoped she would not inquire further into the matter. I didn't like the idea of beginning my acquaintances by mentioning that my father had been shunned from his old, wealthy family for marrying my mother, a woman without title or dowry. I had only ever seen the outlands of Hoth estate, my father's family seat, even though he had, technically, inherited.

"My name is Marigold Florelli," she said, thoroughly buttering her roll. "The Florellis are one of the oldest families in Dernmont. My father knew the queen's cousin."

"How nice for him," I answered, not sure how I was expected to respond to that. The oily salad of greens before me looked unappetizingly full of hairy little sprouts, but I heaped some on my plate anyway.

"How old are you?" asked Marigold.

"Fifteen this autumn."

"Is that right?" she said with disinterest. "I was fifteen last Evenfrost. Several months before you. How did you end up enrolled here?"

"My aunts saw the advertisement. I need to learn some accomplishments. We can just afford it." The information flowed out of my mouth in a rapid release of humiliation, and I felt my face turning beet red. I stuffed a bite of salad in my mouth and tried not to gag on the flavorless, prickly texture. Marigold's mouth hung open at my unfashionably honest response. I swallowed and kept talking just to keep her from asking another question. "Anyway. Those are the reasons, since you asked. Why did you come to this school?"

Marigold smirked. "Miss Tepsom is well acquainted with a family friend and asked mother as a personal favor if I could be her pupil. She said I would be a good example to the other young ladies who might not have been as gently bred as I am." As this was only the second student I had met, and both seemed rather insufferable, I was beginning to wonder what gentle breeding could really mean.

"Oh," was all I could think of in response. I carefully used my fork to pull bones out of my hunk of cod as she talked.

"It's obviously necessary," she said serenely, thickly buttering another roll. "I see now. So, why are you wearing black? Are you in mourning?"

"My parents died years ago, but the main reason is economical," I answered. The truth was embarrassing. At least my aunts always phrased such matters delicately, which kept me from saying something vulgar like, "Black wool is the cheapest."

Marigold's unimaginative prying into my background was tiresome, but not as intrusive as Rubia's had been, so I eventually relaxed. By the end of the meal, she had extracted all the uninteresting details about my life that she could by simply asking. She wanted to know about my parents, their occupation and connections, where I had lived, and what my house had been like. I could see a glazed sort of light in her eyes as she asked, then told me why her corresponding situation was better, then asked again. My outpouring of honesty to her every question seemed to satisfy something in her.

"Well, I can see you desperately need me as your friend," she said smugly.

"Why is that?" I asked tightly, folding the napkin on my lap.

"Because you come from a rude, obscure background. And you speak very baldly, which is borderline uncouth. And I have succeeded overwhelmingly in our first assignment, while you have failed. And an acquaintance with me—"

"Would mean a constant stream of impolite questions? As pleasant as that sounds, I think I'll do better without your help, Marigold." I spoke calmly, although my stomach was trembling as if I had just swallowed some of Aunt Millicent's ham jelly. I was again rejecting one of the first offers of friendship I had received in years. This could not be a good way to start my career at Miss Tepsom's. But the thought of being Marigold's little project was repulsive. "And I think I succeeded rather admirably, in fact. I have learned everything about you that you asked of me, as well as the fact that you have an excessive fondness for butter and gravy."

With a gasp, Marigold put down the spoon she had been licking gravy off of, and her soft pink flush darkened. "You . . . oaf!" she spluttered, then craned her neck side to side as if to see if Miss Tepsom or anyone else had witnessed her embarrassment. I didn't know if she was hoping they had, or not.

"Never mind, Miss Hoth," she hissed at me, laying her spoon down next to her plate, which had been scraped meticulously clean of all traces of gravy while she had interrogated me.

"You will *not* enjoy the benefit of my friendship." With that, Marigold turned resolutely to the tablemate on her right and determinedly inserted herself into the conversation that girl was having with another classmate.

I bit back a sigh and looked up to see the girl with the bright dress and frilly pinafore smiling at me in amusement. I looked away quickly, not ready to fail another friendship before it could start.

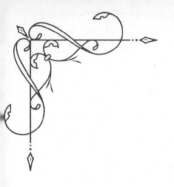
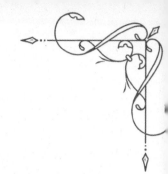

3

M Y   F I R S T   M O N T H   A T
Miss Tepsom's seemed to inch by. We rarely left the school, except to visit the shops on Plight Street for an hour at the end of each week. As I had almost no coin to spend, and we weren't allowed to explore the city, this quickly lost its appeal. The dense air and high city walls sometimes seemed to close in around me.

With Rubia as my roommate, however, I at least gained endless practice in carefully wording my truthful responses. Unless caught terribly off guard by her intrusiveness, I could hold back the urgent response crowding my brain long enough to consider my phrasing. I still had to answer with pure honesty, but sometimes I could minimize the damage.

The students were usually separated into two classes, taught only by Miss Tepsom and Miss Selkirk. Miss Selkirk was hopeless at music instruction, although she played the harp beautifully, and only a few with prior knowledge or talents were able to benefit from her music lessons. After the first few lessons, during which it was obvious that no one would be learning anything, we spent each music hour listening to Miss Selkirk play the harp, and sometimes being told to pair off and dance with one another. Attempting to dance a reel, accompanied by a harp and partnered with my roommate— the tiniest girl in the school with as little skill as I had—highly ranked among my least favorite experiences.

I hoped every day to see the sword case open, to find out that we were going to be using them, but the case remained untouched in the corner. During the few opportunities that I had to sneak into the music room alone, I found the case to be locked.

Due to my unwillingness to be drawn into conversations, and my dislike of questions, I began to develop a reputation for surliness. I was, therefore, left alone by most of the girls. Although this suited my well-developed sense of self-preservation, it combined with the lack of fencing lessons to wring every bit of hope out of me. I was hard-pressed to decide if I would be more miserable at home being lonely and henpecked by the aunts, or bearing the honorary title of school pariah at Miss Tepsom's.

A few weeks into my new life, I was struck by a massive headache (an occasional side effect of Rubia's badgering). In misery, I trudged into Miss Tepsom's classroom. It was as sparse as the rest of the school: bare wooden floors and walls, and a blackboard in the front. Today, the chairs were pushed back to line the walls around the room, and I suppressed a groan as I fell into a chair near the door. When the floor was cleared, that usually meant Miss Tepsom had devised some stilted, improvisation scene for us to act out—such as a debutante and a dowager at a ball, or the meeting of an eligible young man's parents. She expected full participation, and all I felt capable of doing was curling up and staring blankly at the floor.

This is what I was doing when she entered the room and rapped me smartly across the knees with her quizzing glass.

"That's quite enough of that vulgar posture, Miss Hoth. You would be laughed into the street if you attempted such carriage in a home of class and breeding." She floated past me as she spoke, and I winced as I sat upright.

"All right. Marigold and Vivian, you shall be our first performers."

Vivian, who had given me a friendly smile at our first school lunch, had warm brown skin, glossy curls, and wore abundant lace on her pinafores. She and Marigold, in her chignon and crisp silk, stood and gracefully walked to the center of the room. They looked at Miss Tepsom expectantly.

"Today, you will practice the art of information extraction. I know, it sounds positively conniving, but this is why you are here. To rise socially is a feat that cannot be accomplished if you only know what people want you to know. Knowledge is power, and powerful women rise."

Miss Tepsom's eyes were positively shining, and her voice rose several notches in fervor. I glanced around, wondering if Tepsom's ardor struck anyone else as slightly alarming, but no one else appeared disconcerted. Vivian nodded pleasantly, waiting for Miss Tepsom to go on and give them their scene.

"Scene," she began, "a drawing room in the North End, belonging to the widowed mother of a lord, whom neither of you have met. You have both been invited to the lady's salon as special favors to your mothers. For the sake of this exercise, imagine that you have no prior knowledge of each other. You want to know, does the other know the lord? Have they been introduced? Are they attached? What are their prospects as far as the lord is concerned? Who has the upper hand?"

Miss Tepsom continued unleashing her scene, outlining the motivations of the actresses in excruciating detail until my head spun. She lost me at *salon*, and I simply sat in aching exhaustion and hoped the scenes would take too long for everyone to have to participate.

It almost worked. I dozed through about four different scenes, which, to my inattentive observation, seemed to be girls just talking coyly while pretending to sip lemonade. I yawned widely, but the peak of my yawn was interrupted by Miss Tepsom's cutting voice.

"Miss Hoth. *Miss Hoth!*" She repeated sternly, apparently not conscious of the fact that people cannot speak while finishing up a yawn. "Kindly close your mouth, correct your unattractive slump, and proceed to the floor. You are next."

I snapped to sudden alertness. The class watched with smirks which were now too familiar when attention was on me. Bracing myself, I stood and walked to the center of the room. A few of the girls giggled, and I remembered that I had made not the slightest attempt to tidy my hair. I hastily pushed it off of my face, where a few strands were beginning to cling to a sheen of sweat.

"And . . . Rosalie—Miss Montshire. Join Miss Hoth, if you please." A tall, thin girl who dressed as modestly and plainly as a governess walked to the center of the room, her face turning slightly green. I was not the only one who disliked the attention. "Now," Miss Tepsom continued. "We have only a few minutes left, so no hesitation. Begin."

I had absolutely no idea what the assigned scene was. Anything Miss Tepsom said at the beginning of class had been lost in a fog as I whiled away the hour. I gave Rosalie a slight nod, to indicate that she should begin. I would simply have to catch on.

Rosalie self-consciously smoothed her blonde braid and gave a little cough. Straightening her shoulders, she began, "How do you know our hostess, Miss Hoth?"

"Oh, we went to school together," I brazened immediately, trying to sound as snooty as she did. Titters rose around me for some reason I could not fathom.

"Indeed?" Rosalie asked, her cheeks reddening as she shot a look at Miss Tepsom. "You went to school with Lady Hendrick, the mother of the lord?" Furiously realizing that my improvisation was embarrassing me, I refused to let Rosalie ask any more questions.

"No. And where did you go to school, Miss, er, Rosalie?" I asked, forgetting my classmate's surname. Another wave of malicious giggles rose from around the room.

"Something *absurd* would have to happen for Hoth to get invited to a salon in the North End," Marigold stage-whispered from behind me. I ignored her and focused on Rosalie's burning cheeks. My performance was embarrassing her as well.

"I went to Miss Tepsom's School for Gently Bred Young Ladies," she answered dutifully.

"And where is that?" I asked, trying to run out the clock.

"On Plight Street," she answered.

"I see."

Rosalie cleared her throat, looking slightly panicked at the lull in our incredibly boring, staged conversation.

"What is your family like, Miss Hoth?" she asked in a strained voice, a fixed smile on her face.

I froze. I couldn't believe I had not foreseen this eventuality and kept talking. Nerves made my symptoms set in faster, and I answered the only way I could.

"Well, my aunts are eccentric, selfish, and tedious, and my parents passed away several years ago," I said, my chest tightening.

"I'm so sorry. How did they die?" asked Rosalie. I stared very hard at her for a moment as my answer filled my mind, pressing against every other thought. I willed the question back into her mouth and hoped spitefully that Miss Tepsom would give her low marks for asking such personal questions. I stared so long that I saw black spots and had to gasp for air before answering.

"Arrows. They were murdered."

Rosalie's mouth opened slightly as mingled gasps and giggles rose from around the room. I forced my expression into one of neutrality. I thought about smiling to pretend that it was a crude joke, but I couldn't. I felt sick.

A loud ringing clanged through the room. Miss Tepsom stepped in between us, ringing her bell determinedly, every note reverberating in my aching head. Finally, she stopped.

"Well, Miss Hoth, I think we should speak after class about your extremely unsuitable sense of humor. Class dismissed." She held my upper arm to stop me from walking away, her fingers digging in like steel pincers. I was taller than most of the other girls, but still Miss Tepsom managed to loom over me, which made her grip on my arm seem all the more menacing.

"Iris," she addressed the maid who had entered the room to replace the chairs in rows. "Please send Miss Selkirk to my office." Iris bobbed slightly in response and sailed out of the room. Then Miss Tepsom turned to the door at the left of the blackboard, which I suspected led to her office, and pulled me through, confirming my suspicion.

Shutting the door behind her, she released me, then went over and sat down in the straight-backed wooden chair behind her desk. She let out a weary sigh and rubbed her hand over her forehead. I hovered awkwardly near the door as she gazed down at her desk for a long moment without acknowledging me. I was beginning to wonder if I should try to edge backward out the door, when her eyes lifted and fixed on me.

"Come here, Miss Hoth," Miss Tepsom ordered in a quiet voice. I obeyed, standing quite still before her desk. "Have a seat." She gestured to one of two chairs pulled up before her desk. I pulled one back with a scrape and sat down. If I was going to be scolded for my performance in class, I wished she would hurry. My head was pounding.

Miss Tepsom looked me over, in much the same way that she had when I first arrived several weeks earlier. Years of never offering a word about myself without compulsion warred with an instinct to explain myself, for once. I would never joke about my parents' death. But once I started explaining, what else would I have to say? So, I sat with my mouth clamped shut, terrified of what she would ask.

Miss Tepsom cleared her throat. "You chose quite an awkward and inappropriate moment to tell the truth, Miss Hoth." I felt my mouth fall open.

She continued, "For now, never mind how I know you were not making a joke. I hope, anyway, that you find nothing laughable in your parents' murder." She studied me with deadly seriousness as I answered automatically.

"No, ma'am," I whispered.

"At this school, it is terribly important that you learn what to say, and what not to say, in a social setting," she went on. I felt my shoulders slump, suddenly too weary for another of her lectures on how to succeed socially. "Miss Hoth." The words were sharp, startling me. She paused, as if deciding what to say next. I sat up straighter, and a shiver skittered across the back of my neck when she finally spoke. "It is not for the reason that you think," she said, her voice quiet now.

The sound of the door opening made me jump slightly, and a breath of air fluttered my hair as it swung shut behind me.

"Ambrosia. Thank you for joining us," said Miss Tepsom, gesturing to the chair next to mine. Miss Selkirk skirted past me and settled gracefully into the chair.

"Good afternoon, Cressida," said Miss Selkirk, smiling pleasantly at me. "What's this about, Lu?" She looked earnestly at Miss Tepsom. "My class was excessively disappointed when I had to pause in the middle of my Rencetti."

"They'll have to wait, I'm afraid," said Miss Tepsom, pinioning her colleague with a significant glance. Miss Selkirk's graceful hands fluttered nervously in her lavender-draped lap. "Although it is ahead of schedule, I believe it is time for the girls to understand their purpose. No doubt you've already heard of the incident that prompts my decision." Miss Selkirk's fidgeting ceased, and she turned a placidly searching eye upon me—for much longer than I could bear with ease.

"No doubt you are right, Lucretia. Shall I fetch the others?"

"You may go and finish your lesson first. After that, please gather them and bring them here." She flicked a hand dismissively at Miss Selkirk, who nodded with a smile, doubtless pleased that she would be allowed to finish her harp performance.

"You need not wait for answers any longer, Cressida," Miss Tepsom said as soon as the door shut behind Miss Selkirk.

"There is a time for patience, and it is clear that we must cultivate yours, but you have been sitting without questioning in admirably silent bewilderment, so I shall satisfy you."

"Thank you, ma'am," I answered, feeling my perplexity growing enormously with each passing moment. I had almost forgotten my headache. I leaned forward, waiting for Miss Tepsom to continue. She did not leave me in suspense this time.

"Your comprehension of the aims of this school are unlikely to be completely accurate, Miss Hoth. You may have noticed that neither Miss Selkirk, nor I, have ever mentioned the king of Dernmont, King Arctus's name. That is because we do not share the loyalty that most of this kingdom holds." She paused, carefully gauging my reaction. I, however, only felt mildly shocked. I had but a passing knowledge of the royal family and little exposure to excessive patriotism. I nodded slightly, to encourage her to keep speaking.

"Our lack of loyalty is not unfounded, but rather the result of confirmed suspicions." I blinked in surprise, but she continued, "We will discuss our findings with you fully in good time. However, this is where it pertains directly to you. Over the past decade of the king's reign, unexplained and unpunished murders among old, respectable families have grown more and more commonplace. These murders, we have found through years of meticulous investigation, are linked. And they point directly to the crown."

Understanding began to dawn, slowly, painfully. Miss Tepsom continued softly, "We strongly believe that culpability for your parents' murder can be placed at the door of the king himself."

I sat without moving, staring through her, seeing what I had been shutting out for so many years. Arrows, with crimson fletching and powerful shafts, flying directly through our kitchen window. One striking my mother as she bent over my father, speaking in his ear. Speaking one moment, crumpled lifelessly on the floor the next. One arrow missed. The third struck my father, as he shouted and shielded me, upsetting the teacups and milk bottle on the table.

Slowly, I shook my head. The king being responsible for the murder of my parents was as unbelievable and senseless as the fact that my parents had been murdered at all.

"I know it is a lot to accept, Cressida." Miss Tepsom spoke slowly and quietly, as if afraid to spook me. "And in time, I will lay all of the information before you. Before each of you."

"Each of us?" She came into focus as the image of our kitchen table with my father's blood pooling across it finally dissipated.

"Half of the students in this school are in the same position as you. Eight of you have lost loved ones to mysterious circumstances . . . circumstances that we believe can be identified as murders ordered from the throne. Do you know who currently owns your parents' land?"

I hesitated, but my chest began tightening and I had to speak. "Officials of the king—they came and claimed it for the crown. The day after my—after they died." Even though we only occupied a tiny cottage on the edge of the empty estate that was my father's inheritance, they had taken it all.

The day reared into my mind, cold and anguished. My aunts had arrived after I'd knelt for hours in that dark kitchen, blind with terror and grief . . . the only one alive in the house. They'd harped and huffed at the king's officials before shooing me, a shaking, stumbling eight-year-old, into a coach. No goodbyes.

I pushed it all aside and met Miss Tepsom's now-gentle eyes.

She spoke in a soft but firm voice. "Each of you deserve justice. And we can give it to you . . . but we need your help."

I shook my head, completely at a loss. "How . . . how can we possibly help?" I asked, feeling so overwhelmed by the conversation that I sat rigid in my chair.

"You are young ladies receiving an education of social

accomplishments . . . or so it shall seem. What could be more innocent? But not only do you all have a shared motivation, you will also develop unique skills to carry out the tasks of agents of this investigation. By the end of your education, many of you will have received invitations to court, affording you close proximity to the royal family, and a rigorous training in all the arts required to spy on the workings of the court. Once there, you will gather the evidence needed for us to proceed with justice."

"Invitations to court?" I sputtered, not sure where to begin with my questions. "But how will that be possible? What sort of skills do you mean? How—"

At that moment, a gentle hand tapped the door, and Miss Selkirk entered, followed by seven of my classmates. Varying degrees of nerves and curiosity played over their expressions.

Miss Tepsom beckoned them in but did not lift her focus from my panicked face. "You will be impressed by the breadth of our connections and abilities. At this moment, you need to trust me. You will learn so much that you never dreamed of knowing, and you will have justice for your parents' murders. Tell me, do you like the sound of that, Miss Hoth?"

The curse brought the answer immediately to my lips. "Yes. I do."

There were sixteen students at Miss Tepsom's, and so far, I'd only had class with the same set of eight. I assumed our classes were divided by ability, or perhaps randomly, and that we would be mixed up at term breaks. I realized after my meeting with Miss Tepsom, however, that the groups would never mix, because we would not be learning the same set of skills. Only the seven other girls in my classes would be trained alongside me to be Miss Tepsom's agents.

We met in the music room together for our normally scheduled class the next day, looking curiously around at each other as we waited for Miss Selkirk to arrive.

"Has everyone met with Miss Tepsom individually since . . . since last night?" Marigold inquired, looking around at us. Her eyes landed on me and flashed in annoyance.

I gave a small smile. I'd been told the secret before she had.

The others nodded, glancing around at each other. Miss Tepsom, clearly unwilling to risk the others finding out by chance, had given a confidential explanation of our true purpose to the students she'd gathered to her study. It had been grimly exciting, I had to admit. She must have decided to speak to the others about their personal motivations for joining her spy network in one-on-one meetings.

"She spoke to me this morning, and I am fully convinced of our mission. Is everyone else committed?" asked Rubia. Her sharp eyes took in each of our faces. "Because I think it is extremely important that we know we can trust one another with this secret." Several of the girls nodded vigorously. Rubia went on, her voice growing fiercer, "I don't know about the rest of you, but I have a father and two brothers to avenge. As the next in line, I will not allow this injustice to go unpunished."

Her words were like a slap of icy water. I'd known she was proud of her older brothers, whom she spoke of often. I hadn't known that they were dead.

There was a silence after her pronouncement, and no one else offered the details of their own motivation. Rosalie looked away, her eyes shadowed. I pressed my lips together and fought back the image of my own parents' murder as the reminder of what we all had in common sliced through me.

"I don't know how anyone could do such horrible things," Vivian said, her dark eyes troubled. "I want to be useful."

"We will be," Rubia assured her. "I don't know what

Tepsom told *you* all, but with the connections between us and the strings her network can pull, we can get very close to the crown."

"How close?" Marigold's eyes narrowed. "I have no intention of becoming the king's mistress, or anything vulgar like that. I have my reasons for committing to this league, but intend to preserve my honor!"

I snorted, which had the unfortunate effect of drawing attention to myself.

"What do *you* know of it, Hoth?" Marigold asked scornfully, her cheeks reddening.

"Not much," I answered. "None of us do yet. I just don't believe Miss Tepsom has that sort of spying in mind."

Marigold turned her head deliberately away and began to address the others, when the door opened, and both Miss Tepsom and Miss Selkirk entered the music room.

Miss Tepsom crossed over to the mantel and turned to face us, while Miss Selkirk seated herself by her harp.

"You are all now aware of your purpose as our pupils at this school," Miss Tepsom began, as brisk and breezy as if she were giving an embroidery lesson. "This may sound exciting to you, and well it might be. But it will not be easy. You will have to work twice as hard as the other girls, because you will be learning twice as much. You will not be abandoning your classical studies, you will be adding your . . . less conventional . . . classes to your workload. And we expect the highest of achievements from all of you in every subject."

Eugenia Portram, a girl with thick, red-gold hair, raised a tentative hand. "Please, Miss Tepsom, why do we have to learn what the other girls are learning? Surely we won't need diction, or music, or history, or—"

Miss Tepsom cut her off with a raised hand before the list could continue. "You need to not only pass as young ladies of advanced breeding and accomplishments to be a useful spy, you need to *be* young ladies of advanced breeding and accomplishments. Your cover would disintegrate the first time you attended court if you knew nothing that the other successful society ladies know. Your very civility would be called into question if you could not dance a light and graceful reel at a ball. The history you will learn of this kingdom and its royal family will solidify the urgency of the mission in your minds. The art of conversation, and yes, genteel flirtation, will be among your most useful tools in extracting information. When done deftly, the target will not even realize what he has revealed." Marigold shot me a look as Miss Tepsom looked around at us with hard, bright eyes. "You need this education *more* than the others do."

I raised my hand, clearing my throat and ignoring the prickle of sweat on my brow as the others looked at me. Miss Tepsom sighed in resignation as she was forced to pause in her lecture again. "Yes, Cressida?"

"Why are the other girls here? Isn't there a risk that they will notice something strange?"

"That is a good question, one that I had every intention of addressing," Miss Tepsom answered shortly. "The other young ladies are here to lend credence to this establishment. They are highborn, with noble families and bright prospects. You will forge friendships and bonds with them that will serve you well in the future. You are under the strictest charge not to let a single one of them suspect that your lessons are different from theirs. If asked why you need to spend more time at your studies, you will say you need extra tutelage in a respectable subject. Is that understood?" She pierced each of us with a stern eye, tapping her quizzing glass against her palm. "If word of our true purpose here became known, your families might face even more danger than they've already suffered."

Vivian raised a hand. "Miss Tepsom, do our families know?"

"Know what, Miss Guildford?"

"Well . . . about all of this."

Her brow furrowed slightly. "Some of them do. You all represent a variety of backgrounds, but many of you are missing one or both parents. We used our discretion to decide which families to consult on our choice to recruit you. Those guardians who are aware will likely reveal this to you when they see fit. None of you are to speak of this outside of school, otherwise." This was met with an uncomfortable silence. I wondered if Aunt Fenella or Aunt Millicent knew.

Miss Tepsom continued, "On top of your usual studies, you will learn the arts of subterfuge. You will become experts in coding and conversation, you will learn how to distract, deceive, and disappear, figuratively speaking. You will learn the necessarily cruder arts of drugging and self-defense, should your mission turn dangerous. You will learn how to extract information seamlessly and to insert yourself into places you have no lawful business being. In short, you will learn every point of being a spy. As we discern your personal talents, some of you will receive additional training.

"Now. If there are no more questions–" Hands shot up around the room. Miss Tepsom frowned. "Let me rephrase that. Further questions will have to wait, as I have a lesson to teach. You will now apply yourselves to a dance lesson with Miss Selkirk. Ladies." Without another word, she strode out of the room.

"This is going to be so much work," Vivian groaned as we stood to partner with each other for our dance lesson.

I nodded wordlessly, unable to keep a smile off my face. My ears were ringing with an exhilaration I could not explain. My nerves tingled with the anticipation of learning such unusual skills. But as Miss Selkirk began plucking strings and calling out steps, and I predictably stepped on the patient Vivian's toes, a slow dread began to grow, leaching the excitement out of me. Somehow it hadn't occurred to me yet: the condition that I'd lived with for so long was so much a part of me that I sometimes forgot about it.

How could someone without the ability to lie ever become a spy?

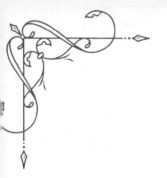

4

THEY'D DRAWN THE CURTAINS.

Aunt Millicent gazed down at the pouch in her sister's hand. I looked also, my head beginning to pound in fear. The room was very silent and still.

"Will it work?" Millicent whispered. "Will the effects be permanent?"

"Only one way to find out," Aunt Fenella said sagely. She removed from the pouch a small, yellowed, and wrinkled sachet. "From what I understand, the powder will go directly to the bloodstream and stay there, forever circulating."

"We are giving a gift to the world. This uncivilized land needs more integrity, and the girl shall be a blessing to all." Aunt Millicent's eyes shone in excitement and her voice squeaked slightly.

With a withering glance at her sister, Aunt Fenella set the sachet inside the single teacup on the tray. My throat started to tighten anxiously as I watched her pour pale tea over the sachet. Aunt Fenella stared into the cup for a long moment, her lips pursed.

A damp, muddy aroma began to rise from it, and I coughed. The aunts both looked at me nervously. Aunt Fenella stood and pushed the hot cup into my hands.

"Drink it up," she said in a falsely cheery voice, as if I had not just witnessed her spike the cup with some unknown ingredient.

I stared at her, then slowly held the cup over the carpet and *began to turn it over. A drop escaped onto the floor before Fenella lunged at me and grasped both the cup and my hand with her much larger one.*

"Drink it up." She gritted her teeth as she pushed the cup toward my face. Somehow, the two of them got the nasty brew down my throat. I thrashed a bit to try to escape them, but I feared getting burned and didn't fight as hard as I could have. I swallowed, and a bitter taste scoured my tongue. Then, everything went dark.

Oblivion nearly engulfed me. I felt as if I had been shoved under dark water for a frightfully long moment, but then, finally, bobbed back up to the surface. I gasped involuntarily when my vision cleared. The aunts were sitting primly on their settee, watching me intently. The curtains were open again. I sat up and coughed. The burnt aftertaste made me gag.

"I want some water," I croaked. I flushed as I tried to swallow past the lump in my throat and blinked away the tears stinging my eyes. They ignored my request and put their heads together, whispering for a moment.

Aunt Fenella turned to me after the brief consultation. "Now, Cressida. Did you steal an entire tin of biscuits from the kitchen this morning?"

"Yes."

I blinked several times, shocked that I had truthfully answered the question, which was bound to get me into more trouble. A smile began to curve Aunt Fenella's mouth.

"I thought as much. And have you, or have you not, a box of your parents' personal effects hidden under a floorboard in your room?"

"Yes, I have," I answered immediately. I shook my head slowly in confusion.

"Tell me how you like living here, child," Aunt Millicent asked softly, her eyes shining.

I looked at her mutely, my heart pounding. I would not

answer. I kept my lips clamped shut, but felt a sudden need for air. I gasped, but nothing could get past my throat, which seemed to be closing up. My response surged to my brain, consuming me as I fought for air. In a panic, I squeaked out, "I hate it here." My windpipe opened and I gulped air into my lungs.

The aunts stared at me, mingled irritation and satisfaction oozing off of them. Heat flooded my face, and I wanted to tear out of the room, but I couldn't move, couldn't do anything.

I couldn't lie.

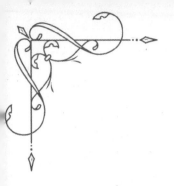
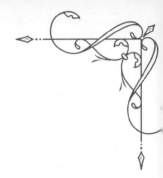

5

THE DREAMS CAME EVERY NIGHT now that I was hyper-aware of my predicament. Now that it was no longer merely a social nuisance. Scene after scene of my years growing up under the thumbs of two old maids, who had nothing better to do than force mundane truths out of their unfortunate charge, haunted my restless nights. The very thought of learning to spy and avenging my parents was the greatest thrill of my life. I knew better than to tell anyone that I was a liability, even if that seemed like the honorable path. I'd noticed that, after asking enough questions, people subconsciously noticed my propensity to answer them all with painful honesty, and became insatiable. I didn't even have a very interesting life, but to be completely truthful about oneself—feelings, motivations, and background—was unheard of in society, and was therefore grabbed at like the last sweet bun at breakfast.

If someone found out the actual truth—that I could not lie even if I wanted to—the power they would hold over me would be unbearable. I couldn't tell Miss Tepsom *now* that I wouldn't be able to spy for her. She would ask why, and my secret would be out. I had to learn how to work against my curse, or at least, work around it.

Our first spy-related lesson was at the hour that we usually met for decorum lessons with Miss Tepsom. However, as we sat waiting in the sun-streaked room for Miss Tepsom to arrive, and hoping that this would *not* be another decorum lesson, the maid Iris entered. She shut and locked the door behind her, then strode to the front of the room. As we watched, puzzled, she carefully removed her apron and maid's cap and tossed them inelegantly into a chair behind her. She faced us in her prim black gown and smoothed her blonde twist of hair. She looked calmly around at our startled expressions.

"I am Miss Rush," she said in a clear, firm voice. "In this classroom, you will call me Miss Rush. Outside of this classroom, you will not acknowledge me except in the usual ways that you might acknowledge a housemaid, and I will be known to you as Iris. Is that clear?"

I nodded slightly, feeling amused. A few other students nodded.

"Are you a maid or not?" asked Marigold insolently, without raising her hand.

Miss Rush looked at her for a moment, her expression unreadable. "Do you think I am?" she finally asked.

Marigold didn't answer, then finally raised a shoulder in a shrug.

"In this school, I am what I need to be. Right now, I am here to teach you the art of undercover deception. If you believed up until this moment that I was nothing more than a housemaid, then I have given you a fair demonstration." The corners of her mouth lifted ever so slightly. "And you will give me the respect afforded a teacher. Next time, raise your hand and wait for me to address you, Miss Florelli," she said.

Marigold reddened.

Miss Rush continued smoothly, "Lessons with me will be unscheduled, with some exceptions. That means, I will occasionally take over the hour that is usually Miss Tepsom's or Miss Selkirk's regular lesson, in favor of giving you one of my . . . *special* lessons. The few that are scheduled are every third music lesson. If you have disposable clothes that can be worn for exercise, I advise you to bring them to those lessons.

For today, I hope you have paper and pencils, because you're going to want to take notes."

Apart from music, dancing, and embroidery, Miss Selkirk taught, to my utter humiliation, the art of flirtation. She said it would, in appropriate moderation, be extremely useful at court. I blushed and stammered through each exercise while the others exploded in giggles. Miss Selkirk ended our first lesson in a bit of a huff, telling each of us to show up ready to seriously flirt next time if we indeed meant to be spies.

Miss Tepsom still taught us history, literature, and decorum. Every lesson was colored with ways to use the subjects to our advantage in our future occupations, from coding messages in works of poetry and verse, to manipulating a social conversation in order to seamlessly extract information. Her history lessons held me more in thrall, as she uncovered the ways in which the king's approved curriculum differed from the reality of his reign.

I knew the general basics of Dernmont history, patched together from what I remembered learning from my parents, and the few dusty volumes in my aunts' limited library. I knew that the reason we were a diverse kingdom was because centuries ago, Dernmont had been an active center of immigration for reasons unknown. We were not an easy country to access. Forbidding, nearly impassible mountain ranges cut our western and southern border off from the lands beyond, and the vast Wulfestar Sea spread to the north. Our only close neighbor was the kingdom of Porleac, and we were on civil but distant terms.

Whatever had drawn immigrants to our land centuries past was buried, dead to history and irrelevant to the present. We were no longer sought, and all of our trade had to be conducted via the Porleacan harbor, which had caused more than one dispute over the years. We shared a holiday with Porleac, called Evenfrost, instated in honor of some peace treaty of a thousand years ago, to celebrate our allied status and memorialize our dead. In Dernmont, though, it had morphed into a celebration of family, patriotism, and remembering loved ones long passed.

"How many of you have read a history book?" Miss Tepsom asked us. A few hands lifted. "Did you find them to be detailed? Comprehensive?" No one responded. I had quickly learned that when Miss Tepsom addressed the whole class, my symptoms left me alone. I'd also learned when to discern if she wanted an answer to her questions, or if she was setting up a lecture. This was clearly the latter.

"Another question. How many of you have read a book that was written outside of Dernmont?" The silence following this question felt slightly more confused. A few girls glanced at one another.

"You will not find a detailed, thorough history book in the whole kingdom, just as you will not find a single book that was inscribed elsewhere."

"Why not?" asked Rubia, her whole body alert.

"Because King Arctus is far more controlling than he would have you believe," Miss Tepsom said. "The history books you've likely read, or have been taught from, are trite reproductions of the royal family's version of Dernmont's history and its relationship with the rest of the world. They herald centuries of peace, ever since the treaty with Porleac ended some dustups over trade ports. They wax eloquent over the goodness and beauty of our land, which brought many to undertake perilous journeys across the mountain ranges to reach our kingdom of good people and bountiful harvest. Piffle!"

She adjusted her spectacles. "They tell of neighborly dealings with Porleac, celebrating a long-held peaceful alliance with the country that, by the way, has something King Arctus wants. The ports. You have doubtless read dry tomes full of a history filled with nothing but love for king and crown. Yes, Rosalie?"

"But—how could one king reinvent our history? Mightn't there just not be much to tell?"

"Quite so. It clearly has not been just *one* king. This practice of lying to the people has been a characteristic of the royal family of Dernmont for quite some time, I believe. And as our heritage is the product of rich immigration, where are the travelers now? Immigration to Dernmont is a thing of the past. And where are the books, the histories, the literature of those other lands? In Dernmont you will find one story, inscribed on Dernmont vellum in Dernmont ink. Stamped with the king of Dernmont's seal." Her cheeks flushed as she spoke.

A heavy silence followed these impassioned words. We rarely saw Miss Tepsom look more than slightly ruffled, but this topic clearly disturbed her. It all sounded a bit far-fetched to me. A conspiracy to stifle the history of Dernmont, going back many centuries?

"Why?" The word popped out of my mouth, laden with all of the confusion and skepticism that Miss Tepsom's fervor ignited in me.

"Raise your hand before you address me again, Miss Hoth," Miss Tepsom said, her countenance smooth once more. "*Why* is an excellent question." Her light eyes roved over the room. "It's also an excellent reason to investigate, don't you think? I do not mean to be unfeeling, but why were your loved ones murdered?"

No one moved, or spoke.

"You do not know why, but you wish to, am I correct?"

I wasn't sure if she was addressing me specifically, but her eyes bored into mine, and my symptoms began to take over my other senses.

"Yes, ma'am," I replied, wishing I could remain silent. Her eyes stayed on me a moment more before speaking again.

"You will find the answers that you deserve. You all will.

Not knowing the why of it does not erase our responsibility to seek truth."

She looked around again, twitched her shoulders a bit, and resumed her brisk manner.

"We may not have the truth in the king's approved historical documents, but there are other ways to piece together the facts. My contacts and I have spent years compiling evidence—stories passed through families for generations, correspondence, and other materials—that point to the crown's grasping nature throughout the generations. Bloody, underhanded campaigns against not only Porleac, but the king's own subjects, for various purposes, are written all over the true history of this kingdom. I can tell you these stories, show you these bits of historicity. The *why* may be different for each instance, or it may be the same. But not knowing it does not erase what's been done. Not knowing why cannot bring your loved ones back, nor the lands that the crown coldly took from your families."

Miss Tepsom's future lessons were not always so scandalous, so charged with the exciting tension that filled the room when she spoke such vivid treason. But occasionally, she brought to class a piece of evidence she or one of her contacts had collected, and they painted a sinister story of our kingdom, an ongoing drama of dark deeds swelling underneath a tranquil surface. And our families were at the heart of it.

I had few previous theories concerning my parents' murders. I'd asked Aunt Fenella several years ago who she thought could have killed them, and why. Her answer had been a perfunctory implication that because we'd lived in dangerous proximity to the no-man's-land that divided the eastern border of Dernmont from Porleac, my parents had brought predictable violence upon themselves. Mercenaries, spies, and thieves were said to infest the forest on the border, and our general nearness to scalawags and ne'er-do-wells tied up the mystery for my aunts. The more I learned from Miss Tepsom of the secret, bloody, power-grasping crusades wrought by generations of our royal family, the more it added up. I still didn't know why, but our home had been seized by officials of the king before my parents had been in the ground a day, and I knew now that my story was not unique.

The third music lesson after we met Miss Rush (as Miss Rush) had us all in a collective frisson of nerves. Several of the girls were dressed in slightly plainer clothes. None of us had any idea what Miss Rush could have meant when she advised us to dress in disposable clothes. I dearly hoped she had been speaking hyperbolically, as nothing I owned could be considered disposable. Nevertheless, I felt alert with anticipation, and hoped that an idea forming in the back of my mind was correct.

When we entered the room, the chairs were pushed back around the wall, as they usually were for a dance lesson. It became immediately clear, however, that dancing was not scheduled for the hour. Miss Rush, dressed in a pair of breeches, was fencing. A grin broke over my face as my hope was realized. The case of swords I'd happened upon my first day was standing open in the corner, inviting us to take up weapons and swing them around. We did not do this, at least not immediately. The fencing match playing out before us was far too thrilling for any of us to do anything but stand in a clump by the door and watch with bated breath.

Miss Rush's fencing partner was a young man. Brown and lean, with laughing eyes but a serious mouth, he parried and attacked with grace and enthusiasm.

With a final thrust and an almost imperceptible wrist-flicking motion, the young man disarmed Miss Rush, and her foil clattered to the floor. He stepped back, lowering his sword arm and wiping perspiration off his brow with the other arm. "Well met, Miss Rush," he said with a courteous nod. "You almost bested me."

"Another moment and I would have, but for that last move. You'll have to teach me." She picked up her foil, looking slightly irked. Not a hair was out of place, but her cheeks were red with exertion.

"I'd be happy to teach you, as well as your pupils," he said, turning with some amusement to the clump of gawking girls. Eugenia stepped forward with clasped hands and shining eyes, while Marigold snickered at her.

"Yes," said Miss Rush. "Girls, I would like to present Mr. Emric Theon. He will not be available for many lessons, but while we have him, you shall learn the art of fencing. Those with a propensity may develop further in future lessons with Mr. Theon or myself, but most of you will simply be taught the basics. None of you shall discuss anything with Mr. Theon but fencing. Now, pair up."

As often occurred in dance lessons, I was left to pair with Rubia. As roommates, we accepted our natural pairing with resignation.

Mr. Theon and Miss Rush walked between us, handing out foils, having us test the weight and balance before settling on one. Mr. Theon handed me a blade as Rubia was experimentally whacking hers against her hand.

"I wouldn't do that," he advised, eliciting an eye roll from her.

I held my foil awkwardly, not sure what to do with it. I felt instantly disappointed in myself. I'd hoped, as soon as I realized what the lesson was to be, that I would be an obvious natural. I had yet to shine in any of my other studies.

"Here," he said, immediately whisking the sword back out of my hand. "Try this one. You're one of the tallest, you might need a longer blade." He handed me another sword, and I wrapped my hand around the grip. It was heavier than I expected. He slid the foil he held into a scabbard on his belt and readjusted my hold on the weapon, showing me to turn my wrist up. "Now, lunge," he instructed when I was holding the sword correctly. He demonstrated, gracefully lunging and miming the thrust of a sword. I copied him, and he nodded in affirmation, but Rubia, standing opposite me, yelped. She swiftly used her sword to whack mine away from her abdomen, where I had nearly jabbed her.

"Gentle with the weapons, young lady," the young man admonished Rubia. "You seem to be unscratched. However, we do have an imbalance of heights in this pairing. You." He nodded at me. "What's your name?"

"Cressida," I answered automatically, and wondered if I should have added, "sir." However, as Mr. Theon did not look to be more than a year or two older than I was, addressing him so formally felt silly.

"Cressida needs to work with a longer blade," he said to Rubia, "and you won't be able to outreach her arm, at least not without considerable speed. I'm going to pair you with Miss Rush. Cressida, I will partner with you, if you're agreeable."

"Fine," Rubia snapped, setting her sword against her shoulder like a tiny soldier and setting off to find Miss Rush.

"Our height is more compatible, so this will give you an advantage over practicing with a classmate," Mr. Theon said to me as he took Rubia's place opposite me. "Not to mention, I'm particularly good at this, so I imagine you'll benefit from that as well," he added with a wink. I flushed and felt myself automatically hunch a bit, as I did when my height was pointed out. He was a few inches taller than me still, which was welcome as I usually towered over all the other girls, but I suddenly felt like a tree tangled up in petticoats.

"Now." He raised his voice so the rest of the class could hear him. "Stand, like so," he said, gesturing at his graceful stance, with one foot slightly ahead of the other. "Hold the hilt with your wrist up. It is awkward at first," he said gallantly when Marigold promptly dropped hers. "So, I suggest that you practice the hold, letting the sword rest lightly in your hand. Once you feel comfortable, attempt a few lunges." He demonstrated on the word *lunges*, thrusting past me. "Watch my feet," he instructed, demonstrating again. "Right foot forward. Practice the lunge and the grip. Thrust next to your partner, not at them," he advised quickly as Rubia lunged forcefully at Miss Rush, causing the teacher to leap backward to escape the blade.

A cacophony of rustles, grunts, and clatters as swords hit the floor ensued, and for the next ten minutes, Mr. Theon watched us lunge, circling the group once or twice to give pointers and readjust grips.

"Now," he said, resuming his place opposite me. "Cressida and I are going to attempt a hit. One of us," he gestured to himself, "will lunge, or attack, the other will parry. Cressida, when you block my advance, I want you to try one of these three sword positions, to try to push my blade away," he said, demonstrating with his sword. I nodded nervously. "These are dull, but we are without protective armor or padding, so our hits need to be light and controlled."

He assumed his starting stance, with one hand resting lightly behind his back. I just focused on not dropping my foil. "En garde," he said, raising his sword.

Suddenly, unable to bear waiting for his attack, I lunged, aiming my sword at his shoulder. He raised his sword and blocked mine, but just barely, pushing it to the side. His eyebrows rose in surprise, but he recovered quickly and lunged forward with incredible swiftness. I barely managed to raise my sword to the position to block his, but pushed back with enough force to make him take a step backward. I held my own against another attack, and almost succeeded in tapping his chest, but he quickly adapted to a defensive role. My parry against his third lunge was too slow, and his sword touched my shoulder.

He grinned and held out a hand to shake mine. To my surprise, a small applause broke out over the watching class.

"I admit, I had not expected that," he remarked. "You're a quick learner. Now," he addressed the class, "I want the rest of you to attempt a bout with your partners. Remember the footwork and grip that you have been practicing. One of each pair will lunge, the other will parry, or block, your partner's weapon. You can then counterattack, and the first to attack will then parry."

He turned back to me. "Shall we go again?"

"Yes, if you're up for it," I answered, just a bit cheekily.

He grinned again. "Absolutely."

◇ ·· ———————— ·· ◇

The next day, I was feeling more buoyant than I had felt yet at Miss Tepsom's, and even Marigold's sneering asides about my future prowess as a female fencing sideshow couldn't pull me back down. In fact, the comments, followed only by a couple of weak snickers, served to brighten my mood further.

Although learning my true purpose at the school had lightened the dreariness to an extent, it had not lifted the heaviness brought on by my clumsy attempts to catch up to the others' social skills. My quick progress in our first fencing lesson had brought some much-needed relief to a so-far stifling school experience.

I sat in Miss Rush's class on lock-picking (a much more complicated topic than I had expected), and ignored Marigold's breath on my neck as she hissed her unimaginative invectives, egged on by Rubia's snorts.

Vivian, who was seated next to me, leaned over and whispered, loudly enough for Marigold to hear, "She's just jealous, Cressida. Marigold dropped her sword at least four times yesterday. I hope I'm partnered with you next time." I looked up in surprise at the amusement in Vivian's eyes as she folded her hands primly on top of her desk, ignoring Marigold's insulted gasp.

Vivian flashed an innocent grin over at me. "In fact, maybe we could—"

"Miss Guildford." Miss Rush's voice cut through the air.

Startled, Vivian glanced up at the diminutive teacher. "Yes, ma'am?"

"Perhaps you have experience in this matter. Please make your way to my desk and give us a demonstration of what I just performed."

"Demonstration?" Vivian asked in polite bewilderment.

A nervous giggle rose in my chest, and I held my breath so it couldn't escape.

"Unlock the box," Miss Rush said with unnerving patience.

"Of course." Vivian rose and made her graceful way to the front of the room.

Displayed on the desk was an array of tools we might find at our disposal: a hairpin, a hatpin, and several small daggers of varying lengths and widths. She mulled over her choices, then selected a hatpin. She held it up confidently for the class to see, and Marigold scoffed behind me. My lips twitched at Vivian's display of false confidence. She bent over and stuck the hatpin into the lock and gave it an experimental jiggle. Nothing happened. Vivian immediately discarded the hatpin and picked up the largest of the daggers. This did not even fit into the keyhole, so she quickly abandoned it. Miss Rush sighed audibly enough for the whole class to hear her annoyance. With dogged determination, Vivian gave every tool on the desk a try, angling and twisting the hairpins and daggers around unsuccessfully. I watched in tense amusement, appreciating the fortitude with which Vivian ignored the giggles of our classmates and tried to repeat the demonstration she had failed to watch. Finally, Miss Rush stepped forward with a guttural sigh and directed Vivian back to her seat.

"How might you have been more successful, Miss Guildford?"

she asked, her blue eyes snapping.

"By not being distracted by Marigold and therefore able to watch your demonstration in peace," Vivian answered promptly.

"Next time, I suggest you rise above such distractions," Miss Rush said dryly. "Miss Florelli." She interrupted Marigold mid-snicker. "You may try next."

After a long hour of our suitably chastened class learning the basic mechanics of four different types of locks and how to jimmy them open with a variety of instruments, we filed out of the classroom. I couldn't help the nervous thrill I felt at the fact that Miss Tepsom fully expected us to put these skills to use.

Someone grabbed my arm in the hall outside the classroom, and I instinctively shook it off, before seeing that it was Vivian. She smiled sheepishly at me.

"Sorry, I didn't mean to scare you."

"Oh . . . you didn't. Thanks, by the way. For putting Marigold in her place," I added, smiling back a little nervously.

"Oh, any time. I love putting Marigold in her place." Vivian tossed her hair over her shoulder and smiled. "Which brings me to a question I have for you. You can say no if you want, but I hope you won't." I waited anxiously. Vivian looked excited. "I was wondering if you might like to be my roommate?"

I stared at her, agape, wondering if this was a practical joke. I was grateful for her phrasing, as it did not elicit a forced response from me.

She continued in a rush, "I thought that maybe, since I'm currently rooming with Marigold," she lowered her voice, "and, frankly, she gives me a headache but seems to get along with your roommate, and I think *we* would get along well—that perhaps we could tell Miss Tepsom that we'd benefit more from each other's company and suggest a swap?"

I was shocked at her hopeful tone. Vivian had always been pleasant to me, but none of my classmates had shown much interest in actually befriending me, especially as I generally dissuaded any such notions. Anxiety began to build alarmingly inside me. I realized that, as she had not asked me a direct question, I was being silent for longer than was polite. Vivian looked down at her shoes for a moment, then back up at me, waiting uncomfortably. I shook myself out of my inability to act and decided to take her offer at face value.

"Of–of course!" I said. Vivian's smile grew warmer. "Rubia and I aren't the best match," I went on, awkwardly truthful in spite of myself. My roommate's most recent spate of questionings, while still inane, had grown alarmingly embarrassing. "It would be fun–and we could study together." I felt shy as my excitement at the idea grew.

"Yes! You could give me some extra pointers on fencing– well, the footwork, anyway!"

"And you could teach me how to pick a lock!" I responded. She chortled in a decidedly unladylike way. I grinned, relieved.

"I'll schedule a meeting with Miss Tepsom," Vivian said, pleased and proper again. "Thank you, Cressida!" She gave my shoulders a quick hug, further surprising me. Even if Miss Tepsom said no, it seemed as if I had truly made a friend worth having.

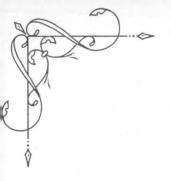

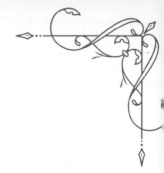

6

WITH PURE INDIFFERENCE from Rubia and only mildly offended resistance from Marigold, Vivian moved into my room, and it was instantly a more cheerful place to be. She was conversational, but did not ask a stream of uncomfortable or rude questions. A protective shell seemed to have grown around me, one that I could not completely shed even with Rubia out of my room, but at least it was one place where I could come close to relaxing.

However, living with Vivian forced me to become more social. I struggled not to see this as a drawback, but Vivian was an open-spirited girl who seemed to genuinely enjoy getting to know others, and I wished I could emulate her. She staunchly defended those whom she considered to be worthy, and I was grateful to be included in this definition. So, although solitude was where I felt safe, I tried not to scare off the friends she introduced me to.

One rainy afternoon, I had sought my solitude by pretending to study in the library, while instead devouring a volume of Dernmont fairy tales. Books were expensive, and my aunts had never allowed fiction in the house. I realized on the first day that I found the school library just how much catching up I had to do. The book was lovely. All Dernmont books were hand-scribed by talented craftsmen, but this one had been inscribed by an artist with a particularly loving hand, who had added detailed illustrations along the margins.

A polite throat-clearing interrupted my concentration. I looked up to see Vivian taking a seat on the bench next to me, with Rosalie and Eugenia sitting across the table from us.

"May we study with you?" Rosalie asked politely.

"Of course," I said trying to hide the cover of my book.

"Miss Tepsom's class on drugging powders had my head spinning. Do any of you have notes from that lecture? Cressida? I think I saw you taking notes," said Vivian.

"Yes, they're upstairs," I answered.

"What are you studying?" she asked curiously, peering down at my book.

"Um. Fairy tales," I responded, feeling my cheeks go red.

Eugenia laughed. "Whatever for?" she asked, pulling out a sheet of parchment from a copybook and handing it to Vivian.

"Just—out of interest, I suppose," I said. "I'm not studying— just reading."

"Are they good?" asked Rosalie anxiously.

"Yes, some are," I said. "I've never read most of these, although I remember my mother telling me a few of them." Rosalie nodded and smiled politely. I wished I could return to my solitary reading.

"You've probably already memorized the notes, Cressida." Vivian flashed a smile. "You know enough by now that I'd rather eat Miss Selkirk's five-bean cake than study. You and Rosalie are two peas in a pod, though. I caught her reading an alchemy text yesterday in her spare time!"

Rosalie's cheeks grew pink. "Well, they don't teach us any of the basic sciences here, unless it pertains to—you know, spying . . . I just thought the theory would be helpful, especially when we're working with drugging solutions. You know, interactions of properties can be a fascinating study, but Miss Tepsom doesn't think it pertinent." She took a short breath and stopped talking abruptly.

Vivian nodded, her eyes slightly glazed.

Eugenia snorted. "Personally, I wish we could get more exercise," she said affably. "Once a week at the stables is not nearly enough. Combat lessons with Miss Rush are dull, and we haven't seen Mr. Theon in weeks. All of this study is making me feel sluggish."

"Cressida has!" offered Vivian proudly. I felt my face redden. "She was selected to have private fencing lessons due to her natural talent."

Eugenia's mouth dropped open as I weakly attempted to make a protest. But the lessons had occurred, precisely because Mr. Theon insisted that I was a quick study.

"I'm so envious!" Eugenia exclaimed. "Not that I'm a natural—I dropped my sword three times last time he was here," she added ruefully. "But he's *entirely* handsome and we don't get much practice interacting with men."

Vivian howled with laughter that she immediately muffled, and Rosalie covered her face in mortified amusement as Eugenia regarded me with frank jealousy. I felt my face blaze with embarrassment.

"Men!" Vivian crowed. "Mr. Theon is fine enough to look at, but if he's a day over sixteen—*maybe* seventeen—I'll eat my bonnet."

"Close enough," Eugenia shrugged, unperturbed.

"Oh! Cressida, before I forget." Vivian produced an envelope and handed it to me. "Miss Tepsom gave me your post."

I took the envelope, surprised. I had not heard a word from my aunts since I moved to school months ago. I opened it as the girls' giggles died and they compared their class notes in hushed tones.

I broke the seal on the envelope and opened it, scanning down to the bottom to see the signature. It was from Aunt Millicent.

> *Dear Cressida,*
> *I hope this letter finds you well and in good spirits. I hope you are minding your manners and*

*have sewn a good pinafore for yourself. I do so
want you to make us proud. Please write to us
at your convenience and tell us all about your
school. What are your teachers like? Do you
enjoy your studies? What are you studying? Do
you have friends? Do you hear any interesting
news? What is it?*

I looked up from the letter in annoyance. Even at a distance, and after months of no contact, Aunt Millicent wanted only to use me for my submission to the truth. I stared at the words thoughtfully and realized that no symptoms had set in when I read her questions. I smiled slightly at this victory. Apparently, a question was useless in writing. I continued reading her thorough list of questions, satisfied by each one that I was not compelled to answer. She closed with reassurance that I was not overly missed.

*Fenella has asked me to write that you are to
stay at school over the holidays. Our Evenfrost
celebrations are simple and boring for you
anyway. They know what is best for you at this
time, and will contact us should a need arise. We
have transferred stewardship of your clothing
allowance to Miss Tepsom to manage. Do stay
in correspondence with us, Cressida.*
        Your faithful aunt,
        Millicent.

I didn't want to be hurt by this, but pain gnawed deep inside that my only remaining relatives would prefer that I keep my distance.

"From your family?" Vivian asked gently, and I realized that my hurt was undisguised.

"Yes," I said, folding up the letter and tucking it into my book. "My aunt."

"What does she say?" Eugenia asked curiously, oblivious to the quelling look that Vivian shot her.

I sighed. "She tells me to stay here over the holidays and asks about twenty questions about school." I glanced down at my book, feeling a twinge of returning satisfaction. "But it's no matter. I don't have to tell her anything."

My sessions with Emric, as he asked me to call him after our first lesson, greatly improved my first several months at Miss Tepsom's. I was good at fencing, as evidenced by our sparring sessions, during which he genuinely had to fight to maintain an upper hand. He also instructed me in knife fighting and dagger throwing, and taught me the variations of fighting styles that were unique to other types of swords. His encouragement left me glowing from the inside out with the knowledge that I was finally good at something—even if that something was decidedly unladylike. By the end of each bout, my muscles were taut, and adrenaline pumped through my veins like living fire. But the highlight of my school career ended rather abruptly.

Without warning that the lessons were about to end, Miss Tepsom informed me one evening that Emric was being used elsewhere and would not return to teach. I resumed my extra lessons with Miss Rush, but she was short-tempered with me, and my enjoyment faded. She could not, however, deny that I was by far the most skilled with a blade of all the pupils. So, in spite of her obvious impatience, we continued the private combat lessons throughout my boarding school career of the next two years, until I had obviously surpassed her own expertise. She ended the final session (during which I had beaten her soundly at every match) with the flippant comment that while I would probably make a shoddy spy, at least I had a future as a bodyguard.

During my time at school, per their request, I did not return home to visit the aunts during the summer or winter holidays. Aunt Millicent sent me a few letters each term, occasionally adding a brief message from Aunt Fenella. I wrote back, but I did not miss them. Their letters grew sparser when it became clear that I was not compelled to answer any of their questions, and my feelings toward them soured even more. They encouraged me to stay and apply myself to my studies, and I knew that if I were to return to their prying questions, I would never be able to keep the nature of my education a secret. But eventually, the letters stopped altogether.

I never grew truly comfortable at school, as I could not completely drop my guard in conversation, but by the fall that I turned seventeen, I realized that I was as at home at Miss Tepsom's as I could ever hope to be anywhere. I was on civil terms with most of the girls in my classes, even friendly with some, which was an accomplishment that I knew I owed to Vivian. Those of us training as spies knew that we all had a common reason for why we grew so dedicated to our education. The tragedies in our pasts bound us together, though most preferred not to speak of them. A few new students arrived at the school at the beginning of each new year, but none were added to our number.

Early in our third year, Miss Tepsom addressed our class with a flush of excitement ruffling her usually unyielding exterior. It was after dinner, and the other students were upstairs studying or gossiping. The black, opaque music room windows were all firmly shut and locked—but I could not help the shiver that danced up my spine, or the rolling feeling in my stomach.

"Tonight, I am pleased to announce the first mission any of my pupils will undertake. Four invitations to the royal court of Shoncliffe Castle have been secured, thanks to the extreme effectiveness of our contacts." A rustle of gasps rose from the gathering of students. My heart flipped in unwilling excitement at the mention of the palace on the white mountain. "As it is the first mission, we have carefully selected which of you will embark upon it. The chosen four will spend the next month in preparation, and then the mission will truly begin. The rest of you will return home at the end of term for an extended Evenfrost break. Do not be disappointed, for your skills will be tested yet." Her pronouncement was met with a tense silence as we waited for her to reveal the names. She straightened her spectacles and looked at us calmly.

I fought the fluttering hope in my stomach. I would not be chosen. I would stay at the school, as I did for every holiday, unless they sent me home to Ramshire.

Hands shot up around the room, and for once, Miss Tepsom appeared pleased by this. The nervous voices of my classmates jarred against my ears. My mind felt so full as to be almost blank, as Marigold's cool voice rose above the others' and commanded attention.

"What are our stories? Are we arriving as individuals or as a group? Are we to be ladies-in-waiting, or simply guests, or—"

Miss Tepsom stopped her with a hand. "Two of you have very specific roles to play. Vivian and Rosalie." Marigold opened her mouth to demand more information, a petulant furrow between her brows, but Miss Tepsom continued, "Vivian and Rosalie possess the nobility of blood and flawless accomplishments to be considered as future brides to Prince Roland."

A stunned silence almost reverberated through the room. I felt my mouth drop open slightly. I had not the slightest idea that any of our interactions with the royal family would reach such intimacy. Slowly, Rosalie rose, trembling and shaking her head. She was an excellent student, but introverted and anxious. Miss Selkirk rose as well, put an arm around Rosalie's thin shoulders, and guided her to another chair in the back next to her, where she whispered softly to her. Those who were not staring at Rosalie were staring at Vivian, who kept her eyes on her hands in her lap and took deep breaths.

"Why them?" asked Marigold. "My father—"

"We all know plenty about your family by now, Marigold, thank you," said Miss Tepsom firmly, silencing her. "I have manifold excellent reasons for my choices. Now. We are sending two others, as ladies-in-waiting. Rubia and Cressida."

My whole body froze, and the silence in the room expanded uncomfortably before Miss Tepsom continued, "Cressida will be the companion of Rosalie, and Rubia will attend Vivian. Miss Montshire and Miss Guildford will have more access to personal conversation with the royal family, but you, as their attendants, will have the advantage of less scrutiny and more freedom to investigate." I stared straight ahead, unwilling to see the disappointed faces, the disbelief that I had been chosen.

"You are all valuable players and will get your opportunities. But if jealousy and a misplaced understanding of the importance of your goal at this school shades your performance in your lessons, I will withdraw you from consideration for future missions immediately." The lamps were burning low but reflected brightly in her animated eyes. Vivian, looking overwhelmed but composed, stood and retreated to the back of the room to sit by Rosalie.

The feeling of *realness*, of an actual mission to the court of King Arctus, threw me into a near panic. A listener at the door or window, as unlikely as that seemed, would hear the actual plotting of traitors. Or at least, potential traitors. And it was probable that those who investigated the morality and secret deeds of the royal family danced very close to the label of traitor. I squashed the thought.

Miss Tepsom focused her attention on Rubia and me. Rubia, sitting a few chairs away, seemed to be quivering with excitement. "There will be other maidens vying for the hand of the prince, and while our aim is not for him to actually *choose* Vivian or Rosalie, we want him to remain interested enough to interact regularly with them. You both will be expected to be unfailingly loyal to your lady. Your loyalty to them begins now, and you will train to attend them for the next month. There will be much more to go over and prepare, and we will begin tomorrow morning. I suggest you all get a good night's sleep."

She strode toward the door, then turned and made one final pronouncement. "I hardly need add that it is more important than ever that your classmates learn nothing of your true education here. It is vital that you keep your guard firmly in place. There will be time enough to discuss the arrangements. Now, to bed."

She opened the door and waited silently as we stood and filed out. I glanced at Rosalie and Vivian, the only two who remained seated. Miss Selkirk was speaking quietly to them with a reassuring smile on her face, but Rosalie still wore a fixed expression of fear, and Vivian seemed to be lost in her own thoughts.

My stomach turned over as I ascended the stairs. By now, we were quite used to speaking of nothing in particular the minute our classroom doors closed, but this evening no one said a word. This was a thick, ill-at-ease sort of silence. I realized with a fervent rush, as Marigold sulked into her room, that I was eternally grateful not to be Rosalie or Vivian right now. I never realized how frightening it would feel, receiving our mission with actual details. And if I was told that in a month I would be expected to flirt with the prince, I would probably flee straight out the front door. Miss Tepsom may have tried to make little of the distinction between our roles, but I knew with a cold certainty that, for whatever reason, Rosalie and Vivian had been awarded the most dangerous.

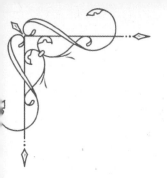
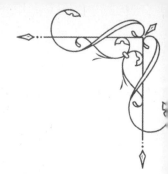

7

ONE WEEK BEFORE THE START
of our mission, the school was completely clear of any students
other than Vivian, Rosalie, Rubia, and me. Although we had
the school to ourselves, Miss Tepsom refused to lift its usual
clandestine rules and procedures.

"The very last thing you need right now is to get out of the
habit of being secretive," she said.

So, our meals and social hours were still preserved for
nothing but non-spy-related conversation and civilities. One
chilly morning, in spite of the holiday being weeks away still,
Miss Selkirk dared Miss Tepsom's disapproval by brewing
lementhe, the delicious, traditional drink of Evenfrost, likely to
ease the tension enfolding us day by day. It helped, in a small
way. The sharp, sweet scent and flavor of the creamy, spiced
tea reminded me of my childhood holidays.

The rest of the time, we were drilled in coded conversations,
lock-picking, handling light sleeping drugs, dancing, flirting,
combat (more frequently for Rubia and me), and every other
skill that our teachers thought necessary. I thought they all
were beginning to seem rather nervous as the week progressed,
which did nothing to assuage my own nerves.

The four of us were summoned to a private counsel with
Miss Tepsom in her office one evening, to clear up any final
uncertainties pertaining to the mission. I couldn't help but fret
over the state of my wardrobe as she detailed the volume of

social engagements, most including royals present. Finally, I swallowed my pride and raised my hand to get to the bottom of it.

"Yes, Cressida?"

"I'm curious about—that is, how are we meant to dress and—pack for our mission?" The other girls were respectfully unresponsive to my embarrassing question.

"Well, we will cover all of that, but as a brief overview, you will be well stocked with receptacles for clandestine messages, invisible ink—which is unreliable and should only be used if absolutely necessary—many-pocketed skirts, boots, corsets, and girdles for smuggling and weapon-concealment purposes, what unobtrusive weapons we can stock you with—"

"No, ma'am," I interrupted, my face reddening.

"What do you mean, *no*, Miss Hoth?" Miss Tepsom asked sharply.

"I mean—I don't mean no to all that, I mean, that wasn't what I meant. I meant, how are we to pass as ladies-in-waiting at court if we—some of us—don't have the suitable wardrobe?"

"Ah. A trivial matter, of course, but during this month of preparation you will be fitted and lent clothing for the occasion. We are currently in communication with some excellent suppliers who are willing to contribute to our mission."

I bristled slightly. Money, and appearing to have it, was only a *trivial matter* to those who did not have to worry about it. But her answer satisfied my practical fears.

"What do we do if we have a body to dispose of?" Rubia asked promptly as Miss Tepsom drew breath to change the subject.

There was a pregnant pause as Miss Tepsom digested the question, and I wished nervously that she looked more shocked by the idea.

"There are some things that even I cannot prepare you for, and something as morbid and undesirable as your suggested scenario is one of them. You will have a contact at court, who

will be at your disposal to assist in unforeseen circumstances."
Rubia opened her mouth, presumably to posit a follow-up
question, but Miss Tepsom held up her hand.

"Before we get into your questions, I need to detail the main
aim of your mission. Finding out anything pertinent that you
can is helpful, but broad. For this specific mission, we want you
to focus on the acquisition of a map, or a set of maps, or even
simply the location of these maps, if they are not at the castle."

"What maps?" Rosalie asked, her voice strained.

"I am afraid it will be difficult for me to give you a clear
picture of what you're looking for, but I believe the land
seizures that the crown has conducted in past decades are
related to one another. The specific purpose is as yet unknown
to us, greed notwithstanding, but the proof is very likely in maps
of the estates and land parcels that were seized. Or, possibly,
a map of a larger area with these specific locations marked.
These maps could lead us to further information regarding the
motives, and also provide proof of the king's misdeeds. You
have approximately a month to complete the mission, as the
invitation only extends through the Evenfrost season."

I digested this information through a new wave of fear.
Spying on our royal family was now beginning to feel real and
dangerous, especially now that our charge was so specific. I
wasted the rest of the meeting half-listening to the other girls'
questions, and forming none of my own.

Vivian grew more and more quiet as our day of departure
approached. This was generally unlike her, even when
something was bothering her, and I didn't know if the right way
to help my friend was to leave her to her thoughts and internal
preparations, or to draw her out. I compromised by chatting
about the mission in the least worrying way. I wondered aloud
about the journey, the climate on Mt. Vindeca, our attire,
our rooms, how many forks we might be expected to know
how to use. At times, this helped draw her out of her fearful

ponderings, and at other times, I sensed that she dearly wished for me to shut up.

What Vivian likely didn't know, was that all of these inane-seeming details actually were worrying me. I had never tried to pass as nobility outside of school and could not even fathom the environment I was about to be thrust into.

The question of our apparel, one of my many concerns, was soon answered. The seamstress who had taken our measurements several weeks prior arrived during the week to fit us all in our court wardrobes, and this rattled me as much as it excited the others. In spite of the others having suitable access to finery, we all would be borrowing the gowns from Miss Tepsom's supplier, as they contained copious hiding spots for weapon, message, and evidence smuggling. I was secretly relieved to not be the only one wearing borrowed attire.

At my appointed hour, I arrived in the music room, which had been transformed into a dress shop for the day. Miss Selkirk ushered me in and bade me strip down to my corset and chemise behind the screen she had set up before the fireplace. I shivered in my underthings as I stepped onto the seamstress' low stool. I was, by now, quite used to snide comments about my height and figure, and was not looking forward to the experience of being analyzed and given a failing grade.

The seamstress was a small, wisp of a woman with a greying frizz of hair pulled into a haphazard chignon. Her eyes shone with a fervent dedication to her work as she took one more set of measurements and muttered to herself.

"This one is ready for her season, isn't she?" she remarked to Miss Selkirk as she pulled a deep blue gown out of a case and shook it out.

"Oh, yes. Cressida was always a little ahead, and I think the other girls were a bit envious, weren't they, dear? But now is the time to look like a woman, and you're ready!"

I blushed furiously, wishing I could cover myself a little

better. I had few delusions that jealousy had anything to do with the rude comments my form had invited, but they had definitely slowed down when the other girls began to mature.

Miss Selkirk presented me with a full, green petticoat that looked meant to be seen. After I tied the strings at my waist, the seamstress held the blue dress up behind me and instructed me to slide my arms into the long, fitted sleeves. It fastened at the front, closing completely down the bodice, then the skirt was slit down the middle to reveal the green petticoat. The seamstress stepped around me, tucking and pulling here and there, till she nodded with satisfaction. I had never worn a dress that felt like it fit in all the right places. It was not tight, nor short at my wrists, it did not cut and strain. It was snug at my waist, but smooth instead of bunched up.

"Would you like to have a look, Cressida?" Miss Selkirk asked warmly. "You look splendid!" She indicated a long, standing mirror near the screen, and I stepped off of the stool and over to it.

As embarrassed as I felt about it, I could not stop the smile that came to my face as I looked at myself. I did not look ungainly. I looked bright, and strong, and really . . . well, splendid. The color brought out rich tones in my hair and complexion and deepened the brown of my eyes. The skirt fell with a pleasing weight and swayed easily when I moved. I did not want to look as pleased as I felt, but I could not help it.

"Let me show you what's special about this gown." The seamstress sidled up next to me. She gently peeled the top layer of the sleeve back at the wrist to reveal a fitted underlayer, and in between, a thin, tough sheath, hidden from view by a slight flare of fabric past the wrist. There was another on the other side, and well-disguised pockets at the hip and in the petticoat.

They had me try on three other gowns as well: a rich aubergine dinner gown with a square neckline and lace at the cuffs, a lavender overdress, suitable to fashionable daytime socializing, and one ball gown. I felt a nervous blend of excitement and trepidation when I saw this last dress. It was a deep, entrancing crimson, like a claret in crystal, with a wide neckline. The sleeves had a fitted underlayer, and a top layer that draped gracefully from the elbow on down. These sleeves were also well equipped for weapon concealment. The gown was heavy, but easy to move in, and thoroughly eye-catching.

Over an hour after I entered the room, I left with Miss Selkirk in tow. Between the two of us, we were loaded up with gowns, gloves, chemises, a cloak, a pair of dancing slippers, and a pair of boots with ankle sheaths. I knew the wardrobe was only on loan for the mission, but I felt as if I had just robbed a seamstress' shop.

Miss Selkirk paid me special attention that evening while Vivian had her fitting, showing me how to put up my hair and chatting idly. I felt a maternal warmth radiating from her, but also a jittery sort of nervousness. It put me on edge, in spite of her gentle hands winding and pinning locks of my hair.

"Of course, fashions have changed so much at court, that maybe you won't need to know how to do this anyway," she murmured around a pin in the corner of her mouth. "Your hair is so much like mine, I can show you a few tricks to keep it up securely."

I eyed the elaborate creation she sported that day and decided not to stick too closely to her advice.

She continued, "I'm sure you're more than ready, with all of your training. The main thing you have to focus on, Cressida, is conversation. You stay awfully quiet, and while that is wonderful for listening and gathering information, you're simply going to have to be able to ask the right questions and make the right connections. Do you feel ready for that?" I couldn't see her expression, but her voice had grown more serious, and I felt my shoulders tense.

"No," I answered immediately, then winced and tried to soften it. "I mean . . . it is not one of my strong suits. I hope I can do it."

She was quiet for a moment, tucking wisps here and there

into the arrangement of hair she had built on top of my head. "Cressida, why do you shy from conversation?" she asked when she had finished.

I felt my chest restricting, and my throat seemed to swell. I tried to think of how to rephrase the jumble of words rising to my lips. My vision grew dark and fuzzy.

"I don't like questions. I am . . . uncomfortable talking about myself." I knew it sounded nearly rude, as if I resented her for asking. I knew, however, that I had been extremely close to revealing my curse, and inhaled sharply to rid myself of the dizziness. I held the breath a moment, terrified that she would ask why.

But she did not. Instead, she said, "Then you must practice. You are meant to be extracting intelligence anyway, but sometimes one must appear willing and even eager to speak of oneself. Although, we do not want you, strictly speaking, talking about yourself, while at court. Near the truth gives the note of truth and circumvents suspicion. Have you studied your story?"

I nodded, relief coursing through me. I began to immediately babble about the backstory that I had been given. My parents' exclusion from the respectable, but now nearly extinct Hoth family was scandalous enough that Miss Tepsom had created a somewhat more dignified background for me. I knew that it would not hold up well under inspection, and that I could not actually get away with lying about my name, but the teachers seemed confident that as ladies-in-waiting, Rubia and I would not be scrutinized. Rosalie and Vivian had genuinely impressive family trees.

I was to imply that my parents were modestly wealthy landowners in the east and that I had met Rosalie at school. The only part of this statement that was not true was the word wealthy, as well as the implication that my parents were still alive. I knew that if I rattled off a lie about myself before being questioned, I could manage it. I also knew that if someone asked a direct question about my parents' occupation, or any other detail, I stood a significant chance of being discovered. I would have to tell the truth.

"Remember, as always, to work as a team," Miss Selkirk was saying. "If one of you is found out, it would jeopardize the others. Rosalie and Vivian, of course, have the most to lose if suspicion is cast upon them. If remaining modestly quiet serves you best in conversation, employ it, but do not shirk from using everything you have learned, should the situation call for it." She walked around to face me and examine her handiwork. "You look like such a lady, Cressida," she said kindly, admiration shining on her pretty face. "I know you will make us proud."

"Miss Selkirk," I began hesitantly, "may I ask why I was selected?" I paused, unsure if I needed to go on. She knew that the other girls all had better connections to nobility, or were nobility themselves, and many, if not all of them, had more natural polish and gentility than I.

She looked at me in perfect understanding and seemed to choose her words carefully. "Miss Tepsom made the final selection, but you were one of our top choices as soon as we began planning this mission."

I couldn't hide the confusion that crept over my face.

She continued nevertheless, "Gentle breeding and social charms are essential, of course, but we were ultimately looking for spies. You might be last in my class on flirting, but you were top in almost every class of technical skills. Lock-picking, drug-mixing, code-writing and deciphering, intelligence-gathering, physical combat . . . you were dedicated to your studies, and that consequently paid off. It was not difficult to see who would be more interested in going to court for the sake of it, and who was applying herself to the necessary skills to complete the mission. As everyone does, you have areas that require improvement, but that does not mean that you are not well equipped."

I gazed at her, genuinely confounded, for a long moment

before I remembered my manners. "Thank you for the encouragement, Miss Selkirk. And the hair instruction." I managed a small smile, which almost turned into a grimace when I caught a glimpse of the extravagant construction on my head in the mirror.

Miss Selkirk bent forward and gave me a small hug. "You're going to do us proud, Cressida. Protect the others as we know you can do best, and together your team will accomplish something great," she said. She then bid me goodnight and rustled out of the room, leaving me alone in the lamplight.

I had, thus far, been counting on my acquired ability to melt into the background and remain quietly unobtrusive to serve me in the upcoming weeks. The picture Miss Selkirk painted of me was one that I longed to be true—an intrepid spy, wielding her carefully honed skills to avenge her family. Practically, I knew that I had learned my lessons well, and the tools I now possessed could indeed yield success on this mission.

I also knew that I was taking an immense risk. I had kept myself from dwelling on the consequences if I was found out and had told myself that they would affect only me, that I could handle it. But now, I forced myself to acknowledge what I had been ignoring. I was not only risking my own safety, but Rosalie's, Rubia's, and Vivian's, as well. No matter how well I had learned my lessons, those skills could never be put to use. I was a liability and could easily put the entire mission, and all those involved, in great danger.

Suddenly I was seething. Anger at myself, but even more so at my aunts, overwhelmed me. I got on my hands and knees and dug my old portmanteau out from underneath my bed, cracking my head on the bedframe and dislodging my towering coiffure in the process.

I was used to the tension of living with my curse, of always being on the edge of discovery. My mind worked through horrible scenarios on sleepless nights of the things people could make me say. But, somehow, those had always been trivial, personal scenes of embarrassment. I had blocked off the part of my brain that knew I had far greater things to worry about as an agent of Miss Tepsom. Somehow, my small success at navigating the curse at school had soothed the realistic fears away.

I dusted off the portmanteau, my heart thudding painfully against my too-tight corset. Still sitting on the bare wood floor, shedding hairpins, I lowered my head against the bed, trying to calm myself and catch my breath. I sucked down air in a panic, but it wasn't right, it wasn't enough.

This evening had confirmed many things that I felt I should have figured out already, but there was no more time to dwell on my extraordinarily ironic ability to lie to myself. I could not go on the mission. There were actual lives at stake. The penalty for treason was death, and what we were doing, and what our teachers were doing, would easily be ruled as treasonous if discovered.

Taking a deep breath, I stood and peeked out the window. The streetlamps were lit, the townhouses up and down the street appeared to be dark and quiet, and the street was empty. I fiddled with the clasp of my portmanteau until finally it released, and cracked open the aged leather case. I flipped it over to dislodge any spiders or dust balls, pulled my dresses off their hooks, and began cramming my few belongings inside.

I stowed the portmanteau back under my bed, hung all my new dresses, and laid down, pretending to be asleep under the covers when Vivian came in twenty minutes later. She readied herself for bed quietly and fell asleep almost as soon as her head touched her pillow, as she usually did. I waited another fifteen minutes to make sure she was deeply asleep, before crawling quietly out of bed and pulling my packed portmanteau out from underneath it.

Then, heart hammering, I tossed my cloak over my arm,

softly opened the door, and stepped into the hall, refusing to look back at my friend or the pile of beautiful clothes that I was leaving behind.

I took the stairs that led toward the music room. The light tapping of my shoes against the wood, and the creak of nearly every stair—a loud squeak emitted from the fourth from the top—almost sent me into a black-out panic. When I finally reached the bottom of the stairs, I stood motionless outside the music room door, listening for any sign that I had awakened someone in the school.

After a long moment, I crept forward and pushed open the door, which was mercifully unlatched. The seamstress' box, screen, and cases full of gowns were still set up in a jumble of shapes and shadows. I moved quickly around the obstacles and finally reached Miss Selkirk's harp, which stood in front of the window, my destination. I was well aware that the sash and lock were broken on this window, as Miss Selkirk grumbled about it every time she sat down to play. The harp, ever the mortal enemy of my ears, now seemed an even more sinister adversary. It would be risky to attempt to move it; it was a heavy, unwieldy instrument, prone to alarming, echoing *twangs* when disturbed. But it was so very close to the window. I stood for a moment, the urge to hurry rising within me.

I set down my case and cloak, and straddling either side of one end of the harp, lifted up with acute deliberation. I held it up for a moment, my fingers sweating and aching, then inched ever so slowly to the left, and set it back down, several inches further from the window. I wiped my hands on my skirt, then picked up my portmanteau and cloak, and slid between the harp and the window. Elated that I was nearly there, I pushed my hand against the sash and forced it up.

Tossing my cloak and case onto the dark ground outside, I sat on the sill, then cautiously slid through, taking great care not to let the window slam shut behind me. I lowered the sash slowly, then crouched against the brick wall for a moment to catch my breath. The air was sharply cold against my throat, and a rush of relief coursed through me.

I threw my cloak over my shoulders and gathered my belongings, then stood and stepped carefully around the wall, keeping to the shadows as I moved toward the front of the house. I paused at the corner of the house, unsure if I was willing to step into the light of the streetlamps at the front. But there was no other route to take, and I would quickly find shadows again.

I hurried forward—and ran straight into a person striding around the side of the house. It was Miss Tepsom.

She startled for a moment, and then her eyes widened as she took in the sight of me, cloaked and guilty, with baggage in tow. An expression of disappointment crossed her shadowed features.

"Come," she said, then turned on her heel and led me up the front steps and into the school. I did not consider disobeying, but my mind churned in an urgent panic as I followed her through the door and down the darkened hall.

I stood near the door of her office, clutching my bag as she lit a lamp and set it on her desk. I knew I had to talk first, before she could ask questions. As soon as she started asking, and she definitely would, I would have no choice but to answer. It was too optimistic to hope that she would word her questions just right—I had been lucky for years, but that couldn't last much longer, and especially not now. I took a deep breath, set down my case and cloak, and meaning to stride but achieving more of a totter, I approached Miss Tepsom's desk and sat down opposite her.

The lamplight glinted against the small spectacles that she sometimes wore, turning her eyes into two opaque, white ovals. Her mouth was a line cut into stone.

"Miss Hoth—" she began in a steely voice, but I interrupted

in a panic, throwing my hand up the way she so often did to quell a student.

"Please, Miss Tepsom—I just . . . if I could just speak," I said awkwardly, nearly rising out of my chair in my desperation to keep her from asking me anything. I did not wait for her consent.

Near the truth gives the note of truth and circumvents suspicion. I decided to give Miss Selkirk's advice a try.

"I spoke with Miss Selkirk this evening. We discussed my strengths and . . . those areas which need improvement. I've been thinking it over, and I don't think I am ready. I struggle so much conversationally still, I'm quite positive I will not be able to pull off the deception and that I will endanger the mission and the other girls. In spite of all your lessons, I'm afraid that when it comes to it, I won't know what to say to fool and manipulate people, much less discover anything useful." I felt my face flushing and my heart pounding even harder than when I had been sneaking through the music room. It felt so near to a confession. I was dancing so close to the truth, and all she had to do was ask the right question. I couldn't hold her off of talking forever.

She stood, pushing her chair back with a scrape, and walked around the desk to sit in the chair next to me. My hand shook as she laid hers on top of it.

"I'm not a coward, Miss Tepsom," I said, desperate for her to believe it, for it to be true. "I wouldn't have tried to leave if I didn't believe the other girls to be in danger because of me—because of my incompetence."

"Cressida," she said firmly, and I sucked in a breath, terrified of what she might say but powerless to hold her back. "What you have to remember, is that no one expects girls fresh out of boarding school to navigate the society of court perfectly. You will be indulged and underestimated. I depend upon that fact. They do not know of your deadly skill with a blade, the way you know exactly what to look and listen for. You will be the poisoned chalice sitting at their right hand—unobtrusive . . . unexpected." Her eyes grew grave. "I have to send you, Cressida. You are my peace of mind."

"What do you mean?" I asked in confusion.

"You all will be on high alert and dedicated to your mission. Your specific charge is that you make the safety of your team the highest priority. I have no one else to send for this task. The protection of your friends is your responsibility, and if I send them without you, then I am sending an incomplete, cracked set of agents. Rubia, whose natural inclination toward stealth does her credit, was also chosen for her combat skills. She has improved admirably this year, but she alone will not be sufficient."

She stopped and watched my face. I stared at my hands, unwilling, even now, to tell her that whatever protection I could bring would not withstand the danger I might also bring down on my classmates. But I felt that I had run out of options. I looked up and nodded, willing her words to be the only relevant truth.

She smiled, then said, "Miss Hoth, I would not have discovered your flight this evening if I had not just stepped out the front door myself. I was awake, but heard nothing. This is a good sign of your skills being put to good use. I only have one note."

I blinked, a little baffled to find my attempted escape turning into another lesson.

"Naturally, I appreciate your candor. But in the future—on your mission, I should say—*if* discovered someplace you are not supposed to be, I recommend that you lie."

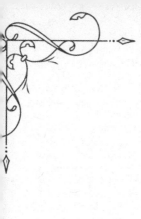
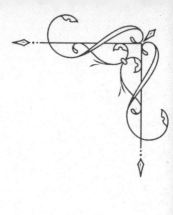

Part
Two

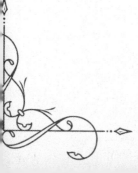

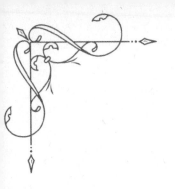
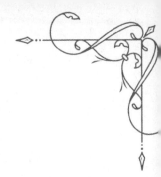

8

THE DAY WE SET OUT
for Shoncliffe Castle was bright and savagely cold. Vivian
and Rubia left the day before Rosalie and I did. Our carriage
rocked us gently over the road, which grew chalk white as we
slowly ascended the frozen mountain, and we were sheltered
from the bitter winds by the trees that hunched over the road.
I remembered my father giving me a small, polished white
stone, long ago, and telling me that it was a piece of the white
mountain. That memory, the timbre of his voice and the
gentleness of his fingers as he dropped the stone into my palm,
filled me as we continued to go upward.

Finally, the road smoothed into a wide drive, and we swayed
through the tall iron gates and onto the long, curving driveway
when the sun was high in the sky. Shoncliffe Castle was set
on the south side of Mt. Vindeca, looming above Savinrue,
surrounded by a high wall of white stone. I had seen its shape
from a hazy distance many times from town, but had only an
impression of turrets and walls.

The carriage was surprisingly well insulated, and the soft, rich
interior made me feel like a princess out of a storybook. Rosalie,
in fact, very nearly held that role, and she looked the part with
her blonde hair curled and arranged demurely, a wide-hooded
cloak swathing her long frame in velvet. But her eyes still held
a glint of fear, which drove my personal concerns to the back
of my brain as I worried about her upcoming performance.

She and Vivian had spent the last week in almost constant coaching with Miss Selkirk and Miss Tepsom. Her panic of the night she discovered her role seemed to have compacted into a controlled anxiety, which I believed could easily pass as a natural nervousness at meeting the royal family—unless she lost control of it, of course. I knew it was part of my job to support her and help her cope, but right now, I wasn't sure how to do that. Rosalie and I were friendly, but had never grown close, nor even particularly comfortable with each other.

I smiled at her in what I hoped was an encouraging way as the carriage slowed, though my own heart began to pound. I leaned my head against the window to try to get a glimpse of the palace, but from our angle, all I could see were walls of cut stone.

"You look beautiful, Rosalie," I said, hoping to hearten her. She did not blink and still looked like a frozen facsimile of a lady, but then she exhaled ever so slightly and managed a small smile. I adjusted my hood and wiggled my numb toes as the coachman called the team to a gentle halt.

The footman opened the door of the carriage, and I waited for Rosalie to exit first. She took a breath, then stepped out gracefully. In a momentary burst of stubborn panic, I considered staying in the carriage. As this was obviously not an option, I accepted the footman's white-gloved hand, and somehow made my way out of the carriage and onto the bright, scrubbed flagstones in front of the palace. The cold of the stone seeped immediately through my slippers, and a chill shot up my body, mocking me for bundling against the wind. A pair of maids in long, black dresses with crimson aprons bowed to Rosalie, then indicated we should follow them inside. I glanced up quickly before stepping under the stone arch before us. The palace was a monstrous edifice, ornately carved, but I only got the briefest glimpse before being led inside.

The arch led into a dark hallway, almost a tunnel, and there were long, narrow, glassless windows set at intervals that looked out into a bare courtyard. Arches of stone, carved with worn and ruined scenes, lined the tunnel. It smelled damp, and the wind shot in streaks through the windows and howled along the passageway. In that corridor, I could forget that it was a sunlit day.

The maids walked at a brisk sort of trot, and we rushed to keep up with them. Finally, we came to the end of the passage and entered through a high set of heavy wooden doors. Footmen in red and black held the doors open for us as we passed through.

My head buzzed with questions. Would we be taken directly to the royal family? Would we be staying together? When—and how—did we get started? I shook the questions out of my dizzy brain, forcing a sheen of composure to encase me.

Rather than a room, we had entered another corridor, this one wider and brighter. The maids turned to the left, and we followed. The thick, red carpet laid over the stone floor was a small relief to my freezing feet. There were wider, glassed-in windows to the left, revealing the vast courtyard, and we passed several arched doorways, set deep into the stone walls to the right.

I tried to take note of the route, the number of doors we passed, which staircases and turns we took, and noteworthy architectural details, but I quickly lost my bearings.

The maids finally stopped before one door along another softly carpeted corridor. One of the maids stood like a sentry at the side of the door, and the other turned a bored eye toward us and asked politely, "One of you is Miss Montshire, and the other her companion, I presume?"

Rosalie nodded quickly without further explanation. The maid eyed her with what almost looked like skepticism for a moment, then said, "This is to be your room, which you will share." Rosalie nodded again, and the maid turned a large key into the lock, then gave the door a hard shove.

"What is your name?" I asked as we followed her into the room, hoping I sounded pleasanter than I felt.

"Sylvie," she answered. She stepped aside to let us pass. Rather than follow us in, she spoke again from the doorway. "You've a bell to summon me if you need anything. I will be seeing to your luggage now and will bring your itinerary as soon as I receive it. Ma'ams." She bowed again, then turned and left, shutting the door behind her.

The room felt silent in an empty sort of way as soon as the door closed behind Sylvie. I glanced at Rosalie, who was staring at the door anxiously.

"The maids here bow," I remarked. "I have no idea what to expect now." She shot a nervous look at me, then, to my shock, emitted a sharp, short giggle. I smiled.

She looked around the room, appearing a bit more relaxed now. The chilly room was as large as three of our bedrooms at school put together, with a bed at each end, two vanities, a standing mirror, and two intricately carved wardrobes. There was a small settee next to a little round table in the middle of the room, with a dark fireplace in the wall behind it. I walked to one of two windows and looked out. The view was, unfortunately, obscured by high stone ramparts.

"You don't mind being my roommate, do you?" Rosalie asked after glancing at the ramparts out of the second window.

I shrugged out of my cloak, then changed my mind and wrapped it back around myself as the cold sank into my skin. "Of course not," I said. I walked slowly around the room, wondering if I ought to be investigating anything yet.

Rosalie sat down on the settee, her expression growing tense again.

"I wonder if Vivian and Rubia have a room on this floor too," I commented. She didn't respond, and I sat down next to her.

"I am not sure I know what I'm doing, Cressida," she confessed.

"I don't either," I told her. "I mean . . . theoretically I do," I clarified. "But I'm having a terrible time picturing myself doing it."

"Yes, that's exactly it," said Rosalie. "When we were being coached this week, Vivian seemed to know all the right questions to ask, and the right answers to the questions she was asked. She has so much more confidence than I have."

I had no idea what to say and hoped this was a moment in which she would appreciate silence. She stared at a bowl of pink roses on the tea table with an odd expression on her face. I reached forward and picked up a folded card, which was stuck half under the glossy clay bowl.

"This is probably for you," I said and handed her the card. She did not take it. Slightly impatient, I opened it myself and read the contents, which had been scrawled in a bold, hasty hand.

Miss Montshire, please accept these roses as a welcome gift. I look forward to meeting you and anticipate the great pleasure of getting to know you. Until this evening, Roland.

"Roland. The prince," she said softly. Her eyes grew wide. "Great pleasure . . . Cressida, you don't think that I'm going to have to, that he means—"

"No, Rosalie. No," I interrupted firmly, my impatience growing slightly. Quelling and soothing Rosalie might turn into a full-time job, and I had a head full enough of my own doubts and fears. I took her hand.

"Listen to me," I said. "You've been given a big job. But Miss Tepsom wouldn't have chosen you if she didn't think you could handle it, and she certainly wouldn't have sent us on this mission if it meant we would have to do unseemly, compromising things. We are . . . intelligence agents. Nothing worse. You pretend, really pretend that you are here for no other reason than to meet the prince and hope he considers you for a bride. That's enough to be getting on with. The rest of us will handle the actual spying until you're comfortable with your role.

"And," I added, knowing that she needed to hear it and knowing that it was quite true, "I will protect you. All right?"

She gazed through me for a moment, then met my eyes with her round, blue ones, and nodded firmly. I released her hand, and my breath. My mission had officially started.

Sylvie, followed by footmen bearing our luggage, brought us tea and an elegant itinerary, written in glistening crimson ink on heavy parchment.

"I'm sorry there was no fire lit, ma'ams," she said primly, and proceeded to light one while we drank our strong tea and studied the ornate itinerary. It included a schedule for the evening.

Introductions: Winterberry Drawing Room was followed by *Dinner: Silver Dining Hall,* and the evening ended with *Coffee: Sedgewood Salon.* Rosalie's brow was furrowed.

"Sylvie," I asked, "will you be showing us where to go?" She did not answer for a moment, and I glanced at Rosalie nervously.

Sylvie rose from the fireplace, where a flame had finally caught and was eating through the kindling. She slipped her hand into a pocket beneath her red apron and produced another folded parchment.

"I almost forgot to give you this: a map of the castle. The rooms are labeled. Will there be anything else, ma'ams?"

I took the map she held out, and Rosalie shook her head with a soft thank-you. Sylvie left quietly.

"Oh heavens," I muttered as I unfolded the map, which was much larger than I'd expected. It took us nearly five minutes to find our location and several more to find our destinations.

The three-story palace looked labyrinthine on the map, but after close inspection, it began to make some sense in my mind.

"What time is it, Cressida?" Rosalie asked suddenly.

"I'm afraid I have no idea." I looked around for a timepiece with mounting trepidation. "Late afternoon sometime?"

"We'd better start getting ready for the introductions, don't you think?" She seemed as if she was waiting for me to tell her what to do.

"I think that's a good idea," I said.

We selected sides of the room and began to busy ourselves with unpacking our bags and airing our evening gowns. I laid the aubergine gown across the deep, richly embroidered coverlet of my bed, then paused and took a deep breath as I looked down at it. I would help Rosalie through this, but the task tightened around me like a corset several sizes too small.

I finally located a small clock tucked behind some intricate, white stone-carved ornaments on the mantel, and we could breathe a little easier as we readied ourselves. We helped lace each other into the complicated bodices of our gowns, Rosalie's a shining peach silk of cascading layers that brought out the blush in her cheeks. I twisted and pinned my hair into place with trembling hands. When there was no more cause or time to stall, we stepped out of our room into the hall. Somehow, I had ended up the proprietor of the map, and Rosalie waited expectantly to follow me. Feeling completely outside of myself in the borrowed gown, knives in my boots and sleeves and a lockpick in my hair, I set off with false confidence down the hall.

We only made one wrong turn, and corrected immediately. It was difficult not to take our time. The stone passages were profuse with carved figures, gargoyles, and paintings depicting scenes ranging from historic and religious, to literary and mythic. The brilliant tapestries, all overcome with crimson but interwoven with golds, blues, greens, and black, told even more vivid tales, but we did not linger.

Finally, we reached a set of doors which were held open by footmen and matched the location on the map of the Winterberry Drawing Room. It was brightly lit and humming with conversation, so I assumed I had led us correctly. I looked at Rosalie, whose face had become a mask, but a lovely one, bordered by her carefully arranged golden curls.

I gave her hand a squeeze. "I will be right behind you," I assured her softly, then fell a step back as we approached the doors.

We had learned the protocol from Miss Tepsom. Whisper your name to the footman, and he would lead you to the family. Or something like that.

Rosalie quietly announced her name to the footman, and her voice did not shake. He nodded and leaned over to whisper in the ear of another gentleman in a powdered wig, whose gold-striped, black uniform looked slightly finer than the footman's. This man bowed to us.

"Do follow me, madams," he said cordially. My heart leapt into my throat as I stepped through the threshold into the bright room.

It was well-named Winterberry, for everything from the silk-covered chairs and settees, to the cut-glass wine cups and jeweled accents on the chandelier, were a berry-bright shade of red. The hangings on the wall shimmered an almost golden pink, with a deep red beneath. There were about twenty other people in the room, socializing gracefully. Placid smiles did not crack faces perfectly set with powder and rouge, voices did not rise above a light titter. I felt relieved that I was not overdressed, although the dark shade of my elegant aubergine gown was an anomaly. Brightly colored silks and patterns were draped over the ladies, and the men all wore formal, if less colorful, coats and breeches, topped with snowy cravats. Some of the older set sported rather dusty-looking wigs of dubious-looking origin, and I was fervently thankful that one had *not* been a part of my own costume.

The king was easy to spot. He did not sit on a throne, or even a place of precedence, but he laughed louder than the others and wore a voluminous-sleeved, peacock-blue jacket that was nearly a royal robe itself, open at the front to allow his cravat room to tumble in a perfect waterfall. His round face was red, expressive, and half-buried beneath a greying beard. We followed our escort directly into the king's circle.

The fellow we followed bowed low, then rose with a click of his heels.

"Who have we here, Fenwick?" the king asked, peering around the man pleasantly.

"At the invitation of the prince, Miss Rosalie Montshire, and her lady-in-waiting, Miss Cressida Hoth," Fenwick announced us grandly, stepping aside.

We made low curtsies as the four or five courtiers who encircled him stepped back slightly. They remained near, however, looking us over curiously. Anxious heat engulfed me and prickled over my skin.

The king looked for a place to set his brimming wine cup and finally settled on the arm of a settee nearby, where it was quickly rescued by a lady behind him. Then, to my shock, he reached out and cordially shook Rosalie's hand, causing her to flush deeply.

"Terrible pleasure, Miss Montshire," said King Arctus jovially, then reached around and shook my hand as well. I hoped my shock was not as apparent as it felt. His grip was firm and brief, a quick sensation of my hand being swallowed then released.

"My wife, Queen Ceridwen," he said, turning to the lady who had rescued his glass. He allowed her room to stand next to him and put his hand on her back. She was pretty and slightly plump, with graying blonde hair set with one or two silver ornaments, and a simply cut gown of sky blue. She smiled serenely at us, her eyes pleasant in a misty, faraway sort of way, but did not offer her hand as her husband had. We each curtsied to her.

"Fenwick, would you say the ladies' names again?" King Arctus turned apologetically to us and tapped the side of his head. "I always need to hear them more than once before they stick."

Fenwick proceeded to introduce us again, during which time it felt necessary, but also embarrassingly excessive, to curtsy a third time.

"Delighted, my dear," said Queen Ceridwen to Rosalie, darting a quick smile at me as well. "You must meet Roland, but I am afraid you have arrived too early."

My stomach clenched in mortification at the idea that we had boldly walked into a private party. But then she smiled more warmly.

"You see, my son does not care to make an entrance until we have all begun to wonder if he ever really existed." Rosalie offered a faltering smile in response, and I felt my muscles relax ever so slightly. "Meanwhile, do enjoy yourself, and we will introduce you the moment he arrives."

She nodded grandly at us, then turned to a lady on her right and resumed a quiet conversation. The courtiers closed in once again around their king, and somehow, we managed to gracefully slip out of the royal ring.

I spotted Vivian mingling on the other side of the room, with Rubia hovering nearby, and I nudged Rosalie. A sheen of sweat had begun to glisten on her pale forehead, but relief broke over her face when she saw Vivian, and she nodded to me that we should make our way to her. I led the way, as it was obvious that Rosalie was waiting for me to.

I was walking with such purpose, craning my neck to see around the courtiers in my way, that I nearly ran into a tall figure that strode directly into my path and stopped there, forcing me to stop also. The gentleman stood gazing down at us in satisfaction, a red glass glinting in his hand. I wanted to glance at Rosalie, feeling that I should at least appear to take my cue from her, but she was directly behind me. Hiding, almost. I dropped into a curtsy, having no idea the station of the man before us, and Rosalie's gown rustled behind me as she followed suit.

"One of the prince's many delightful selections, I take it?" the gentleman asked smoothly, taking my hand and bringing it to his lips. His pale blond hair was impeccably coiffed, and he was crisply dressed in a black coat and vibrant purple waistcoat. His age was a mystery to me. He could have been anywhere from an elegant twenty-five to a well-preserved forty.

Rising from my curtsy, I answered abruptly, annoyed at his presumption. "No. I am not." He looked down at me in bemusement, saying nothing. "Allow me to introduce my lady, Rosalie Montshire. The most delightful of the . . . selection," I said, turning my shoulder to allow Rosalie to come forward. I felt like a recalcitrant girl's mother when she did not move.

"Enchanted," the gentleman said with a bow, taking Rosalie's hand and drawing her forward. "May I fetch any refreshments for you and your companion? The prince will, I am sure, take excellent care of you—once he finally arrives," he said smoothly. He slid his gaze back my way and winked conspiratorially. "He does like to make an entrance." I bit my tongue against the urge to dismiss the man and move on, but felt that Rosalie needed to at least make a pretense of leading.

"Would you be so kind as to introduce yourself first, sir? We would not like to inconvenience someone with whom we are not even acquainted," Rosalie replied. The evenness of her tone caught me by surprise.

"Lord Eston," the gentleman answered with another courteous bow. "I am overfond of berry-sherbet claret," he raised his glass apologetically, "cards, and am impatient to a fault. I apologize for my precipitate familiarity. Now, we are the best of friends. How may I be at your service, my lady?" His blue eyes twinkled playfully at Rosalie.

"It is lovely to make your acquaintance, Lord Eston," Rosalie answered with a smile that was only slightly tense. "A glass of berry-sherbet claret would be delightful."

"Excellent." He smiled down at her, then over at me. "I will see that you are both served." With yet another bow, he slipped away through the crowd.

Rosalie took in a quick breath, then exhaled. "Oh look," she said with some relief. I followed her eyes. Vivian and Rubia were approaching us. We all looked at each other in a brief, panicked moment of indecision, then Vivian nodded.

"Miss Montshire, Miss Hoth. How good to see you again," she said warmly.

"Lovely to see you as well," Rosalie responded, and I nodded, my stomach tightening automatically.

"You look lovely," Rubia said to Rosalie in what was probably meant to be a reassuring undertone, but it came out rather menacing.

"We are waiting for a lord to bring us drinks," I said softly.

"Well done," Vivian approved, nodding.

We attempted small talk as we waited, but nerves flattened the conversation. I tried very hard not to feel as if all eyes were on us, although it was difficult, especially considering the pair of gentlemen openly ogling from halfway across the room. One, in a striped waistcoat, held a quizzing glass to his eye as he surveyed our party, and nodded in satisfaction as the other smirking young man whispered in his ear. I angled my face away from them and tried to join in the forced exchange, but an awkward silence had settled over our anxious group by the time Lord Eston appeared, bearing a glass, and followed by a footman with a tray.

I accepted a foaming cup from the footman, immediately soaking the fingertips of my gloves with sticky crimson liquid. I realized, upon taking my first sip, that Miss Tepsom's education had been woefully lacking in preparing her young charges for the taste of wine. I swallowed quickly, then forced my expression not to twist as if I had just sucked the center out of a lemon. The other girls took it in stride, although Rubia had me worried when she emptied her glass in three swigs. I prayed she had enough experience to know when to stop before the wine affected her judgment.

The ringing of a bell interrupted the conversation that Lord Eston was attempting to resurrect. "Ah! Dinner," he said. "Would you do me the honor of allowing me to escort you?" he asked Rosalie gallantly.

Two silent footmen, who were beginning to remind me of chessmen in their red and black livery, opened a pair of doors at the opposite end of the room, and guests were pairing off and wandering through.

"I—well, thank you—" Rosalie began. But she was saved from having to formulate a response when the doors we had entered were suddenly flung open with alarming force, and a rather disheveled young man in evening wear burst through. Another young man strode in at his heels.

"Yes, yes, I can announce myself Fenwick, thank you!" the tousled young man said, shooing the eager butler who immediately descended. "Prince Roland has arrived, and just in time for soup, I hope!" he said grandly as he jogged into the room. He pulled up short near our party and addressed Lord Eston in a low voice.

"Tell me mother has already gone in?" he asked anxiously, peering around Eston's tall frame. "I've bungled it again, and it simply won't fly this time." His face, while stressed, was merry like his father's, and a bit pink, as if he'd had a few cups of wine already. His slightly unkempt hair was blond, and I noticed a bit of the queen around his eyes. If he had not announced his identity, I believe I would have recognized him anyway.

"You are quite safe, Your Highness," Lord Eston answered Prince Roland gamely. "Her Majesty was the first to enter the hall and is no doubt awaiting you there."

"Of course." The prince clapped Eston on the shoulder. "I daresay I was meant to meet someone again tonight, wasn't I?"

"You have arrived fortuitously at her feet, Highness," said Lord Eston, gesturing to Rosalie. Fenwick flapped around the perimeter of our party, no doubt anxious to do the job he was assigned. Lord Eston ignored him. "May I introduce Lady Rosalie Montshire."

Rosalie had, thankfully, taken advantage of Prince Roland's state of confusion to gather her own bearings, and was waiting serenely for her introduction. Her poise made me proud, in spite of my own churning stomach. We all dropped into curtsies.

"Have I? That's great luck, although I suppose it would have been luckier if I knew how to behave. My apologies, my dear lady. Rosalie. Miss Montshire. Prince Roland, at your service." He made a surprisingly elegant bow. "And Miss Guildford, Miss . . . Feldingham, delightful to see you again." He muffled his voice uncertainly as he stumbled over Rubia's surname, but recovered himself well. He then turned and smiled warmly at me, where I waited quietly at Rosalie's side. "I presume this is your attendant?"

"Miss Cressida Hoth," Rosalie introduced me.

"Delighted. I've a man, though who knows where he's gone off to." He smiled around at all of us.

"I'm right here, Your Highness," came a dry voice directly behind Prince Roland. The prince jumped rather exaggeratedly and turned to allow the young man access to the circle. My heart thudded to a stop.

"Ah, there you are, Theon. Ladies, I'd like to introduce you to my right-hand man, Mr. Emric Theon." Emric bowed. My mind whirled with the surprise of seeing him again. He'd been on the verge of young manhood when last I saw him; now, he'd crossed the threshold. I wondered why Miss Tepsom had not mentioned that he would be here also.

"Ladies," said Emric, almost dismissively, with a shallow bow. His courtly clothing was simple, but somehow on him, the black of his jacket and the crisp white cloth at his throat was striking. "Your Highness, we should go in, before your mother devises a punishment for me."

"Ah yes, my whipping boy. Joking!" he said reassuringly, patting Rosalie's back familiarly. "May I escort you in, my lady?" he asked, offering his arm.

She looked panicked for a moment, glancing up at Lord Eston.

Eston smoothed the awkwardness by immediately offering me his arm. "And would you be so kind as to accompany me, Miss Hoth?" he asked.

Rosalie took the prince's arm with a small exhale, and I took Lord Eston's. Emric led the way, solo, and we followed him into the dining hall.

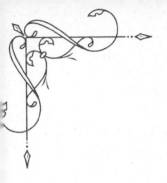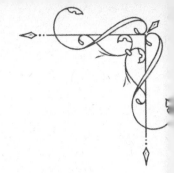

9

BY THE SECOND COURSE, I was positive I would not be able to handle the stress of the mission for the rest of the evening, let alone the next month. Lord Eston kept up a steady flow of conversation on my right, and Rubia, on my left, was muttering her observations to me in such terms that nearly made me pass out from anxiety.

"I mean, that's him, right? I'm sure it is. I would recognize that physique anywhere." I tried to kick her under the table, and unfortunately, was not sure who I succeeded in kicking, because it did not seem to deter her. I'd questioned Miss Tepsom's judgment in sending *me* on this mission, but it was Rubia's indiscretion that could be the death of us.

The table was a dazzling light in the center of the dark hall, and the backdrop to every guest was heavy blackness, with the silent shapes of footmen rippling through the room. Golden-rimmed dishes and goblets shone robustly. Fragrant white flowers tumbled down the center of the table, and silver candelabra towered at intervals.

Emric was seated across the table and a little to my left, and I did everything in my power to avoid his eyes. When I did accidentally glance his way a time or two, his attention was firmly elsewhere. He was seated next to a pretty, red-haired young woman, and he kept his eyes on her as they conversed.

"That's a delightfully unique name, if I may say so, Miss Hoth. Cressida, was it?" Lord Eston had decided to start asking me polite questions about myself. It was time to put my untested conversation-maneuvering skills to the test.

"Yes," I answered quickly, and immediately mirrored his question before he could ask more of me. "And what of Eston? That name is new to me as well. Can you tell me its origins?"

"It is unfamiliar to you?" He raised his eyebrows. "How interesting. Eston is a very, very old name, and also the name of my estate near the Porleacan border. My mother chose my given name from among her own family. Beaufort."

I nodded, unsure how to respond. I was unfamiliar with the estates surrounding my childhood home, but as we also lived near the border, his response worried me.

"And where are you—ah, lovely." Lord Eston's attention was diverted to his plate.

My stomach clenched as a footman leaned discreetly between us and set a dish before me. It contained a trio of petite chops, artfully arranged on a large cabbage leaf, glazed in something that looked sticky-sweet, and drizzled in broth and thin cream. As grand as the food appeared, I could not discern hunger from nausea in my current state of anxiety. The food would not distract my dinner companion indefinitely.

I could not help but glance again at Emric then, and this time, his eyes were on me. He looked away quickly. My stomach tightened even further. Conversation waned only slightly as the guests tucked into their meal.

"So, you have not told me where you are from, Miss Hoth," Lord Eston said with a smile when the lamb had been cleared away. Panic struck as he spoke, and a footman placed dishes of fig pudding heaped in cream and caramel sauce before us next. Although it was the most delectable dish I had ever seen, my mouth felt as dry as if it were stuffed with dust. Then I realized that while Lord Eston had, in fact, asked me a question, there were no symptoms. He'd asked without *asking*.

"Evenrock," I answered through my dry throat. It was not

true, and not what I had planned to say. But it was, hopefully, far enough away from Lord Eston's estate that he would not expect to be familiar with the area. "An old estate, but a very dull little place."

As I spoke, I realized how difficult it was to avoid the stare of a gentleman directly across the table from me. He appeared to be one of the men who had been openly staring before dinner. He watched me with interest, seeming to find me a fascinating point of focus, with no regard for my discomfort. I forced my attention to remain on the guest to my right.

"I quite understand," Lord Eston was saying. "I consider my family home to be quite dull indeed, but the king seems to enjoy it for the hunting. The royal family have been frequent visitors at Eston Hall for generations, and I am not deaf to the compliment."

"How nice *that* must be," sighed the lady on Lord Eston's other side. "Really, it was my poor, late husband who was close with their Majesties. But they do take pity on me and invite me to the odd dinner party, occasionally." She did little to disguise her sour tone as she wiggled her way into the conversation.

"To the appreciation of us all, Lady Bern. May I present Miss Cressida Hoth? Lady Bern is another dear friend of the royal family." He deftly introduced the lady to me, and she leaned over him curiously to see me better. Her brown hair was set in poofs over her ears, with, to my mystification, a tall powdered wig set on top. A large, gilded butterfly, nearly large enough to pass for a hat, adorned one side of her wig. She looked almost insultingly intrigued as she looked me over, raking me with her pale blue-grey eyes.

"A pleasure, my dear."

"How do you do?" I responded, unsure what else to say. She followed my eyes, then flicked hers up to my hair.

"You must think that wigs are a fading fashion. I've heard some of the others say so, but I have done extensive research on the matter. They will *always* remain the height of style for nobles."

"Your confidence does you credit," I responded with a stiff smile.

Done with me, she leaned close to Lord Eston, clearly bent on maintaining his attention. "Is this another of the prince's prospects? Do you think His Highness will be able to make a choice this time, Lord Eston?" she purred. I strained to hear his response.

"Let us hope so, for the sake of Her Majesty," Lord Eston replied with a sigh. "As you doubtless have heard, the king's brother remains unstable. It would give their Majesties great peace of mind to see Roland's line flourish."

Lord Eston almost caught me leaning suspiciously close to catch his conversation when he suddenly turned back to me.

"I am so pleased to see how lovely and charming Miss Montshire is. Three months ago, seven young women came to visit for a month. The prince did not form a lasting attachment to any of them. Their Majesties do not wish to force him to wed without affection and are hesitant to pressure him further," he said, tossing back the last of his wine.

"How many have been invited this time?" I asked.

"Only four, I believe." He nodded across the table subtly. "The slim brunette directly across, she was the first to arrive. Lady Adella. The sweet-faced girl sitting next to the queen is Lady Vivian—oh, but you've met her. And the, er, autumn-haired lady in blue silk next to Theon is Lady Tilda. All, I might add, are of Dernmont."

I said nothing, wondering at Lord Eston's observation. It was interesting that all the contenders for the prince's hand should be from his own country. An alliance with Porleac would be a fortifying move for the kingdom and lessen some of the historical unease between the two countries.

The king, at the head of the table, stood, and all conversation fell respectfully silent.

"My wife and I shall repair to the Sedgewood Salon to take

our ease, enjoy some entertainment, and I hope, revel in your good company. You are all most welcome to join us at your leisure."

Queen Ceridwen stood and gracefully took her husband's arm, and they strolled the length of the table and out a door on the opposite end of the room from where we had entered. Others followed immediately. Among them, the gentleman across the table with the determined gaze.

Lord Eston inclined his head to me graciously. "It has been a great pleasure making your acquaintance, Miss Hoth, and I hope to continue to do so during your stay." I gave a smile in response, and he joined several other courtiers as they left the table and followed their sovereigns.

"Well he had lots to say, didn't he?" Rubia said in an undertone as Lord Eston slipped out the door. Most of the dinner guests had already risen and were making their way to the salon. I noticed that Prince Roland escorted Rosalie.

"Who were you sitting next to?" I asked Rubia as I stood. It felt as if I had been encased in stone for the past hour, and my muscles desperately needed to unkink.

"I don't know, some old fellow in velvet that smelled like dog. I was busy listening to your conversation."

I followed her in resignation to the doorway the courtiers had all exited. There was a candelabra in a sconce near the door, but the short passage between the dining hall and the salon was dark. I stepped through the doorway into the passage as Rubia trotted ahead, and immediately felt a hand grasp mine firmly.

I smothered a gasp and turned sharply, tugging my hand away. I slipped my fingers around the dagger in my wrist sheath.

"Who's there?" I asked in a hushed voice. A tall figure took a step closer to me. My eyes adjusted to the dark and I saw that it was Emric, his cravat bright amid the shadows.

"Shh. It's just me." A slight smile crinkled his eyes.

I took a deep breath and exhaled in relief. "You startled me,"

I said, pushing the dagger more securely back into its sheath. "Emric, I had no idea you were here. What—"

"I'm sorry, Cressida, we can't talk yet. I wanted to tell you that if any of you need anything, or have learned something important, you may contact me to meet through your maid. She'll think it's a rendezvous of a different sort." His voice was calm, but barely audible, and he stepped closer so I could hear. The evenness of his tone was belied by an urgent intensity in his eyes.

I wanted to ask about his mission, but instead I simply replied, "I understand." Then, because I couldn't help myself, I added, "I didn't think that you recognized us."

"Good," he answered, then turned toward the salon. Then, he paused and said lightly over his shoulder, "But I'd know you anywhere, Cressida."

I was holding my breath again, and didn't release it until well after he was through the door. I nervously tugged at my sleeve, adjusted my tight bodice over my aching ribs, and went through the passage into the salon.

I was relieved to find the lighting low, the well-spaced candles casting a soft orange glow rather than a bright, golden one. My entrance seemed to go unnoticed. I scanned the room, noting Lord Eston and Lady Bern standing near the king, and Emric against the wall near Prince Roland, who was conversing with the red-haired Lady Tilda.

Rosalie and Vivian had found one another and were sitting on a settee not too far from where I stood, so I made my way over to them. The walls of the salon were paneled in golden wood, and its spicy aroma drifted through the smells of candle smoke and perfume. I took a seat on a stiff, brocade chair near Rosalie. Vivian looked up and smiled at me, her eyes sparkling in excitement.

"Have you seen the itinerary for tomorrow, Cressida?" she asked. "In the morning we all picnic! The guests of the prince, and their attendants."

"Picnic?" I asked in disbelief. "In the dead of winter?"

"Prince Roland described it to me at dinner," said Rosalie. "He said a mountain picnic is his favorite, no matter the season." My brows drifted up in amusement. Prince Roland, no longer a faceless royal, was not as we had expected.

"What else did he say to you?" asked Vivian, leaning forward. "I met him last evening but barely spoke to him. And you were escorted by him into dinner!"

"Honestly . . ." Rosalie's eyes dropped to her lap. We both leaned in closer to hear her. "I don't remember most of it. This is all too–too much. I don't think I am going to accomplish anything here." She drew in a shuddering breath and quickly dashed away a tear that clung to her eyelashes.

I glanced around quickly, then slowly reached forward and patted her arm. "Rosalie. You are doing just fine. This is the first night, and–"

The room suddenly quieted, and I realized that this was the wrong moment for this conversation. I straightened as the stillness in the room was filled with the plucking of harp chords. A stocky woman, draped in rubies, stepped onto a low dais and began to sing. The woman's rich contralto was robust, but soothing, and I kept an eye on Rosalie as she took several calming breaths.

Some of the guests continued to talk quietly among themselves, and the entertainment did not deter two gentlemen from continuing to socialize. The man who had found it amusing to openly stare at me during dinner, and his companion with the quizzing glass, strolled toward us and affected bows. We all followed Vivian's confident lead and stood, then curtsied.

The smug expression on the face of the man with the quizzing glass was mystifying. His companion smiled around at all of us.

"Lord Petran, of Wulfeport, at your service, my dear ladies," the quizzing glass fellow said, swinging his accessory jauntily by its chain. "And this Mr. Lupei. We must assume that at least some of you are here for the prince's delectation, but we are terribly eager to make your acquaintance for ourselves." He appeared younger close up, in spite of his stiffly elegant costume. His pale, ginger hair had been smoothed away from his face with some sort of stiffening product, but frizzed a bit around his neck. His companion, Mr. Lupei, bowed a second time when he was introduced.

"I am Lady Vivian Guildford, and this is my companion, Miss Rubia Feldingham," Vivian responded smoothly. There was a slightly awkward pause after their hands were kissed, then Rosalie remembered herself.

"Oh. I am Miss—Lady Rosalie Montshire, and this is Miss Hoth," she said stiffly.

The gentlemen kissed our hands, and I froze nervously when Mr. Lupei lingered, glancing up at me as his lips hovered over my hand for a fraction of a moment longer than felt proper. His long, dark hair brushed over my fingertips.

"We are delighted to make your acquaintance, and hope for the pleasure of socializing with you further," Mr. Lupei said, showing a neat set of white teeth when he smiled.

"How long are you at court?" Lord Petran inquired, his eyes flicking over each of us.

"Through the Evenfrost holiday," Vivian answered. She offered nothing more, but smiled serenely.

"Excellent! Well, we shall leave you to the music for now, and anticipate with pleasure our future encounters," Lord Petran said with feeling, bowing once more. Mr. Lupei followed suit, and the gentlemen departed. We sat and looked at each other, our collective unease palpable.

As we applauded the third song of the set, Vivian leaned over and whispered, "I almost forgot! I have something I am supposed to give each of you. Can I visit your room after this?" She raised her eyebrows and lowered her voice even more significantly. "Preferably when your maid is done assisting you for the evening."

Rosalie nodded nervously.

I gave Vivian the direction, and she nodded in satisfaction. "We're on the same corridor. I'll find you."

It did not take Sylvie long to complete her duties and leave. She lit a fire, then asked if we needed help undressing. Conscious of my hidden weaponry, I assured her that we did not. She bowed and bid us goodnight.

Less than a minute after she left, there was a quiet tapping at the door. I rushed to it and opened it, and Vivian squeezed quickly inside. "I was just around the corner waiting for her to leave, thank goodness she went the other way!" she gasped, her cheeks flushed.

I ushered her in, thinking perhaps she was being a bit dramatic. I noticed then that she was wearing a heavy cloak and wondered in exasperation if she was *trying* to look suspicious.

"Where's Rubia?" I asked.

"Asleep already. She enjoyed that claret sherbet a bit too much. I'll fill her in later." She went to Rosalie's bed and heaved something from under her cloak onto the brocaded coverlet.

Rosalie and I approached curiously. Vivian was unwrapping laces that were wound around a leather satchel, her fingers shaking slightly. She flipped open one side of the faded leather, and then the other. It opened like a book, but instead of pages, it contained pockets. There were six pockets, and each contained a small, flat, corked and sealed bottle.

Vivian held her hands above the satchel, as if she were the proprietress of the bottles, but afraid to touch any of them. "You remember the lesson we had on herbs, powders, and potions?" she asked. I nodded.

"If you can call it that." Rosalie snorted. She had always been dissatisfied with Miss Tepsom's perfunctory skimming of all subjects scientific or alchemical. "But she told us she hadn't been able to acquire the drugs she wanted to send with us," she said with a frown.

"Right. But on the day that I left, Miss Selkirk gave me these. She said they had just arrived. She warned us to be extremely cautious with them and only to use if absolutely necessary. Cressida, I think this one is specifically for you." She pointed to a tall, thin bottle about half-filled with a dark liquid. The other half of the bottle appeared to be full of smoke.

Vivian looked at me. "If necessary, you're to dip the tip of a stiletto dagger in this potion," she went on. "It is not lethal unless a large amount is used, but even a prick of a blade dipped in this potion will induce a deep sleep, one that could take many days, or longer, to escape. I think she called it Nemere." She lowered her voice to an anxious whisper. "I'd say be ever so careful with this one, and don't touch your blades once you've treated them!"

I drew the smooth bottle gently out if its pocket and held it up before me. No light from the fire could be seen through the liquid or the smoke. I controlled a shiver as the weight of our task continued to drape itself over me, and wondered what circumstances could induce me to use the Nemere. I wondered what Miss Tepsom expected.

"Rosalie," Vivian said, carefully picking up a bottle filled with a pale, speckled powder, "you and I are to keep hold of these." She indicated that there was another just like it. "This is the truth powder. Verum."

I nearly dropped the bottle I was holding and stared at what Vivian was handing to Rosalie.

"It can be dissolved or steeped in liquid," she was saying.

I felt my palms become slick, and I quickly slid the Nemere into my inner petticoat pocket before I dropped it.

"How does that one work?" I asked unevenly.

"Apparently, it becomes impossible for the one who ingests

it to lie. These two are the follow-up." She pointed to two matching bottles of a green powder, as bright as fresh sage.

"That's the antidote?" I asked breathlessly.

Vivian glanced at me curiously. "No, there's no antidote required. The effects of Verum should be temporary. This powder is for forgetfulness and is supposed to make the last half hour you experienced a bit of a blur, if used sparingly. If one were induced to speak truths they did not mean to speak, they might easily become suspicious. This is touchy, as there might not be an opportunity—"

"Or they might leave, or call for help, or—" Rosalie broke in anxiously, staring at the bottle in its pocket.

"Right," said Vivian, her eyes darting between me and Rosalie, her fear becoming more apparent. But her voice was resolute. "One of those things might happen first. But if possible, if they don't notice that something is strange in time to do something about it, we try to dose them with the forgetfulness drug, Lethen. If it works, it should help remove suspicion."

We stood together silently, contemplating the satchel of drugs.

Eventually, Rosalie said, "We were never trained on powders this powerful. What are they? Herb? Mineral? Something else entirely? I wish we knew more if we're to wield them as weapons. Do we dare drug a royal?" Her face was white.

Vivian took a deep breath. "I know it feels too real, too dangerous, but this is what we're here for. We can skulk around all we like, eavesdrop, try to get in their confidences, or try to slip into private rooms to search. But I think this is the most powerful tool that we have at our disposal, and we should use it. Using the truth powder is the only sure way of discovering if they truly are responsible for the murders in our families."

I was shaking my head vigorously. A numbness had washed over me. "Don't do it," I said hoarsely. Rosalie and Vivian looked at me in astonishment.

"Cressida, you look positively green! What is it?" said Vivian.

My head began to pound the minute she asked the question and I dug my nails into my palms, willing myself to remain calm, and deflect further questions as I answered in the only way that I could.

"Too harmful. I've never heard of . . . Verum . . . specifically, but . . . but I don't believe its effects are temporary." My deepest truth danced on my tongue, but the symptoms receded as I spoke. I stumbled over my words to keep them from asking another question.

"I–I've heard of truth potions. My aunts . . . they . . . dabbled. I've never heard of one with only temporary effects. And there can't be that many."

Vivian's expression grew sober. "Of course, we don't want to risk such a thing, if that is true." She paused. "But would Miss Tepsom and Miss Selkirk have given it to us if they did not know exactly how it works? I don't believe so." She furrowed her brow. "Cressida, I know how frightening it is. But Rosalie and I are most likely to be the ones taking the risk. While you need to be keeping your ears and eyes open as well, your primary goal is to protect us. I know it feels innocent enough, but this place is full of intrigue. We have to be willing to act."

I looked at Rosalie. She was more cautious. She would agree with me.

But Rosalie was nodding slowly. "She's right, Cressida. Miss Tepsom knows what this powder will do. And I have to remember why I'm here. It's for my father." Her hand hovered momentarily over the bottle, nestled into its quilted pocket, then she drew it out and wrapped her slender fingers around it.

I felt a wave of nausea. I wanted to wash my hands of it all and let Rosalie and Vivian take the responsibility. But I was here, fully a member of a treasonous plot. And that wasn't what bothered me. The Verum, innocent as salt and pepper in its little wax-sealed bottle, taunted me with its very existence. How could I let them inflict it on somebody else?

But Vivian made a good point. Miss Tepsom knew the drug. Could there really be more than one concoction capable of such a power, but different from the one used on me? I, too, remembered my reason for being here under these conditions. The memory of my parents' gentle hands holding mine provided a cold clarity that comes with pain. If I was going to be a party to this act that frightened me so much, I would not simply stand back. I would be there, to either stop them, or help them.

"At least, don't do this alone," I said. "I know you have to get the prince by himself, but on the chance that he suspects before you can administer the Lethen, you will need protection. Let me be there. I am the closest thing to a bodyguard that you have."

Vivian nodded in agreement. "Rubia considers herself my bodyguard, and she is handy enough with a sword, but she is a bit . . . zealous. There's no way I would entrust the Nemere to her. It might have to be done in the moment, if an unplanned opportunity arises, but if at all possible, you should be there at the ready. At least, if we can't administer a dose of the Lethen, you can prick him with your blade and he will sleep. Then we can leave the palace before he wakes up and remembers that he revealed vital information."

"Preferably after finding the maps," inserted Rosalie.

The fire glowed low in the hearth and the burning logs snapped at the silence. There were too many variables. We were clutching at strands of a plan, unprepared for the gravity of this mission. We were plunged in over our heads, charged with discovering royal secrets. The idea of needing a plan of escape had not occurred to me, nor had it been presented. We had envisioned a smooth, crafty extraction of information, all the while being perceived as nothing but the most innocent of young guests. The defense lessons, the weaponry, in spite of the exciting scenarios my imagination conjured, had felt like unnecessary precautions.

Vivian pulled out one of the bottles of green Lethen and placed it in Rosalie's hand. She stowed her own bottle of Verum inside her sleeve, thought better of it, and retrieved it, tucking it in between the other bottle of Lethen and another small, thin bottle, which appeared to contain more of the Nemere. She then began hastily wrapping up the satchel with the remaining potions inside. Her movements were rushed, and she was showing considerably more anxiety than when she had arrived.

"Well, I'd better go. If we need to communicate, we will have to plan it carefully ahead of time again, and keep our social interactions brief," she said as she moved to leave. Rosalie and I nodded wordlessly.

"See you tomorrow," Vivian whispered, and cracked the door open.

I hurried forward and put a hand on her shoulder. "Better let me check first," I said, my nerves vibrating at how easy it was to make a mistake. Vivian stepped back while I peeked into the hallway. I went out and down the hall to peer around the corner to make sure no one was around to see her leave our corridor. The passage was clear, so I beckoned to Vivian, who scurried out of our door and down the hall, looking awkwardly hunched with the satchel tucked under her cloak.

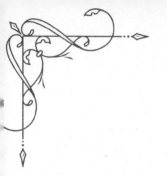

10

WE DRESSED WARMLY for the picnic, which was scheduled for late in the morning. I was grateful for the sturdy fabric of my gowns; our seamstress had done an excellent job of blending practicality with the romantic court styles. I could have done with less complicated lacing up the back of my bodices, however. I tucked a throwing knife into the ankle sheath deep in my boot, strapped my wrist sheaths and slender stiletto daggers between two layers of sleeves, and pulled long leather gloves over the cuffs.

I contemplated the bottle of Nemere for a long moment in indecision, its strange gases swirling and twisting above the dark liquid. With reluctance, I wrapped the small bottle in a handkerchief and tucked it into my petticoat pocket.

My cloak was heavy and dark and felt like armor when I draped it over my shoulders. As the castle was embedded in the mountainside of Mt. Vindeca, I wondered with trepidation if we were really going to be traipsing around the frozen mountain on the prince's whim.

We were directed to meet in the Wulfestar Hall. I located the hall on our map, and Rosalie and I found it with only a couple of wrong turns. The front of the castle faced south and stared down the mountainside toward Savinrue. The Wulfestar Hall was on the east end, the furthest wing from our quarters. The palace truly felt like a labyrinth as we navigated hall after hall and passed one forbidding, closed door after another. But the layout was beginning to take shape in my head, and I could visualize the way the silent, red-carpeted halls skirted around ballrooms and galleries, drawing rooms and music chambers.

The Wulfestar Hall was a long, high-ceilinged room with massive fireplaces carved into three walls. Thick, stone columns stood at intervals throughout the hall, and tall, gleaming windows lined the outside wall, rising above the ramparts.

The view was breathtaking, drawing our gaze away from the town to the south and toward the rural, untamed countryside. The land sprawled to the east, a haphazard quilt of unevenly fenced farms clustering at the foot of the mountain, spreading broader and wilder toward the northeast. The trees and hillsides thickened in the distance, blurring our view of the border between our country and Porleac. The land was frozen now, especially in the heights of Mt. Vindeca, and the ground was a pattern of white and brown. Winter was not long, which was fortunate for the farmers and those in the country who suffered through it. It traveled down from the mountain and froze the earth each year for a furious, fleeting season of ice.

I'd found I liked the mildness of winter in town. At the southern foot of the mountain, Savinrue was blocked from the worst of the winds off the Wulfestar Sea, to the north. The town lit up this time of year with fires and braziers at every turn, the shops filled to bursting with Evenfrost drinks and fashionable furs. Townsfolk and vendors made the most of their craftwork to hawk every possible easement of the season. For those with a home and a hearth, it felt rather like a long holiday, despite the bite of ice.

The very idea of leaving the castle, but remaining on the frozen mountainside, awoke in me a fear of the elements, and I had to sternly remind my brain that ice was the least of my concerns right now.

"Are you sure this is it?" asked Rosalie, her voice echoing as she looked around the hall. "There's no one else here."

"I think we're in the right place," I answered, drinking in the view from the window nearest to me. It was clear and bright, the sky brilliantly blue, but the glass was as cold as a sheet of ice. If I squinted, I could just barely make out a slice of grey-blue to the northeast. I wondered if it was the sea. The sound of voices broke the vast silence of the hall. Rosalie and I turned expectantly to the door.

Prince Roland entered, chatting amiably with Vivian and Rubia.

"I hope we have not kept you waiting!" he exclaimed when he saw us, and I was relieved to see the flush of wine gone from his face, and no trace of unsettling repercussions. He smiled warmly at Rosalie and swept a courtly bow. She curtsied, and I followed suit.

"You've met Lady Vivian and her companion, Miss Feldingham?" the prince asked, sweeping an arm to encompass the ladies surrounding him.

"Yes, Your Highness, we are acquainted. How are you, Lady Vivian?" Rosalie responded with quiet composure.

"So glad to see you, of course!" answered Vivian, in high spirits. She looked merry and natural in her fur-lined cloak and muff. "We shall have an excellent time." She turned to the prince. "So, this hall must be named for the Wulfestar Sea?" she asked with interest.

"Indeed, madam. So named, because this is the only common room in the castle from which the sea can be glimpsed."

We were joined then by Lady Adella and Lady Tilda, each accompanied by a lady-in-waiting. The number of young women surrounding Prince Roland was becoming overwhelming; I thought it no wonder that he was having difficulty making a choice. Prince Roland introduced us to the petite, brunette Lady Adella, then the ice-eyed, ginger-haired Lady Tilda.

Emric, cloaked in heavy black wool, had slipped unobtrusively into the room and strode toward a set of double doors set between two high windows. Glancing out one of the windows near the door, he called back to us, "The coaches are here, Your Highness."

"Thank you, Theon! You and I share a solemn privilege, to escort these fine ladies. Let's not lose even one today!" Prince Roland chuckled, and the ladies around him seemed to have varying reactions of amusement and nerves, which resulted in an awkward titter emitting from the group. He offered Lady Tilda his arm. "Shall we, ladies?" he said, and marched regally to the doors.

Emric gave one of the doors a rap, and two footmen pulled them open from the outside, seeming to struggle with an icy wind that wanted to slam the doors shut again. A precarious flight of stairs sloped down to a curved drive, where two black carriages waited. The familiar Dernmont coat of arms was emblazoned on the sides of the conveyances in shining white, red, and gold filigree: two red roses crossed over the image of the white mountain. The teams of shaggy mountain horses stamped their giant hooves, and breath steamed forcefully out of their nostrils.

The stone steps had been salted and sanded, but it was a difficult descent, wrapped as we were in petticoats, heavy skirts, and cloaks. The prince, Emric, and footmen made gallant endeavors to make sure no one slipped. Finally, the large party reached the bottom of the steps without mishap, and we were bundled into the coaches.

Vivian and Rubia were in one coach with the prince, Lady Tilda, and her companion. Rosalie and I shared the other with Lady Adella and her apprehensive-looking lady-in-waiting. Emric was the last to step up into our coach. He looked briefly around with a strained sort of smile, then sat down in the empty space next to me, near the door. As there was very little available space, we were packed in and uncomfortably cozy. Outside of the wind, the cold was bearable. The collected breath of the five passengers in the coach steamed up the windows almost instantaneously.

"Mr. Theon," asked Lady Adella's companion from the opposite seat, "Where exactly are we picnicking today? Surely not on the side of the mountain?" Her voice shook with cold.

"Not exactly, no," Emric answered in his pleasant, rich baritone.

"Not exactly?" Rosalie asked in surprise.

Emric smiled. "Prince Roland has a favorite haunt, and I believe he enjoys the stark beauty of it in the frozen months. The Monastery of Rounelith. The monks there are happy to allow parties to traipse through the halls and grounds, as long as we do not disturb their private apartments. The views are incomparable."

"Rounelith?" Rosalie asked in surprise. "The site of the pool with healing minerals?"

Emric was silent for a moment before responding. "I've heard there is a spring on the grounds that is sometimes sought for healthful purposes, although I've never experienced this for myself."

Rosalie's eyes widened, and I knew she was recalling whatever she had read on the subject.

"Does he not—not fear the sacrilege of picnicking at a holy site?" Lady Adella leaned forward to ask, her expression slightly appalled.

"Not at all," he reassured her. "I understand your concern, my lady, but the monastery and the castle have long been on such terms."

All further conversation ceased as the ride became almost unbearably rocky. The carriage was making a steep ascent, and the road felt treacherous. The coachmen encouraged the horses onward as the brakes scraped to prevent the wheels from slipping on the icy scree. As much as I wanted to see where we were going, and the views surrounding us, I felt a cowardly relief that the windows were too fogged for me to see exactly how great a danger the road presented.

We drove in tense discomfort for about a quarter of an hour before the road leveled somewhat, and the team pulled up sharply. Emric unlatched the door and hopped down, then flipped down the step for us to use.

"Miss Hoth?" He held out his hand to assist me out of the carriage. I took his offered hand and hoped that he couldn't feel the grip of my dagger, which was digging into my palm beneath my glove. My hope wasn't worth much, however; his fingers lingered directly over the hard lump there, and his eyes flashed into mine for an instant. I smiled serenely at him as he released my hand. My heart pumped wildly in my chest, belying what I hoped was a calm exterior. Emric helped the rest of the ladies out of the carriage, as Prince Roland gallantly did the same at the coach ahead.

We had climbed nearly a mile up into the ice-crusted mountain. The evergreens were thick to the north, and nestled up against them was the monastery: a low, rambling edifice of ivied, crumbling stone, surrounded by a dead hedge. To the east, the vista we had viewed from the Wulfestar Hall in the castle spread before us, only far more vivid and breathtaking. The brilliant blue of the sky seemed to cast silver and jewel tones over the entire landscape, and I wondered how much brighter and more beautiful it would look during summer.

Inside the walls, barren gardens adorned the front of the monastery. Bare-limbed fruit trees stood as still, lonely sentinels along the path that Prince Roland led us down, directly to the monastery. When he reached a pair of tall, finely carved wooden doors, he lifted the heavy knocker and released it. I was a little surprised, since I had rather expected a footman to announce his presence, or perhaps for the prince to simply stroll in. A small silence followed the knock, and then, the sound of a bolt scraping. The door was pulled open with a creak by a diminutive fellow who made a low bow. He nearly disappeared into his massive wrappings of rough wool and pulled his hood up over his tonsured head as he straightened. He swept his hand wide to usher us inside.

"I apologize for the icy breeze we bring with us, Brother," Prince Roland said as we filed in quickly.

Emric shut the doors behind the footmen, and for a moment, I could see nothing as the outdoor light was extinguished. My eyes adjusted quickly, however, as we passed out of the vestibule and into a long chamber. Low, narrow windows allowed some light into the barren stone hall. The dank, old smell of damp earth and stone assailed my senses, and an odd wave of comfort washed over me. It reminded me of my father's workshop, where I used to sit on his workbench and carefully polish old stones and metal bits as he tinkered in his leather apron.

The monk led us down the center of the chamber, where a small huddle of holy brothers, all wrapped in the same undyed wool robes, sat hunched over piles of manuscripts, conversing in heavy, hushed drones.

"Brother Arin has taken a vow of silence," came a whisper over my shoulder, and I turned to Emric, who nodded toward our guide. "He's not spoken a word since joining the brotherhood."

"Why ever not?" I asked, startled. Emric suppressed a grin as I looked around in embarrassment. I had not exactly whispered.

Emric kept his own voice much quieter. "The personal sacrifice aids in his devotion, I suppose."

"Have many of them made that sacrifice?" I asked, and wished for a moment that I had been sent to a monastery instead of to my aunts' house. I would have preferred not talking at all to being forced to answer endless slews of questions.

"Only a few others, I believe," he answered as we approached the clump of monks at the end of the room. "Though they have all given up much."

The prince stopped at a respectful distance as Brother Arin went forward and tapped on the shoulder of a white-tonsured old monk. The man looked up in surprise, so engrossed had he been, then got to his feet with the aid of those around him.

"You do us honor, Your Royal Highness," he wheezed. He walked toward us, his gait labored.

"I am terribly sorry if we have disturbed you, Father Harrick.

My father said he would send word. Our messenger bird did not fly off course, I hope?"

Father Harrick waved the apology aside with a gesture that looked like it unbalanced him slightly, and Brother Arin grasped his arm. "Not at all, young prince. We received word. Her Majesty's birds never fail to find me, but the days blur and I forget easily. You are all most welcome. I doubt our little hut will have much to entertain, but what we do have is utterly at your disposal."

"We shall strive to stay out of your way and cause no bother, Father," said Prince Roland warmly. "I'd like to show the ladies around, and then picnic at the east end, if it will be no trouble."

"Please enjoy yourselves." He gazed mistily over our party. His presence felt at once solemn and comforting. "Our monastery and grounds are humble, but echo with the rich history of our land." He paused, then raised his hand, closing his eyes. When he spoke, his voice carried the weight of a benediction.

"May the white mountain open your heart and close your wounds. May its stones bring you truth, and in truth, may you find the peace of its Creator and the courage He imparts." He opened his eyes, and they crinkled into a smile. "And may each of you receive a clearer sight before you descend."

Prince Roland bowed graciously, and Father Harrick was led back to his seat and circle of companions.

The blessing of Father Harrick attained, we followed Prince Roland to the east wall and through a low doorway cut into the rough rock. I noticed Rosalie looking around with interest and wondered if she would be bold enough to ask to see the spring. The door led to a dark, wide passageway.

Roland spoke in a low voice as he led us down the corridor, which was so dim and long that I could not see the end of it. "They aren't terribly easy to see, but try and have a look at the tapestries that line these walls. The scenes woven into the wool are the product of thousands of years of history. You may have seen some like these at the castle, but many of these are much older. The monks want them displayed, but also preserved for future generations to study." I glanced at the wall, determined not to meet the eyes of any of my companions. Doubtless, they all wondered the same thing I did: whether the tapestries only displayed history approved by the royal family, or something truer.

The prince offered an arm to Vivian and began strolling ahead, bending his head toward hers slightly as he spoke in a tone only she could hear. I noticed a sniff and twitch from Lady Tilda, and she moved quickly to follow him, her companion in tow. I suppressed a smile and realized what a difficult task Prince Roland had before him. How could he possibly choose a bride from a party of young ladies when he was obligated to spend equal amounts of time with all of them, always chaperoned? And he was certainly heavily chaperoned today, as there were twelve in our party. I fell behind slightly, allowing a little breathing room between myself and the slow-moving cluster of ladies following the prince.

The tapestries were large—perhaps as wide and as tall as the massive double doors at the entrance of the monastery. They were illuminated dimly by thick, fragrant beeswax candles set into sconces in the wall between each, with a solid length of wall separating the hanging and the flame. It protected the tapestries from fire or smoke damage, but it also made them rather difficult to see.

"So very . . . educational," Lady Adella commented, a slight sneer in her voice as she ran her fingers over a tapestry she was passing without stopping to look at it.

"Oh dear." I cringed slightly.

"Is something wrong?"

I started. I hadn't realized I was close enough to anyone to be heard. I recognized Emric's voice, however, and my face grew hot as I was forced to truthfully answer him.

"Well, yes. I'm afraid that Lady Adella will damage the tapestries if she keeps touching them carelessly. I imagine our hosts would be quite disappointed if that were to happen. And rightly so," I added.

"And I imagine you are right." He raised his voice. "Lady Adella! Hands off the hangings, if you please."

She turned sharply, and in the soft light of the candles, her cheeks turned a dull red. Without answering, she turned back around and strode ahead.

"Oh dear," I sighed.

"There you go again. Now what is it?" Emric said with amusement. I glanced up at him, at the easy smile that I had not seen for two years, but had not forgotten. My stomach flipped; likely because I'd given him the opportunity to ask me questions twice in a row.

"Well, now you've offended her," I answered. "She will probably rake her fingernails over the next few, just to teach you a lesson."

"I don't want that on my conscience," he said earnestly, peering ahead. "No, she appears to have lost all interest in the tapestries."

"How many are there?" I asked as I ran my eyes over a clunky scene of men falling off horses and a fellow with a spear through his eye. Dark threads that traced the shape of billowing smoke clouded the border, with the stiff forms of fallen soldiers beneath it. It couldn't be easy to depict dramatic historical battles in woven form.

"I believe fifteen or sixteen. A few religious scenes, but most are battle scenes and landscapes, I'm afraid, so I'm sorry if that doesn't interest you."

I hitched my shoulders. "I confess I am unlikely to recognize many of them, but the history is interesting nonetheless. Doubtless more interesting if I understood the context a little better." I tried to relax my tense posture, though I felt the need to be even more guarded than usual. I knew very little about Emric's mission, and had no idea what he knew of mine.

"Perhaps, but it is understandable if you don't. The wars between Dernmont and Porleac are numerous, but not terribly varied."

"All of these are depicting wars with Porleac?" I probed. "I knew that there has not always been peace, but did not realize we had fought many wars."

"Relations have been tense for centuries, but of an actual history of war, I've read only vague references. Given the ongoing tension over trade ports and harbor tax, perhaps we have been fortunate not to have seen war in our lifetimes, or that of our parents," he said quietly, stopping before one of the religious scenes. Even in the dim light, the gold of the halos and brilliant blues and reds of sky and robes and blood took my breath away. It was so vivid for so ancient a thing.

"Your teachers were doubtless occupied with teaching you more eminently useful skills," Emric said.

"I suppose so," I said, not daring to look at him. It was true that our history lessons had been few, focusing on the foibles of our royal family for the past few generations. Our social and spy skills took precedent.

"Which subject in school was your favorite?" he asked conversationally.

"Fencing," I answered immediately, my nose inches away from a scene featuring a bright, caged menagerie ringed by a battle. A lion in the center held up a silver cup. I had no idea what it symbolized. Realizing what I had just said, I stole a glance at him, holding my breath.

His lips twitched forcefully, as if to contain a grin. Relieved, I checked that no one was near. The rest of the party had wandered at least two tapestries up the passageway.

"I'm sorry," I whispered.

"No need," he whispered back. "I had hoped you'd say as much, but I suppose I didn't expect that you would. However, I am glad to hear it. Did you keep up your . . . studies?"

"Yes, but infrequently," I said. He had stopped walking altogether, and I couldn't decide if I should follow his lead or continue walking at a casual pace before we fell suspiciously behind the others.

He leaned in to take a closer look at the tapestry and spoke in a voice so low it was nearly inaudible. "I was extremely surprised that your headmistress sent you this season. I did not believe that it was her intention to send you ladies yet."

I looked up at him in surprise, then remembered to pretend to inspect the hanging as well. "Why not? This is what we have been preparing for. We have information to collect and the sooner it is obtained, the better," I whispered. Struck by a thought, prompted by the tapestry I was glancing over, no doubt, I asked suddenly, "Do the king's men use arrows? What color is the fletching?"

"Some. Red and white, I believe. Crossbows are their standard, however," he replied, glancing curiously at me. Instead of pursuing my question, however, he glanced at the party, moving ever gradually further away, then back at me. "I fear you were sent precipitously. You don't have to tell me, but I still need to ask—what is your objective, and your strategy?"

I kept my eyes firmly ahead of me, although the moldy weaving blurred before me. My throat became tight and my head swam as I remained silent. When I could bear it no longer, I hoped that this was a minor crime, confessing secrets to someone on my own side.

"Maps . . . and Verum," I finally said, my voice tight. I was furious that my curse had made me name the truth powder as our strategy; although, reluctant as I was, it was the only one we'd truly discussed so far. I glanced at Emric.

His eyebrows went up. Then, seeming to realize how far

behind we had fallen, he started walking. I remained at his side, waiting impatiently for a response.

"Do you have experience with Verum?" His expression was a courteous mask.

"Some," I answered automatically, and my lungs constricted unpleasantly.

There was a pause. "Be careful," was all he said.

We walked on in silence, and I realized how important it was for us to begin gathering as much information as we could. Emric had asked about strategy, and other than the Verum, we had none. Our training had covered many facets, but we were woefully underprepared. It was as if Miss Tepsom had mixed up several ingredients to bake a cake, then flung a handful of the mixture haphazardly into a hot oven.

My jaw tensed. The situation was not ideal. We were officially on our mission, stocked with weapons and potions and a thirst for justice. We couldn't just leave and head back to school to demand better preparation and another chance to try. We had to collect the information we needed, now, and complete the mission.

The corridor of tapestries ended at the entrance to a greenhouse. By the time Emric and I caught up to the others, Prince Roland was delightedly showing the ladies at his heels all of the plants that the monks managed to cultivate throughout the winter. I followed Emric down a dirt path that led to the center of the greenhouse, where a small woodstove stood, its iron belly glowing with embers. There were logs and chunks of wood set around the stove at random, and the footmen from the carriage had already brought some large picnic baskets inside.

"Please be seated, everyone!" Prince Roland called out genially, then plunked down on a mossy log.

"How delightfully rustic!" Lady Tilda exclaimed, her face a concentrated mask of enjoyment. She gingerly sat on the log near the prince, pulling her burgundy cloak tightly around herself to allow as little fabric as possible to touch the damp wood.

"How is it so warm in here?" asked Rubia to nobody in particular, throwing her hood back off of her dark head.

It was Emric who responded. "Well, I would not presume to know all the secrets to the monks' talents, but not only do they burn wood in that stove when they can spare it, but the king provided this thick glass for the walls and ceilings, which absorbs the sunlight and traps its heat inside. This face of the mountain gets a surprising amount of sunlight. The hot spring is extremely useful and radiates heat into the air. Also, you may have noticed that we stepped down into the greenhouse. That is because it is dug into the earth, which—"

"So, lots of ways," Rubia interrupted, turning away in boredom.

"Hot spring?" Rosalie asked, her blue eyes alight with interest.

"Oh, of course," Prince Roland interjected from his perch. "The famed, healthful springs of Rounelith. It isn't quite all it's cracked up to be, but you all must try a sip while you're here."

Rosalie and I followed a footman to the eastern end of the greenhouse, where a hole no larger than a serving platter was cut into a ledge of stone. Steam rose in curls from the cloudy, white water that bubbled within. A crumbling statue of a raven, carved in white stone, stood over the spring. The dutiful footman knelt and dipped a silver pitcher into the water. I waited for Rosalie as she knelt and gave the spring a thorough inspection. She arose after a moment with her face pink, and her expression more genuinely animated than I'd seen since we learned of our mission.

We then followed the footman's path back to the center of the greenhouse and accepted small cups of the water as they were passed around. Rosalie inspected her water closely before drinking, and I took a cautious sip. It was the temperature of rapidly cooling tea and tasted strongly of muddy water. The rest of the ladies took an obligatory sip before setting their nearly full cups aside. From the corner of my eye, I caught Rubia pouring hers into the soil of a potted plant.

Vivian spoke brightly into the ensuing awkward silence. "You were right, Your Highness," she said, taking a seat near the prince. "The view is absolutely incomparable." She gestured to the stunning sprawl of scenery that lay to the east, perfectly framed through the thick glass panes of the greenhouse wall. The rocky outcroppings that jutted to the south of the monastery were of a pure white stone that shone brilliantly where the sun struck it.

The footmen handed around plates of tiny fig and cheese sandwiches, light cakes, and cups of spiced wine poured from flasks. I was relieved to remove the dirty taste of the hot spring from my mouth. The prince seemed to make a genuine effort to give Vivian, Rosalie, Tilda, and Adella equal measures of his attention, and I saw that it was quite the cumbersome balancing act. Lady Tilda stuck as close to his side as she could and inserted her own comments into any conversation the prince began. Lady Adella sulked slightly when she was not part of the conversation, and seemed to want to be drawn in. Rosalie's strategy seemed to be to stay on the outskirts and listen, and Vivian was putting her best foot forward, sticking close and attempting to get the prince to talk about his family.

My head spun with the difficulty of our charge, and I told myself sternly not to get discouraged. We had a month for Vivian and Rosalie to achieve their task, but if this was the prince's method of courting, it was going to be a very tricky month.

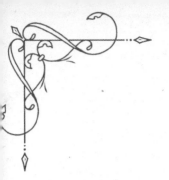

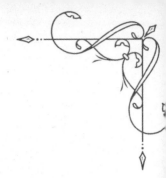

"WE'VE BEEN HERE A WEEK and have only seen the royals at dinner and at the monastery. *You two* need to make yourselves more exciting!" Rubia said sternly to Rosalie and Vivian, causing the former to turn a deep shade of magenta, and the latter to drop a piece of shortbread onto her lap.

The four of us were in a lavender-papered, cozy drawing room down the hall from our quarters. We had passed the last few days taking it in turns to comb the library for clues (although Rosalie admitted she had spent most of her time devouring the alchemical texts and scientific journals), but to no avail. It had been something to do, but of course the royals were unlikely to leave evidence of their misdeeds lying about. As several days had passed in an uncomfortable dearth of events, we finally decided we needed to meet. There was small risk of being overheard in the drawing room, as we rarely saw others in our hall. I paced near the doorway and popped my head out every few minutes, just to be safe.

"That isn't fair, Rubia," Vivian chided, reclaiming her shortbread.

Rubia's lips thinned. "I heard Prince Roland invite Lady Tilda to tea with him last night, and the evening after our picnic, I heard him invite Lady Adella to be his partner for cards."

Vivian raised a finger in objection. "I was his partner last night in the Sedgewood Salon."

"Excellent, and did he happen to tell you where his family keeps their secret documents over the table?" Rubia retorted.

"We need to be patient," Rosalie said. I saw that she was attempting a serene demeanor, but her eyes were panicked and pleading.

I wandered back toward the doorway. The hall was still empty.

"Why?" asked Rubia. "We were taught to sneak. So, let's sneak around! At night! Find the king's study, find those maps! Why are we all waiting on Vivian and Rosalie's flirting skills to improve?" she asked, her voice rising carelessly.

I squeezed my eyes shut in exasperation and checked the hall again.

"Cressida! You're making me nervous, stop obsessing!" Rubia snapped at me suddenly.

I stared at her until she turned away in a huff.

"Rubia," Vivian said with controlled patience. "I don't think we are that desperate yet. We have tools at our disposal, and sneaking into the king's private study at night, where we would probably be arrested on the spot if discovered, ought to be near the bottom of the list!"

"What do you suggest?" Rubia demanded.

I wondered if Vivian had decided to tell her about the powders. It seemed likely that Rubia would be in favor of using the Verum immediately, if so.

"You're right about it being time to act. Rosalie or I have to get the prince on his own, and we can only do that by making ourselves more interesting somehow. But once we have him alone, we can't just rely on manipulating the information out of him. We need to use the tools at our disposal. Miss Tepsom supplied Rosalie and me with what we need. I'm sorry we've been letting you down so far, but I promise, we will succeed. We have time."

A wave of nausea swept over me. I had no ideas to offer that would make Vivian and Rosalie consider not using the Verum.

I had racked my brain over and over, but had come up empty and more annoyed with myself every time.

"It feels like time is running out, but we still have three weeks. We can't panic now," said Rosalie, emboldened after Vivian's contribution.

"How do we get his attention?" I asked, hoping to skirt around the potential topic of Verum. "Has anyone at least learned what his interests are this week?"

"Dinner. Wine," Rubia began intoning, checking off each item on her fingers. "Monasteries. Greenhouses. His valet *really* likes greenhouses—"

"He likes fencing," Rosalie broke in tentatively.

"As if that can help us," Rubia said, plopping down on a settee and reaching for a biscuit.

"No, it might, though," Rosalie persisted, to my surprise. I checked the hallway again, then moved closer. Vivian handed me a cup of cooling tea. "He seemed to enjoy talking about it, and I wasn't sure if I should act like a young woman with no prior knowledge of the sport, or if I should try to use what I know to stand out. Maybe if I bring it up again, show that I have more than the usual amount of knowledge or interest, he might . . . want to give me more attention?" She finished with her cheeks flaming, then added quickly, "Or maybe Vivian should do it. Just an idea."

"No," I broke in suddenly.

Rosalie looked up at me in surprise. "What do you mean?" she asked uncertainly.

"Just that . . . I think you should do it. I know more about fencing, and I can help you stand out. And—" I desperately did not want to say *and keep either of you from dosing the prince with Verum,* but I had to continue. My head began to pound as I tried to arrange my words. "And I don't want us resorting to anything drastic yet. This is a good plan." I sucked in air as my symptoms receded. It had been true enough.

"It isn't a plan, not yet!" scoffed Rubia.

"No, but it could lead to more," said Vivian. "If Rosalie catches the prince's attention with her fencing knowledge, he might decide he wants to get to know her better. This is a good idea, Rose!" she said, leaning forward and putting a hand on Rosalie's, which was trembling slightly. I barely stopped myself from rolling my eyes. I felt sympathy for Rosalie's situation, but I wished she would get herself under control, otherwise Prince Roland would never be able to see past the stammers and blushes to find a girl to pursue.

I coached Rosalie before dinner to supplement her cursory fencing knowledge, which was understandably sparse, since Rubia and I had been the only girls to practice beyond a few lessons. I refreshed her memory, however, and also told her as much new information as I thought she could hold.

She surprised me that evening. I hadn't expected her to manage it, but for the second time, she was seated right next to the prince at dinner. Her strategy was simply to be in the right place at the right time. She stuck as close as glue and giggled determinedly at every jocund word out of Prince Roland's mouth, and when dinner was announced and the doors to the dining hall were flung open, he almost had no choice but to offer her his arm.

She brought up the topic of fencing easily, a revival of their previous conversation, and it seemed to move elegantly and naturally from there. I tried not to look like I was listening so closely to their conversation and focused my attention on the palate-cleansing ginger ice placed before me.

"You astonish me, Lady Rosalie," Prince Roland said, his voice warm but with a hint of teasing. "I had no idea I'd piqued your interest in fencing to such an extent."

"My brothers have an excessive dedication to the sport. I couldn't help but soak it in somewhat, and I confess, they made an unwilling devotee of me," she said demurely.

"I'd love to offer a demonstration for your entertainment, if you'd like." I held my breath as Prince Roland spoke, and glanced down the table to make sure Lady Tilda and Lady Adella were not close enough to express an interest as well. They were several seats down. Lady Adella was looking curiously in our direction, and Lady Tilda was locked in a fairly loud conversation about the monastery with Lord Eston, doubtless hoping that her raptures about the site would reach the prince's ears.

"Oh, did you visit Rounelith?" Lady Bern's voice sailed across the table, and the prince's smile froze somewhat. "I should dearly love to pay the place a visit, you know! I've heard so much of its history. And the monks must be so quaint!"

"A dull place for a party, madam," groused the court chemist, Mr. Creedling, who sat at Lady Bern's right, and fought with a pained expression to hold her interest.

"Perhaps next time we will be invited, dear lady," Lord Eston answered her in a mollifying tone.

"I do hope so!" she responded pointedly, and finally turned back to the disgruntled chemist.

Prince Roland cleared his throat and leaned toward Rosalie. "Would you be interested? You could bring Miss Hoth and witness a bout between Theon and me. I don't mean to presume that you would enjoy such a demonstration, that is, but if you *are* interested—"

I was surprised to hear the insecurity creeping into the prince's voice, and I noticed his father, several seats down at the head of the table, had stilled his conversation with the queen and was watching the prince intently. The prince glanced at the king, then quickly back at Rosalie, a polite smile on his face.

"I would be delighted, Your Highness!" Rosalie responded,

her voice confident in the face of his sudden shyness.

"It's settled then!" he said happily. "Tomorrow?"

It felt like success, to hear the prince awkwardly, with genuine interest, invite Rosalie to a nearly private activity together. I looked at Emric in triumph, but his solemn eyes, dark with the shadows of the room, were fixed on Rosalie.

That evening, the Sedgewood Salon was festooned with Evenfrost greenery, and the spicy scent of lementhe wafted through the room, gnawing an empty, homesick pit in my stomach. I used to help my parents make our little holiday brew. Missing them could strike from nowhere and threaten to squeeze my heart to the point of physical pain.

I took a deep breath and looked around. The furniture in the salon had been rearranged to make space for a dance floor. And, indeed, a dance was called and the musicians began a rambling introduction. My mouth grew as dry as dust. I dearly hoped to avoid dancing. I watched as the prince led Vivian, her color high but her expression serene, onto the dance floor as his first partner. Rosalie, standing close to me and fiddling with her gloves, breathed a sigh of relief.

"I won't have to dance just yet, then," she murmured.

"Sorry," I grimaced, nudging her elbow. Lord Eston was making a gallant beeline for her. Her spine stiffened, and she plastered on a sweet smile.

"Miss Montshire." Lord Eston bowed low over her hand. "Would you do me the very great honor?"

"Of—of course," Rosalie replied, and Lord Eston led her to the floor.

I moved to a settee and sat down, relief coursing through me as the dancers began and no one asked me to join them. Emric was paired with Lady Bern, who wore an excessively satisfied expression. Her mouth moved continually throughout their stately set, and I suppressed an amused smile as I watched.

Sooner than I had expected, the dance ended, and the

couples bowed to one another. The musicians called out the next dance, a more complicated one, and I watched nervously as Emric led Lady Bern to the settee near mine. She released his arm and sat, not close enough to have to acknowledge me, but near enough so that I could hear.

"All I'm saying, is *I've* never met this supposedly mad brother, have you? How do we really know, anyway?" Her voice beseeched Emric as she took her seat.

"Thank you for the dance, Lady Bern," Emric bowed. "You have given me much to think about." Her eyes narrowed as he turned away. I sat stiffly, hoping he was off to find another partner, but he instead turned deliberately to me and drew near, a light of mischief glinting in his eye.

"Miss Hoth." He bowed. "They are calling the next dance."

I shook my head infinitesimally. "So they are, Mr. Theon. You, I'm sure, will require a rest now." I injected some steeliness into my tone to deter him.

"Not at all." He grinned. "And that was a challenge if ever I heard one."

"It really wasn't," I said, growing more nervous.

"And I'm never one to turn down a challenge," he continued, his eyes glinting playfully.

Behind Emric, I saw Mr. Lupei, approaching me with clear intent. Before Emric could extend the request that he seemed to be working up to, Mr. Lupei was upon us. He nodded courteously to Emric, who looked vaguely startled.

"Miss Hoth! Delighted to see you this evening. You are stunning," he said without shame.

"I–thank you," I responded.

"Do me the honor of a dance?"

"Oh, I–of course," I acquiesced when no immediate excuse appeared out of thin air. I glanced at Emric, who smiled dispassionately.

"Enjoy your dance, Miss Hoth," he said politely. He bowed

again, then walked quickly away through the smoky candlelight.

Mr. Lupei took my arm and led me back to the floor, where couples were lining up for an elegant court dance. I stood next to Vivian, whose partner was the prince. Mr. Lupei's eyes were bright with interest as he took his place opposite me, and I realized too late that this dance was well suited to conversation.

He began the moment our hands joined and we took our first turn through the sedate set. "Where are you from, Miss Hoth? You have such a striking appearance."

I took a deep breath before answering, and my chest grew tight. "East. I hail from the east side of Dernmont." It was difficult to pay attention to both the steps and the conversation, which allowed him another opening.

"How coy you are! Very well, girl from the east, you have my attention," he said, smirking down at me and holding my hand firmly when it joined his again. We passed through a maze of other couples. "What sort of life is yours? I'm intrigued."

I swallowed, my mouth dry, and tried to push all my concentration into the words that leapt into my mouth. I stepped on Vivian's toes rather sharply in the process. "My life—is one of travel, and change, and unexpected challenges," I answered, testing the words cautiously. "I was raised by old aunts, sent to school, and am now here. An exciting progression, as you can see." I smiled, relieved at my own answer.

He opened his mouth to respond.

"I find myself fascinated by your own story, Mr. Lupei," I said quickly. "What part of the kingdom do you call home?"

"You do well to wonder, Miss Hoth," he said, his voice amused. A lock of dark hair fell over his eyes. "My father was Porleacan, and I have spent my time in many homes all over Dernmont and Porleac. I consider myself, however, wholly Dern."

"How interesting!" I replied, determined to keep him talking about himself. "Were you educated, then, in Dernmont?"

"With the prince, in fact! Petran and I met His Highness at

school and then served at sea together." The pride in his voice was open and abundant. "I have many a story about our royal scallywag, if you're interested!"

"Very," I responded with a smile.

Mr. Lupei happily dominated the remainder of the conversation during the dance, as well as the next quarter of an hour afterward. He fetched me a cup of hot lementhe and sat much too close, but required little of me conversationally. It seemed I had hit upon his favorite subject. I was finally rescued by Vivian, who interrupted to tell me that Rosalie needed me. I took leave of my enthusiastic companion and followed her across the room.

"There is no message from Rosalie. I just noticed him leaving you less and less room on that settee and thought maybe you needed rescuing," Vivian whispered, a polite smile plastered across her face as we moved through the crowd.

I thanked her fervently.

"Although, I must say, Cressida, I'm impressed! He was clearly set on learning all about you during that dance, and you turned it around on him so neatly I almost missed the transition. Well done," she said softly with a small smile.

I returned a strained smile, far too anxious to feel a drop of pride. The interaction with Mr. Lupei had felt like walking a tightwire over a pit of vipers, and the night wasn't over yet.

After escaping the evening unscathed, I passed a fitful night, anxious for the morning. The prince had asked Rosalie and me to meet him and Emric in the Winterberry Drawing Room for the fencing demonstration after breakfast. When grey daylight finally drifted through our windows, we dressed in the cold hush of our room. I slid my daggers into place and added a lockpick pin to my coiffure.

Ready, we walked through the palace in tense silence, acknowledging the few courtiers and servants that we passed. After a quick bite in one of the small, court breakfast areas, we made our way to the Winterberry Drawing Room. I noticed Rosalie's back stiffen as we approached, and her step slowed slightly. Before we reached the door, I put my hand on her arm.

"Rosalie, you did an excellent job last night, and you're going to do well again today. We're really getting somewhere now," I said, hoping to infuse her with some confidence before she met the prince. To my surprise, her lips pressed together in annoyance and she stepped away from me.

"I know none of you think I am able to accomplish anything. You don't need to manipulate me into doing my job," she said stiffly.

"I wasn't—" I began, then stopped. Put baldly, that was exactly what I'd been trying to do, but she didn't need to take it so hard. We all had a job to do.

"I'm just trying to encourage you," I started but then stopped and nodded toward the door. It was ajar, and low male voices were drifting out. Rosalie walked softly toward the door, then glanced back at me. I jerked my head to the side, and she nodded and slipped quietly to the left of the door, where she was unlikely to be seen from the inside. I followed and moved in next to her.

"I just need to wait out the month, Theon," Prince Roland was saying. "I know it's going to be a hard sell, but Father won't listen if I try to tell him about her with our guests here. Not when he has such high hopes for some of them." The prince's voice was tense, unconfident, nothing like the cheery, bold tone we had grown used to hearing.

"But . . . you remember his reaction at the end of the last visit. Can that really be the best time, when he is sure to be even more angry this time?" responded Emric's voice, lower than the prince's.

"Have you a better suggestion, Theon?" Prince Roland shot back. "I begin to wonder if I should tell him at all. Maybe I should just go—"

"No. Leaving will solve nothing. Send for her. And send for her now. It won't be smooth, but I honestly believe that sooner is better."

"I—I can't yet. I need to be patient. I can ride this out, I can convince him—at the right time."

"I just think—"

"Seriously, drop it for now, Theon. I need to be cheerful today. Where are those girls anyway?"

The sound of footsteps growing closer startled us out of our eavesdropping position, and we quickly moved several feet away. I barely managed to compose my guilty face before the prince flung the door open. As he did so, I lowered my head and began whispering in Rosalie's ear.

"Look excited. Gossipy," I whispered, not caring if she did not like if I took charge. We needed to mask our flushed faces somehow, and expressions of excitement were our best bet. She instantly giggled, her eyebrows high as if I were imparting something juicy.

"There you ladies are!" Prince Roland bellowed. "We'd begun to think you'd gotten lost."

"I'm so sorry, Your Highness," said Rosalie breathlessly, dropping into a curtsy. "We're terrible dawdlers."

"No apology necessary, Lady Rosalie," he said warmly and ushered us into the Winterberry Drawing Room. Emric offered a bow and we bobbed curtsies again.

"Why have we met here?" I asked, glancing curiously around. The drawing room was artfully arranged with furniture and expensive decor, excellent for a social gathering with the royal family, and completely unsuitable for a fencing match.

"Because the private quarters of the royal family are not on the map you've been given," the prince answered with a smile.

"I have a solar which I use expressly for the purpose of sport and exercise that I would be delighted to show you. Provided you can each keep a secret. It probably isn't entirely appropriate, but we are well chaperoned. Lady Rosalie?" He indicated a door at the far end of the drawing room. He beamed down at her. She smiled brightly up at him, almost startling me with the sudden force of her charm.

"I'm terribly intrigued, Your Highness. And discreet, of course. Lead on."

"Excellent! Let's be off, then." He marched around settees and armchairs, and finally led us through the door, with Emric bringing up the rear of our party. The door led straight into a rather dark interior corridor, very long and curving, the stone walls heavily lined with labeled portraits of lesser-family relations and ornately framed paintings of mountain scenes. A rather large portrait of a limpid-eyed dog with a bow around its neck struck a random chord of amusement within me, and I held my breath to keep from laughing as I followed Rosalie's soft steps on the thick rug.

The prince turned abruptly down another corridor, this one better lit with lamps, and with a rather more appealing décor. The rug was a bright berry red and the walls were hung with gold and cream draperies that absorbed the cold from the stone walls and insulated the corridor.

"Up this way!" Prince Roland announced suddenly, turning to the left and disappearing up a stairwell.

"Watch your step," Emric warned behind me. The stairwell was narrow, twisting, and steep. The steps were roughly cut, sloping rock.

"Watch your step!" came Roland's muffled echo of Emric from somewhere ahead and above. I clutched my heavy skirts and pulled them out of my way with one hand, bracing myself against the cold stone wall with the other.

"This is the oldest, unrenovated part of the castle," Emric

informed me. "I mean, it's all old, but they've neglected updating this particularly treacherous stairwell for some reason."

It seemed to wind and climb ever upward. My corset felt like it was growing tighter, and I struggled not to heave and wheeze like an ox.

Finally, we reached the top, where a wooden door with a low lintel stood between us and our destination. There was an arrow slit on the wall next to me, and I peered through as the prince sorted through a ring of keys. A sliver of sky was all that I could see, blue and cloudless and cold.

I turned back to see the prince fitting a large iron key into the matching keyhole. "I get excited every time I come up here," he said. "And I live here!" I couldn't help but smile at his enthusiasm. He turned the key and pushed open the heavy wooden door.

The prince stepped through and flung out an arm. "Welcome to the solar, ladies," he said.

I followed Rosalie into the room. It was a vast circle, unadorned except for a narrow, faded tapestry bearing the royal coat of arms hanging on the far wall. The floor was scuffed, worn wooden boards with no rugs. All around the room were windows—wide, thickly paned windows, the glass so clear that it almost appeared not to be there. The room was bright with the light that poured in; as spacious, empty, and bare as it was, it felt as peaceful as a meadow.

I followed Rosalie directly over to a window, drawn to the sunlight. The view was stunning from every angle.

"We must be at the uttermost top. In the turret that you can see for miles!" Rosalie exclaimed, unguarded and delighted. She drifted from window to window while I remained mesmerized at the first, in awe of the endless spread of sky.

"The very same, my lady," Prince Roland said with a laugh. "Could you see the castle from your school?"

"Our building is not tall enough to allow us to see over the

townhouses across the street, I'm afraid. But we've seen it
many times while visiting the shops. Look, Cressida! It must be
one of those!" She pointed excitedly out one of the windows.

I broke away from my window and joined her, the mention of
our school causing my stomach to clench. It was not possible to
pick out the school amid the rows of tiny rooftops and forest of
chimneys, like matchsticks, but I smiled vaguely in the general
direction she was pointing.

"And did you enjoy school?" the prince asked cordially, his
hands folded behind his back. I was pleased to see him looking
at Rosalie, certain that my symptoms would set in if he were
asking me.

"Oh—well enough. I don't know anyone who really loves
being at school, do you, Your Highness?"

"Please. You must call me Roland, at least here. And you're
absolutely right, Rosalie. School is a dreadful bore and I, for
one, am happy to have it behind me."

A light scraping drew my attention to the other side of the
room. Emric was standing near a wide, glass-fronted case full of
gleaming fencing foils. He had removed his black coat and was
standing in his crisp shirtsleeves, in the process of returning a
sword back into its space in the case. With a quick glance back
at Rosalie and Roland, I left them to their conversation and
wandered over to join Emric at the case.

"What was wrong with that one?" I asked, peering into
the case.

"Nothing. It just isn't my favorite," he said, carefully pulling
another out of the case and immediately handing it to me. I
wrapped my fingers around the smooth leather and enjoyed the
thrill of holding a sword again. I adjusted my wrist and held it
in a relaxed, yet firm grip.

"Is this one your favorite?" I asked as he ducked back into
the case.

"No. But it should be yours," he said, emerging with a grin

and another foil in his grip. "It should be the perfect weight for you. Give it a try."

I looked back at the prince and Rosalie, where they stood in conversation with their backs to us. Emric nodded at me in encouragement. Stepping back, I lunged, thrusting with the sword and then executing an imaginary parry.

Emric nodded in approval. "Elegant," he said, pulling on a pair of leather gloves. "You must have had an excellent teacher." I thought perhaps I imagined a wink as he said this, and I pursed my lips to suppress a grin. "A satisfactory one. I have a natural talent," I said primly.

"I'd have to agree with you," he remarked. "It would be nice to spar and see where you are, but I suppose you'd like to keep your talents hidden."

"It would probably be for the best," I said, carefully handing the foil back to him. "Do you and the prince spar often?"

"It's one of his greatest interests," he replied as he replaced the foil in the case. "I was hired as his instructor, and somehow moved on from there to valet. He drags me up here to practice as often as he can."

I desperately wanted to ask more. I wanted to know more about his mission, how long he had been here, and what he'd discovered. But not only was Prince Roland in the same room, he was now approaching with Rosalie.

"You ready to show these ladies what it looks like to lose with dignity, Theon?" Prince Roland flashed a grin as he removed his heavy, plum coat and flung it carelessly to the side.

"I'm going to have to press that jacket later, you know," Emric said with a pained expression.

"And you'll do an excellent job, as usual. Top-notch. No better presser to be found, I've said it before and I'll say it many times to come."

Emric chuckled. He walked to the center of the solar, twirling his sword expertly, and I caught Rosalie's eye and shared an amused glance, hoping she was no longer angry with me. Our eye contact was short-lived, however, and she looked away quickly. I walked over and stood uncomfortably at her side as Roland selected his weapon. I liked Rosalie, and it felt imperative that we be able to work together as a team, especially during an opportunity like this, but her sudden snit irked me.

Perhaps she had been right—perhaps I had been handling her delicately, even manipulatively, in order to get her to play her part with the desired results. But our mission was serious, and we were underprepared. I was tired of watching her shrink away in fear from the task at hand while I did my best to prop her up. Although I had to admit, she showed far more determination today.

The gentlemen bowed to one another and assumed their stances. Emric held his free hand loosely behind his back, while Roland held his up in the air theatrically.

"Are you sure you don't want a mask today, Highness?" Emric asked as he lunged forward, beginning the first attack. "I wouldn't want to be responsible for marring your royal face— I'd likely get thrown out of the castle, never to return to press your jackets." He grunted slightly on the last word, parrying an aggressive counterattack from the prince.

"I see your point, Theon. But if I wore a mask, where would be the fun in that for the ladies?"

I elbowed Rosalie, and she giggled, only slightly belatedly. I determinedly kept my eyes on the sparring pair so as to avoid her probable annoyance.

The banter dissipated as the duel grew more intense. The prince was, without a doubt, an excellent swordsman. A sheen of sweat broke out on both brows, and they used the full length of the solar as their attacks and counterattacks drove one another back and forth. Emric seemed to possess a degree more control; I noticed his efforts to steer the duel away from Rosalie and me when, at one or two points, the prince's exuberant footwork brought the slashing blades a bit too close to us for comfort.

Finally, with a flick of the wrist that I remembered from the very first time I saw him fight, Emric unburdened the prince of his weapon, and sent it clattering to the floor.

"Have a care!" Roland said with a breathless laugh, bending quickly to retrieve his foil and inspecting the steel. "That's one of my best blades."

"Maybe one of these days you'll learn to hold on to it," Emric returned, grinning and wiping the back of his arm across his forehead.

Rosalie began a polite applause, and I joined her, feeling slightly silly. Roland swept a bow in our direction.

"I'm sorry you ladies had to see that," he said. "Something went horribly wrong, as my intention was *not* to lose spectacularly. The prince is humbled."

"Not at all, Your Highness. I mean, Roland," said Rosalie warmly. "It was thrilling!" She glanced briefly at me and then back up at the prince. "Your footwork is impressively controlled, and your parries are so fast!" I did not completely agree with her analysis, but it was well put.

Prince Roland beamed. "You do know something, then, don't you! Would you like to give it a try?"

"Oh! I—" She looked at me as if for help or permission, neither of which I knew exactly how to give without displaying an odd reversal of our roles.

"You'll enjoy it, my lady," I offered. "You've always said that you wished your brothers would give you a lesson!"

"Ah, yes. That's right, I do always say that. I'm just—"

"Don't worry, Lady Rosalie, I won't let you be harmed. Let's go have a look at the swords, shall we?" Prince Roland said with encouraging excitement. Rosalie followed him hesitantly to the case.

Emric approached me. "Would you also like a lesson, Miss Hoth?" he asked. I looked up at him, unsure if he meant it. He was grinning mischievously down at me. "Best not, I suppose. You'll either outshine us all or feign clumsiness and drop the precious swords all over the floor."

I nodded, amusement bubbling through me, heightened by my tightly wound nerves. "I would like one." I had to respond honestly as the answer threatened to choke me. I hastened to add, "But yes. Best not. Maybe another time."

He nodded, and his grin faded slightly. He glanced over at Rosalie and Roland, laughing over their lesson, then back at me. He shifted uncomfortably, then tilted his head toward the sword case, indicating I should follow him. "Look . . ." he began quietly, picking up an oiled rag from a bench near the case and carefully smoothing it over the blade of his sword. "I need—that is . . ." He paused for such a long moment that I had to force my hands not to fidget.

"Can we talk in private?" he finally said, glancing quickly at my face. "Tonight, maybe? It's just, I have to speak to you, and I can't while—" He pursed his lips and shook his head, frustration spelled out in his furrowed brow and tense jaw.

"Um—" I almost shot a look over my shoulder, but could hear the laughter and swords clanging still, and stopped myself. "Yes, we can talk. How?"

"The drawing room in your corridor. Can you meet me there at one?" He carefully replaced his weapon in the case as he spoke in a quiet, yet casual sort of voice.

"Yes. I can do that," I said, ignoring the exciting dance of nerves inside me.

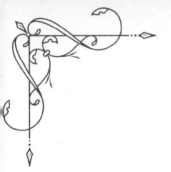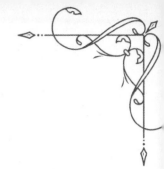

12

ROSALIE WHIRLED ON ME
the moment we entered our room and I shut the door behind us.

"Well?" she asked, her face determined.

"Well . . ." I prompted, confused.

"My rapport with Roland. Do you think we accomplished anything today? Do you think we'll get him alone again?" Her eyes were bright and focused.

"I think it went well today," I said, trying to sort through the words that fogged my mind and wanted to pour out of my mouth. "I don't know if we accomplished anything yet"—she began to visibly wilt at my words, so I pushed on encouragingly—"but I do think he enjoyed your company, so of course there's a chance we will get another opportunity like this one. We just need to decide how to use it when it comes."

"Oh, I know how to use it." Rosalie walked over to the window near her bed, her movements deliberate. I wondered if she was working to hide her anxiety from me now.

"How?" I asked, surprised.

"Verum," she answered promptly. "I would have used it today, but there was obviously no opportunity. I mean, I wondered what would happen if I got some onto the tip of a sword, and then nicked him—accidentally, you know—while we were sparring, and—"

"Rosalie!" I interrupted in alarm.

Her head swiveled to me, her eyes wide. "What?"

"That's a terrible idea!" I blurted.

A dull flush crept over her cheeks and she turned back to the window. "Thank you, Cressida. Once again, your confidence in me is overwhelming. I didn't notice *you* doing anything useful today, unless flirting with Mr. Theon is your idea of helping!" She stared stonily out at the battlements as she spoke, her voice tight.

I took a deep breath and went over to her, sitting on the bed. "Rosalie. I'm sorry, that was not what I meant. It's just that we don't know everything about Verum. Actually stabbing the prince with it—"

"I didn't say anything about stabbing him. I said nick, as in slightly scratch," she retorted. "I've been studying the Verum, and it is definitely a mineral composite. It ought to work in the same way as the Nemere, although I need some time to study that one, too, but hypothetically, it just needs to get into the bloodstream one way or another."

"Right. Hypothetically." I shut my eyes briefly in frustration. "Scratching the prince with what amounts to poison, with no understanding of the full effects of such an action, would be reckless."

Her spine stiffened even further, and I tried softening my tone. "I know you're nervous, and impatient. I am too. And I know you're hurt that I haven't had confidence in you. And I really am sorry. I just . . . I think we're all on edge because we don't see this going anywhere quickly. I honestly think you did an excellent job today, laying the groundwork for a friendship with him, piquing his interest. We both just need to be patient. And not do anything rash."

I felt like a hypocritical fool as I spoke. I knew my words were reasonable, but I was having a hard time agreeing with them myself. The need to act was creeping up on me like an itch I desperately had to scratch. The silence following my words was ringing. I sighed and rose to retreat to my side of the room, but Rosalie suddenly uttered a suppressed sob. She took in short breaths and clutched her forearms as if she needed to hold herself together, and I realized with a rush of compassion how lonely and terrified she was.

I didn't know how to be her friend. But I stepped forward and wrapped my arm around her shoulders anyway, because it looked like maybe she needed it. I felt her thin frame shudder as she buried her face in her hands. She eventually moved away and faced me.

"Thank you, Cressida," she choked, pushing the heel of her hand against one of her red eyes. "I'm sorry—I don't know what's wrong with me."

"You've been given a heavy assignment," I said. "There's no Miss Tepsom here to steer us. It's hard. And even though your job is scary, you're not in this alone. None of us are, and we probably need to stop acting and feeling like we are." Most likely, she was missing her parents as well and didn't want to fail them—same as me. I felt an uneasy twist in my gut as I spoke, knowing that if I really believed my own words, I would tell her about my meeting tonight. But I didn't.

She nodded and took a deep breath. "We'll get this done together. I'll try to hold his interest enough to get another afternoon alone. Next time, we'll make sure to have tea." I smiled at her attempt at confidence, and felt sick inside.

We returned late from dinner that night and immediately readied ourselves for bed. It was half past twelve by the time we blew out our candles, and I lay as still as possible, trying to listen for Rosalie's breathing to grow deep and even. The timepiece on the mantel ticked heavily, noisily, and half an hour felt like an hour. It was one o'clock exactly when I finally was able to confirm that Rosalie slept. My intention had been to slip back into my dress. I was not particularly comfortable meeting Emric in my nightgown, but slipping into my dress unaided was not an easy feat, and I was already late. So, I settled for grabbing a dressing gown and securing it tightly over the nightgown.

I stepped into my slippers, then exited the room with only a slight screech of the wooden door. I walked silently down the corridor, moving slowly to test the floor for creaky spots, until I reached the drawing room.

The door was open. I peeked around the corner and saw no candles or lamps lit. The only light was a haze of moonlight that misted in through the window, and it didn't illuminate much. I cautiously stepped into the room, feeling anxiously vulnerable, not knowing if the room was empty or not.

"Cressida?" came a low whisper, giving me a slight jolt.

"Emric?" I asked in a quieter whisper. I sensed his movement closer to me now.

"You did know I would be here, right?"

"Yes," I said, and exhaled slowly. I still couldn't see him. "Where are you?" I whispered uncomfortably.

"Trying to get to you without cracking my shin on a tea table," he said.

"Sit down on the settee if you're near it," I suggested, stepping hesitantly forward, wishing my eyes would adjust more quickly to the darkness.

"Which settee?" he asked in a loud whisper.

"The one near the tea table that you're about to turn over." I heard the painful sound of bone whacking against wood, and I held my breath to contain a laugh.

"Right," he grunted, and the couch emitted a muffled sigh as he sat—or fell—down on it.

"Stay there," I whispered. I headed in the general direction of the settee and promptly collided with a sharp edge.

"Tea table there," he said mildly.

"Found it," I said, clutching my shin and sitting down heavily.

"I don't want to spook you, but I'm going to slide just a bit closer so we can talk quietly. Is that all right?"

I nodded, then realized in the ensuing silence that it wasn't enough. "All right," I said finally. I felt the settee dip slightly as he moved closer.

"Thank you for meeting me. I know it's not very proper–I hoped you wouldn't be too scandalized. But I needed to talk to you."

"It's fine," I said. "Go on. And I have questions for you, if you don't mind me asking when you're finished."

"Very well, then." He paused for a moment. "I've been here on a similar mission to yours for over a year now. I've been collecting certain information. It . . . it goes deeper than I'd originally thought, this game we're playing. Listen, Cressida, you girls need to leave."

"What?" I exclaimed, holding tightly to a handful of my robe on my lap. "Why?"

"It's hard to explain, and I think it's better if I didn't. I just–I don't think Tepsom knew what she was doing in sending you here. We need to figure out a way to get all of you away from this place as soon as possible."

A blend of irritation and confusion rippled through me. He thought we couldn't handle our mission. He thought I couldn't handle it. And I'd been excited about meeting him, believing he thought me a valuable enough agent to share intelligence with, believing he saw me as useful and needed my help.

I tamped down the surge of embarrassment. I didn't need him to need me or believe in me. "We have a job to do," I stated firmly, "and we're going to see it through. Unless you have something useful to share with me, I'm going to go back to bed."

"Please. I'm deadly serious, Cressida, I think it's for the best if you leave. I know you have personal stakes, I know your parents were–"

I drew in my breath sharply, but that wasn't what cut him off. A shift of light and shadow near the doorway told me that someone carrying a light was approaching. I froze as I heard soft footsteps.

Emric moved quickly, tugging me toward him. "Sorry about this." His words became clear when he wrapped an arm around me.

My blood pumped riotously as he held me tightly. The circle of yellow light grew brighter and smaller.

"Oh, for heaven's sake," came the irritated voice of Sylvie, and I took the natural opportunity to move away as the maid came nearer and squinted down at us. Hot wax from her fat candle threatened to drip all over us.

I pulled my robe tighter around my neck and glanced at Emric. The embarrassment that must have been scrawled all over my face was definitely not an act, but it would serve. Emric only grinned rakishly up at Sylvie.

"Excuse you, young lady," he said, appearing to almost enjoy the intrusion.

Sylvie emitted a loud snort. "I knew you were rough," she said nastily at me. "It's easy to spot the girls who play around. Only respectable sorts are welcome here, you know."

Emric stood slowly and made a show of buttoning his loosened collar. "Now, that's not called for. But as a well-paid sneak who's several floors away from the servants' quarters past midnight, are you really one to talk, Sylvie?" She narrowed her eyes at him. "I hear things," he informed her. "I don't care for the way you spoke to this lady, so unless you want some of your own exploits to come to light, you will either speak only courteous words to and about her, or nothing at all. Do we understand each other?"

Sylvie shot a disgusted look at me that undermined every word Emric had said in my defense, but gave a curt nod of agreement. She affected an extremely pious sniff before leaving us once again in darkness.

As soon as her footsteps faded, I jumped up and made my

way toward the door, heedless of the injuries I could sustain. But Emric stopped me at the door.

"Cressida, please, wait a moment." I peered into the hall but could see only darkness. It seemed to me that anyone could be lurking and listening. "I'm so sorry about that. I couldn't think of another way to explain our meeting. I had hoped she wouldn't recognize you, anyway."

"No need to apologize, it was well played," I said coolly. "Destroying Rosalie's lady's reputation would ensure that at least one of us leaves the castle, maybe even half the team."

"That wasn't my intention. I swear."

"Goodnight," I said, needing to escape to my room.

"Cressida." He took hold of my arm. "I need you to give me the Verum."

"*What*?" I shook his hand off of my arm.

"Please. I know this hasn't . . . gone—" he growled suddenly in irritation. "Please, think about it. You girls should leave. But if you won't, I need you to give me the Verum. Or even just the location of the Verum, and I'll handle the rest."

His face was barely visible, his eyes in shadow. I wanted nothing now, suddenly, but to be in utter and complete control of the Verum. And my mission. Emric would no longer be a part of that.

"You'll have to handle the rest without my assistance. Goodnight."

I walked toward my room, moving as quickly as I could without tripping in the dark. I paused for a moment when I reached my door and stared down the black hall until I was positive that he had not followed me.

◇ ·· ———————— ·· ◇

The trio of flutes from our entertainment and Lord Eston's determinedly attentive conversation was still echoing through my pounding head when we returned from the next evening's salon. Sylvie was even scarcer and less enthusiastic in her service than usual after she caught Emric and me supposedly having a tryst in the drawing room, but she followed us to our room and helped Rosalie out of her gown. When she stonily, yet determinedly, approached me to attack my laces, I forestalled her with a hand.

"I'll manage on my own," I said quietly through clenched teeth.

Sylvie snorted. "Very well." She looked around. "Here," she whispered. She handed me a tiny roll of parchment, then exited immediately. I glanced over at Rosalie. She was occupied at her basin, washing her face. Turning my back to her, I quickly unrolled the parchment, which was no longer than my pinky finger. The handwriting was a light, minuscule, elegant scrawl.

> *Pear Tree Parlor. 1 a.m.*
> *Bring the Verum. Come alone.*

◇ ·· ———————— ·· ◇

I did not undress this time, nor did I have any intention of smuggling the Verum out of our room. I had been to the Pear Tree Parlor, on the east end of the palace, once before, and I had no desire to be caught walking across the castle in my nightdress and robe. I told Rosalie that I intended to stay up and read, knowing that I'd never be able to lace myself completely back into my gown if I undressed. I felt a small twinge of guilt in not telling her my plans, but had a mad fear that she would grab her truth powder and come along.

I shook my head and suppressed a yawn as I crept into the dark hall. These middle-of-the-night meetings were ridiculous, and all the more infuriating because I knew that I could choose *not* to go. I doubted Emric would come and knock on my door in the middle of the night to check and see if I received his note if I didn't show up. And I was still angry with him. But, while he was clearly desperate for the Verum and likely going to renew his urgent warning for me to leave, this time he might intend to explain himself. Or even simply offer a token of information to appease me.

I had several reasons not to leave my room, and so I felt foolish as I trudged, rather than glided like a sly shadow, to my rendezvous. I barely acknowledged in the back of my mind that there was something else that drew me to meet Emric again. But no—what I coveted was that bit of information he was going to give this time, that slice of truth to try to scare me into leaving. I needed to know what he knew.

The door to the Pear Tree Parlor stood ajar. Moonlight shafted through tall windows in the corridor, but it was dark as pitch inside the room. I wondered why, this deep into the palace, this far from living quarters, a candle could not have been lit. I pushed open the door and stepped inside. A chill slid across my neck.

Hands grabbed me roughly from behind, and the door slammed shut behind me.

A large hand clamped tightly over my mouth, and the other held both my wrists sharply behind my back, twisting them at the wrong angle. I swallowed a whimper at the pain, and a sweat broke over my brow. I struggled to breathe around the hand that was squeezing my face.

"Give me the Verum," a hoarse whisper hissed in my ear.

My blood boiled in a sudden red rage, and I stomped on the foot that was lodged against my ankle. My assailant grunted, but only twisted my wrists tighter. He then let go of my face.

"Shhh." A sharp tip of a dagger sank into the top layer of skin behind my ear, and traveled to the back of my neck. Panic couldn't quite numb the warm trail of blood blossoming under the hot sting of the blade. "Do you have it?" His breath was hot in my ear.

I lurched forward, trying to escape the knife, and it caught the edge of my ear, slicing smoothly. The pain robbed me of my breath for a moment, and my symptoms began to set in before I could breathe again, let alone talk. Finally, I gritted out through a haze of pain and dizziness, "No. I don't have it."

He tightened his grip on my writhing wrists and wrapped his other arm around my neck, holding the knife roughly against the side of my scalp. His rough face burned against mine as he hissed, "Where is the truth powder?"

I finally managed to pull one of my wrists free and began clawing at the arm around my neck. I hated every word that tore out of my throat, but I hated more the idea of falling in a dead faint at this brute's feet. "Rosalie and Vivian have it."

He pushed the knife against my scalp, and I felt another trickle of blood ooze from the stinging wound as he managed to catch my arm again in a grip somehow harder than before. "All of it?"

"Yes," I gasped, and angry tears rolled down my cheeks, my fury choking me as I spoke.

"Where are they keeping it?" he demanded.

"I don't know." Almost as soon as the words were out of my mouth, he released his hold and shoved hard against my back. I fell, sprawling on the wooden floor, striking my chin. The door opened and closed before I could struggle to my feet.

I lurched forward, groping the smooth door in the dark and wrenching it open as soon as I found the handle. There was no one in sight in the corridor. I took my skirts in hand and ran back the way I came, heedless of the noise I made as my slippered feet slapped and skidded along the floor. It was a circuitous route, and at every turn, my skin crawled with the possibility of an ambush, even though I knew my attacker was done with me. I choked on an angry sob as I remembered my stupid confidence on my way to the parlor, of how I'd held my thoughts of Emric. I hated myself for those thoughts, and for leaving my room. But just then, I hated Emric more.

Vivian and I sat alone in our drawing room the following morning. I couldn't talk to Rosalie about it, not yet. I let both of them down in a spectacular fashion, and I needed my first confession to be to my friend. We had a few minutes to spare before we were expected at the queen's weekly luncheon.

"It was him. It had to have been," Vivian said breathlessly, then clutched at my arm. "Rubia said she saw Mr. Theon in our corridor last night. I didn't think about it at the time because I was dead tired, but he must have been considering breaking into our rooms."

My heart seemed to suddenly grow five times heavier. I'd turned last night's incident over in my mind again and again, because I didn't want it to be Emric who had attacked me. But want was not fact, and I couldn't afford to lie to myself.

Vivian put her arm around me and hugged my shoulders. As I had known she would be, she was immediately forgiving, more so than I deserved. "I'm so happy you weren't hurt," she said. I tried not to look as uneasy as I felt at the words. "You weren't hurt, were you?" she asked, a note of anxiety in her voice.

"A little," I was forced to say. "He wasn't particularly gentle, but nothing that won't heal quickly."

"You look exhausted." Vivian sat back and eyed me. "I imagine you couldn't sleep after that."

"Not much. I needed to make sure he wasn't going to search our rooms," I said, rubbing my eyes. Once back to my room, I had unearthed the Nemere from deep within my wardrobe, where I'd been hoping to forget about it. I'd come too close to splashing the poison all over myself as I dipped my dagger into the bottle, and then spent the rest of the night either peeking into the corridor, or sitting on the floor in our room, listening closely at the door. "I must have fallen asleep a few times though, because I didn't see anyone."

I avoided Vivian's eyes. "I'm—I'm so sorry that I told him," I said, feeling the useless hollowness of the words.

"Cressida! He might have hurt you even worse! He might have killed you! Then what good could you do for any of us?" She leaned forward. "You did the right thing. I'm glad you told him. Well, I'm not glad that he *knows*," she clarified at my arched brow, "but I'm glad that you complied and then he left you alone." She shook her head. "I thought that Emric was our ally. I thought we could trust him."

"We don't know for sure that it was him," I said without conviction.

"He'd asked you for the Verum, though . . . right?" she asked.

I stared out the window, which revealed nothing but stone battlements and an iron-grey sky, and nodded.

"Yes. He asked for it urgently. I know it looks like it was him. And it probably was." I turned back to her, my anger and my frustration calcifying until I was nothing but steely resolve. Or so I imagined.

"We need to get that Verum hidden," I said. "The whole case of potions ought to be put away where no one can find it, so no one can give away its location. They're too powerful, and we have no experience with them. And now someone else wants access."

Vivian furrowed her brow. "But we're meant to use them. We're never going to get the location of those maps otherwise. We can't do what Rubia suggests and sneak around in private royal quarters, hunting for them with no idea where to look. They could be anywhere!"

"Maybe this was a ridiculously underplanned mission to begin with!" I suggested restlessly.

Vivian's face darkened in a rare expression of crossness. "Maybe. But we were given tools for a reason. If we don't discover the location of those maps, within the month, we will return to Miss Tepsom empty-handed, with no evidence against the king. Our families deserve better!" Her irritability gave way to insistence.

"Someone knows about the Verum! And possibly about the rest. I don't know what his purpose is, but if he were on our side, I don't think he would have threatened me with a knife." I was barely keeping my temper in check. I took a deep breath. "Keeping it nearby and using it is reckless."

"My father's throat was cut," Vivian said unexpectedly. Her eyes were tearful.

A shock ran through me. "What?"

"I know we've never talked about it much. Just to say we had parents who were murdered. I know we each have a story. I can't get mine out of my head, especially not while I'm here. His throat was cut, and I found him. Grey . . . slumped over the bench he'd made for my mother."

I looked at her, frozen. "I'm so sorry," I finally whispered.

She shook her head, sweeping the room with her eyes. "With no remaining heir, the crown technically owned the estate, although I never believed they would be so cruel as to claim it. Historically, that isn't done. Courtesy and kindness to widows is preached. Respect for old families. But in reality . . . we were compensated, of course, but our home was taken; we were abruptly turned out." Her eyes continued roving the room as she spoke, and her breaths came quicker. "Miss Tepsom made a convincing case against the royals. Aggressive land seizures immediately following the death of landowners and heirs. I know we don't have all the facts yet. But if it's true . . . they dearly deserve to pay for their crimes. And there's no way to find out for sure except one." She turned to me then, and all the pain that she carried behind the gentle brightness of her dark eyes brimmed to the surface.

"I know this is important. I just . . . I don't want anyone

getting hurt, and the Verum seems like a reckless choice," I said weakly, apologetically.

"You're usually so bold, Cressida!" Vivian dashed away a tear from her now-flashing eyes. "This caution isn't what we need from you right now. We need to act, and we need you with us. Why don't you want us to use the Verum?"

An icy current ran through my veins. I had dropped my guard, the ever-present shell that protected me from personal questions . . . from the one question I never wanted anyone to ask.

"Well?" She looked me square in the face, and I watched as her anger ebbed away, replaced by concern. My throat became tight, my head pounded. I pressed my eyes shut, then opened them again. "You're losing color," Vivian said, taking hold of my shoulders.

"I don't want you to use it because I think someone used it on me once," I whispered in a rush, gasping for a breath. "It was a long time ago, and it was horrible." Her hands dropped away, and she regarded me, blinking rapidly as she formed her next question. I clasped my hands together. "Please don't ask me about it."

Vivian stared. "Why didn't you tell me?" she finally said.

"I—I don't like to talk about it," I said. "I know that isn't fair. I know that by now I should have, that I owe that to you."

"I'm sorry that happened to you, Cressida," she said earnestly.

I desperately wanted to run out of the room before she could ask another question. I stared at her warily.

"I wish . . . I wish you had felt comfortable telling me. I really do."

My heart ached when she looked down, the hurt rolling off of her. Then she lifted her head. "But as awful as it may have been, we can't sacrifice our only option because you had a bad experience."

I said nothing, knowing that she was right, because I hadn't given her the whole story. She deserved the whole story, even if it meant telling her that the truth curse had never worn off. But I had pulled my armor back around myself so tightly that it wasn't going to budge—unless she asked the right question. Our friendship could never be the same if she knew.

Finally, I nodded. I truly had nothing else to offer in lieu of the Verum. I'd hoped that Emric had collected information that he would share, and that with our combined efforts we could find a way to learn the location of the maps without resorting to Verum.

"Just for now, please hide it well. And bolt your door at night."

Vivian nodded a little sadly, then silently stood and left the room.

I returned to my room to find it empty, and wondered if Rosalie had gone down to the queen's luncheon without me. I checked my appearance in the mirror before I left again. Shadows darkened the skin under my eyes, and my complexion that usually glowed next to the violet of my day gown looked pallid and dull. A fresh bead of blood was welling up on my nicked ear. I held a handkerchief to it for a moment, then went and knocked on Vivian's door. She opened it immediately, smiling anxiously at me.

"I'm ready!"

"Where is Rubia?" I asked as Vivian shut the door behind us and smoothed her curls.

"With Rosalie," she answered, looking at me in confusion. "Isn't she?"

"I don't know," I said with a shrug, as we headed down the corridor to the stairwell.

"I hope everything goes well with the prince," she remarked as we descended.

"I don't think he will be at the luncheon, will he?" I asked. "He wasn't last week."

"Well, I expect not, as he invited Rosalie to a private lunch today. Private, except for the attendants." She glanced at me, puzzled. "You didn't know? I wondered why she asked Rubia to accompany her, but I assumed you knew about it."

I stopped in my tracks at the foot of the stairs and faced Vivian and her startled expression. "Where were they meeting?" I asked breathlessly.

She bit her lip. "I'm not sure."

"Go on without me. I'll see you at the luncheon. Maybe," I said before I bolted.

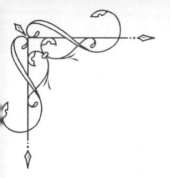
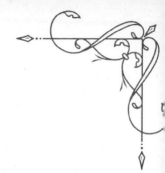

13

I HAD NO IDEA WHERE
they would be meeting. There was so much of the palace that I
hadn't seen yet. But things seemed to be fine between Rosalie
and me now, so the only reason she could have for not telling
me about this meeting would be the Verum. She planned to
use it on him today, and she believed she could do so in the
company of Rubia and Emric. I hadn't told her yet that we
couldn't trust him.

I ran faster, brushing roughly past a footman as I rounded
the corner to the Pear Tree Parlor. My heart stopped for a
moment when I saw the door, ajar as it had been last night.
I checked inside. The only occupants were a pair of maids,
dusting and polishing the already gleaming surfaces of the pale
wood furniture. I stopped short when I saw them, started to
turn, then changed my mind.

The maids looked up at me and immediately bowed. My hair,
which I had given hasty attention today, had mostly escaped its
twist, and I was probably a somewhat alarming sight. I cleared
my throat.

"I'm looking for my mistress. Lady Rosalie. Have either of
you seen her?"

The blonde, young-looking maid, who had been dusting a
tea table, said, "Please, ma'am, is she the one who is having
luncheon with the prince today?"

"Yes, she is. She forgot to tell me where they are meeting," I said, implying that I was meant to join them.

"I believe they are meeting in the Wulfestar Hall, ma'am," the maid reported. "I remember cook saying how inconveniently far from the kitchens it was for a meal to be served, but the prince likes the view, so he dines there with friends sometimes."

"Thank you!" I said gratefully, pleased that it was a part of the castle I knew how to find.

As I left, the nasal voice of the other maid followed me out of the room. "She's probably just looking for Mr. Theon. I've heard whispers about the two of them . . ."

I winced and turned left down a thickly carpeted corridor that I believed ran east and west and ought to take me in the proper direction. Of course, Sylvie had not kept her mouth shut. So much for Emric's threat that he would reveal things about her—or maybe that was all a show for my benefit to begin with. Trying to figure out Emric's motives made my head spin, and I forced my thoughts to the task at hand.

I had to slow down a few times when other servants or courtiers came into view. I already looked wild, I possibly had a reputation beyond the servants' quarters, and I did not want to excite any more interest. My breath caught in my throat when I passed Mr. Lupei and Lord Petran exiting a room, and I kept my head down in an effort to remain unnoticed.

I came to the end of the hall and was just about to breathe a sigh of relief, when I glanced over my shoulder. Mr. Lupei and Lord Petran were still visible, walking slowly, and clearly watching me. I quickly faced forward again and considered trying to lose them. It felt stupid to assume as much, but now I felt as if I were being followed.

Then I spied a pair of bright, rosewood double doors and the familiar seafaring tapestries that flanked them. I was pretty sure this was the entrance to the Wulfestar Hall, and there was no time to try to lose any possible pursuers. They were likely just going in the same direction.

I pushed the door open and looked inside the vast hall. A table was set up near one of the massive windows, with four people seated around it. I took a deep breath and walked toward them, my heels clicking loudly against the cobblestone floor. Everyone turned to look at me, and I resisted the urge to fix my hair and avoid Emric's eyes. Rather, his were the first that I sought, and I filled my stare with venom. He looked back, bewildered.

"I'm so sorry to interrupt, I know it's terribly rude of me," I said as I reached the table, turning my focus to the others. Rubia shook her head in disbelief. Rosalie stared at me, her eyes wide and round. "I need a word with Lady Rosalie. I'm afraid it's urgent."

"Miss Hoth! It's delightful to see you. You're not interrupting in the least, I will send for another setting," Prince Roland said, as he and Emric rose politely. He nodded to the bewigged footman hovering near, and the fellow marched past me toward the doors.

"I don't wish to intrude," I protested. "I simply need to speak with Lady Rosalie." Rosalie said nothing for a moment. Her eyes on mine were anxious. Finally, she stood. "I beg you excuse me," she said timidly.

"Of course, take all the time you need." Prince Roland smiled warmly at her, taking his seat.

"Thank you," she said, and went with me down half the length of the room.

"Where is it?" I asked her gently when we were out of earshot. "This is important, Rosalie. Please tell me you don't have the Verum with you right now."

She looked at me gravely for a long moment. Then, she looked down at her hand. I followed her gaze. She was just barely opening up a clenched fist, where a small, empty bottle lay in her palm. A wave of nausea swept over me.

"You *used* it? You used *all* of it?" I whispered loudly in utter dismay. She closed her eyes for a moment, and I saw how scared she was.

"Rubia did it. I passed it to her when she prepared the prince's drink and I distracted him. I took the bottle back and—oh, Cressida. I should have talked to you about this instead of bringing her. I knew you didn't like the idea. It was reckless . . . I did fill her in on the way here, but I forgot to tell her not to use all of it. And now it's gone. He—he acted strange for a moment, as if he wasn't feeling well, then recovered." Her eyes were stricken and pleading, and she held the empty bottle tightly. "This is our only chance. Can't you see, Cressida? I know you don't like it, but we have to take advantage of it before it wears off."

I looked at her grimly, crossing my arms to tuck away my shaking hands. "We won't have to worry about that. If that stuff was temporary to begin with, it's going to take a good long while to wear off if she used the entire bottle." A lifetime, maybe.

"This. We need to use this." Rosalie fumbled in her pocket and revealed the small bottle filled with the bright green forgetfulness powder—Lethen. I shook my head, my breaths coming short. "Who knows what will actually happen if we mix these. Rosalie. This is the prince, and we've just given him a powerful drug that we know very little about, left him alone with Rubia and Emric—who we can't trust, by the way—and now you're talking about giving him another powerful drug. We can't just—"

"We can't trust Mr. Theon? Why?"

"That's not—" My words changed. "I think he attacked me. He asked me to give him the Verum. I can't tell you any more now, we have to get back to the others. I don't know what we're going to do, but we have to do something as soon as possible. And we can't let Emric know."

She nodded tensely, and we walked back to the table.

"I don't know. In his study, I suppose? What an odd question, Miss Feldingham," Prince Roland was saying, his voice puzzled. "Why would you want to know where my father keeps his maps?"

I looked at Rosalie in a panic, and we practically ran to the table.

"Rubia, I think it is time you joined the others at the queen's luncheon," said Rosalie with forced cheer. "We know how badly you wanted to, and Cressida is here now."

Rubia shot us a look that was both dark and haughty. "Seriously, you two? You can't get anything done. He isn't going to remember this." She leaned in closer to the prince.

"Documents, then? Where does he keep documents that he wouldn't want just anybody to read?"

"I don't know," Prince Roland said, his voice thick with confusion. "I believe his steward locks them away somewhere, but—"

"What is this?" Emric interrupted, his face as cold as stone. "What's going on?"

"Tell me your deepest secret," came Rubia's ringing voice, talking over Emric.

"Rubia!" Rosalie and I shouted together. My head felt as if it were filled with a swarm of bees. The first moments of my own curse thickly crowded my consciousness, and I almost feared I would black out. The betrayal . . . the burnt aftertaste . . . and my windpipe closing as I clung desperately to my meager secrets, my privacy, and my independence.

"Elin." Coldness rippled over my body at the bewildered, forced tone of Prince Roland's voice. He stared at Rubia with a look of horror on his face.

"Explain. What or who is Elin?" she demanded.

"Elin is the woman I love. What's going on, what is this?" The prince's voice became frantic as he put his hands to his head.

"Your Highness, please come with me," I urged. But Emric jumped up to help the prince to his feet.

"Actually, you should come with me," Emric countered firmly. The prince stood, looking around in a daze, his discombobulation apparent. I stood, uncertain. I couldn't let Emric take the prince anywhere on his own in this state.

"Come, Rubia." Rosalie grasped Rubia's arm and tried to tug her out of her seat.

"No! This is our only chance to learn something from the prince. He might not know where the maps are, but we need to keep trying!" Her voice was belligerent, almost maniacal now. "Prince Roland, did your father order the murder of Count Feldingham the second and his sons?"

"No! I mean, I–I don't know," came Roland's automatic response.

The insolence of this attack by Rubia stole my breath. The forced responses came right in front of Emric, whose allegiance was murky at best. I gauged the distance between myself and Emric. He held the prince's arm, his body taut and poised for action. I glanced at Rubia, who was next to me now, drawing a breath for her next question. Snapping through the fog of indecision and panic, I acted. Drawing my dagger swiftly out of my sleeve, I pressed it carefully to the side of Rubia's neck. Rosalie screamed, then covered her mouth with her hands as Rubia dropped to the floor.

The room was deadly silent as Rubia fell, and I caught her awkwardly, then settled her head gently on the floor.

"You killed her?" Prince Roland gaped at Rubia's limp form in horror. Emric stared at me in disbelief.

"Of course not," I said breathlessly, kneeling down to check Rubia's pulse. It was slow but steady. Relief coursed through me, strong enough to make me lightheaded. "She's just asleep," I said to the stunned and silent onlookers. I tilted Rubia's head slightly to examine the tiny prick I had made a couple inches below her ear. A tiny drop of blood beaded there. I wiped it with my sleeve, and the mark was invisible. My heart pounded wildly. I had just berated Rosalie for using a powerful potion on the prince, and then I used Nemere on Rubia, my own classmate and ally. But my resolve warred with my fear. She had poisoned the prince and was determined to exploit every secret he held in front of Emric. I couldn't let her. But she looked so small, lying in a heap at my knees. Like a child. I fought for air.

"You're all incredibly reckless." Emric's voice was dangerously low. "Bloody stones of Vindeca. You used Verum on the prince, didn't you? *Didn't you?*" His voice grew in force.

"Yes." I exhaled the word, automatically submitting to my curse. I hadn't done it, but my comrades had. And my curse knew that there was no difference.

"Used *what* on me?" Prince Roland asked.

"We gave you a truth powder," Rosalie answered him, her eyes frightened.

"Verum. He said you used Verum. Are you *mad*?" The prince looked at Rosalie in revulsion.

Emric's dark eyes flashed at me. "Now will you listen to me, Cressida? You girls have to leave the castle immediately."

"And leave you to whatever you're plotting?" I retorted, rising to my feet with my dagger still in hand.

But Prince Roland's voice boomed over mine. "You can't be serious, Emric? They know about—that is to say—they committed treason. They're not going anywhere!"

A door slammed behind me, and I spun around. The footman, laden with plates, had returned. Lady Tilda shimmered into view behind him, walking arm in arm with Lady Bern. The footman took one look at the tableau before him and immediately turned on his heel and left the room. The ladies walked forward, and the sly smirks on their faces faded when they encountered us, Rubia in a heap, and Prince Roland's arm firmly in Emric's grip. I was not sure if they saw my dagger, which I immediately hid in my skirts.

"Your Highness—" Lady Tilda began, concern creasing her smooth brow. Lady Bern's eyes narrowed suspiciously.

Prince Roland shook Emric off and straightened his neckcloth. "Ladies, good afternoon," he said before Lady Tilda could ask a question. "Miss Rubia here has had a fainting spell and has not recovered yet. Please enlist some footmen to take her back to her room, and summon a physician, if you would?"

Taken aback, Lady Tilda and Lady Bern looked around at each of us, their expressions bewildered.

"Of course, Your Highness," said Lady Bern after a pause. They executed deep, elegant curtsies, then hurried back out of the room together.

"Why didn't you send for guards?" Rosalie asked hesitantly as soon as the door closed behind Tilda.

"Because I have not decided what course to take, and I do not want a single courtier to know the condition you have put me in." His eyes were fierce. "And that is the last time you or your companion will address me again, or I'll have you gagged. Is that understood?"

Rosalie's cheeks flamed, but she didn't answer.

"Emric, take the ladies up to their room and stay there until I send up a guard. I will stay with Miss Feldingham until the footmen retrieve her, then I will confine myself. Hopefully I can wait this out."

"I'll find you as soon as I'm able to leave Miss Montshire and Miss Hoth." Emric delivered a short bow, then walked toward me. "Cressida, your dagger, please."

Remembering the violence I endured only a few hours ago, I was tempted to strike him with the dagger instead of handing it over. But Prince Roland could easily change his mind about calling for guards . . . and what Emric did not know, was that although the Nemere-dipped stiletto might have been my most potent weapon, it was not my only one. Without dropping my gaze, I held the smooth handle of the dagger between two fingers and let it dangle, point-down, over his waiting palm as if I would drop it. He quickly moved his hand, and deftly plucked the weapon out of my fingers. I glanced at Rosalie, who looked terrified, yet alert.

"Shall we?" Emric asked formally, holding out his hand to indicate that we should go ahead of him. With no choice but to comply, Rosalie and I quickly walked out of the Wulfestar Hall, with Emric at our heels. I forced myself not to look back at Rubia, still crumpled in a heap and lying as still as the dead.

We walked back to our room without a word. When we arrived at our door, Rosalie turned to Emric.

"Will you please come in? We need to talk." He glanced between us, his expression stony, then gestured for us to precede him into the room. After entering, I let my hand inch down my leg as he turned to secure the bolt. As the lock clicked into place, I whipped the dagger out of my boot and pressed it to the side of his neck.

"Turn slowly and drop the dagger you took from me. Drop it on the floor right now," I hissed the words to mask the fear in my voice. I followed his movements and kept my dagger against his neck as he turned to face the room. I pushed the blade so that a drop of blood welled up under my knife. He reached carefully into his jacket and pulled out the Nemere-dipped stiletto.

"Drop it," I repeated.

He dropped the blade to the floor, and the steel clattered against the wood.

"Kick it away from you," I said, my pulse hammering.

Emric lightly kicked the knife across the floor with the toe of his boot, far enough that it slid under Rosalie's bed.

"Rosalie, would you—" I began, but my request was cut short by Emric grabbing my arm and forcing it down to my side. He spun me and wrapped his other arm around my neck, squeezing my wrist until I dropped my dagger with a gasp of pain. I rammed my elbow as hard as I could into the soft spot just below his sternum. He fell back against the door, then bent over as he gasped for the breath I had knocked out of him. Twisting, I rammed my knee up into his forehead. Rosalie hurried over to the bed to retrieve the dagger.

Rushing back, she pulled me away from Emric as he staggered forward. "Stop!" Rosalie ordered, clutching my arm and holding my poisoned dagger out in front of her. "If you come another step closer, I'll use this!"

Emric winced and put his hands on his knees for a moment. "Fine. Truce," he panted.

"Cressida. What's going on?" Rosalie asked, holding the weapon firmly, although her voice shook as she spoke. "Why do you say we can't we trust him?"

"Yes, I'd like to know the same thing," Emric said, standing up straight, eyes boring into mine.

"Because he attacked me last night," I said curtly. "Move slowly toward the fire and sit," I instructed Emric.

"*What*?" Rosalie exclaimed.

Emric took a step toward me, ignoring my order and the dagger. "Attacked you?" he said sharply. "If you're referring to the night we met in the drawing room, that was far from an attack, it was—"

"Get back!" Rosalie brandished her weapon.

"Sit down," I ordered.

After a pause, Emric sat down on the settee.

"You met him alone?" Rosalie asked me, mystified. I crossed my arms. I knew it was mulish, but I wouldn't apologize for not inviting her into my confidence. Not after the scene she had just instigated.

"Yes. Twice."

"We met once, Cressida," Emric stated flatly.

My stomach flipped over. I felt so strongly that it had been him. And I had to be able to trust my instincts. I reached into my pocket and pulled out the tiny roll of parchment and handed it to Rosalie. She unrolled it hastily, then she glanced up at me.

"This isn't signed."

"May I see it?" Emric asked her politely. She handed it to him, and he scanned it. "Cressida, you met someone alone, after midnight, when you didn't know who they were?"

"It was you."

"Except it wasn't." He leaned forward, his voice tense. "Did they hurt you?"

His question irritated me. "Yes. A little. But I'm fine. How can you prove to me that it wasn't you?" I challenged.

"I can't," he said. "I was . . . well, actually, I was nearby last night, keeping an eye on your corridor."

"What? Why?"

"I was keeping an eye on your rooms. To make sure you were all safe. The point is, I have no other alibi. But why would you think I would do such a thing?" His expression was incredulous.

"You're the only one who knows we have the powders," I said, "and you wanted me to give you the Verum. The person I met last night was extremely bent on getting it from me. Not to mention, you seem to like meeting at that time of night."

"But I would never resort to hurting you—"

"Wait a moment," Rosalie interrupted us. "Here." She handed my stiletto back to me. I held it carefully, uncertain if I was still holding Emric captive anymore. Rosalie, unexpectedly, went over to her wardrobe and began rummaging inside it. I kept my eyes on Emric and held the dagger firmly at my side.

There was the barest hint of amusement in his eyes. "You're a hit first, accuse later kind of girl. I can't say I'm surprised."

I glared at him. There was a bright red mark on his forehead, courtesy of my knee.

"I wouldn't have to be if you had cooperated to begin with."

Emric shrugged. "I'm guessing you'd have done the same if you were me."

"Well, I'm very much not you," I retorted as Rosalie came back to my side, having found whatever she was looking for.

"Look at this," she said, watching my face carefully as she handed me a tiny roll of parchment, identical to the one I had handed her. I looked at her, puzzled, and she held up the first one. "They aren't the same note. But they are the same. Look at it."

I unrolled it, and my stomach plummeted as I read the message.

> *Pear Tree Parlor. 1 a.m.*
> *Bring the Verum. Come alone.*

"When did you get this?"

"The night before last. I should have told you," Rosalie said.

"But you didn't go, did you?" I asked in alarm.

Rosalie shook her head. "I didn't know what to make of it, but . . . it seemed like a foolish thing to do," she answered simply. I swallowed. Extremely foolish.

Emric stood. "The night before last is when we met, Cressida. At one."

"Yes, I know," I snapped. He didn't need to spell it out for me. "I realize that you couldn't have been planning to meet two different women at the same time at separate parts of the castle." My cheeks were burning.

It was clear that whoever had sent Rosalie's note had also sent mine. The tight scrawl was unmistakably the same. I slid my Nemere-dipped knife carefully into my sleeve sheath and glanced briefly up at him, unable to hide my embarrassment. "Sorry about your head," I muttered.

"Why did you want Cressida to give you our Verum, though?" Rosalie studied him.

"Because it's a big problem." His voice was grim. "An even bigger problem now that you two dosed the prince with it."

"Cressida didn't want me to," Rosalie said honorably. "That's why I took Rubia today. I let her do it because of her proximity to his drink. I—I didn't mean for her to use all of it."

His eyes flew wide. "She used all of it? How much was there?" Rosalie timidly held up the bottle. It was just small enough that the quantity could dissolve in a full cup, and completely empty.

"This was full."

Emric threw his hand over his eyes.

"We didn't know!" Rosalie protested. "And—and I thought you were on our side. Shouldn't we have used the opportunity to get some information out of Roland?" I could see the guilt flaming over her cheeks in spite of her defensive words.

Emric slowly shook his head. "There's a lot more going on here. I believe it's far too dangerous at this point to use the Verum on the royals, or to even have it in the castle at all. I know it's hard to know whom to trust, but please try to trust me on this."

I regarded him. "Can you explain?"

"I can try, but not yet."

"Why not?" I demanded.

"Look," he said impatiently, frowning at me, "I didn't want you to use the Verum on the prince for multiple reasons, not the least of which is the appalling recklessness of such an act. You're both in real danger right now, do you realize that?"

I said nothing, but Rosalie drew herself up. "We risked our lives for a reason, Emric. You need to give us a very good explanation why you followed the prince's orders rather than letting us question him."

"And I will. For one thing, I didn't want to make an outrageously bad scenario even worse. I will come back as soon as I can, and then I will explain. Meanwhile"—his eyes darted to both of us—"the prince is in a precarious situation and needs supervision." He strode toward the door and unbolted it.

"Wait!" I said. He turned back impatiently as I ran over

to my wardrobe and fished deep into the pocket of my spare petticoat. Finding what I needed, I ran back to him and held out the slim bottle.

"Do you know what this is?" I asked.

"I believe so," he responded warily. His eye flashed up to mine. "Is this what you used on Miss Feldingham?"

"Yes, and I don't believe it was harmful." My throat tightened, but I continued, "It will put him into a deep sleep. He won't be forced to respond to anyone. Someone wants to use the Verum and was willing to hurt me to get to it. The effects of his dose aren't going to be fading any time soon. Only use a drop . . . if he agrees."

Emric considered me for a moment. Then he took the bottle, tucking it into his jacket as he left the room.

I turned to Rosalie and the expected shock on her face.

"Why did you give him the Nemere, Cressida?" She put her hands up to her temples. "Nothing makes sense."

"I know," I told her. "And I know you probably don't want to trust my instincts right now, but I think he should give it to Prince Roland."

"What? Emric scolds us for dosing the prince with Verum, and now he's planning to use an even more dangerous drug?"

"He'll offer it as an option, yes. Think about it. Rubia had time to throw some pretty specific questions at Roland before she—"

"Before you poisoned her?" Rosalie finished, cocking her head.

"Right. Before I administered the Nemere, she asked Prince Roland what he knew of the maps and her family's murders and the whereabouts of important documents. The Verum forced a truthful response out of him. He didn't know."

"So, he wasn't ever going to be able to help us to begin with." Rosalie's voice was wooden.

"Not only does that make our task next to impossible, it means we are not hurting our own cause by putting him to sleep for a while. And . . . he seems like an honorable man, with secrets that have nothing to do with us. We can both see that by now. And someone in the palace unaffiliated with us is after the Verum, so Prince Roland is in danger if anyone were to discover that he's been dosed."

"So the Nemere is to protect him."

I nodded, taking a deep breath to try to calm my agitation as I struggled to convince myself that I'd done the right thing. "No one can question him and exploit him for whatever secrets he *does* know, or that they desire, for reasons we know nothing about. We had our reasons for being suspicious of the royal family, but someone else's motives for wanting that Verum could be completely different."

"Motives we want no part of." Rosalie dropped down on her bed.

I nodded soberly. "Exactly."

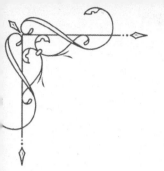

14

A GUARD ARRIVED AND STOOD
outside our room shortly after Emric left. An hour passed and
Emric did not return. Rosalie and I tried to wait patiently, but
our speculation only made us more restless. Finally, around the
time Sylvie might bring us an afternoon tea tray, we heard a
knock at our door. I looked at Rosalie nervously. She hurried
to the door with me at her heels and cracked it open.

"Rosalie? Cressida?" Vivian's voice was pitched high and
strained.

"Let her in!" I urged Rosalie, and we stepped back as Vivian
entered the room.

Rosalie popped her head out the door once Vivian was
inside and looked down the corridor. "The guard is gone," she
said as she shut and bolted the door.

"Yes, I came as soon as I noticed," said Vivian. Her cheeks
were bright and she held her hands clasped together. "I saw
the guard an hour or so ago, but didn't know how to find out
what was going on, so I've been checking every few minutes. I
ran over as soon as it was clear. There's something wrong with
Rubia!" She looked at us in near panic. "She won't wake up.
We've sent for her mother."

A wave of nausea swept over me.

"But is she all right?" I asked, doused in a cold fear. "Is she
breathing well, is her heartbeat strong?"

"She seems to only be sleeping, nothing more. But she

won't wake," Vivian said with concern. "Do you know what's going on?"

"Yes . . . but not enough," I said. "Let's sit down, though. We need to tell you what happened."

We sat on the settee and chair by the empty fire grate, and Rosalie cleared her throat, taking the lead on the story. I was relieved. I felt so confused, yet so responsible for the mess we were in, I didn't even know where to start.

Vivian listened in silence, nodding occasionally for Rosalie to continue. She did not interrupt to ask questions, and Rosalie was thorough. Rosalie finished by telling Vivian the last thing we knew—that Emric had left, taking the Nemere, promising to return with an explanation.

"I'm still confused on some points," Vivian said slowly. "If Emric is here for the same reason we are, why wouldn't he let you take advantage of the Verum? It's unfortunate that Rubia mishandled it, but—"

"We don't know about Emric yet, but the answers to Rubia's questions were enough for us to know that the prince isn't going to be able to help us find what we need," Rosalie explained.

Vivian flung up her hands. "Well, what on earth are we going to do? None of us are going to get a private audience with the king or queen. We don't even know where their private quarters are. We're down a teammate. What do we do?"

"We leave," I said.

"What?" Vivian said incredulously.

"At least Rosalie and I have to leave now," I clarified. "Emric may have used Nemere on the prince, but when he wakes up, he's going to want to deal with us. And even if he doesn't wake soon, Lady Bern and Lady Tilda saw us after Rubia had collapsed, and who knows what they overheard. Likely it won't stay a secret that a guard was posted outside our door. We are bound to be considered a problem by the time the day's out." I leaned forward. "Also, something else is going on, since someone knows about the Verum and wants it. It isn't safe here anymore."

"But our mission," Vivian protested, pain catching in her voice. "We won't ever get another chance like this."

"Maybe not. But I think now we have another job to do," I said carefully. "I don't think the prince is going to recover from that Verum without an antidote . . . if there is one." I swallowed hard before continuing. "All evidence points to him being innocent of any of the crimes his parents may have committed, and we've cursed him. Possibly for life." I knew I was opening myself up to questions. I also knew that, for once, I didn't want the truth forced out of me. I wanted to give it freely.

I cleared my throat. "I know . . . I know that you've both wondered why I have been so unwilling to use the Verum. For our mission. And—" I struggled to find the words. "You have every right to question it. I need to tell you something. Something I should have told you a long time ago." I tried to steady my trembling voice. "I shouldn't even be on this mission, because Verum was used on me when I was eight years old. And the effects never wore off."

My friends gaped at me in disbelief.

"*What?*" Vivian blurted. "That can't be true. We would have noticed by now. Wouldn't we?"

"But you didn't," I said. "I spent years believing that my curse would be discovered at any moment, but I learned how to handle it. Some might have wondered if there was something strange about me. Rubia couldn't seem to stop asking personal questions, but people usually don't ask questions that would be ridiculous to answer."

"But we're friends. We've been friends for a while now. I can't understand why I didn't see it." Tears were shining in Vivian's eyes now. I had never felt more exposed in my entire life.

"That's why you never seemed to have many friends . . . other than Vivian," Rosalie reflected. "You didn't want questions. You do have a little bit of a reputation for being blunt, but it makes sense now."

"This is why you told your attacker where the Verum was," Vivian realized suddenly. "Not because he frightened it out of you, but simply because he asked." Her face shadowed. "Cressida . . . I can't believe you came here."

"I know. I shouldn't have come . . . I'm sorry I've put everyone in danger." Tears were in my own eyes, and a lump in my throat. The curse of telling the truth had turned me into a most dishonest person.

I dashed the tears away and looked earnestly at the two of them. "That's how I know what danger the prince is in. Someone else here knows about the Verum, and we don't know what their purpose is. A presumably innocent royal is now in real danger."

"And there's no antidote?" Rosalie glanced uneasily at Vivian. "Nothing that came with the powders . . . for the Verum or the Nemere?"

Vivian shook her head. "I just assumed both wore off in time."

I felt twitchy with unease. I, who knew that the Verum did not wear off, had also administered the Nemere without foresight. "My aunts who gave me the Verum said there was no antidote. But there has to be a way I can fix this."

I pushed my hair back from my flushed face and tried to catch my breath. I might, eventually, be glad that I chose to tell Vivian and Rosalie the truth, but for the moment, I wanted nothing more than to crawl under the covers of my bed and be alone. A ridiculous thing for a spy to want, really. I had taken a calculated risk, and now I had to be alert.

"How? Cressida?" Vivian demanded. "Fix it how? You have no idea where to find antidotes, none of us do."

"I don't know yet, but they need to be found!" I said. Desperation rose in me. "We could go to Miss Tepsom, or my aunts. Maybe they didn't know about a cure, or maybe they lied to me. They had that luxury," I said bitterly.

"So . . . you've never told a lie? Since you were eight?" Rosalie asked, looking at me with more curiosity than dismay.

"Not exactly . . . just not a lie that I couldn't back up if someone asked me a question. I have to answer direct questions truthfully."

"Or what?" probed Vivian. She paused a moment. "I guess I want to know what we've done to Roland."

"Some painful symptoms set in. If I hold out long enough, I can't breathe and pass out or have a fit. I usually panic and answer before seeing how far they would go, but I feel like I could die the longer I try to resist."

"Oh, Cress . . ." Vivian's tone changed to instant sympathy. The pity in her eyes was worse than the anger I knew I deserved for putting them in such a predicament.

A light knock on the door made me jump. I looked at the girls in consternation. "I know I don't really have a right to ask this, but please don't tell anyone about this. About me."

"I'm not happy about where this has gotten us, but knowing you weren't forced to tell us means something. And I appreciate that," Vivian said quickly.

Rosalie nodded. "We won't tell anyone."

I whispered my thanks as I went to answer the door, where the knocking had persisted. As soon as I withdrew the bolt, Emric pushed inside and shut the door quickly behind himself.

At the sight of him, Vivian jumped to her feet. "Well! You'd better have some answers for us!" She strode toward him. "So you wanted Cressida to give you the Verum, and you did not want us to use it on the prince? You worked with Tepsom and Rush. We *are* on the same side, right?" she challenged.

Emric held her off. "We are on the same side," he said patiently. "However, I have been Roland's valet for long enough to know that we aren't going to learn anything about the royals' past misdeeds through him. Verum is a dangerous weapon in the wrong hands. It's dangerous to even know about it. And because I believe the wrong people want it, we have to get it out of the castle." He looked at me. "We also have to get you two out. Lady Tilda is already telling anyone who will listen that she saw something fishy and thinks that Rosalie is to blame for Roland's current—er—state."

"She knows he's been dosed?" I asked, shocked.

"No—that's not the state I was referring to. He and I discussed the danger he was in, and he has secrets—innocent secrets as far as we're concerned, but again, dangerous if known by the wrong people. He agreed to use a drop of the Nemere." Emric's face grew pale as he spoke, likely mirroring my own. "I did so, then fetched help, telling them that the prince won't wake. Someone is going to figure out what happened pretty quickly, with Rubia unconscious as well. What with Lady Tilda pointing her finger at you two, and Roland ordering a guard outside your door before he took the Nemere, we have approximately no time left to wonder when they'll arrest you."

"What happened to the guard?" Rosalie asked. "How are we supposed to get out of the castle?"

"I dismissed him to other duties. And I know a few things about this castle that might help us get out unseen. I have—well, half a plan. We'll make up the rest as we go along. But we have to hurry."

None of us moved. I didn't like the sound of half a plan.

Then I looked at Vivian. "Are you coming with us?" I asked.

She bit her lip, thinking. "I don't think so," she finally responded. Of course she wouldn't. Vivian was brave and determined. And not as embroiled in Prince Roland's misfortune.

"Why not?" Rosalie pressed. "It can't be safe here for any of us anymore."

"But I am not implicated, at least not yet. Only you two have an actual reason to flee."

"Vivian, please." I knew that it was in vain. Her jaw was set and her eyes were steely. But I had put our entire team in danger and was shaken by the idea of leaving her behind, essentially alone.

"I'm not throwing away our only remaining opportunity to stay close to the situation and keep digging." Her calm tone was belied by the tension in her features. I nodded reluctantly, knowing that I could never force my friend to give up her mission.

It might have been my imagination, but a hum of voices and stirring activity seemed to be rising from the lower wings. I felt an itch to get moving.

"What about you?" I looked at Emric. "Once we're gone, suspicion is sure to fall on you. Lady Tilda also saw you with Prince Roland shortly before he was given the Nemere."

"I have to stay," said Emric. "I'm investigating a lead here. It might be nothing, but I can't drop it yet, not when I'm close. But we'll figure out how to communicate with you two once you're out, especially if we find anything. I have some contacts."

"So—pack!" Vivian commanded suddenly, shooing us. Then she pulled Rosalie and me in for a crushing hug. "All right, now pack!" she said upon releasing us.

Rosalie and I looked at one another, and a silent resignation passed between us. She turned to her wardrobe and began to hastily pack.

"I'll be right back," said Vivian, and she slipped out of the room.

I ran to my wardrobe and pulled out only what few garments I could fit in my smallest bag. I didn't know how long we'd be on the mountain, but I knew I would be glad of any extra layers. Emric moved about anxiously.

"Can I help? Need me to fold anything?" he asked as I wadded up a petticoat and crammed it into the bag, then fastened the straining top with some effort. I silently handed him the bag, then shoved every dagger I had into the hidden sheaths in my dress, wrists, and boots, and pulled my cloak around myself.

Vivian returned the moment Rosalie and I were done. Emric let her in with another cautious glance into the hall.

"This is the rest of our store. I think you need to get it out of the castle." She pushed the leather case of powders into my hands. I agreed and slung the strap over my shoulder so that the case hung over my back, underneath my cloak.

Making a quick decision, I pulled out my dagger that had been dipped in Nemere and held it carefully out to Vivian. She looked at it for a moment, then took it without a word, nodding her thanks. I didn't like leaving her alone, but giving her the weapon helped a little.

"And you need to promise to communicate with us all from now on," Vivian told Emric as she wrapped the dagger carefully in her handkerchief. He raised his eyebrows.

"We might be in less trouble right now if you had trusted us," Rosalie agreed. "We have to be able to work together from now on or this is going to turn into a bigger mess."

Emric's face turned slightly pink, but his voice was steady. "I'm sorry. You are both absolutely right. Vivian, I will tell you everything I learn from now on, and we will work out how to communicate with our friends. Does that sound fair?" Her expression held a graceful acceptance of his apology, and he slid back the bolt.

We followed Emric through the dim, empty corridor, and down the south-end stairs. Rather than descending all the way to the bottom, he turned and paused at a narrow door that stood between the first and the third floor. I had always assumed it led to a broom cupboard. He opened the door.

It *was* a broom cupboard. Rosalie and I glanced at each other in confusion as Emric stepped inside, shuffling the brooms and rags and buckets out of his way. A nervous giggle bubbled up into my throat, but I swallowed it and stuck my head into the dark cupboard.

"Uh . . . Emric? Did you lose something in here, or—"

"Through here, quickly please." He stepped back and gestured to the corner of the cupboard.

"I'm sorry?" I said in confusion, stepping inside and peering closer at the corner, wondering if we were walking into a ridiculous sort of trap. Then, I understood. Emric was pushing aside a rough, grey board that matched the stone of the walls. Behind the board was a threadbare curtain.

"Please. Go through there, I will be right behind you." He leaned the board against the opposite wall and held the curtain aside. "Oh. We'll want that," he remarked, swooping down and snatching something from the floor just inside the dark opening. It was a fat, half-melted candle stuck in a brass tray. Emric let go of the curtain and pulled a flint and bit of steel from somewhere on his person. Kneeling down, he struck it several times until the candlewick caught. He handed the candle to me and beckoned for Rosalie to join us in the broom closet.

"Step just through the opening but don't go on yet," Emric whispered. The candlelight threw wavering shadows across his face, which couldn't hide the tense lines of his mouth or the worry in his dark eyes.

I turned sideways to squeeze through the narrow opening and was relieved when it opened up into a slightly wider passage. We could hear as he shut the door, affixed the board back over the opening, and finally let the curtain drop.

I had noticed a heap of something on the floor, and now Emric picked up what turned out to be two heavy cloaks and handed one to each of us. I threw the dark cloak over my other one. It was damply chilly in the castle, but it would be deathly frigid outside on the mountain.

"We have to be quiet as we walk," he cautioned. "This passage is one of a few that loop the castle, and many spots share a wall with an occupied room. I admit, I am not familiar with the whole of the passage network, but I do have an idea of how to get to a seldom-used room on the ground floor. We can get you out a window from there."

I resisted the urge to shoot a panicked glance at Rosalie. But I had no better plan. I handed the candle to Emric as he slid past me in the narrow space to take the lead. I pushed against the fear that threatened to clamp down upon me. The heavy, dust-hung air choked me. I kept my eyes trained on Emric's back as we made our careful way down the narrow passage.

I didn't like the thought of leaving Emric behind, any more than I liked leaving Vivian. Mere hours ago, all I had felt toward him was a hurt, betrayed anger . . . but it had dissipated. I now felt like the worst sort of fool to have suspected him of attacking me on so little evidence. After helping us escape and dosing the prince with Nemere, any further good he could do here seemed hardly worth the risk.

"Do the king and queen trust you?" I asked in a hushed voice as we followed Emric through the dusty, but barren passage. His broad back blocked most of the light from the candle.

"Can you hold the light up?" Rosalie requested from behind me, after stumbling into me for the third time.

Emric held the candle up and to the right to allow us more light. It illuminated the filthy, cobweb-hung walls. "I don't know," he answered my question. "That is, they have trusted me enough to do my job, but I don't know if they'll continue to trust me under the circumstances."

"Are you really sure you should stay?" I asked. I kept my head down to watch my steps carefully, so as not to step on his heels.

"I have to stay," he replied. "I'm trying to put some pieces together, and I think I'm close."

I waited, hoping he would continue.

"I want to explain . . ." He forgot to hold the candle up, which caused Rosalie to huff her annoyance in the darkness behind me and brace her hand against my back. "It just hardly makes any sense to me yet." He stopped and turned slightly. I felt a rush of frustration. I thought about badgering him with reminders that he had promised to be more communicative.

"What do you remember about your attacker?" he asked, surprising me before I could urge him to disclose specific details.

I thought briefly. "Male, obviously. Rude. He carried a knife. His cheek was rough. He whispered. I couldn't place his voice because of that."

"Anything else?"

I closed my eyes, recalling the cold terror of that night, of the moment the hands grabbed me, the arm wrapped around my neck. I remembered freeing my wrist and scrabbling against the assailant's arm and hand.

"He wore a ring," I realized, then added, "but that can't help much. A lot of men at court wear rings."

"True. Do you remember what finger he wore it on?" Emric asked.

"I think it was his little finger. A flat signet, maybe. And I felt lace at his cuffs. He was definitely a courtier, or noble of some sort. Well," I amended, "I suppose some of the higher grooms and footmen also wear lace cuffs." I paused, coming alongside Emric to get a look at his expression. "Do you think you know who it was?"

Emric shifted his footing and rubbed his hand across the back of his neck. "I don't have enough to go on yet. But we need to keep moving," he said suddenly. I glanced back at Rosalie, who shot a discouraged look at me, and we fell back behind him as he moved ahead with the candle.

Everything was tangled up and murky. We came to investigate the royals, yet we now fled them, but left friends behind to protect the prince, while still spying. There were no longer two distinct sides of the board now—the pieces had mingled, the colors bled.

There was no more conversation as we moved more slowly

through the next passage, sensing movement and indistinct, muffled voices through the walls on each side. Finally, we passed the occupied rooms, but had to move more carefully as the floor began to slope rather steeply downward. I assumed we were nearing the ground floor and, hopefully, the room Emric had in mind.

"I don't exactly have allies in this place," Emric said quietly, turning slightly as he walked. "But I have contacts with their own secrets. One of them is a groom waiting in the woods on the east side of the castle, with two ponies. Once I get you out of here, go due southeast as swiftly as you can. Keep out of sight until you get to the groom. I advise you not to speak to him, but take the ponies. Then, get far away from the castle, quickly.

"What do you know of the journey down the mountainside?" Rosalie asked.

"By pony, easier than on foot, but you don't want to be caught on Mt. Vindeca overnight. It's too cold and the ponies will stumble and possibly lame if you try to ride them in the dark. Try to find the road, but stay out of sight of anyone travelling on it. The king might become suspicious enough to order a search for you, so you'll need to stay out of town, or at least out of sight if you must go into Savinrue."

As Emric spoke, his voice suddenly sounded louder, as if it was amplified. Then, a cold draft blew the candle out. A chill skittered across my neck, both from the sudden darkness, and the drop in temperature.

"What happened?" Rosalie whispered as we stood as still as statues in the dark.

"I'm not sure," Emric replied. I heard him take a cautious, shuffling step to the left. "There seems to be another branch of the passage that I hadn't noticed before my candle blew out."

"How did your candle blow out?" I asked. "It's nearly airless in here."

"Not down this way, apparently," Emric replied, and I heard

him take a few more steps away from us. "I want to see where this leads."

Rosalie and I followed hesitantly. The darkness felt isolating, and it grew significantly chillier the further we went. We slowly trailed the sound of Emric's voice and footsteps. I put my hand out and gingerly touched the wall. It was cold and rocky.

"This is fascinating." Emric's voice echoed slightly ahead of us. A dim, grey light began to lift the heaviness of the darkness, and I could almost make out his outline. "Shoncliffe hasn't seen war in a long while," he said. "But such was not always the case. It would stand to reason if, in times of siege and war, the king and his men made use of a secret exit—"

"A sally port," Rosalie broke in, her voice colored with interest.

"Right," said Emric. "The tunnel would be used to escape the castle, or to stage an ambush by allowing the king's men to come up behind the attacking army. The kingdom has been at relative peace for centuries, with no castle sieges for even longer than that. If this is what I think it is, it might well be forgotten—abandoned and unmanned."

I silently processed this, impressed by the idea in spite of my utter unwillingness to be in the dark, freezing tunnel. Emric walked slower now, and we shuffled carefully to avoid a collision as the floor sloped steeply downward. Finally, it leveled out. It was unmistakably lighter and colder inside the tunnel. Ahead, a dim but obvious vertical line of light was visible, and an icy wind moaned up the passage. When we were within several yards of the source of light, Emric stopped. "Wait here while I investigate what's ahead."

Rosalie and I stood still and watched as he slowly approached the light. I wrapped my cloaks tightly around me. A damp smell of earth and rot thickened the air. As I watched Emric's vague shape, it suddenly disappeared.

Ignoring his warning, we rushed forward. As we approached the line of light, it seemed to grow brighter, and faintly illuminated what appeared to be a wall of solid rock. I reached out to it, puzzled. Suddenly, Emric's head seemed to appear from out of nowhere. I startled, then realized that he was leaning around a corner that had been completely camouflaged by the rock. The line of light was a narrow opening between the end of the tunnel and the rock wall just past it. Emric was standing in open air, wedged in between the rock wall and a stony outcropping on the outside of the tunnel.

"This way!" he beckoned, then turned and slid through the gap.

I followed, with Rosalie right behind me. The rock wall extended a few feet past the opening of the tunnel, and once we had stepped past it, we were standing outside in the icy wood next to a vast boulder. I turned and looked up. Shoncliffe stood a couple hundred yards up a steep incline, and the high wall shielded us from the castle's windows. It might not, however, hide us from wall sentries.

Emric jogged several feet further into the wood, then looked back, studying the entrance to the tunnel. He came back, shaking his head with a bemused look on his face.

"Genius," he said over the wind. "The boulder conceals the tunnel entrance without closing it off completely." One look at our strained expressions, however, told him that we would each prefer to discuss the merits of the hidden sally port at a different time. "Right. You two should be on your way. The groom should be . . ." He pivoted slowly, then pointed east.

"Thank you," I said quickly. "Now please go back right away and get far from us, as soon as you can."

"Yes!" said Rosalie. "Once we're missed, you need to be cleared of any involvement." She looked at him. "Thank you for helping us this far."

He released his breath in a puff of steam. "All right. Be careful." His dark eyes met mine, then he slipped back behind the boulder and into the tunnel.

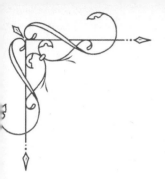

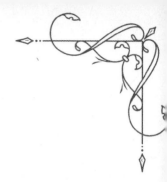

15

I GLANCED BACK UP AT THE
fortress, massive and forbidding under the steely sky. No guards
were visible, but that didn't mean that none were in a position
to take notice. A bitter wind howled and battered us.

"We have to move further into the trees. And fast!" I tried
not to shout.

We pulled our cloaks tightly around ourselves as we
clambered down the incline. It grew slightly less steep as the
trees thickened, and an icy crust of snow coated the wood. We
made our way easterly, straining our eyes for any sight of our
contact in the thickening forest.

I shivered as the wood closed around us. My parents had
spoken of Mt. Vindeca frequently, and with reverence. But I felt
only a growing fear of the mountain. The wind that thrashed the
mountainside, cutting through the trees here below the palace,
moaned and sighed eerily through the stillness.

A scrape of red on the grey and white canvas surrounding us
caught my stinging eyes. I blinked hard, staring further down
into the trees and catching a slight movement. I nudged Rosalie
and pointed, just as the pale face of a man peered from around
a thick tree trunk. Spotting us, he motioned to us. We made
our way down the snowy incline, grasping at branches and
slim trees for balance until we reached the spot where the red-
liveried groom waited, holding the reins of two shaggy-haired
ponies. Their golden coats were thick and dull, their pale manes

were tangled, and they stamped impatiently among the trees that hid them so well.

The groom had the reins of the ponies slung over a low branch, and he straightened when we approached, rubbing red hands together. "About time," he said, too loudly. "It's frigid out here." He shifted his weight back and forth nervously.

I studied him for a moment, wondering why he looked so familiar. Then I realized that he was the footman who had attended the prince's party in the Wulfestar Hall only hours ago, minus the wig.

Rosalie spoke up. "Thank you for waiting," she said quietly. "And for your silence."

He smiled at her. "Did I agree to that? I'm pretty sure it's worth more to me if I go back *with* some information, right? Where are you ladies headed?"

Rosalie shot an alarmed look at me. "We're just . . ." She faltered as she tried to think of a believable lie.

"Going to be like that are you? Save the stories," he said nastily. He reached around and pulled a large dagger out of the back of his breeches.

I raised my eyebrows at the entirely impractical hiding spot for a pointy weapon. Keeping my hands inside my cloak, I slowly drew the remaining dagger out of my wrist sheath, my heart racing.

"Now," he said, taking a step toward us. "What are your names, and why are you scampering off? Tell me, and I won't raise the alarm *just* yet."

Rosalie's eyes went wide as he directed the question at me. "Freya! Her name is Freya. Mine is Lady . . . Ros . . . worth. Please don't tell anyone you saw us—" Rosalie continued to babble as the answer to his question flooded my brain, and my lungs constricted. I considered how long I could fight it, but we'd be in worse straits if I fainted and left Rosalie to deal with the wayward groom on her own. I appreciated her effort to drown out my words, but it was no use.

"We are Cressida Hoth and Rosalie Montshire. We are leaving because we'll be arrested if we stay," I ground the words out through my teeth. Curse my curse.

"Lady Rosalie, eh?" he said. "That's something. He'll be very interested to hear that."

"Do you mean the king?" Rosalie asked faintly.

"Of course not."

"It will be common knowledge who left soon enough, so I can't imagine your information is worth that much," I remarked.

"Perhaps. But I have your admission of guilt as well." He leveled his gaze at us. "Anyway, three names will be worth a good payoff."

"Three names?" Rosalie asked sharply.

"You two and your accomplice. We've been watching him for some time, and now he's made his move. Traitor. Now, just one thing before I decide if I should actually let you go." He suddenly grabbed me and pushed me hard against a tree, pinning his forearm against my throat. The strap of the potion-case dug into my neck. "What did you two do?"

Of course, he had to ask me. I stared into his bright blue eyes, fringed with fair lashes. My vision darkened at the edges. I wished desperately that I had given Rosalie a dagger. There was nothing she could do without prompting him to kill me and then move on to questioning her. My throat squeezed shut, and my head began to feel muffled and heavy.

"Go on and faint," came the scornful voice of the groom, seemingly from far away, although I could feel his breath hot on my face. "I only need one of you to give me answers." He put pressure on my neck and shoved the dagger under my chin, pushing it in hard enough for me to feel a hot sting as it pierced my skin. I shifted blindly as adrenaline coursed through me, telling me to act.

"We poisoned the prince," I gasped, then rammed my dagger in between his ribs.

The groom sucked in a sharp breath, choking and clawing at the dagger, buried high in his left side. His arm against my throat slackened, and I pushed him, hard. He fell, shuddering and twitching in the snow. Rosalie clapped a hand over her mouth when she saw the dagger sticking out of his ribcage. Oxygen flooded through me, clearing my vision.

I forced myself to breathe and my legs to move toward the groom, then dropped to my knees beside him. I hovered my hands uselessly above his body as Rosalie circled him and knelt beside me. I wrapped my hand around the hilt of the dagger, braced my other against his chest, and pulled. The dagger scraped and stuck against bone, and I almost vomited when it finally came out, dripping dark blood over the snow.

"We need to–to stop the blood–" My teeth chattered, and I wadded up the edge of my cloak and pressed it against the seeping wound.

Rosalie put her hand on my arm. "I think he's dead, Cressida," she said hoarsely. "I think he was dead before you pulled it out."

I stared at the still body, at the blood streaking my hands that pressed my cloak against the dead man's wound. I nodded numbly.

Rosalie crawled over to his head and held her hand under his nose, then sat back quickly on her heels. "He was going to kill us, or hurt us, or turn us in to whomever he works for," she said, her voice small but firm. She stayed next to me as I held my cloak uselessly against the groom's side. I knew it didn't matter; I just couldn't move.

Several minutes passed before I finally lifted my hands, stiff and numb. I raised my eyes to his face. He had overlarge ears and had nicked himself shaving under his chin. I looked away quickly. Tears I didn't remember shedding froze in trails on my cheeks.

"We can't stay here, Cressida," Rosalie whispered.

"I need to do something with the body," I whispered back, hardly able to speak.

"Yes," she agreed. "And quickly." She stood, face pale but determined.

"No," I told her, stumbling to my feet, my blood surging through my veins again. "You need to go. Now, as quickly as you can."

"What?" Rosalie said in confusion. "*We* need to go. After we hide the—the body."

I laid a hand on her arm. "It's most important that you leave. You're the one primarily under suspicion. But Emric's in more danger than he knows, and I need to tell him. If we both wait to hide the body and then find Emric, we're not getting out of here and down the mountain before dark. We've already lost too much time. If you leave right now, you might have a chance. And you can get to Miss Tepsom's."

"Cressida—no. You can't go back, especially after—especially now! We both need to get away from here!"

I was unyielding. "Just you. I will meet you at school as soon as I can. If that's too dangerous, Miss Tepsom will know where to send you. Either way, I'll find you, Rosalie. Then we can plan what's next." I bent down and started stripping the groom's red jacket off of him. Rosalie watched me for a moment, then turned.

"Wait." I fished into my left boot and drew out a dagger, holding it out to her. She hesitated, then took the dagger and hurried over to the baleful ponies, pulling the reins of one down from the branch. "Find the road and try to stay near it but out of sight from it, if you can," I reminded her.

"You too," she said, looping the pony's reins around her hand and preparing to lead it down the hill to less steep terrain. "Please be careful, Cressida!"

"I'll see you soon," I said as she led her pony down the wooded mountainside. I uttered a prayer that she would find the road, then wadded up the coat, stuck it into a shallow hole, and covered it quickly. The body was going to be considerably harder to conceal, but I didn't have time to do it thoroughly. Hopefully, without the red livery, he would stay camouflaged for the time being. Choking on panic and bile, I threw heaps of snow, leaves, and rocks over the body.

I listened to the still wood around me as I worked with raw, numb fingers to hide a corpse. I thought of Rosalie, too, on the mountain alone; I needed her hard-won courage to soak into me now.

Finally, the groom was completely covered, and I stood back to survey my work, thinking how absurd it had seemed to me when Rubia had asked Miss Tepsom how to dispose of a body. I felt that I could also use Rubia's tenacity in this moment, but couldn't bear to think any longer of the girl I'd drugged.

There was an unnatural-looking heap at the foot of the tree the groom had pinned me against, but hopefully no one would be searching the woods for him any time soon. I was about to turn away, when I saw fingertips peeking macabrely from the snow. Stomach rolling, I pushed them deeper with the toe of my boot, and kicked more snow to fully cover them. I blinked back panicked tears and tried not to think about how wolves would probably dig him up in a matter of hours or less.

I walked over to the now-impatient pony and, shushing gently, buried my frozen, sticky hands in its shaggy mane. It stilled its shifting hooves and tossing head. I glanced at the steel sky. It was impossible to tell how late in the day it was now. It felt as if a week had passed since we had come into the woods. I closed my eyes and bent my head down, resting against the pony's withers, and breathed in the scent of straw and musk and dirt.

I had sent Rosalie away, while knowing now more than ever that I was not qualified to be giving orders. I'd thought myself the capable one between us, but I had just caused a monumental problem. I'd committed murder, leaving Rosalie to escape the mountain on her own. I was no leader, and I wasn't even an effective protector. Separating from one another might have seemed strategically unsound . . . but Rosalie had good sense, and she'd agreed. Maybe she was beginning to understand what I already knew: being caught in my company was more dangerous than being caught alone. I was a worse liability than even I had imagined.

I squeezed my eyes shut to bar tears from spilling. The moment of the killing looped through my brain. The decision to kill, followed immediately by the action. I'd known what I was doing, and I couldn't decide if that knowledge would make it easier or harder to live with.

I allowed myself four or five deep breaths, then raised my head and shook off what I could dislodge of my inner turmoil.

I gave the pony a final pat, wishing that I could return him to his warm stall. But not only was that impossible without being seen, I might still be able to use him in my own escape, if that ever occurred now. I picked up my abandoned pack and the case of powders, and shoved them deep into a gnarly, frozen bush, berating myself for not sending the drugs with Rosalie. I'd get them on the way out, God willing, but I was not going to risk being caught with them on my person inside the palace.

Using the just-visible castle as my guide, I made my way back toward the hidden tunnel. It seemed to take longer to reach than it had to find the groom and the ponies, and panic began to mount as I frantically scanned the frozen, rocky incline for the entrance. It was remarkably well concealed, but finally I recognized the boulder.

I scrambled up the hill, keeping an eye on the castle wall looming above me, and willed myself not to be seen. I reached the ice-glazed boulder and slipped out of the biting wind and into the passage.

The darkness enfolded me. There was no chance of having a

light at all this time, but I slammed a mental door shut against the fear that accompanied that thought and rushed determinedly up the cold passage. I slid my hands along the cold rock of the wall as I climbed the underground hill. Finally, the air grew warmer, and my hand found the corner that marked the end of the tunnel.

I closed my eyes unnecessarily and pulled every jittery ounce of my concentration to a singular point of focus. My breathing evened and my heart rate slowed as I envisioned the map of the castle that we had been given on the day we arrived, that I'd studied many times since. Mentally, I traced the path that we had taken to reach this tunnel. Shortly before we'd found the way out, we had passed a room that I had believed to be the Winterberry Drawing Room. There had been several branching-off passages that we'd passed before reaching that point, and if I had everything straight in my head, then the second branch to the left should be the one I was looking for.

My sight could not adjust to the darkness—it was so complete that I could not make out a single shape, although my eyes strained optimistically. I faced the direction I believed to be correct and held my hands out to my sides, tracing my fingers lightly along the walls as I walked, so that I would not miss a branch of the passage. The air grew warmer and closer as I moved further and further into the heart of the palace, and a suffocating panic threatened to steal over me. I had not felt this smothering fear the first time I had walked this route, but this time I was alone in the dark, and desperately fighting off the disorientation that would accompany my fear.

I whispered a soothing chant to myself as my fingers passed over dusty cobwebs and tangled, furry clumps that shot shivers down my spine. *"Second on the left. Second on the left. Second on the left."*

Finally, my left hand found an empty space, and I knew that I had passed the first branch. With a flood of relief, I walked faster, ignoring the silken webs and less pleasant, unknown sensations that scraped through my fingers. But a growing uneasiness soon replaced the relief. It seemed too far, my brisk walk felt too long. I must have miscalculated. I had been depending on nothing but my own memory, which I had not prepared for this task. I was trapped and lost in the bowels of the castle.

I halted, standing as still as a statue, feeling as if I were suppressing a dreadful truth. We were almost certainly under suspicion by now, if not being actively hunted. Rosalie was embarking on an icy, dangerous mountain descent all alone, Emric was in danger from whomever had the groom in his pay. And the groom . . . was a dead body freezing under the snow that I had heaped on top of him after shoving a knife into his lung. Or heart. The murder I was guilty of had been brutal, and I wasn't even sure of the particulars at this point.

The truth that played itself through my brain could not steady me, nor distract from the panic that was threatening to overwhelm me completely. It could not get air into my lungs; it could not make me think straight. The truth of this day was a hateful, ugly thing.

I sank down onto the cold stone floor, the weight of the rock-hewn castle above pressing me down. With agonizing slowness, I worked through the shallow breaths and the churning hate and disgust that plowed through my brain, my whole body. Finally, with measured, concentrated effort, I breathed evenly. The self-loathing had not relented, but I could—and must—move. I was no safer here than I would have been hunkering in the woods. Emric was no safer while I hid like a rat in the castle's secret passages—which were possibly not a secret to all. If Rosalie and I were searched for in earnest, someone might know to check here. With exhausted determination, I pulled myself to my feet, ignoring the instinct to curl up and never move again.

The panic and loathing were chased with an overwhelming

sense of foolishness. I placed my hands back on the walls and took a step, then another. Another, and another—and my left hand again fell through empty air. I had sat and wallowed and panicked not five paces from the passage I sought.

I gasped in mingled relief and frustration, and turned down the branch, walking slowly and listening with my ear close to the wall on my left. It was not stone, but wood. There were no sounds of activity. My hand passed over a ridge of cold, rusted metal, and I jerked away from the change in sensation.

I stumbled and caught myself hard against something. Kneeling carefully, I ran my hands over the rough step of stone I had run into. My heart leapt—I'd found exactly what I was looking for. This passage ended in a narrow, steep, winding staircase. I held back my skirts and climbed, hugging the wall and feeling out every step with precision. Finally, my straining, aching eyes were rewarded. A dim light spilled in a ghostly patch across my path. I knelt down and found the source: the bottom seam of a door. I held my breath and strained to listen, desperately unwilling to emerge from the passage, dusty and filthy, with bloody hands, into the wrong room and the shocked, genteel presence of a courtier.

I refused to stay there listening for long, however. All was quiet on the other side, so my fingers found the seam of the door, and I worked it open, pulling it inward. I was unsurprised to find myself facing the back of a tapestry. I pulled my cloaks around me like armor. Then I took a deep breath and pushed the tapestry aside.

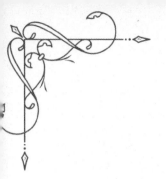

16

THE DAYLIGHT THAT FLOODED

the solar struck my eyes, and I sucked in my breath in an audible gasp of relief when I realized that I had gambled and won. Emric was there, alone. He stood in his shirtsleeves at the other end of the solar, and he whipped around when I gasped.

"Cressida?" His hair was wild as if he had been tugging it in frustration, and his face was tense and hard lined. I pulled the passage-door shut and let the tapestry fall back over it. Emric came right over to me, and his eyes widened in shock when he took in my appearance. I had a fleeting rush of embarrassment when I realized that my hair was probably ten times wilder than his, and I was filthy and bloodstained. But how I looked was the last thing that mattered at this moment.

"Why are you here? How did you get up here? Were you seen? I've been watching for the groom to return, and hoped I had missed him, but almost was anxious enough to head out and check—"

My head spun. "Because you're in danger, I followed the passage, of course, and I pray I was not seen. But I don't know." My face flooded with a rush of heat as I baldly answered his stream of questions. He blinked.

"What do you mean I'm in danger?" He asked, after a pause. "Wait. You don't look so good. Come sit down." He led me toward a chair near the sword cabinet.

I answered as I followed him across the room, unwilling

to endure a moment of my symptoms by not satisfying the truth immediately. "The groom worked for another party. He was going to—to reveal everything he discovered about our escape, including your involvement. I don't know who he was working for."

"What did he discover? He threatened you?" Emric stopped walking. "Where is Rosalie?"

The overload of questions caused a wave of nausea to wash over me, and I closed my eyes to shut out the dizziness as I answered, "He learned our names, and why we are under suspicion. Yes—he did. Threaten us. Rosalie is on her way down the mountain."

A fresh surge of shame and horror threatened to overwhelm me. He was about to ask more about the groom, and I'd have to tell him what I'd done. I wanted to be imposing and confident—and not have to tell anybody anything I didn't want to. But instead, I was loose-limbed and shaking, dizzy, and sickened by our predicament and my own actions. By my vulnerability and the hateful curse.

Emric was silent a moment, watching me, then he gently placed his hand on my back. "Here. Sit." His unreadable eyes were on the dried blood that streaked and stained my fingers and the backs of my hands. I sat in the chair he indicated, and he sat opposite me. My memory spun back to our lessons at Miss Tepsom's, growing easy in his company, laughing with him while we rested between duels. His face was harder now, with no trace of laughter.

"Cressida, I understand you took a great risk to come back here, and we have no time to lose. I have a lot of questions. But you should take a minute. Tell me what I need to know when you're ready."

My blood thundered in my ears as he watched me closely, leaning forward and resting his elbows on his knees. I couldn't read his expression or comprehend his words. But he needed answers, and he wasn't going to drag them out of me. I couldn't even begin to disentangle the swirl of thoughts and feelings that provoked.

I swallowed, feeling hot and awful in my layers of cloaks and hidden daggers, my filthy hands and wild hair. But I met his eyes.

"I killed the groom."

The words sounded harsh. But Emric didn't even blink, and I continued in a rush, "He questioned us—and said that he would be delivering every word to his employer. He seemed to be contemplating delivering us to him as well. He became violent and threatened me—us—with a dagger. I fought back . . . and killed him. I hid the body—not very well—in the woods where we met him. I sent Rosalie down the mountain because she had to get away from here. But someone here likely already knows that you secured the groom to meet us and help us escape, or they're already suspicious. The groom said they'd been watching you. That person will be waiting for a report. You aren't safe here and should leave with me now, before night falls. And before the body is found."

I stood, my purpose renewed. He now knew what he needed to know, and I could breathe.

Emric also stood. "You're probably right. But I don't like to leave Roland in this state. I truly believe he is innocent, you know," he added, glancing at my face.

"I believe you," I said. "But you can't help him much when suspicion falls on you. We can figure out how to best protect him, and cure him, and everything else once we're out of here."

"You're right," Emric relented. He paused. "Thank you for coming back for me, Cressida." He abruptly went to a tall wooden cabinet that stood near the regular door of the solar, and knelt down to open a pair of cupboard doors at the bottom.

"Fortunately, I'm relatively prepared for a hasty retreat." He pulled out a small leather satchel and a neatly folded woolen cloak. I glanced out the window to see the pale streak of the western horizon dimming through the trees, the sky darkening from steel grey to iron. Emric fastened the cloak around his neck and then motioned to me.

"Come over," he said, going to the sword case. There was a small washstand next to it. He glanced at my bloody hands. "You need water before we go back into the passage—to drink and to wash with."

I poured some of the chilly water into the washstand basin, plunged my hands in, and began scrubbing hastily. We looked suspicious enough without one of us being bloodstained. When I had finished, my hands were stinging and pink, but mostly clean. I accepted a tumbler of water from him.

I thanked him, then asked, "Can we leave soon?" The idea of Rosalie, alone on the mountainside at nightfall, was reopening my nauseating jitters. "Perhaps I shouldn't have left Rosalie alone," I worried. "If we hurry—"

Emric stopped me. "We are unlikely to be able to catch up with her. With any luck, she will be off the mountain by full dark. Which is possible if she found the road and encountered no obstacles." He lifted a sword carefully out of the case—a short, broad, unattractive weapon compared with the fencing foils—and slid it into a leather scabbard which he strapped around his waist as he continued, "We won't be so fortunate—I agree that we need to leave the castle, but we have a rough night ahead of us."

"All right, but let's go." We crossed over to the tapestry and were about to push open the secret door, when there was a click and scrape from the door on the opposite end of the solar.

Emric swore under his breath. Without pause, we both pushed at the narrow door before us. I entered first and stepped aside to make room for him on the top step.

The tapestry dropped behind us, just as we heard the wooden door scrape along the stone floor on the other end of the solar. I gently put my hand on the back of the tapestry to still its swaying, and my heart stopped as the sound of boots thudded across the floor. I moved to slowly push the door shut, but Emric put his hand on mine, stopping me. I looked up at him, barely able to make out his face in the dark, but saw him shaking his head. He wanted to know who was in the solar. I stood perfectly still, and Emric leaned in, bracing his hand against the wall.

It sounded like more than one pair of boots that marched across the floor, but I could not tell how many.

"No one here." The voice was male, unfamiliar. "With his room empty, too, I'd say he must have fled with the ladies."

"Probably in league, eh? Poisoned the prince together. But why?" Came a thin, reedy voice—disconcertingly, much closer.

"Not our job to speculate. Report his absence, and I'll set the guard around the perimeter and have them search the forest. The traitors must not escape, especially if the prince dies from the poisoning."

The boots stopped, too close to the tapestry. I held my breath, feeling Emric's body tense beside me.

"Right you are, sir," the thin voice responded. The footsteps receded, and the solar door thudded shut. I waited a moment, listening hard, before releasing my breath.

"All right," Emric whispered. He pushed the door shut carefully. Its outline was a vague ribbon of light that barely broke the heavy darkness. I didn't care for the trepidation that the return to the passages released in me.

"Who else knows about these passages?" I asked.

"I have no idea. Most likely Roland. He actually dropped a few hints that prompted me to explore, but we've never discussed them outright. I discovered them on my own months ago, but have never heard them mentioned, seen them on a castle blueprint, or met another soul using them. That doesn't mean that they are a secret to the royal family and the guard, though."

"What do you suggest?" I asked anxiously. "The guard is

mobilized—they'll be in the woods before we can reach it. They might find the—the groom." I swallowed hard.

"But if we stay in the passages, there's a chance they will be searched as well, if they are known. I don't like the idea of waiting like trapped rats."

"Then let's head for the sally port while we decide what to do next. I don't like it in here at all." I started down the steep and narrow stairs, clutching at the jutting stones of the wall with one hand.

"Cressida, if you hadn't come back when you did—"

"Don't thank me again yet."

By the time we had made our careful way down to the bottom of the stairs and into the muffled air of the passageway, any sliver of light from the solar door had evaporated, and darkness pressed against me. We kept our voices to a whisper.

"You didn't happen to leave that candle anywhere near here, did you?" I asked.

"I have one here," he answered, and I heard him kneel and rummage through his satchel. Although every inch of me was impatient to leave, I stood still in the utter darkness, waiting for him to strike a flame.

In a moment, I heard the scrape of the flint, and the wick caught. The pitiful, hazy yellow glow flooded me with relief; I wouldn't have to navigate back in complete darkness. Emric stood and slung his satchel over his shoulder, his shadowed face grim, his dark eyes anxious.

"I know we need to go—but I think you need to see something before we move on."

"What?" My instinct to flee the castle drummed harder.

Emric went a few paces down the passage, then stopped before a dusty section of wall. His candlelight revealed an ancient, rusted iron lock. The ridge of metal that I had touched on my way to find him. I bent down and inspected it. It appeared to be unlatched, its keyhole scraped as if by a determined effort to pick it open.

"Did you do this?" I asked, glancing up at him. He nodded. I saw that it was wood instead of stone, with rusted hinges at the seam. Emric handed me the candle and used both hands to push against the door until it loosened and swung inward.

"What is in there?" I asked, as the dark pit of the open door gaped before me. Whatever it was, it was directly below the prince's solar.

"I came across this room rather recently. And—" He hesitated. "I have been unsure what to do with what I found." Emric took the candle out of my hand and stepped into the dark, stone chamber. I followed, trying to still the twisting nerves in my stomach. Bat droppings littered the floor, and I determined not to look up. I flipped my hood up over my head.

"It's the full breadth of the solar," Emric said. He held the candle near a section of curved wall. Mounted on it were racks of what appeared to be very ancient, filthy arrows. The sparse and dusty fletching was crimson, and the heads of all but three were missing. These three were very peculiar. Rather than a traditional arrowhead, a glass bulb was fastened to the tip of each.

Emric moved away from the wall and made a slow arc with the candle, attempting to illuminate the whole room for me, bit by bit. The walls were hung with many rusted, dust-coated weapons: swords, crossbows, and spears. The spears and crossbow bolts had the same strange glass bulbs at the ends. Dirty banners draped the walls, stitched with a seal that was similar to the emblem of Dernmont, but not quite the same. I could barely make out the coat of arms, but it seemed to include crossed arrows with the strange bulbed tip, with the mountain in the background. On the far end of the room, a row of shelves lined the wall, housing stacks and stacks of scrolls.

"This is indeed strange," I conceded, "but couldn't you have told me about it on the way?" At any moment I expected guards to come barreling down the stairs and appear in the doorway.

"I–suppose," Emric said. "But our chance to investigate here is nearly gone. I hardly know what to make of it myself. I wanted you to be able to see what I've found with your own eyes, not just take my word for it. I know that it is hard to completely trust anyone right now."

He searched the shelves of scrolls, then pulled one out with great care and inspected it. It was clearly very old parchment, loosely rolled, as if the seal had been broken and it had been unfurled already. "I didn't mention this earlier because, not only is it completely baffling, but I am not sure who should know about it. It seems dangerous knowledge to have."

"You're probably right . . . although I don't understand any of this." I waved a hand at the room at large. Emric handed the candle to me again.

"I want to show you this," Emric said. Then he caught my agitated expression. "I think we need to wait a bit before we leave the castle anyway," he said, and began to gently unroll the scroll.

He was likely right. The woods surrounding the castle would already be full of soldiers hunting for us. Perhaps if we gave them a while to search the perimeter, we could escape when they dispersed. Perhaps.

I nodded, although my fear was a knot in my chest, refusing to loosen. I glanced down at the top of the page that Emric held. In brown, faded ink, but a bold hand, official lettering was scrawled across the top.

> *Outlawed in use and in memory: Verum, Lethen, Nemere, and all variations and concoctions thereof.*
>
> *Never again shall the mines of our most powerful substances be plundered for use of peasant, soldier, or royal. Sealed, they shall remain forgotten, and upheld only in the*

memory of the crown and its descendants, for the sole purposes of caution and betterment.

Never again shall Dernmont be known for her prowess in Mineral Alchemy Arts or Warfare, nor for the healing of her stones. Any acknowledgement of such a history or possible future shall be regarded as Treason.

Porleac will do well to heed our Lementhe Treaty in all its particulars, and any heir who finds she has not will be compelled to secret action of military nature.

Mystified, I looked up at Emric. "Lementhe Treaty?"

Suddenly, the sharp call of a bugle and the clanging of a bell seemed to reverberate throughout the entire bones of the castle and shake the dust from the walls.

I grasped Emric's forearm. "We need to leave!"

He rolled up the scroll hastily, then crammed it into his satchel. My breath caught tightly in my chest, and I frantically scanned the shelves of scrolls. We were in enough trouble without being caught with documents that were clearly top secret, but I desperately wished to know more.

"This will have to be enough for now," Emric whispered, and we reluctantly left the wall of scrolls and shut the door to the secret room behind us. We knew we were hunted.

We turned right down the passage and hurried through the dark. Emric reached back and took my hand firmly in his. I was thankful, in spite of the heat that flooded my face.

"Do you remember how far from here?" he asked in a whisper. I slid past him to take the lead.

"I think so." I moved faster, more confident now that I knew where we were. I ran my hand along the wall, noting when we passed the thinner walls of the Winterberry Drawing Room. Shortly beyond that, the floor steeped, then my hand found the cold corner of the tunnel.

"Here," I whispered. I pulled him through the dark opening.

When we reached the end of the drafty sally port, there was no dim line of light outlining the entrance, and I realized that full darkness had nearly fallen. I couldn't decide if this made me feel better or worse.

"Are you ready?" Emric asked softly.

I nodded. He blew out the candle and, releasing my hand, stepped into the narrow space between the boulder and the icy outcropping. I could just see the shape of him, inching his way along until he was standing at the edge. He stood there a moment, then slowly leaned his head around. I pulled my hood up and slid into the space next to him.

"It looks clear," he said, pulling his own hood up over his dark head. I followed as he stepped cautiously out from behind the boulder.

The wind was biting, and it would be full dark in a matter of minutes. We scurried down the rocky, sloping incline until we reached the near cover of thicker trees.

"We need to avoid the spot where you met the groom," Emric said.

I glanced back at the castle, its grey towers and walls solid and forbidding as the mountain. The bright top windows were just visible from here: the fortress awake, alert and watching. I was anxious to get further into the wood, away from Shoncliffe.

"Why?" I asked. "Well, I know why, but the pony might still be there. We might need him." I thought also of the case of powders I had hidden.

"They most likely already found the pony," Emric replied, and I knew what he was choosing not to say. That they had likely found the body of the man I killed, as well.

I swallowed. "But how do we find the road down the mountain?" I asked, shivering in spite of my two cloaks.

"Not down the mountain," Emric said. "Up."

"What?" I said blankly. "But—"

"It makes the most sense at this point to get to shelter and avoid the guard at all cost, right?" Emric said, tipping his head slightly to see my eyes under my cloak. His were bright in spite of the darkness.

"Right," I answered automatically. Emric shook his head suddenly, his face tense.

"What is your idea?" I asked impatiently, but then I held up my hand suddenly to stop him from speaking as a flash of movement caught the corner of my eye. I whipped my head to the left, where I had seen the movement, and Emric turned to search the shadows of the trees behind him. He gripped his sword hilt and stepped backward slowly, keeping a thick tree at his back. Suddenly, a figure lunged out of the darkness with a bellow. Emric dodged to the side as a guard with saber drawn rammed his shoulder against the tree Emric had been standing in front of a split second before. I pulled my dagger out of my wrist sheath and launched a kick at his back with all of my might. He sprawled to the ground, and Emric placed the tip of his sword to the back of the guard's neck.

"Not a word, my friend," Emric instructed. "A call to your comrades could cost you your life." Then, so swiftly that my breath caught in my throat, he flipped his sword so that the blade was up, and thudded the heavy hilt into the side of the guard's head. The red-liveried body went limp, and a sick feeling swept through me.

Emric bent down and extracted the guard's saber from his hand. "Cressida," he said shortly, and tossed the weapon to me. I caught it, mercifully by the hilt, and Emric quickly removed the belt and scabbard from the guard's waist. He stood and brought it to me. I could not control the shivers that rippled through my body as I stared at the prone form on the ground. I could feel Emric's eyes on my face, but I didn't move.

"You should wear this," he said quietly. He reached into my cloaks and slid the belt around my waist, his hands swift and efficient. The belt was too big to buckle, but he cinched it and looped it tightly, then finally looked back at me.

"He's alive," he said, reading my fears. "Is that too tight?"

"No. It's fine," I said, and sheathed the sword as Emric stepped back.

"Do you remember how to wield a saber?" he asked, miming holding one in his fist, then bringing it down in a diagonal slash.

I nodded, smiling slightly as I recalled his lessons. "We really need to move," I said, stepping past Emric, past the body on the ground. Every nerve of my body was buzzing with the need to get deeper into the darkness, away from the castle and the guards roaming the wood.

"The monastery," he said, following me. "To the east."

I slowed my walk and looked into the dark wood. "All right," I said. "Lead the way."

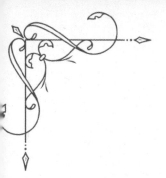

17

A DEAD HAND IN THE SNOW,
sightless blue eyes. The sickening scrape of blade against bone.
I blinked hard, over and over again, to remove the images
from my mind. My eyes ached from straining in the dark as
I endeavored to aim my steps in Emric's footprints. At some
point in the night, icy chunks of snow had made their way into
my boots, and above the misery of the cold seeping through
my stockings and the chafe of the leather against my heels,
rose an absurd anxiety about the damage the water would do
to my dagger blade. My throat and chest ached with the harsh
cold that I sucked into my lungs. Every physical irritation,
every ounce of pain served to distract me from the images of
dead men left in our wake, but only momentarily. Had Emric
and I each killed a man during our attempted escape? Were
we a pair of murderers on our way to seek refuge in a holy
place? I hoped that he, at least, was guilty of nothing more
than a stunning.

A wet, sharp branch slapped against my face, jolting me out
of my fixations of guilt.

"I'm sorry," Emric said over his shoulder. As we climbed up
the mountainside, he had been chivalrously holding branches
aside for me, to do anything to make my path easier. We
were avoiding the road, where the king's patrol could ride by
at any moment, but taking it would have been considerably
smoother going.

"Have you given much thought to what I showed you?" Emric panted.

I could barely muster the energy to respond. "Some," I managed.

He paused and leaned against a tree. "What do you make of it?" he asked as he caught his breath.

I took my own deep breaths and tried to wiggle my numb fingers and toes as I thought, but they didn't seem to move in response to the order my brain sent. The wood was exceptionally quiet, muffled by the deep layers of snow and ice, and the panic that had been chasing me for the past two hours began to recede a little.

"I have no idea what the weapons on the wall were all about." My voice sounded hoarse. "But the document certainly seemed to imply that the substances that we were given . . . hold a significant place in Dernmont's history. Its *actual* history."

"And are now highly illegal—even the knowledge of them," Emric added.

"Is that why you wanted us to hand the Verum over to you?" I realized.

He nodded. "I found that room just a few months ago and have been attempting to study the scrolls whenever I could. You girls were in enough danger on this mission without possessing something that would instantly condemn you if discovered."

"Miss Tepsom didn't warn us about them." My brain felt as if it was overflowing.

"Perhaps she didn't know the extent of their danger. I would bet this stuff has been around on underground markets for centuries, no matter how badly the king wants it only under his control. Tepsom was certainly right about Dernmont's history being rewritten." He pushed his hood off his head and shook snow from his hair.

"And—if the Verum and Nemere have been around for centuries, perhaps antidotes exist as well?"

"I hope so," he said. "We will need to start by asking Tepsom where she got her hands on such substances."

Without further conversation, we continued onward. My mind was awake now, wild with the possibility that an antidote existed. The thought pushed me on, in spite of my frozen limbs and aching muscles.

The wood thinned a bit, and the moon lit the snow around us. I brushed more icy pine needles out of my face and looked up. We were finally within sight of the road that led up to the monastery, just beyond a frozen stream. Emric turned and offered me his hand to help me over the stream. I chanced a glance at his face.

"Normally blue suits you, but I don't think that color is doing you justice tonight," he said, his light tone at odds with his serious expression.

I just looked at him quizzically.

"I'm just teasing you. Your hands are turning blue—and your lips. We need to get you warmed up as soon as possible," he said, gripping my hand and stepping gingerly over the icy stream. A log had frozen in the middle, its branches jutting up like black arms reaching out of the ice.

We forged on through the muddy, freezing slush gathered near the stream. Trees obscured most of our view, but just through them, I could see the pale strip of moonlit road.

"We'll be pretty visible once we're on the road. Better approach it carefully to make sure it's clear, then move quickly."

We set off immediately through the trees and slowed as we drew nearer, and the light that illuminated the road spread thinly over the edge of the wood. I strained my ears for the sound of voices or hoofbeats, but the wind over the open road was strong enough to muffle such sounds.

Finally, we emerged from the forest and into the biting wind of the unsheltered road. It glowed white in the moonlight and shone a clear path all the way up to where the monastery sat, pressed snugly against the protective trees on the mountainside.

"Let's hurry," Emric urged. "We need to minimize the chance of being seen from the monastery, or someone coming from behind. Can you run?"

"Yes," I said hopefully. Thankfully, my numb and shaking legs cooperated. The road to the monastery was steep, and icy shards of pain shot from the soles of my feet up my legs.

I never thought to wonder what we would do when we got to the monastery, until we had almost reached it. When we were close enough to be in its shadow, I laid a hand on Emric's arm and he pulled up short.

"How do we get in? And then what?"

He pointed to the back of the monastery. "The greenhouse."

We walked briskly, but silently, around the side of the monastery, until we had reached the east side where the glass-walled greenhouse connected to the ancient stone structure. Emric felt his way along the walls to the outside door. The moonlight slanted across the greenhouse, reflecting off the top, illuminating patches amid the shadows inside. He found the door, and the latch clicked open easily.

I followed him inside, and my body immediately began to thaw. The stove in the center of the greenhouse was empty, but the air was considerably warmer and gentle compared to the mountain-lashing wind. Emric quickly shut the door behind us, and the silence of the space was full and enveloping, disturbed only slightly by the hushed bubbling of the hot spring. Every pain my mind had been telling me to ignore came screeching into focus, and I felt a moment of real panic that my legs wouldn't hold me up another second. The last thing I wanted to do at this moment was wilt like a hothouse flower, so I braced my hand against the edge of a wooden table covered in clay pots and took several deep breaths of the clean, earthy air.

"Let's find a spot to rest," Emric suggested. We prowled around in the shadowy greenhouse for a few moments, and

I felt as if I were wading through a daze. I almost wondered if I had fallen asleep outside in the snow and was comfortably waiting to freeze to death.

Emric spread his cloak on the ground near the steaming hot spring. Its white raven guardian glistened in the moonlight.

"Here," I said. "I have two, remember?"

I picked his cloak up and gave it back to him, then took off my top cloak and spread it out on the ground. It was stiff with ice on the outside and the groom's blood on the bottom, but the inside was only slightly damp. We sat down on it and leaned against a log which had been placed near the spring.

After a few moments, I realized that in spite of the rise in temperature, I was still shivering. I still couldn't feel the tips of my fingers or toes.

Emric glanced at me. "Are you warm enough?"

"No," I answered immediately, ever truthful. "I'm better though," I added. "This is a good spot."

"I wish we could light a fire in the stove," he said. "That probably wouldn't be wise, though. We should try to rest. We can leave right before daybreak."

I shuddered involuntarily at the thought of going back out to face the wind and ice. I thought of Rosalie and desperately hoped that she made it down the mountain and into town before night fell. I didn't like to think of the state she'd be in if she hadn't.

"What do we do after this? After we get down the mountain?" I asked.

Emric was silent a moment, scraping his boot back and forth across the hard-packed floor. "I'll see you back to Miss Tepsom's. She will know what your next move should be, I imagine."

"And you will . . ." I prompted.

"I have to find the antidotes."

"How?"

"I will ask Miss Tepsom what she knows when I take you to her, and go from there," he responded.

I felt irrationally irritable at the thought of going back to stay at Miss Tepsom's . . . it looked like a dead end for me. But I'd told Rosalie I'd meet her there, and he had no reason to include me in his quest.

"Do you . . ." He stopped, then started again. "I'm wondering if you know about any other leads I should pursue," Emric said, each word deliberately chosen. I peered at him suspiciously through the darkness. He had worked awfully hard to not phrase his question directly.

"No. How would I?" I asked.

"I just have been wondering . . . if you have any memory of some prior experience that could help us. Your family's land was seized, after all, and I can't help but wonder if those seizures might mean something."

"As was yours, I presume," I commented. He said nothing, but his eyes watched me carefully. "Why else would you end up spying for Tepsom?"

"Yes, our home was taken—I was recruited to avenge my father. Ambrosia was too," he added, staring into his hands laced around his raised knee.

"Ambrosia?"

"Your teacher, Ambrosia—Miss Selkirk. She's my older sister," he said quietly.

I blinked, surprised that I never realized the connection, although now I could easily recall a resemblance in their golden-brown complexions and arresting features.

"Our father was murdered, and my mother died shortly after. After that, I wanted nothing more than to leave. Our home was 'reclaimed' by officials of the king, as they told Ambrosia. I suppose with me out of the picture, it did appear as if the crown rightfully owned the land. Although my understanding was that in such cases, it was customary for the king to grant the land to the remaining family. That didn't happen, and I was too hotheaded to stick around and try to claim my rights.

"My sister went to stay with a friend, and I left for Porleac when I was sixteen. I worked as a hired guard—a mercenary. It was not an entirely noble profession, but my skill with a blade kept me well paid and on the move. After about a year, I received communication from my sister that there was an opportunity for us to seek justice for our father's murder. I wanted to ignore it—but out of fear for my sister, who had already been recruited, I came home. My name isn't Theon, and hers isn't Selkirk. It's Dantis."

I listened attentively, grateful that he would offer me his story. "How did you end up teaching us?"

"Ambrosia introduced me to your headmistress after I arrived home. She convinced me of the mission to investigate the royal family's interest in our lands and put me to work training you. Shortly after I began that, as you know, I was placed in the palace." He paused for a moment before continuing, his voice strained. "I know what it sounds like. It sounds like I was aimless and angry, following whoever offered me vengeance."

"None of us knew what we were doing," I said. "It's all so tangled up. How do we really know what to do with all of this? Our families were killed. I don't want anyone else to die, especially because I stepped into something too deep for me."

"I know. But we can find out more," Emric stressed. "We can find out the truth of this. And once we find irrefutable proof of the crown's culpability, we can go on from there."

"But how are we supposed to do that? We also need to get Prince Roland the antidotes. I know, in spite of everything, you're still loyal to him."

"I don't believe he shares whatever guilt rests on his father," he responded firmly.

"You said you think that Prince Roland hinted about the passages. Do you think there's a chance he wanted you to find them?"

"I think that he wants someone to share secrets with," Emric said slowly. "He's very alone, you know. He dropped enough hints for me to find that room—carelessly, it seemed, but I have to believe he knew what he was doing. I never found the opportunity to let him know that I had. Once, he'd been drinking and was in a bit of a mood, and he mentioned the burden of royal secrets hanging over him that he barely understands. His mind is heavier than he lets on. He's in love with a girl from Porleac, and it's put him in a tough spot."

"Elin?" I asked, remembering the name. "Then why—"

"He hasn't figured out how to tell his father, hence all the prospective brides being trotted in. As good as it could be for the kingdoms to unite in this way, he's fearful his father may never consider such a match."

We sat in silence for several long moments. I wondered if he was falling asleep. I knew that I had to rest before we left the greenhouse, but I was growing more and more alert. My blood felt like it was fizzing and sparking through my veins as I tried to understand and organize everything in my mind. Nothing was clear, however, no matter how I turned it over.

Emric suddenly spoke. "Cressida, I would like to ask you something."

"All—all right," I said, swallowing hard.

"I don't want to make you tell me anything you don't want to," he said gently. "I'm not even sure how this works, and I'm afraid if I ask you directly you will *have* to tell me . . ."

He knew.

I remembered how deliberately he had tried, more than once, not to ask me a direct question. I realized now that I should have known. I was so used to people looking right past it, enjoying its benefits or hating me for it, but never really seeing it.

"It's all right." I was making a decision that frightened me. "If you're wondering if I have been dosed, or cursed, with

Verum, then the answer is yes, I believe I have." I swallowed, my mouth suddenly dry. "So I have to tell the truth."

"Cressida . . ." he said awkwardly. "I'm sorry if I made you tell me—"

"You didn't. But thank you," I said, fighting off a wave of panic. I hadn't felt so overwhelmed when I'd told Vivian and Rosalie. But for some reason I wanted him to know. Telling him filled me with a perplexing, terrified relief.

"Thank you for telling me, then. Do you want to talk about it?" he asked, then winced. "Sorry."

"Yes," I answered, surprising myself.

"And I'd like to ask a question first, if I may."

"All right . . ."

"May I put my arm around you?" My pulse quickened. "I have the most honorable of intentions. I'm freezing." I could just make out his gleaming grin, and was thankful that he probably couldn't see the blazing blush creeping up my cheeks.

"You may. But I might not be of much help in warming you up," I answered.

He wrapped an arm around my shoulder and pulled me closer against his side. "Worth a try," he said, and I stifled an embarrassed laugh.

I cleared my throat. "I was eight. I still am not sure why—I suppose because I was sort of a liar—my aunts gave it to me. I don't think they knew what they were doing."

"Eight?" Emric exclaimed, shocked.

"Yes, eight. That's why I was so against using it on anybody to get the information we were after. Its potency doesn't seem to expire."

"Oh no," he breathed. "And . . . if you resist, I assume there are some consequences." He seemed to be making a concentrated effort not to make me say anything I didn't choose to.

"Like death?" I said grimly. "Early on, I had a fit and passed out. I think I was ill for a long time afterward. After that, I honestly have always been too terrified to find out how long I can resist. The answers just pop out. I can't breathe and it feels like it's killing me if I don't answer a direct question truthfully and immediately."

He was silent, digesting the information.

"I am a horrible, dangerous liability on this mission. I know," I said miserably. "I tried to leave school when I realized it, but Miss Tepsom stopped me and talked me into not giving up. She doesn't know the truth, though. No one has ever known until today. I told Rosalie and Vivian before we left."

"You shouldn't have ever had to worry about anything but protecting yourself, and somehow you ended up as the protector of your entire team." Emric's low voice was tense. "Your aunts have a lot to answer for."

"Even so, I did *want* to go to the palace as a spy, and I have to take responsibility for that. I could have gotten out of it, somehow."

"Maybe. But you worked with it, and I am in complete awe of how you've managed your curse. No one would have ever guessed, the way you handle yourself, and handle conversations. It's amazing."

"You guessed," I pointed out, amused.

"I noticed a couple of times when you were particularly blunt, but it wasn't until after Roland was dosed and the effects on him were on my mind that it occurred to me. Your response to my questions when you found me in the solar today was what convinced me that I was on to something." He seemed lost in thought.

"So you have no previous experience with Verum?"

"No, only what I've read since finding the scrolls."

"But you knew we had it?"

"Ambrosia wrote to me. We've only been in rare communication since I came to the palace, but she wrote her concern in the code that we worked out for emergencies. She couldn't go into much detail, but had reason to fear that the powders—the Verum in particular—could fall into very dangerous hands. I wish I had the chance to really talk to her—I sensed a genuine fear in her letter. After what I'd found in that room beneath the solar, I knew we had to get those substances safely hidden."

"They should never have been given to us," I said, frustration rippling through me. "And now the prince—"

Suddenly, Emric's body tensed, and he cocked his head ever so slightly. I automatically held my breath. There was a chinking, scraping sound, like clay pots rubbing together. A prickling chill glided down my neck. We sat in frozen stillness, and Emric's arm grew tight around me. A faint brushing sound followed the scrape. Another person, or an animal at least, was in the greenhouse with us.

The slightest movement could give us away, but every nerve in my body wanted to stand. Emric slowly released me and grasped the hilt of his sword. I inched my hand over to the saber lying next to me on the ground. The brushing sound grew nearer, and then, the dark outline of a human came into view, creeping in a furtive manner between tables of young potted trees. I could see from the shape that he wore a cloak, which accounted for the brushing sound as it trailed across the greenhouse floor.

The moment the figure was visible, Emric sprang to his feet. I followed suit, getting tangled slightly in my damp cloak. I gripped my sword and heard Emric sliding his from its sheath.

The figure was small, I could see as it drew closer—shorter than me, which gave me a boost of courage. Emric and I could probably overpower it. The thought felt foolish almost as soon as it entered my head, upon realizing it was a small and entirely unmenacing monk who approached us. Emric lowered his sword cautiously.

The monk stepped into a patch of moonlight, and I immediately recognized the delicate features of the silent one who had let us in on my first visit.

"Brother Arin." Emric apologized. "I beg your pardon. We never should have trespassed. However, it is too cold a night to spend on the mountain." He confidently omitted the reason about why we would have to spend a night on the mountain if not in the monastery greenhouse.

I held my breath again as I watched the monk's stony expression. His eyes flitted to me, then back to Emric. Then he turned and began walking back the direction he had come. I glanced at Emric, who was watching the monk's retreating back in apprehension.

"We'd better leave," he muttered, sheathing his sword. "He'll be bringing someone back here."

"Wait." I put a hand on his arm. "Look." Brother Arin had stopped and was watching us, unmoving. He appeared to be waiting. "Does he want us to follow him?"

"I'm not following like a lad to the headmaster, whatever he wants," Emric replied, but his voice was uncertain.

I saw the monk's shoulders heave in an annoyed sigh, and he jerked his head to indicate that he did indeed wish us to follow him.

"All right, but I'm curious. You can wait here," I said, sheathing my saber as well and starting after the monk.

"Cressida," Emric said warily.

I looked at him impatiently. "Does it look like he's about to drag us before the king and all our enemies?" I said with some asperity. "He couldn't if he wanted to. I, at least, want to know what he has in mind. We can turn and outrun him if need be, right?"

Indecision chased over his features. "All right. But be on your guard."

The moment we moved toward him, Brother Arin turned again and led the way to the door into the monastery. He pushed it open and beckoned us through into the dimly lit corridor of tapestries.

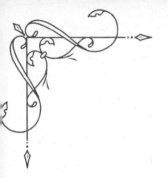

18

THE MONK WALKED SLOWLY down the drafty hall, and I began to question my decision to follow him. One monk might be easy to escape, but a monastery full of them could hold us prisoners while word was sent to the palace. I knew this was exactly Emric's reasoning, but I still couldn't disregard the curiosity that drew me onward.

The monk stopped and looked at me. I noticed he wore a white, chipped-enamel brooch in the shape of a raven on the breast of his robe.

"You," he said. There was a slight gasp from Emric. In shock, I wondered if I had been wrong and he was not the monk who had taken the vow of silence. But his voice fairly creaked from disuse, rasping lightly. "What will you do with it?"

"With what?" I asked in amazement.

Emric stared at the monk, his hand still on the grip of his sword. "Why have you broken your silence? What is this about?"

But Arin's blue eyes never left mine. "The antidote. Tell me what you would do with it if you found it." His voice cracked and wheezed as he pushed through the words.

"How do you—" Emric stepped forward, but I answered immediately, automatically.

"I would use it for myself. And I would give some to the prince."

"How long were you listening to us?" Emric demanded in confusion.

The monk stared at me a moment longer, his expression bland, inscrutable. Then he glanced up at Emric and smirked a little, but did not answer. Instead, he bent down and picked up a dusty oil lamp that sat on the floor by the wall. Then he lifted one of the fat candles out of a wall sconce and lit the lamp with it, turning the wick until it blazed higher. Yellow light spilled over the tapestry before us. He looked at me significantly, then held the lamp close to the tapestry, so close that I tensed at the thought of the ancient hanging catching fire.

"Then you will need the source," came the words.

I glanced over the tapestry, which hung nearly floor to ceiling. I barely remembered it from the day I was here. Emric bent close to the tapestry, studying it with a strange look on his face.

"What is it?" I asked. The weaving was unremarkable, faded greens and browns depicting what appeared to be landscape. Wavy lines shaping mountain and sea, forest and farmland. I leaned in to try to see what I was missing. Then I saw how very detailed the work was.

It almost appeared to be a portrait within a portrait. What looked at first glance to be bland, heavy-handed landscape, was in fact an intricately detailed scene depicting a much larger area. When I adjusted my eyes to this new view, I saw colors. There were trailing rivers of the finest blue threads, so fine that when I stepped back, they appeared to blend into the greens. The greys and blacks of paths and foothills lightly stood out over the brown heap of the mountain. Silver strands made up the castle and the monastery, faint but proud. Further to the right of the mountain were patches of land in different shades of brown, ranging from deep sable to faint gold, and each color was outlined in blue or green threads. When I took in the whole of the tapestry, actually *seeing* it now, it was almost too obvious, and too glorious. A lamp was pushed into my hand, and I held it as close as I dared to the tapestry.

"What the blaze—" I nudged Emric, and he changed course.

"How have I never noticed . . ."

Dernmont was displayed in brilliant, intricate detail.

"It's a map," I said softly. "And—here. Look." My voice shook in excitement. I had found my home. The small village and tiny patch of land where I had lived my happy childhood memories, before being sent to the aunts, were stitched into the beautiful, ancient work of art. Silver threads traced a slender stream that I knew. I stretched onto my tiptoes and looked closer. In that bit of the map, my homelands no larger than an infant's palm, was woven a minuscule deep blue circle with a gold dot at the center.

"Mine has one too." Emric's quiet voice was intrigued. He showed me, to the south of my family's farm, a slightly larger patch of land, the delicate threads nearly russet brown, and within the borders of blue were grey hills and caves, barely visible. A tiny blue circle with a gold dot at the center lay atop Emric's land.

"Is that—" Emric turned to the monk, but he was no longer in the corridor with us.

I looked up and down the hall in surprise. I had no idea how long Emric and I had been examining the tapestry, but long enough for Arin to slip silently away. Perhaps he was fetching another monk. Or perhaps his work with us was done.

"It is, isn't it?" My eyes darted over the tapestry. "It's the map we were sent to find."

"It has to be," Emric said. "This corridor is always so dim. I've been down here a dozen times, paying decent enough attention to these, but I've never noticed the detail on this one. And look—" He pointed at the sconces on either side. Both were angled away from this particular tapestry, toward the ones that flanked it, keeping it in shadow.

"We could be wrong," I considered. "It could just be a detailed map of the kingdom."

"Perhaps. Except none of the estates neighboring mine are

as clearly depicted as ours, nor are they marked as ours are."

"And the Montshire estate, and the Feldingham," I said, indicating the lands I had also found, each detailed, each with a dot.

"This likely means all the other lands that were seized by the king are depicted and marked as well."

We continued to pore over the stitching. Something was growing inside me, an excitement I was almost too afraid to acknowledge. But I couldn't ignore it.

"Why do you suppose the monk asked what I would do with the antidote before showing us this?" I looked at Emric. "That it was so important he actually spoke?"

Emric shook his head. "I don't know, but I'd like to know what—"

"Emric!" I said, grasping his arm. "*You will need the source.* The lands. The king wanted them," I said breathlessly. "Suppose—I mean, I could be wrong, but—" My voice was shaking. I desperately did not want to be wrong.

"The royals wanted mine access. Our lands must hold the mines. That's it, Cressida. You're right." Emric's grin overtook his shadowed face. He held the lamp high so that a yellow pool of light centered on a large circle of the magnificent weaving.

"And so . . . at least one of these marked locations should lead us to the substances that comprise Verum, and, presumably, its antidote," I said, trying to reserve my excitement.

"Where though? I've never known of a mine on my family's estate, and this marking could show anywhere within the borders." Emric examined the tapestry so closely that his nose nearly brushed it.

I squinted at the dot over my childhood home. "It's so small, I can barely make it out. But there's nothing that I remember between this hill and this stream, except a waterfall. The dot could be randomly placed over the land, but if not, I suppose that's where I'd look first—wait a minute." I focused hard on the blue dot where the waterfall should be. Stitched with a single, fine thread, just barely a shade lighter than the rest of the blue dot, was a number. It was in the ancient numerals that we still learned in school but never used, three of them ringing the gold dot at the center.

"One, one . . . three."

Emric put his face next to mine, examining the numbers on the dot. "By the stones of Vindeca. That's amazing." He inched over slightly, looking closely at the dot over his family's land. "One, two, then eight. They're directing us to the location. Eleven miles by three on yours, twelve miles by eight on mine. I could be reaching, but I don't think so. That has to be it."

"This tapestry's ancient, though. The land will have changed, borders will have shifted."

"True." Emric took a couple of steps back, studying the tapestry as a whole, a furrow between his brow. I held the lamp up, trying to let it illuminate the entire tapestry.

I tried to let my eyes adjust and readjust, trying to see the tapestry both ways. Once I saw the intricate map, it was difficult to go back to seeing the tapestry as the heavy-handed landscape I had seen before. I narrowed my eyes, searching for the blue dots, but they were incredibly well concealed if you didn't know exactly where to look.

"Not the most convenient map," Emric remarked.

"Might there be a copy? On paper?" I asked doubtfully.

"If there is, we've no access to it. And I suspect there isn't. Arin broke a vow of silence, and, I imagine, a vow of secrecy, when he showed us this."

"He wants us to help the prince," I said softly. "Why? How would he know Prince Roland was in danger?"

"The king would have informed the monks of the situation before we ever arrived. I should have thought of that. Their messenger birds are very efficient, at least at this distance. The monastery is very loyal to the royal family." Emric frowned at the tapestry.

"I know, but when Rubia administered the Verum, Prince Roland didn't seem to know much."

"Maybe she asked the wrong question," said Emric, glancing at me.

I turned back to the tapestry, moving the lamp slowly over the surface, starting with the top left corner and trying not to miss a single stitch, as if I were reading complicated text.

My trust in Prince Roland did not run as strong as Emric's, but I did trust Emric. If he believed Roland was worthy of loyalty, then I would make it my mission to get the antidote to the prince. An aching fear coiled inside me. What if we found just enough for one? Would I do the honorable thing and give it to the prince, when my own freedom was so near? The thought of losing my chance was too sharp, so I smothered it with my determination to simply find it.

◇ ·· ——————— ·· ◇

We studied the tapestry for most of the remaining night. Our scrutiny was impeded by an overwhelming exhaustion that struck us both, but we continued to push through, staring at the map with dull, bloodshot eyes, reading out our findings in hoarse whispers, trying to commit the locations and their coordinates to memory.

"Cressida!" Emric beckoned suddenly. He was crouching awkwardly; his nose was about an inch from the musty tapestry. "I found another one. Look." He carefully placed his finger on the dot, then straightened and stepped back so that I could have a closer look. I bent to see, and there it was, our ninth dot.

"It looks like it's quite near the border," I said, squinting at it, then squeezing my eyes shut as bright lights burst behind them.

I looked up at Emric. His hair was tousled, and there were shadows under his eyes, but he was alert again, his eyes bright and excited. Whenever we found a dot, it was like a clean breeze swept through me. My meager store of energy emptied into my bloodstream, and I knew that this time, I was on the last push of adrenaline that my body had.

"I think I know where that is," Emric remarked slowly. "It will be dawn in a few hours, and there have to be so many more on here—" He stopped short as he looked down at me.

"Don't stop, I'm giving you my full concentration," I prompted, as my head spun and the floor seemed to tilt.

"No. We're done for now." He plucked the lamp out of my limp hand, where it was dangerously drooping toward the ground. "We need a couple hours sleep or we're never getting down this mountain on foot. Come on."

I did not argue. I simply didn't have it in me to resist the suggestion of sleep when it seemed my body would obey no other command. I shuffled past him down the cold corridor without another glance at the tapestry, with him behind me, holding the lamp aloft.

He lowered the wick when we reached the greenhouse, until the flame was no bigger than that of a trimmed candle. We sat down on the cloak that we had left spread on the ground. I shivered. It didn't feel as warm in here after being inside the monastery for hours. Emric leaned back against the log.

"You can lean on me . . . if you want," he offered, and I practically fell against him, putting my cheek against his shoulder. "I'll wake you up before dawn and we can leave, hopefully before the monks are active."

"But who will wake you up?" I breathed, barely getting the words out before sleep took me. I didn't hear his answer.

◇ ·· ———— ·· ◇

My question had apparently been a valid one, because when I awoke, Emric's chest rose and fell as he breathed deeply. I had an intense urge to relieve myself. As I got to my feet, I noted

Emric was gripping his sword hilt. He must have slept like that the whole time.

The sun was just peeking over the horizon, and it shone in shafts across the greenhouse. The monks were surely up and around by now, but my options were limited, so I crept back into the monastery. The corridor of tapestries was empty.

I forced myself to walk past the map that we had reluctantly abandoned last night. When I reached the end of the hall, I could hear a low murmur of conversation.

The great room that we had been led into on our first visit was straight ahead of me and was clearly where the voices were coming from. I was in luck, however. There was another corridor that branched off of the one I walked now, just before the great room. Behind a narrow door, I found a water closet, rough and somewhat primitive, but it held what I needed. I was also grateful to find that there was a small iron hand pump, with icy water that gushed out when I cranked it up and down. I drank until my teeth ached, and washed as best as I could. As I finished, I noticed a small clay pot on a shelf that contained a couple of stalks of dried lavender. I removed the lavender, rinsed the pot, and filled it with water. Cradling this carefully in the crook of my arm, I exited the water closet with caution.

I hastened down the hall, hugging the shadowed walls and sloshing water. As I was about to turn the corner to the corridor of tapestries, I froze. From outside the monastery came a heavy, many-hooved thudding of horses arriving en masse. There rose a shout of orders being delivered and repeated, and I stood uncertainly, heart racing. A heavy knocking boomed at the entrance, and I lunged down the branch of hallway to my left, now spilling most of the water.

I rushed into the greenhouse, and Emric immediately pulled me over to crouch, rather absurdly, behind a potted fern.

"Where were you?" His voice was tight, his eye on the door.

"I brought you water," I said, handing him the pot with what remained in it. "And there are palace guards here, I think."

Emric choked on the water he was gulping. "*What*?"

"I'm not positive, but that's what it sounds like." The sun had fully broken over the horizon and the greenhouse flooded with morning light. I berated myself for not suggesting that we continue reading the tapestry through the night and then leave before dawn. But our exhaustion had been much too powerful. "We won't get another look at that tapestry," I whispered to Emric as he stood cautiously. I followed suit.

He glanced grimly out the glass walls. Fortunately, the greenhouse was out of sight from the road and front of the monastery. "We need to get into the forest, quickly," he said sharply, quickly wending his way through the pots of plants and tables of supplies and seedlings.

"Will Arin give us away?"

"I have no idea," came Emric's abrupt reply.

Brother Arin's loyalties were confusing. At this point, our own loyalties were confusing. We were running from the royal guard on a mission to help the prince.

Emric scooped up the cloak that we had been sitting on and tossed it over my shoulders. We checked to be sure there was no obvious sign of our presence, then crept over to the door we'd entered last night, and Emric pushed it open.

The morning air was not as painfully frigid as it had been in the night, but it was bitter, and the wind cut straight through my cloaks. In the open air, we could plainly hear the sounds of men and horses. They would be circling and searching the monastery in no time, unless the monks refused to allow it. But that chance was slim, and so I was thankful that the cover of trees was mere yards away from the back of the greenhouse. The tree line began at a steep incline, and Emric reached up to grasp a low branch and pull it toward us.

"Here," he said, and I wrapped my hands around the icy branch, using it like a rope as I scrambled up the incline.

Emric followed immediately behind me, and after an awkward struggle with the branch and slippery hill, we both managed to crawl up onto the forest floor. I turned around and used a fallen branch to swipe away the sign of our climb in the snow. I bit my lip when I noticed the obvious set of tracks leading straight from the greenhouse to the forest.

"Nothing we can do. Except hurry," Emric prodded.

I nodded, and we moved as quietly and quickly as we could through the dense forest. Little snow had made it through the tangled crowns of the trees, so at least our path through the woods would not be as obvious.

We had not gone far before we could hear the shouts of the soldiers, sharp but distant. I glanced anxiously at Emric.

"They've seen our tracks," I whispered. His mouth pressed into a grim line. He scanned the trees behind us, then turned abruptly to the right. I followed, trying to contain my panic.

We headed southeast, moving swiftly and trying not to stumble downhill. Our journey down the mountain would be all the more impossible if we strayed too far north or west. The trees were hard to navigate through, as dense as they grew, but there was no wind in the forest, and I barely noticed the cold now that we were on the move. I strained my ears for any evidence that the soldiers had caught our trail, but heard nothing.

Sunlight filtered in from the east, throwing slanting shadows around the forest. Eventually, the tension knotting my insides began to subside, and I threw all of my focus into the task of getting off the mountain. This far up Mt. Vindeca, the trees were all sharply fragrant conifers, but we encountered thick tangles of spiky, leafless brambles as well, like miniature forests that we needed to circumvent.

The sun climbed higher, and I felt my strength draining rapidly as the adrenaline of our rush to escape the monastery ebbed away. It had been close to twenty-four hours since I had eaten anything, and it was likely the same for Emric. I kept my eyes open for any sign of something edible—berries, or some sort of wildlife. I hadn't seen so much as a squirrel or a crow in the past hour. Not that I would have the faintest idea how to catch a crow or a squirrel, let alone cook one.

The descent was not terribly steep, but the ground sloped downward just enough to make me turn an ankle painfully every few steps if I did not concentrate. The unfamiliar angle of the incline made my calves and joints throb with pain.

Emric halted, and it took a moment for my glazed brain to signal my body to stop as well.

"Listen," Emric whispered, and my blood froze. Had we come this far, wringing out our strength just to run straight into trouble? I tried to steady my breathing, and listened.

Then I noticed the grin on Emric's tired face. I blinked in confusion. "Water," he said. I heard it then, the gentle trickle of a mountain stream. "The air is getting warmer too," he added. "We're on the right track."

I nodded. "This way?" I tilted my head to the right.

He nodded, and we headed toward the sound, going slower now. I strained my eyes for a glimpse of the stream. The trees were finally starting to thin, but only slightly.

"There it is," I exclaimed. The glimmer of falling water was just visible through the trees. We hurried toward it, and the trickling sound was overwhelmed by the gentle rush of a slim waterfall as it tumbled over white rock and plunged to the stones below. The sight of the water frothing into a clear, gently swirling pool made me realize how desperately empty and thirsty I had become. We ignored the spray of the waterfall and dropped to our knees to scoop up the icy water. It was so cold it nearly froze my lips and teeth and tasted of minerals and snow, but it was the most thirst-quenching water I had ever tasted.

After he drank, Emric splashed some of the painfully frigid

water over his face and ran his wet hands through his hair. He shook himself with a shiver.

"You're insane," I remarked, resting on my knees. After drinking, I felt renewed. The aches and pains from our rough descent were momentarily evaporating.

Emric flashed a grin at me. "But I'm awake now. That water is amazing." He rose to his feet. "Now, we need to find—"

"Shh." I held a finger to my lips and pointed into the pool. There, at the bottom of the shallow basin, was a slender, silver fish.

"We could spend the rest of the day trying to catch that thing," I said, staring at the fish moodily and picturing it sizzling in a frying pan, which we did not possess, along with any other tool for catching or cooking a fish.

"True," Emric admitted. "But I'm all for trying."

"Sure." My lips twitched. I could easily rest for fifteen minutes while watching Emric try to catch a fish with his bare hands.

"All right, why don't you find a long stick we can sharpen, and I'll use some rocks to cut off his escape route," Emric began, looking around, eyes bright.

I got heavily to my feet. We were clearly experiencing opposite effects of little sleep or food. He was a fizzing bundle of energy, and I could lie down on the frozen ground and fall asleep within seconds. I watched for a moment as he worked to dislodge a rock the size of his head from the edge of the pool. I glanced wearily around and picked up a stick that looked promising.

Emric was busy constructing a dam across the narrow outlet of the pool. I pulled my dagger from my boot and began hacking at the end of the stick, carving it into a point and hoping that it wouldn't dull the blade too much.

After a few moments, Emric stood back to survey his handiwork. "It shouldn't be able to get past that easily," he declared.

I nodded in affirmation and handed him the stick.

"Well done," he said, examining the point. He crouched by the pool and eyed the fish as it gently swished its tail.

"We need to decide where to go first after we find Rosalie," I said. I felt queasy as my friend rose to my mind. I crouched next to him.

"We should go over what we learned from the map," he suggested as he took aim. He slowly drew his arm back, then in a swift motion, threw the makeshift spear down into the pool. I squinted through the water that splashed into my eyes, just in time to see the silver fish dart toward Emric's dam and slip through easily.

"Stones of Vindeca," Emric said sheepishly. "Sorry about that. I was sure . . ." His inspection of his dam was so serious, I burst out laughing.

"I suppose it was a bit optimistic of me," Emric said, bemused as he glanced at me. "Just hang on to that sense of humor. You're trapped in the forest with a distinctly unskilled hunter."

My laughter dissolved into a smile. "We'll find something. And you did find water."

"That's something," he agreed. His expression grew earnest. "I'm going to find that antidote for you, too, Cressida. Please don't lose hope." A shiver slipped down my neck as he spoke, one that had less to do with the frosty air and much more to do with the warmth in his voice. I had no delusions that this was going to end happily. But I couldn't stop hope from welling up inside me.

"*We're* going to get it. For Prince Roland," I amended. His smile returned, and I looked away, self-conscious.

"About the map," I said. "Do you suppose Miss Tepsom really expected us to bring it to her?"

"I imagine she had no idea it was a floor-to-ceiling tapestry," Emric responded. "But it makes sense why it was her goal. That map, along with the scrolls in that secret room, has massive implications for the crown's motives and duplicity. The lands of the murdered families are marked. Brother Arin's behavior suggests that our guess about what we'd find there is correct. It seems clear that they wanted access to substances so dangerous no one is even meant to know they exist. With that kind of evidence, accusing the royals of murder followed by aggressive land seizures would actually carry some weight. I still think it was insanely careless to send you all on such a dangerous mission, but by the stones . . . you can't deny that she was on to something."

I watched the puffs of steam from Emric's speech evaporate as I turned his words over in my mind.

"Why do you swear by the mountain?" I asked curiously.

"I don't know. I suppose because my father did. Why?"

"Because my father used that expression too. I've just never heard anyone else say it."

"Come to think of it, I'm not sure my father used it the way I do," Emric said. "He spoke almost reverently about the stones of Vindeca. I thought it was funny. Odd."

The phrase had transported me back to a time long forgotten. I stood up stiffly.

"Time to get off of this mountain," I said, shaking off the memories.

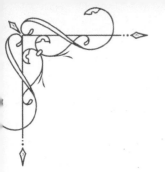

19

W E DRANK AGAIN, THEN LEFT
the stream. Within the hour, we managed to find sparse bushes of winterberries and collected a few handfuls. The blood-red skin was withered and tough, but they weren't dried all the way through. Having something to chew and swallow helped to ease the cramping in my stomach. When we were sure we had widely skirted the monastery and palace, we stopped heading east and tried to navigate true south as much as possible.

Just as the forest thickened again to an almost impenetrable density, I thought I saw a shimmer of white through the pines. I grabbed Emric's arm, slowing his determined progress. "Is that the road?"

He peered through the shadows. "Hopefully," he replied.

We made more of an attempt to move quietly through the underbrush now, in case we were indeed nearer to civilization.

"It is," I whispered when we had moved twenty yards closer. The shimmering white of the road snaked ahead of us, cutting through the wood. It was protected from snow by the intertwining branches of the trees overhead, but the dust of the mountain rock was as white as chalk, and coated the road so that it was impossible to miss.

"Well spotted," Emric said. "We're on the right track."

We kept enough distance between ourselves and the road to maintain adequate cover from anyone who might pass. Our way was quite steep at places, and level at others. The forest was thinning. Scrubby gorse and heather gradually replaced the trees, which made it difficult to find even footing. We were reaching the foothills, and although this was arduous walking, it meant we were closer to town. Unfortunately, it also meant that we were almost in the open.

"Might the king have sentries posted at the foot of the mountain?" I asked as I strained to see the road in the falling dusk.

"He doesn't usually, so I suppose it depends on how great a threat he believes we are. If the dead groom is found, it may be that the king will have patrols on the road at least." My heart dropped at his words. I had pushed the dead man to the back of my brain and let the task at hand clamor to the front.

"Good to know," I muttered.

As twilight deepened, the cover of darkness began to drape over us like a cloak. Dots of light flared ahead, and a cluster of red-roofed houses and shops became visible.

"Look." Emric halted, pointing to the southwest. Yellow lights moved along the road between the city and the foot of the mountain. I focused on the lights and gradually realized that they were torches, carried by guards on horseback who rode up and down the length of the pass.

"Oh," I said, feeling defeated. We watched the patrol for several minutes before Emric spoke again.

"This might be manageable. See how they're only sending out a guard to sweep the perimeter at random intervals?"

"He isn't going very wide, either," I said, observing the guard who had just left the road on horseback. He did a shallow loop with his torch held high, scanning the outlying darkness, and then returned quickly to the road. Another guard did the same on the other side. "We can stick close to the brush and trees further east."

"Right. Ready?" Emric asked.

I nodded, and pulled my hood low over my forehead.

We didn't waste time, as it was now full dark, and we were

headed away from the guards. My legs felt stiff and unreliable as I ran, plowing against heavy skirts and through dried, ice-crusted bracken. Once we had run far enough to be well outside of the guards' patrol, we changed course and headed south over the rough terrain.

We were both panting with exhaustion once we finally came to one of the town's outlying structures, a stable. We stopped to catch our breath behind it.

"We'll need to avoid the main road," Emric said tightly.

"I think we can do that easily enough." I drew air through my raw throat, thinking through the layout of the city. We were entering from the east and should encounter Plight Street before we came near the main road.

We crept from the shadows of building to building, until we were far enough into town that the streetlights shone on us. Concealing our swords under our cloaks, we walked swiftly until we neared the school.

It was the only dark building on Plight Street. The rest of the townhouses and shops were brightly lit and merrily festooned for the Evenfrost holiday.

"What if she isn't there?" I whispered nervously.

"Then we carry on with our plan. The best way to help Rosalie if she's been arrested is . . ." He trailed off uncertainly.

"What?" I prompted, needing him to say something reassuring and true.

"I'm not sure," he admitted.

"What if the school is being watched?" I asked, trying to ignore the unsettling feeling his lack of an answer had brought over me.

"I've been keeping my eyes open. I haven't seen any sentries or guards on this street, at least not in uniform."

Yet another discouraging answer, but he wasn't a miracle worker. I was still glad he was with me, no matter what happened next.

He looked down at me and flashed me a small smile. "All

right," he said. "Let's go get some answers."

Tense with anxiety and exhaustion, I took his proffered arm, and we crossed the street as if we were doing nothing more than enjoying a stroll through the festive city. Our disheveled appearances likely told a different story, so we did not waste any time getting to the front step and ringing the bell of Miss Tepsom's School for Gently Bred Young Ladies.

It was Miss Selkirk who answered the door, rather than Iris. Her pretty face lit up as soon as she saw us. "Emric!" She spoke in a shocked gasp. "Rosalie told us we might expect Cressida, but I didn't think—Oh, please come inside. I'm just so glad to see you!" She ushered us into the foyer, which was lit by a single dark lamp, and gave Emric a fierce hug. I shut the door quietly. The warmth of the moment could not smooth over the undercurrent of fear expanding in the small space.

"Listen," Miss Selkirk's voice was hushed as she released her brother and gave me a quick squeeze, "I've been terribly worried about the two of you since Rosalie arrived. I'm so happy to see you safe—but you need to leave, immediately."

"Leave?" Emric looked at his sister in confusion.

"Is Rosalie all right?" I asked anxiously.

Miss Selkirk clasped both of our hands, while steering us backward toward the door. "She's—she'll be fine—but you two must—" Her words were cut off as the front door opened behind us.

"Ambrosia?" came a rich baritone as Lord Eston stepped into the foyer. In my periphery, I saw Emric slide his hand into his cloak, undoubtedly to grip his sword hilt. I wanted to do the same, but Miss Selkirk was still tightly gripping my right hand.

Lord Eston strode forward, removed his hat, and bent over Miss Selkirk's hand. "How fortunate," he said, glancing over at Emric and me. "Good evening, Theon, and Miss . . . Hoth, was it? How interesting to see you two here together this evening." His brow rose.

"You are here to see Miss Tepsom, my lord?" Miss Selkirk asked graciously.

He withdrew his smirking eyes from my face.

"Naturally. May I show myself in?" He moved toward Miss Tepsom's office door.

"Why don't we wait in here for her? I will let her know you've all arrived." Miss Selkirk opened the door that led to the music room. A ribbon of firelight spilled through the door.

"Where is Miss Tepsom?" I asked.

"She is attending to some business, but I will make her aware of your presence." She pushed the door wide. "Please, come and sit by the fire."

I hesitated in indecision, half-believing that we should turn around and leave. But we had not yet seen Rosalie. I glanced at Emric, whose face seemed cut from stone, then stepped through the door.

A fire flickering in the hearth illuminated only a small patch of the room. It was much as I had last seen it, a harp and piano covered with sheets by the window, a case of fencing foils in the corner, and a bare stretch of floor, dark except for the shafts of streetlight and moonlight that slipped through the drapes.

"Please sit," offered Miss Selkirk.

"Eston," Emric said suddenly, his voice low and steely. "A word."

"In private? But of course."

"Ambrosia too." Emric responded.

I looked up at him in surprise, but his eyes were fixed on Lord Eston.

Miss Selkirk nodded. "Please excuse us, Miss Hoth. Take a moment to warm yourself."

The three filed out the door without a backward glance at me. I inhaled, unsure what to do. After a long moment, the latch clicked. I leapt to the door, wrenching the handle. It had been locked. I stared at the doorknob, the brass glinting in the firelight. Without wasting another second, I ran to each window, finding nothing like the luck I experienced the night that I'd tried to run away. Each window was tightly sealed—even the one with the broken sash was immovable.

I stood motionless by the window behind the harp. Thoughts swirled through my mind, but I couldn't sift through them, couldn't make sense of what was happening, except that we had clearly come to the wrong place. It had felt wrong from the moment Eston appeared. Or perhaps, from the moment Miss Selkirk told us to leave.

Did Emric know that they'd locked me in here? I felt dumb and useless, unable to think, unable to do anything. My body ached from our mountain descent. The moments ticked by as I stared into the fire, tested each window again, listened at the door. The door that led to the upstairs dormitory was locked as well, with not a sound coming from the other side. I narrowed my eye at the lock, trying to peek through, but there was only darkness on the other side. My impatience grew so that I felt like screaming. I flung my cloaks off and clawed at my wrist, finally digging the slender dagger out of its sheath.

The dagger was narrow enough to slide into the keyhole. I worked it into the opening, twisting and prodding relentlessly, feeling for the pieces of the catch. I was growing lightheaded, so I pulled the knife out and forced myself to relax. I closed my eyes, drew a long breath, and slid the dagger in once more, but only slightly, and angled it down and to the right. I finally felt the catch and gently pushed up with the tip of my blade. It released with a click.

I replaced the dagger in its sheath, then gently turned the knob. The door opened to the dark and empty stairwell. I took the stairs carefully, keeping to the edges, and skipping the fourth from the top. The hall beyond was also dark, and very cold. The upstairs must have been shut up completely during the holiday break. I moved down the hallway, noticing the open doors and empty rooms, with their beds stripped of linens. It was as if the school had never been alive with schoolgirls. As if my memories were a lie.

At the end of the hall, however, was a closed door. I stilled when I saw the faintest sliver of light at the bottom. This door was near the other stairwell, and as I approached it, I could hear a faint murmur of voices below. Deciding quickly, I went to the room first.

The door was not locked, and as I pushed it open, I fervently hoped that I would not see Rosalie. The shadows were too deep, the air too cold. I didn't want to find her here.

But there she was. Her slender form lay on a bare mattress, her golden hair matted and her face pale. Miss Tepsom sat on a chair next to her, holding her hand. My headmistress looked up, startled. Miss Rush was sitting on the other bed and stood quickly at my entrance.

"Cressida! Where did you come from?" she demanded, her features pinched with disapproval.

"Downstairs," I answered automatically. I looked back at Miss Tepsom, who was smiling now. "I'm sorry to barge in. Is Rosalie all right?" Rosalie's eyes were closed, but I could not tell if she was asleep. Her chest was rising and falling, and she seemed to be gripping Miss Tepsom's hand.

"Rosalie will be fine. She fell ill. It seems she braved the mountain overnight, and it's left her in quite a state," Miss Tepsom said, looking up at me curiously. "I'm so pleased to see you, although the circumstances baffle me, I admit. It will be good to have some answers."

"Fell ill?" I asked, sick with worry. I sent her down the freezing mountain alone, while I cozied up with Emric for the night at the monastery.

"We are taking care of her as well as we can. We shall call for the doctor in the morning." Miss Tepsom released Rosalie's hand and stood. "Come down to my office and we can get everything straightened out. Miss Rush will look after Rosalie."

I glanced at Iris's thin-lipped expression and felt a surge of nerves. Miss Tepsom ushered me backward out of the door and shut it carefully behind us.

She walked wordlessly down the stairs, rounded the banister, and unlocked her office door. I considered telling her that I had been locked in the music room, but the words stuck in my throat. Before she opened the door, Miss Tepsom turned to me, smiling slightly. She held out both hands to me, as if she wanted me to take them.

"I'm so happy you girls are all right," she said.

I placed my hands hesitantly into hers and attempted to return her smile. But her lips appeared frozen, and the smile didn't reach her eyes. With a movement so quick I had no chance to react, she gripped my hands together, hard, and pulled a loop of garrote wire tightly around them. Then, as she pulled the wire tight with one hand, she pushed a long stiletto against the pulse at my neck with the other.

I was numb with shock as she leaned in and hissed in my ear.

"I have questions for you. And I will kill Rosalie without hesitation if you do not cooperate." She shouldered her office door open and tugged me forward with the garrote wire. It cut sharply into my wrists, and I stumbled forward to relieve the tension.

Lord Eston sat at Miss Tepsom's desk, while Miss Selkirk and Emric stood by the fire. Emric's hand was on the hilt of his sword as we entered, his eyes hard. I felt as if I had been struck when he did not move to help me.

"For heaven's sake, Eston, relinquish my desk to me," Miss Tepsom said wearily.

Lord Eston did not move, but leaned back comfortably in the chair. "Thank you for bringing Miss Hoth, Lucretia. We are ready for her." Miss Tepsom bristled, but wrapped the length of wire all the more tightly around my wrists.

I bit my tongue against the pain, as blood seeped out where

the wire cut into the sides of my wrists. I thought about kicking her, and hard, but her threat echoed in my ears.

Eston went on smoothly as if nothing were amiss, "Our intelligence about Miss Hoth's unique virtue has just been confirmed. She will tell us anything."

The blood froze in my veins. I stared at him as fear rooted me to the spot. I dared not look at Emric. I was unable to comprehend the betrayal.

Miss Tepsom looked at me with an unsettling intensity. "Of course she will. Even before we discovered her condition, I knew that Cressida would be the one most likely to yield information. Always so hungry—so eager to please." Anger spiked within me as she spoke such shaming, unfiltered truth.

"Well, then," Eston remarked. "I propose we waste no more time. Miss Hoth, please have a seat."

I didn't move. "Whatever you like, then." He waved a hand, and a flat, gold signet ring glinted in the firelight. A memory swept through me, followed by a cold shot of realization. The Pear Tree Parlor, a blade at my throat. I sat down.

"Why did you leave the palace, Cressida?" Eston inquired, a smile playing over his lips.

I paused for the barest moment. I should save my strength for resisting harder truths. I took a deep breath, then answered. "Because Rubia dosed the prince with Verum, and Rosalie and I were complicit and under suspicion."

"And why did you kill my groom?" Eston asked in the same pleasant tone.

My head ached with the tears building up behind my eyes. "Because he threatened Rosalie and me. He was violent."

"And what happened to the potions? I had your rooms searched before I descended the mountain myself. And your friend Vivian was useless."

"I left the case hidden by the groom. Did you hurt Vivian?" The words grated against my throat, and I tasted bile.

Emric's voice broke harshly through the thundering in my ears. "You left the potions up at the castle?"

"Yes," I whispered, feeling lightheaded, unable to turn to him.

"Eston, she's slyer than you might believe possible under the influence of Verum. I wouldn't trust everything she says. It may be that she's learned some control over the curse the Verum brings. She made me believe she had the potions." My heart seemed to pause at Emric's words, then stutter to catch up.

"No matter," Eston said briskly. "I care not about the case of potions, especially if you used the Verum up on her, as you said. I believe she has more valuable information for me." He stood and circled the desk, until he was standing in oppressive proximity to me. "Cressida, I'm looking for something. I believe you know what it is. Miss Tepsom sent you to find something at the palace, didn't she?"

"Yes," I said, my pulse pounding.

What use was my training? My years of practice to defend myself and others, if, yet again, I allowed myself to be made helpless?

I stood suddenly, catching Eston off guard. He was bent toward me, and I used his surprise and my momentum to my advantage, stomping my heel down as hard as I could into the top of his soft-booted foot, and bashing my forehead into his with a focused strike that knocked him sideways. I absorbed the blow, but stars still burst before my eyes. I blinked hard and whirled around, intent on reaching the door.

Miss Tepsom stood before it, two wicked blades glinting in her hands. In the brief pause, Eston recovered quickly and threw his arm around my neck, forcing me to look at Tepsom as she brandished the blades.

"If you care for your friend, you will stand down, Miss Hoth," she snapped. "Another display like that and I'll not warn you again before I drag her down here and carve her lovely face while you watch."

The madness in her eyes frightened me more than her words. She meant it. I could do nothing but force myself to be still in response as Eston gave my throat a final, painful crush with his forearm, and then shoved me back down into the chair. A thin rustle behind me suggested that Emric was sliding his sword back into its sheath. Ghosts of tears pricked my eyes, but I refused to let them materialize. I stared stonily ahead, refusing to make eye contact with Eston as he bent over me.

"Now." His fingers held my jaw. "Remind me. What did your headmistress send you to find?" I focused my attention on the red lump blossoming on his forehead.

"A map," I whispered.

"That's right. A map that will lead us to each and every mine, every well, every cavern containing the most valuable potion substances in the world. I know some people in Porleac who will pay extremely handsomely for such information, and gain the upper hand in a long-overdue war against the weak, thankless royal family of Dernmont. Some of the substances pose a much more violent threat than Verum or Nemere alone." His lips curled, and he stroked his thumb over my chin, making my skin crawl. "Cressida . . . did you find any such map?"

I stared at him as the words swelled through my brain, my lips sealed and my eyes burning. My symptoms were already setting in hard. I could refuse to answer at all and just see what happened. I tried to breathe through the nausea billowing through me, but my throat closed. I gasped for air that wouldn't enter. Then, my body began to seize and thrash, bones bashing against the floor, and I knew I was dying. There were shouts and the clasp of hands, holding me tightly.

When I opened my eyes again, I was lying on the floor on my side, a spot of blood next to me. A voice whispered in my ear. I'd felt that voice in my ear before, creeping under my skin. "Another fit like that could kill you, Cressida. Now, I'm going to ask again—"

"You—you attacked me that night at the palace," I interrupted weakly, pushing the words out to stall his question. "You sent Rosalie and me those notes."

"Yes," Eston spoke sharply. "And I shouldn't have been so gentle. Now, about those maps—"

"I'm telling you, Eston, I already asked her about the maps. She didn't find any," came Emric's voice, close by. I held on to it, letting the words embrace me. He was lying to Eston, and even if I never left this room alive, that felt like the most important thing in the world right now.

"She almost killed herself to keep from answering, Emric. She knows something." Eston's smooth voice was edged. "Up you get." He jerked me under the arms and shoved me down into the armchair near the fire. My wrists and head throbbed.

"Eston, you need to stop this, I'll not stand by while—"

"Theon, there are palace guards patrolling this street. Guards in *my* pay. They were told to leave you two alone if you came to the school, but I will not hesitate to have them haul you before the king if you do not desist stalling my interrogation." His voice rose as his ire expanded. "Now, you did well when you dosed this girl, but that will be disregarded if you do not *shut up*."

I didn't know where Emric's lies to Eston were meant to lead. But whether he was truly on my side or not, the sound of his voice cut through my sluggish thoughts and reminded me that the interrogation wasn't over, and I had to keep fighting. My eyes fluttered open, and I tried to pull my sagging body upright in the chair.

Miss Tepsom glided toward me the moment I moved, and knelt in front of me.

"I don't understand," I gasped, struggling for breath, before she could ask me a question. "You already know where they are. You gathered agents whose family estates had been seized by the king—because of the access to these substances, presumably."

"Yes," she acknowledged. "We know where some are. Not

all. But even on those lands of which we are aware, the king has done everything in his power to keep the mines' specific locations secret. To the point of letting the valuable substances sit there, of no use to anyone. If our people are to assault their defenses, we need to know exactly where they are." Her face drew close to me. "Now, listen to me. You can refuse to answer me again, but something tells me that a few more times of that nonsense and you'll be dead. Cressida, do you know where we can find information that we seek? A simple yes or no is all I ask—for now."

In the corner of my eye, I could see Emric moving, and feared he'd do something rash to keep me from having another fit or from answering. "Yes," I said. It wasn't a question worth anyone dying over.

Miss Tepsom's lips curved into a placating smile. Eston started toward us, but Miss Tepsom held up a hand, stilling him. "Thank you. Now. Do you have the maps?"

"No," I answered promptly.

"This isn't so hard, is it?" Miss Tepsom asked, but I saw the agitated shift in her eyes.

"Where can we find the maps—or map?" Her voice was deadly calm as she adjusted her question. Her hands closed tightly over mine.

I held my tongue with effort, almost leaning into the familiar feeling of suffocation that pressed against my chest. Darkness curled over my vision.

"Perhaps we should wake Rosalie and see what might induce her to speak?" Miss Tepsom commented, whether to me or to Eston I could not tell. Fear sliced through me.

"The monastery," I ground out, then gasped for air.

"Where at the monastery, girl? We don't have all night!" Eston shoved Miss Tepsom aside and gripped my forearms, leaning in to me. I convulsed involuntarily as the fit came over me faster this time.

"My Lord Eston, please!" Miss Selkirk hurried forward and pried his hands off of my arms. Her actions distracted from the fact that Emric had his sword half-drawn and was about to lunge forward. I caught his eye and shook my head firmly, fighting through the terror that came with my air supply cutting off, the blood that roared in my ears, and the inescapable nausea.

When I awoke, I tasted blood. I was in the chair still, and frighteningly weak. I lay there helplessly listening to the jumble of voices around me, and perfectly happy to pretend that I was still unconscious. Fingers briefly touched the pulse at my neck.

"We go now. She's wasting our time and would slow us down," Miss Tepsom murmured. "We have enough."

"I'm ready. But I want her with us," Eston growled.

"To keep doing this, and possibly die on the road? Even if she didn't, we'd have to drag her along."

"I'll watch her here," Miss Selkirk volunteered, her voice somewhat nervous.

"Ambrosia, I know I can trust you," said Eston silkily. "But she's sly, and we can't afford to lose her. Theon. You stand guard with your sister. You, the girl, and her friend are all being watched for by the palace guard because I alerted the king to your status as a traitor the moment my groom's corpse was found. I suggest you lie low here, and wait for instruction from no one but me, unless you want to face arrest. I assure you, I will not be speaking on your behalf should you do something stupid. Keep her restrained," he demanded.

"Quickly, Eston," Miss Tepsom urged. There was a shuffle of footsteps, then the door was firmly shut.

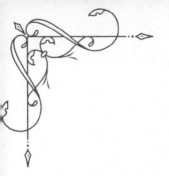
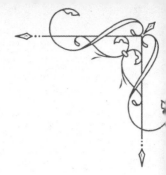

20

NEITHER MISS SELKIRK NOR
Emric spoke for a moment. The heaviness of my limbs began to lift slowly, but the pounding in my skull was inescapable. Finally, the outside door slammed as Miss Tepsom and Lord Eston left the school.

At that, Miss Selkirk immediately said, "Emric."

I cracked my eyes open to see him dart out of the room. Miss Selkirk bent over me, concern etched all over her pretty, round face. "Oh, good," she breathed. "You're breathing deeper now. I'm so relieved. I thought we lost you for a moment there, you were so still."

But I didn't know what to make of Miss Selkirk, so I said nothing, and fought to keep my eyes open. She gently wiped the blood that had trickled from my nose, and then tried to remove the wire from my wrists, so that was a good sign. I heard hurried footsteps, and Emric reappeared in the doorway.

"They're gone. They took guards that had been concealed on the street with them." He rushed over and knelt next to me. "Cressida, please tell me you're all right." He took over for his sister, carefully unwinding and loosening the bloody wire from my stinging wrists. His lips were a tense line.

"I'll be fine," I said, although I could barely get enough air circulating through my lungs to make a sound. "I'm sorry," I added in a whisper.

"I shouldn't have ever let it come to that. I'm the one who's sorry."

I clenched my teeth as Miss Selkirk began applying some sort of salve to my wrists, then wrapped them in strips of cloth.

"I told them too much," I said, taking measured breaths and trying to sit up better.

"They'll never find a thing. They don't know what to look for."

"But the monks," I protested, and a painful regret welled up inside of me. I had sent Eston and Tepsom straight to them.

"Don't worry about them. Some of them are better fighters than the king's own guard, if it comes to that." Emric gave a wry smile. "But I hope it won't."

I looked at Miss Selkirk. She finished tying my bandages, then stood, hands clasped tightly together in front of her. "I don't understand," I said, simply.

"Sit down, Ambrosia," Emric said gently, indicating the chair opposite mine.

"I—I don't even know where to start," Miss Selkirk stuttered. "I'm deeply sorry for my part in all of this."

"You were as deceived as the rest of us," Emric stated.

Miss Selkirk took a breath. "I've been slowly learning more of Miss Tepsom's purposes, but had no idea what to do with the information when I started to realize she had been recruiting us all under false pretenses," she said. "I felt so useless. And, in the beginning, it was a joy to finally be useful. Eston recruited me, you know. His sister and I were old school friends, and I went to stay with her for a bit after Mother died. He visited often and pulled me in with the same story of justice for my family that Lucretia told you girls." She wiped a tear away. "I should have told you, Emric, but I was under the strictest orders not to reveal that he was with our cause. As our plans to investigate the royals developed, Lucretia became secretive, and so intensely anxious for news and action, that I grew more and more alarmed. The safety of the girls was clearly not a priority to her. And when Rosalie showed up and Lucretia began questioning and drugging her—"

"Drugging her?" I gasped.

"Lucretia had her own stash of potions—nothing as powerful as Verum, but she hoped to get the same results. It ended up just making Rosalie sick and sleepy, but she did give up one vital piece of information."

"The fact that I had been dosed with Verum."

"Yes. Miss Tepsom sent for Eston immediately."

"Why did you want to speak to him privately?" I asked Emric.

"To get him away from you in case he already knew, or started asking you questions," Emric replied. "I had my vague suspicions about him, nothing solid. When he showed up here, I knew I had to get him away from you immediately. He instructed Ambrosia to lock you in the drawing room, then introduced himself to me as an ally. He wanted to know what I had learned from you—said he had strong suspicions that you were a turncoat to our cause, and that you'd been dosed with Verum. He wanted to begin questioning you immediately."

Emric pursed his lips. "I knew the truth of your condition would be evident as soon as he began. He didn't seem to know when you might have been dosed—which is why I took credit for it," he explained. "It seemed to be the way to establish his trust. I tried to convince him I'd already questioned you thoroughly."

"He never would have left me in your care if you hadn't," I realized, and Emric nodded.

"I'd hoped to keep you from his interrogation, and also get to the bottom of his motives. But I didn't think or act quickly enough. I admit I didn't expect Tepsom to act as she did. I thought perhaps the four of us could get rid of Eston, but then she brought you in at knifepoint, and I almost couldn't believe what I was seeing."

"I'm so sorry for not realizing the truth of Lucretia's mission," Miss Selkirk broke in, her expression one of painful despair. "I taught the lighter subjects, but I knew the propaganda she taught you girls about our royal family. It was the same story she told us, Emric, and I wanted to believe it because I so wanted my own vengeance on Father's murderer."

A muscle flexed in Emric's jaw. "We still don't know what was propaganda and what is true. Eston and Tepsom may want the mine locations and a war, but the royals still don't look innocent."

"Since you girls went to court, Lucretia had been worrying me," Miss Selkirk said in her soft voice, "carrying on meetings and secret correspondence and keeping me in the dark. She held back any information about her contacts in Porleac, and the substance access as well. I began to do some of my own digging and visited some archivists here in town to hear the official side's story. Of course, I knew that they could be on the king's payroll, but their written records claim that in the cases of the landowners who were killed, the king technically already owned the properties. Upon their owners' deaths, the lands traditionally return to the crown for him to keep or grant back to the families. The latter is usually the case. Instead, after the murders, he paid for the homes at extravagant prices and relocated the family estates."

"Yes. That isn't in direct contradiction to what Miss Tepsom told us, though," I pointed out. "King Arctus might have had the landowners killed . . . because he wanted access to the mines."

"True. I can only speculate why the king would murder the deedholders, when he was willing to buy the properties. Or could enforce their sale. If there was something unique about the properties, I'm wondering if the king removed the families for their own safety."

"That's a kind view," Emric said to his sister. "Then who killed the landowners?"

She hesitated. "I don't know. But it's looking like Porleac wants access to the mines, and maybe even a war, if Tepsom and Eston are reliable representatives . . ."

Suddenly I jerked upright, ignoring the pain charging through my head. "Rosalie. We need to make sure she's all right. Miss Rush is with her right now."

Emric jumped to his feet as he drew his sword. "Where is she?"

"Upstairs dormitory. The closed door at the west end of the corridor."

Emric raced out, and Miss Selkirk and I waited anxiously until he returned. He did so moments later, preceded into the room by Miss Rush, his sword tip between her shoulder blades. Rosalie followed them slowly, ashen faced and holding onto the walls. I wanted to run to her in my relief, but I could not move.

"Sit," Emric instructed Miss Rush. She sat in the hard-backed chair next to Miss Tepsom's desk. "Keep your hands on the arms where we can see them."

Miss Selkirk helped Rosalie into a chair, and I sat up as straight as I could. Miss Rush might not know that I was weakened, and I preferred her to think that she was formidably outnumbered.

"Where is Tepsom? And that snake, Eston?" Miss Rush demanded, looking at Miss Selkirk.

"Off on their own crusade. They've left you," Miss Selkirk replied.

"Of course." Miss Rush snapped her mouth shut and glanced at me, her face a cool mask.

Emric kept his sword leveled at her. "You're going to tell us everything Tepsom has planned," he said.

"Or what—you'll torture me? Your sister will sing at me?"

Her bravado was met with silence. She huffed.

"Fine. I don't care what they're up to, but I'm getting an annoying feeling that I'm not going to get paid."

"Paid?" Emric asked.

"I'm a blade and spy for hire."

"And what did she hire you to do?"

Miss Rush looked speculative for a moment, then lifted a shoulder in a small shrug. "She was going to put me in at court until she realized that my loyalties are easily bought, so she withheld most of her plans from me. I just taught, and did some odd poking around here and there, and got paid more than most teachers do. Of course, the skills I taught were . . . unusual." She relaxed in her chair. "I have no reason to tell you any more."

"I'll pay you whatever your information is worth." All our heads turned in surprise to Rosalie.

"Interesting. And how could you do that?"

"I carry notes from my guardian. They're signed by him, but require my signature as well. I'll sign one, add the amount, and it will be good anywhere in Dernmont."

Miss Rush raised an eyebrow.

"I assure you, it will be worth your while," Rosalie said evenly.

"Very well. I'll tell you what I know, and then I'm leaving."

"Works for me," Emric said under his breath.

Miss Rush ignored him. "You're in luck, because I am terribly adept at snooping, and most of this I found out on my own over the past two years." Her tone grew crisp. "Tepsom is from Porleac. She's known Eston for years from his over-the-border dealings with her family. Neither are good people. Tepsom's family has been involved in the long game of profiting from war for generations, and these substances they're after would be dangerously useful in a war. Her father headed up an independent group of radicals that went after the families that owned these magical mines that Tepsom's grown obsessed with."

My mouth dropped open. "Her people killed our families?" I interrupted. Coldness spread through me. Miss Tepsom had put a knife to my throat. Her betrayal was clear. But she had been the one to throw me a lifeline when I was lost, and offered the promise of vengeance, the gift of purpose. I could barely make myself believe the depth of her deception.

Again, Miss Rush ignored the interruption. "After committing murder several times over, they had a plan in place to locate and access the mines. But the king caught wind of the operation and got to them first. He had them fortified and defended, and relocated the families who guarded them before they could come to more harm. This band of radicals has grown significantly over the years, made up of both Porleacans and rogue Dernmontians. Tepsom's old friend Eston wasn't getting enough done at court, being too known to the king but not entirely trusted. And since Tepsom couldn't get herself in, she cooked up the idea of the school."

With an expression of mild disapproval, she added, "The other two respectable finishing schools in Savinrue experienced some very bad luck, courtesy of Lucretia, which is how she managed to acquire much of her impressive clientele. She'd hoped to use Verum on all of you initially, to see if you knew anything, but the stuff is hard to come by. When she finally got some, Selkirk here had the good sense to get it away from her as quickly as possible." Finished, she sat back in her seat, leveling a look at Rosalie.

"What does she mean?" I asked Miss Selkirk.

"I was not quite so perceptive," she confessed. "Lucretia was beside herself with excitement when the potions arrived, and described their uses to me. I believed that her intention was to send them with you girls on your mission. On the day that Vivian left for the palace, Lucretia was away, so I gave Vivian the case. I felt uneasy about the substances' properties, so I told her that you girls must only use them if absolutely necessary." Her eyes flickered in remembered concern. "When Lucretia returned, she was clearly horrified that I had sent them, although she did her best to hide that fact. She said she would write to her contact at court and have him monitor your usage. I wondered why she had ordered them, if not for your mission, and my suspicions toward her began to mount. I was very confused about whom to trust. I decided to write to Emric, asking him to confiscate the potions and keep them from falling into the wrong hands."

A wave of lightheadedness threatened to overwhelm me, and I steadied myself.

"Do you know anything else of Lord Eston?" Emric asked Miss Rush.

She glanced at his sword and shifted with impatience. "Heir to an old, struggling estate, entangled himself in dealings with Porleacan smugglers who paid well for what black market substances he was able to get his hands on, and presumably had strong anti-Dernmont sentiments. Eventually, he realized he could make even more money selling secrets and fell in with radicals willing to pay for any information that could hurt the crown. This eventually led him to Tepsom. It seems he's been using his family's reputation to ingratiate himself to the royal family by hosting them and being a prominent figure at court, while attempting to spy. He isn't very good at it. From what I gathered, he spends most of his time sowing gossip and rumors to stir up dissent."

Emric glanced at me quickly and gave the shadow of a nod. I understood that her information aligned with his own suspicions concerning Eston. He looked back at Miss Rush, his sword still steadily pointed.

"Any idea why my sister and I are still alive?"

"My best guess? You made yourself scarce back when they first thought the murders would do them any good, the king reclaimed your land as they originally intended, and your deaths would do nothing for them. So, with your sister running afoul of Eston at a garden party or something, they decided simply to use you instead. It seems that heartache is very easy to manipulate, and Tepsom wielded it well."

"Is that everything you have?"

"That's it. Now, I believe Miss Montshire here has some paperwork to see to?"

Rosalie sent Miss Selkirk after her satchel, dug out a crumpled note, and began filling it out. I stood slowly and leaned against

the mantel, as close to the licking flames of the fire as I dared.
Everything hurt. I could feel wisps of strength returning to me,
but I would need food and rest soon, or it was likely to drain
completely away again.

If Rush's information was correct, then the royal family was
innocent—at least of the crimes Miss Tepsom had leveled against
them. Whatever their secrets, the murder of our families could
not be laid at their door. And Miss Tepsom's behavior tonight
had been incriminating. But then, so had Miss Rush's, to a
degree. The woman was currently snatching the barely signed
note out from under Rosalie's pen. She strode out of the room,
slamming the door smartly behind her.

Miss Selkirk spoke immediately upon her departure. "If we
believe what we just heard, then someone needs to warn the
royal family. Tepsom and Eston may be war-bent murderers
who just received some vital information."

"Yes. You're right," Emric agreed somberly. I nodded slowly
and glanced at Rosalie. She jerked her chin in a nod.

"I'm calling for a coach," Miss Selkirk said, striding toward
the door. "The king needs to send troops to the monastery."

"I'm coming with you," Rosalie said. "I'm not sure how it's
going to work, but I want my name cleared."

I was glad to see she seemed in better condition than I was,
but I was still concerned. "Are you well enough, Rosalie?"

"Whatever she gave me was disorienting and took me out
for a while, but at least I slept," she said, then looked anxious.
"I'm sorry about whatever I might have told her before it
knocked me out."

"Not your fault," I asserted. "If I hadn't sent you away
without protection it wouldn't have come to that." I moved
away from the mantel, gathering every ounce of energy that I
could muster. "I won't make that mistake again."

"You're not thinking of coming to Shoncliffe, Cressida?"
Miss Selkirk said in alarm.

"You're in no condition to travel yet," Emric warned.

I shook my head vigorously, the effort making the room spin a little. "I won't send Rosalie off defenseless again. And I'll do my job right this time."

Rosalie raised her voice. "In case you hadn't noticed," she said firmly, "I've managed just fine so far." The unuttered phrase, *without you doing your job right*, hung in the air.

I looked at her, taking in the dauntless set of her mouth, the resolve in her eyes. I couldn't blame her. I hadn't trusted her at the palace, which led to Eston finding out about the potions, Rosalie and Rubia keeping their plans from Vivian and me . . . then dosing the prince. My version of doing my job had been attacking Rubia, my own comrade, and murdering a guard. Then I made Rosalie brave the mountain overnight, alone, and told her to meet me here, which eventually led to Tepsom drugging her and forcing her to reveal my curse.

So . . . she didn't want me to join her now. Fair enough. Not only was I useless to her, I was still cursed. I nodded in mute agreement. Who knew what trouble I would cause for us next.

I watched the fire flicker as I rested my stiff and aching body and listened to Miss Selkirk and Rosalie quietly discuss their plans to leave at first light. Steeping in my guilt and pain, I didn't notice when Emric pulled a chair up next to mine.

"It's going to be a chilly night," he said. "I do believe that greenhouse was warmer than this school."

I said nothing.

He considered me for a moment. "You do know that this mess isn't your fault, right?"

I looked at him then. The words came quietly, without my permission. "No. I did everything wrong. I should never have gone on the mission. I can't believe what I did to Rubia. She was so proud of her brothers and father. She missed them and just wanted answers. I never looked past her intensity enough to realize she felt the same way and wanted the same things I did. Instead, I punished her for it. And Rosalie shouldn't forgive me for how I handled our partnership. I can't believe I thought she'd want me to join her. And I'll never forget, as long as I live—that groom—" Tears were threatening, forcing me to stop talking.

"That groom might have killed you, Cressida. What use was your defense training if not to defend yourself and your friends? Listen, we were all lied to and put in an impossible, confusing situation. Mistakes were made—all around. We did it for our families. Even with a challenge none of us realized, you gave the mission everything you had to avenge your family and protect your teammates." He looked at me earnestly.

"Your worth isn't determined by your usefulness to anyone. You're not disposable based on how much of a liability you are, or think you are. You're a created soul who is as worthy of forgiveness and protection as Rosalie, or Rubia, or the prince. And whether you feel it or not, you're not alone."

I had lost the capability to put my thoughts in order. I closed my eyes as the blessing of his words flooded through me.

"Thank you," I whispered as Miss Selkirk and Rosalie joined us at the fire.

We all spent the night in Miss Tepsom's office, which was the warmest room in the school. After sharing a hastily boiled pot of porridge in the morning, Rosalie and Ambrosia (as Miss Selkirk asked us to call her now) boarded a hired coach and set off for the mountain. Rosalie looked pale and shaky, but she clasped hands firmly with me before departing. From what we could tell, they were not followed. Eston's threat that the school was being watched must have been empty.

"Are you well enough to travel today?" Emric asked me in the school kitchen after they departed.

"Yes. I think so." My wrists had been well tended by Ambrosia, and the opportunity to rest and wash had been refreshing. "The effects of last night have worn off, and I'll be well enough on my own from now on. Perhaps you should follow your sister."

"You do look better than I would have expected after what you went through," Emric remarked. His eyes found the bruise on my forehead, then skimmed over me in a way that I was sure was meant to be clinical, but made my cheeks warm nevertheless. "But I am not planning to join Ambrosia for quite a while. Roland and Rubia, as far as we know, still need antidotes. And so do you. I might not have a clue how to solve all of this business with Tepsom and Eston, but I do know that when I return to Shoncliffe, I don't want it to be empty-handed." He paused. "Do you want to come with me?"

The question made my heart thump with an insistent need to answer the question. There was truly nothing else that I wanted more. "Yes," I said promptly. "Yes, I think we should do that." But where to start? Then I remembered. "Do you still have the scroll you took from that room beneath the solar?"

His face lit. "I do." Springing up, he bounded out of the room and returned in a moment with his satchel. Standing at the table, he dug inside and pulled out the thick, yellowed scroll with care and laid it on the table. The vellum was dry and cracked, but still intact.

Dust and decayed bits crumbled off the sides as I gently unfurled the top several inches. The proclamation that I had read in the castle was at the very top. I unrolled it further, revealing in the same bold hand, a long list of outlawed items. Verum, Lethen, and Nemere were at the top, followed by what seemed to be a list of weapons: bulb-tipped arrows, spears, javelins, poison darts, and something called *dust orbs*.

Emric pointed further down the list. "Do you think those are books?"

I nodded slowly, reading the curious titles.

Dernmont: A History of Healing; Sleep of Death: A Treatise; Sharing Our Wealth; Ancients of the Mines; Dangerous Truth: A Study; Minerals of Dernmont; Lithomancy; The Bliss of Forgetting: Love and Lethen; and *Alchemy of War* topped a very long list that seemed to crawl several feet down the scroll.

"Why, though?" Emric wondered, scanning the list. "Why outlaw these?"

My brow furrowed. "The weapons, the proclamation . . . it all points to a history of warfare with Verum and the others at the center, but so few people even know that they exist now. This couldn't have been—Oh!" As I continued to unfurl the scroll, another, smaller scroll was revealed, tightly rolled and tucked at the center. A small, pinkish smear of grease marked the spot where a circle of wax had once sealed it.

Emric pulled it open gently, leaning across the table toward me so that I could read it with him. In a smaller, less formal script than the other, a faint brown scrawl filled the page of what appeared to be a letter to the king of Dernmont from the Abbot of Rounelith Monastery.

> *May it please Your Majesty to know that the faithful brothers of my trusted order and I have devoted ourselves to your commission, and have taken every possible step to ensure that the Dust Wars and all preceding events have been eradicated from the memories of the people of Dernmont. The Lementhe, as concocted by the most skilled Lethen alchemist of our order, has been widely administered. Steadfast friars of the highest martial excellence have chosen to dedicate their service to the guardianship of mines. We have scoured the kingdom of written evidence, and trust in your decision to prohibit*

outside works from infiltrating and igniting suspicion. We carry the burden of enforcing this, the greatest secret the Crown shall bear, and do not hold it lightly.

Although it has been a long road to reach this point, the road ahead is longer still. Many generations will rise and fall before the remnants of memory truly pass into legend and finally vanish entirely. But we will hold true to our vow, to keep our knowledge hidden unto death, and bury it deep within the secrets of our order. Only with cooperation from the Crown and its direct heirs may we prevent such a devastation from occurring in our lands again.

For the Good of all Dernmont I remain,
Father Cade,
Abbot of Rounelith
Order of the White Raven

"White Raven," I reminded Emric excitedly. The hot spring guardian at the monastery was a white stone raven. Brother Arin wore the shape of one on his robes.

Perplexed, Emric rolled the vellum up again and put both scrolls back into his satchel. "As fascinating as this is, it hasn't given us a lead. We could try the monastery again, but I don't expect the rest of the monks will be any happier to break their vow for us than they would be for Eston and Tepsom and their compatriots."

"So, where on earth do we start?"

"Our leads are sparse, but not nonexistent," Emric replied. "We know now that the substances have been available for a while, for those willing to pay a steep price for illegal potions."

"Of course," I realized. "You think there might be antidotes floating around as well, perhaps in unsanctioned trade channels?"

Hope, like I hadn't felt since I was a little girl plotting impossible schemes to destroy my curse, started to unfurl at the thought that there might actually be a place to start looking. I'd never realized before just how much hope felt like fear.

"I think it stands to reason." Emric's eyes searched my face. "It might be a bit of a rough visit, but what do you say to starting with the people who dosed you with Verum to begin with?"

I hadn't been back to Ramshire in over two years, and it had been almost that long since I'd heard from my aunts. We needed a place to start, however, and they were the only people we knew, other than Miss Tepsom, who had likely procured Verum at some point.

Emric had the idea to search Miss Tepsom's office, and our inspection yielded a purse with a few coins. Perhaps enough to hire a coach. Her desk had been emptied of any helpful correspondence, unfortunately. We packed the coins and what food we could find into Emric's satchel, and I sharpened my knives on the kitchen whetstone. I had no intention of threatening my aged aunts, but we had no idea where this expedition would take us.

"Ready?" Emric asked, smiling when I looked up from inspecting my blade.

"Yes. Armed and dangerous," I replied.

We left the dark and chilly school, concealing our weapons under our cloaks. In my old black school dress, dark cloak, and hidden weaponry, I felt resolute, and a little excited. Perhaps withstanding Eston's interrogation had changed me a bit. Maybe I did hold some control and my curse did not enslave me. And hopefully, its days were numbered.

The sun shone brilliantly and warmed my face as we went to the stables around the corner. We didn't have enough coins for a coach, but the hiring clerk, brewing a pungent batch of lementhe and grumpy at having to be in the office on a holiday, gave us the pick of the horses for the full contents of Miss Tepsom's purse. The sleepy horses for hire were overpriced and unwilling to cooperate with unfamiliar riders, but we eventually got two healthy-looking greys saddled up.

"We just follow the road east, and there should be signs pointing to Ramshire," I said, doing my best to conceal my discomfort atop my irritable horse.

We made our way through the nearly empty streets at a trot. I had completely forgotten that Evenfrost was today until the stable clerk mentioned it, but it was evident now. The streets were deserted because families would be gathered together, united in whatever tiny cottage or spacious hall was the oldest in their families' heritage, clustered around hearths and holiday breakfast tables, raising a glass of lementhe to the mountain and sharing whatever dishes and stories were traditional to their family histories. My Evenfrost memories felt distilled and frozen in the time that I shared with my parents, more distant and faded as the years between expanded. My aunts had ignored the holiday.

Finally, we cleared the last of the town's outlying shops and residences. The road stretched out ahead of us, open and winding through the hilly countryside. The apprehension I felt about returning to the people who had dosed me, and then spent seven years abusing their power over me, was muted by my determination to get my own questions answered. I inhaled a lungful of the crisp air and urged my horse into a canter, enjoying the stinging wind on my cheeks. Perhaps I had no right to feel joy in this moment, with so much at stake. Our friends could be in danger and our mission might be doomed. But mysteries had tugged at me my whole life, and I couldn't help but savor the freedom I felt. Now, I was finally in pursuit of the truth.

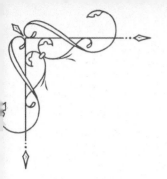

21

I HAD NOT TRAVELED EAST
since I left my aunts, and the countryside was only barely familiar. It was nothing like the mountain, with its white crags of vindeca stone and thick, towering pines. The road grew red, and the occasional groves of trees were barren and brown. By spring, however, they were sure to be flourishing and waving their green heads in the wind, which now blew bitterly across frozen meadows and croplands.

After two hours of steady riding and little conversation, alternating our horses' gaits so as not to weary them too quickly, we came upon a crossroad with a weathered sign, an arm pointing down each branch of the road.

"Ramshire, straight on," Emric read. He looked at me for a moment, then said, "If you need a rest, I'm happy to stop for a bit." I noticed that he had taken care with his wording.

I was tired, but impatient to arrive. "It can't be much further," I said. "My horse seems to be fine, how's yours?"

"Doing well." He gave the mare an encouraging rub down her muscular neck. "Very well, let's keep going." We urged our horses on, and I mentally groaned as my thighs burned in protest. They were clad only in stockings under my skirts, which didn't provide much protection against the friction of the saddle.

Fortunately, my suffering was not prolonged. Ramshire was only about three miles past the crossroad. A flood of uncomfortable memories assaulted me as we trotted into the small hamlet, and my nerves produced symptoms not entirely unlike those of my curse. The village was sparse, so before I was ready, we reached the narrow, tall house on the main road where the aunts lived. The pale lavender paint on the door was peeling, and the lacy drapes were drawn.

"This is it," I told Emric. There was no fence or post outside to hitch the horses to, so we doubled back to the village ale house and tied them at the fence outside. I dismounted, and my stiff, aching legs nearly buckled under me. I had never spent so long on horseback, but I preferred Emric didn't know that, so I hid my discomfort as well as I could. When we returned to my aunts' house, I took a deep breath and approached the front door.

I had seen neither my aunts, nor this house, since I left it years ago. I didn't want to think about why this felt so hard, or why my breaths were coming so short. But the memories surfaced. The long, tedious days of seclusion, yearning for my parents—wishing, at the very least, for the sense of home and security that I'd felt with them. My mind filled with the thrashing and fighting as Aunt Fenella forced the bitter, burning brew of Verum and tea down my throat. And I once again felt the bewilderment over how my gentle father could have had such dreadful sisters.

I knocked. We waited a long moment, hearing nothing, seeing no movement at the windows. I glanced at Emric uncertainly.

"Might they be out? Or even have moved?" he asked, glancing away from the faded door to me.

"I think I'd know if they'd moved," I said doubtfully, completely unsure if that was true.

Emric turned to face the street. "Maybe there's someone we could ask."

My focus remained on the door, my stomach sinking. I hadn't wanted to go into that house. But I would rather go in and revisit the uncomfortable, cold memories of my childhood if it meant finding some answers than leave with nothing.

Then the door opened.

I started, and Emric whirled around. The sagging, lined face of my aunt met ours blankly.

"Hello, Aunt Millicent," I said pleasantly, surprised at my own composure. "May we come in?"

Aunt Millicent's eyes widened. "Ah. Cressida. Home for the holiday for once, I see. How nice." She stepped aside, opening the door wider without a word. She hitched up an uncertain smile and led us into the foyer, which was dark and cold. The house smelled dusty and dank, as if it had been closed up. She did not turn around and speak, but kept walking, passing the drawing room on the left and the parlor on the right. I thought for a moment that she was leading us to the kitchen or dining room, until she began ascending the stairs up to the bedrooms.

"Aunt Millicent?" I asked gently. Perhaps she was growing forgetful. I felt a surge of warmth and sympathy toward the timid soul, living alone with her domineering sister year after year. "Where would you like us to wait for you?"

"Oh, no, you follow me. You'll want to see your old room. Bring your young man," she said, her voice as soft as I remembered.

I glanced back at Emric, who gave a slight shrug. I smiled nervously, and we followed Aunt Millicent up the narrow stairwell. As we reached the top floor, it grew warmer, and there was a light under the door at the end of the hall—Aunt Fenella's room. Low voices in quick conversation drifted from within.

Aunt Millicent stuck a brass key into the keyhole of my old room and jangled the rusty lock vigorously before it clicked open. She pushed at the door and ushered us inside. As I entered the dark, dusty room, I wondered if I should call for Aunt Fenella, who surely wouldn't approve of Millicent entertaining guests in here. Emric had followed me, and we turned to Millicent, who hovered in the doorway. The key was still in the lock.

"Where is your headmistress? Tepsom?" she asked in her soft voice.

I gaped at her as my head started to pound.

"It's all right, Cressida," Emric said quickly. He didn't want me collapsing.

"Headed to the monastery on the mountain, last I knew," I answered.

"Why?" A wisp of her greying hair fluttered whimsically around Millicent's ear.

"To find a map," I answered in a near whisper, struggling to wrap my mind around the questioning. Had Aunt Millicent completely lost her mind?

"Good. That will be enough for her," Millicent said briskly, and retreated back into the hall, shutting the door. Before Emric or I could react, we heard the key turning in the lock.

"Well. That was unexpected," Emric said, breaking our shocked silence.

I shook my head in disbelief. "There must be something wrong with her," I said, almost wanting that to be true.

"Or we've come to the right place for answers. But apparently, we just don't have the upper hand," Emric said, inspecting the lock.

"We can use my wrist dagger," I said numbly, still in shock.

"I can give it a try," he said. I handed it over, and he knelt down and tried to slide the dagger in the keyhole. "The lock is too small for this, I'm afraid," he said.

I automatically reached into my hair and dug around while he watched me, puzzled. Then I yanked away with a frustrated groan.

"Of course it's long gone. I lost my hairpin blade, probably on the mountain somewhere." I sank down onto my old, narrow bed with the faded counterpane.

Emric knelt in front of me. "I know this isn't ideal," he said gently, "especially as they know better than anyone about your curse. But, unless this is, indeed, simply a case of your aunt cracking up, I think we're in a good place to find answers."

"Oh, we're in a good place for someone to find answers. From me," I said wearily. Something about being in my old room made me want to do nothing but curl up and brood over the injustice of it all. But that wasn't going to get us anywhere.

"Who else do you think is here?" Emric asked as voices down the hall continued to drone on.

"I have no idea. I'm so . . ." I put my head in my hands. "I'm so confused," I said through my fingers.

"It's all right. We'll figure this out." Emric put a reassuring hand on my knee. "So, you lived in this house with your aunts after your parents died? Have you stayed in close touch with them?" He flushed. "Sorry," he said, realizing he was forcing me to answer his questions.

"I did live here, yes. I haven't been back here or written much since I left for school."

"I imagine it would be hard to be close to the people who did this to you."

I shook my head. "I have no happy memories of this place. And I have no memories of them before my parents died. Just a happy childhood with two parents—then this place, with two women who seemed respectable enough in the most boring, strict sense. But I suppose they must have been somewhat insane. I mean, who in their right mind would do what they did? They didn't try to have a relationship with me. They only wanted to know things they had no right to know. About my feelings. About my memories. They emptied me of everything that was just mine." A thought struck me, and I sat up straighter and scanned the floor. "They probably even took that by now," I muttered, but I couldn't help but hope.

Emric had the consideration not to ask me what I was talking about. I slid off the bed, then got to my hands and knees and felt carefully around the floor. The wood was grimy with dust, but I kept up my search.

Emric spoke up. "I could help you find whatever you're looking for, if you like."

I was grateful for the effort he made not to directly question. "I'm looking for the loose floorboard where I hid my parents' things. Aunt Fenella knew about it, and she probably took it long ag—" I cut off as my hands touched the familiar, slightly ridged knot. I pried up the edge, which didn't fit quite right into the slat, and the whole board lifted up with a creak and a puff of filthy dust. I ducked my head and coughed, waving the dust out of my face.

Emric crouched next to me as I reached rather squeamishly into the hole. My fingers brushed the tin of my box, and an unexpected relief swept over me. Tears sprang to my eyes. This was all that I had left of my parents. What would they have thought of the person I had become? A murderess with a curse. My relief dissolved into despair, and I held my hand flat atop the cold tin, unable to lift it out and encounter those memories again. I blinked the tears away and swallowed the lump in my throat. Emric sat quietly, saying nothing.

After a moment, I took a deep breath and lifted out the box.

It was covered in dust, which had been disrupted by my fingers, and I brushed the rest of the thick layer carefully into the hole in the floor. Emric stood and pulled the curtain open, to provide what small amount of light the tiny window would allow. The box was an Evenfrost shortbread tin with a faded holiday scene pictured on the front in flaking paint. I smiled involuntarily, remembering my mother washing and giving me the tin when we'd finished the shortbread. She told me it could be for my treasures.

The lid was tight with rust, but it came off after a moment's effort. My treasures were a smattering of memories that I'd nearly forgotten I had. A pang of regret hit me.

The box contained a small, polished white stone that I remembered fishing out of my little knitted Evenfrost sack, a yellowed card with a winter mountain scene hand-painted on the front, an embroidered handkerchief that had belonged to my mother, and my father's pipe.

I picked up the pipe first, smiling at the burst of memory. It was really just his spare that he'd let me play with when it was clean. I had marched around with it clamped in between my teeth and talked like the farmer down the road as my mother protested through her laughter. It was quaint and curved, with a lovely smooth bowl.

I replaced it after a short moment, to stifle the grief that was rising rapidly to the surface. I bypassed the stone and the handkerchief, picking up the card in spite of the heaviness I felt at reading my mother's beautiful penmanship and sweet words.

I had read the card over and over again after my parents' deaths. They'd had no reason to bid me farewell, or write a letter of encouragement or advice. But they had given me the card with my Evenfrost gifts the winter before they died, and I had known the moment I proudly read it aloud to them that it belonged with my treasures.

> *Dearest Cressida,*
>
> *You are, even as I write this, working hard on the gifts you're making for your Papa and me. You're so creative, so thoughtful. You need to know, though, that your heart is our treasure. You're our miracle, our gift, our wild girl, and you always will be.*
>
> *This year, Papa and I want to give you this vindeca stone to remind you always to be true. The stones of Mt. Vindeca symbolize healing and restoration. If you ever feel that you've lost yourself, remember the healing stones of Vindeca (especially this one that Papa polished*

up for you!) and that we will always love you,
and believe in you.

With love, always,
Mama and Papa

I handed the card to Emric, lost in my own thoughts.

"You don't need to share this with me, it's personal . . ." Emric protested.

"No, you should read it," I said. A small line creased his brow as he read the words that had echoed through my heart year after year.

"How could I not have considered. . ." I mused as he finished.

"That's a very thoughtful letter. It must mean a lot to you."

"It does." I glanced up at him. "But what does it mean to you?"

"That you were wild and crafty?" Emric offered.

"Other than that?" I prompted.

Emric looked again. "Well, my parents used to say similar things about Mt. Vindeca. When my father wasn't using it to swear by," he added ruefully.

"Exactly."

"Exactly . . ." Emric asked the question without asking.

"Like we talked about the other day. I haven't heard anyone else ever talk about the mountain like that. I remember that Papa told me to keep my vindeca stone safe, and I thought it was symbolic—sentimental." I met his gaze. "Emric, both of our parents owned land from which powerful substances could be mined. What did they know about the mountain that other people didn't?"

He looked doubtful. "Like you said, it's probably symbolic—a generational thing."

"Or it's a *real* thing," I responded, knowing how crazed I sounded. But the connection my brain had made couldn't be derailed. I had to know, I had to find out, somehow, if the stone of the mountain was special.

Emric looked at me pensively, almost as if he didn't think I was crazy. "May I?" he asked, indicating the vindeca stone. At my nod, he lifted it out and inspected it closely.

A turn of the rusty lock made us both jump. I shook my head fiercely at Emric, and he shoved the stone deep into his jacket. I prayed there was a pocket in there somewhere. I crammed the card into my own pocket, slapped the lid back on the tin, and shoved it back into the hole, covering it loosely with the floorboard just as the door opened. I winced, thinking of my mother's handkerchief and my father's pipe, haphazardly crammed in the tin, but I stepped over the hole to cover it with my skirt.

The door swung open, and there was a small shuffle in the hall as Millicent stepped aside, and Aunt Fenella sailed past her into the room.

She wasn't as physically intimidating as I remembered. Her height and girth seemed somewhat diminished, and what used to be a magnificent pile of stiffly coiffed dark hair was now a severe, grey bun. My instinct, however, was to step back, but I stood my ground as she approached.

"Cressida Hoth, what are you doing here?" she demanded, wasting no time.

"We want answers about the Verum you gave me," I began, but Emric interrupted sharply.

"You will not direct another question at Cressida, madam. We are happy to have a civil discourse, but I must insist you do not treat us like prisoners, or stoop to interrogating your niece, whom you recklessly abused."

Aunt Fenella looked at Emric, her nostrils flaring. "You brought a protector. How charming."

"Cressida doesn't need—" Emric began with a huff, then bit off the angry words. I stopped myself from tossing him a warning look. He was attempting to get himself under control, although I sensed the tension in his stance.

"So, you're still under the influence of the Verum," Aunt Fenella said, watching me beadily. "How fascinating. We wondered if it would ever fade. Apparently not, as it's been the better part of a decade."

"Why did you do it?" I countered.

"As an experiment. And to get answers. Verum was hard to get a hold of—still is—and its effects were little studied. Who better to test the long-term effects on, than a child? Of course, nothing changed, and the subject grew boring. I see that's still the case." Her lips pursed.

"You were curious, so you decided to test a powerful drug on me, your young niece?" I asked. The callousness of her tone shocked me. I'd never received affection from Aunt Fenella, but I had never doubted her familial loyalty.

"Well, you're not really our niece, you know," she responded calmly.

I stared at her, uncomprehending. "What?" I said finally.

"I said you aren't really our niece. You were an asset, and a useless one. You proved to be just as unhelpful as a test subject, too."

The room seemed to be tilting as I slowly comprehended her words. "Why did I come live with you?"

Emric placed a steadying hand on my back.

"We were quick to claim you as family. No one looks too closely when someone offers to take an unwanted orphan off their hands. I was surprised that you didn't question the fact that you'd never met us."

She was so complacent in her contempt, I felt I was drowning in it. "Why?"

She ignored my question. "Millicent says that you told her that Tepsom is at the king's monastery. Why?"

"Because she is looking for something there," I snapped the words at her as anger began to overtake my confusion. "You're out of practice interrogating me."

Fenella raised her brow. "I have it on authority that she believes she's located the maps we need. Is this true?"

"I don't know what she believes." My head began to immediately pound. "I mean—yes." I clenched and unclenched my fists. Emric and I were both armed, and Fenella was aging and frail. And because Fenella was aging and frail, the thought of attacking her, deceitful brute that she was, didn't sit right.

"Who else is here?" Emric demanded. I could tell he was trying to shift the improbable power that she seemed to hold over the conversation.

"My contact. A liaison between Tepsom's branch of operations and ours," Fenella answered blithely. "We usually communicate via post—coded, of course—but this matter required speed. Is Miss Tepsom alone?" She looked directly at me, her face almost pleasantly expressionless. Like an unobtrusive auntie on a teatime call.

"No," I answered.

"Who is with her?"

"Lord Eston and some palace guards loyal to him," I answered impatiently. "What do you mean *branch of operations*?"

"I'm obviously not going to answer that," Fenella said, putting her hand on the door with a cold smile. "*I* don't have to. You're not to be trusted with any more information. You must make for a rotten spy," she remarked. "Well, tell me, before I go. I'm getting old and something may have slipped my mind. Is there anything else I'd like to know that you're not telling me?"

"I do not know," I answered but lifted my chin. "You haven't explained a thing about your role in any of this, so how do I know what you'd like to know? It looks like you're the one who's a rotten spy, or whatever it is you think you are."

Fenella took her hand off of the door and came slowly toward me. "You always were a useless little wretch. I wasn't sure what to do with you. But I just decided." She reached into her apron pocket and withdrew a small pouch. It looked disconcertingly like the one that she pulled out years ago to stir into my tea. Or, it looked the way it did in my imaginative memory.

Emric stiffened, and his hand went to his side. "What is that?"

Fenella untied the top of the pouch, and I instinctively put my hand on the hilt of my sword, despite the fact that I felt unwilling to use it on Fenella. "This is the raw, powdered stone we call Nemere. Undiluted, it's extremely powerful, I imagine, with untested results." She raised her chin in the pompous way that I remembered too well. "I have made great strides in my substance studies, but even I only have theories about how to reverse the effects. You proved to be a boring test subject the first time, but perhaps not this time." She loosened the drawstring.

Emric and I drew our swords at the same time, but couldn't extend them without running her through, so we held them awkwardly in front of Fenella as she exposed a small mound of dark dust that was nestled in the bag. She glanced at our faces and smiled brazenly.

With a startling clatter, the door burst open behind Fenella, and a petite lady entered the room. Fenella did not move to see who was behind her. "You're interrupting, Millicent. Leave."

"Ma'am, I apologize for the intrusion, but I've had an urgent communication from the monastery." I stared in shock at Iris Rush, who stood with a weapon in her hand. A burning anger flared in my chest, and I itched to smack her sword out of her hand with mine.

Fenella still did not turn, but now clenched her fist over the powder, her eyes darting between Emric's face and mine, choosing her target. "Thank you, Iris. I will be—"

The hilt of Miss Rush's sword clunked sharply against the side of Fenella's head, and I gasped as she crumpled to the floor with a thud. "No need. You stay right there," Miss Rush said curtly as she sheathed her sword. "Why hadn't either of you done that yet?" she asked irritably. "That stuff isn't to be trifled with. She wasn't messing around, you know. Crazy old bat." She shook her head at Fenella, lying motionless on the floor, the dark powder leaking from the bag and staining her open hand.

Emric and I kept our swords out, and he now raised his, though mine lowered. I was completely bewildered.

"What is going on?" I asked in exasperation, grateful that Fenella had not managed to throw raw Nemere dust into our faces.

"I decided I was too interested to disappear into the night." Miss Rush shrugged, tossing a blonde curl out of her eyes, and crouching down to examine Fenella. "I searched Tepsom's room and found a stash of correspondence, then left at first light to get some answers out of these two. They'd never seen me, but I brought along a couple of their letters to prove I was a contact. Turns out this is just a stopping point, and occasional communication center for Warwick, which is what I've gathered their operation is called. They were chomping at the bit to receive any word of some action, so I dropped some hints that Miss Tepsom needed reinforcements in the hope that they would provide me with the names of their other contacts so I could pretend to pass on the rallying call. No luck so far, but I imagine the information is here somewhere, and the palace would probably pay handsomely for those names. Along with the evidence I gathered from Miss Tepsom's room."

"I don't think they'll be paying you for deciding to be patriotic at this point," Emric pointed out.

Miss Rush shrugged again. "Can't hurt to find out. I'm terribly good at sneaking off, if not. Besides," she tossed over her shoulder as she turned to the door, "you two managed to give the palace guards the slip. How hard could it be?"

I glanced up at Emric, surprised to find a crooked smile on his face. "Let's find your other aunt," he said. I said nothing.

"The other old bat," he amended. We joined Rush, who was striding down the hall to the door at the end of it. She swung it open without knocking, and we followed her inside.

Millicent stood quickly from her seat by a small fire, knocking over a cup of tea and clutching her shawl to her chest. "Where is Fenella?" she asked, looking at me fearfully. I despised her for remembering to ask me specifically.

"On the floor," I answered curtly.

Both Rush and Emric had drawn their swords, and once more, I followed suit, no reluctance this time. "Your sister apparently has a stash of dangerous substances." Miss Rush's eyes pierced Millicent's. "Tell me immediately where they are, as well as all of your correspondence with agents of Warwick. Or we'll use these." She leveled the sword tip at the woman.

Millicent did not hesitate. She pointed at the mantelpiece, where a brass candlestick and a biscuit tin sat. When no one moved, she took down the biscuit tin and held it out uncertainly.

"Hand it to Cressida," Emric commanded. Millicent met my eyes for a brief instant, her expression hunted. I snatched the tin out of her wobbling grasp. "We've got her covered, Cressida," Emric said. "You have a look."

I glanced at him, as he kept a steady eye on Millicent. In that ridiculously wrong moment, I realized just how much I loved his face.

It struck hard, that thought, and my face grew warm as I fought a smile.

I managed to sheath my sword and set the tin on the tea table. Emric and Rush herded Millicent a few feet away from me. The biscuit tin looked meek and civil, like one that had been bought in a very innocent shop. I gingerly lifted the lid.

Inside were four small pouches, plus a circular imprint in the dust where a fifth had sat before Fenella removed it. Each pouch had a small tag, scrawled labels written in faded ink. *Nemere. Lethen. Lethen. Verum.* The pouch labeled *Verum* was slightly deflated—only half full. A shiver ran through me. One of the ones labeled *Lethen* looked almost empty. I carefully loosened the drawstring and glanced inside. It was full of a fine, light green powder. If there was an antidote in there, it was not labeled as such. Tucked next to the Nemere was a scrap of paper, on which the words: *one part VD, one part raw N* were scrawled. I replaced the lid and held the tin firmly.

"She has a small stock of substances here, all in powder form," I said, after clearing my throat.

"Anything that looks like antidotes?" Emric asked. I shook my head as my heart sank.

"Are there antidotes to these?" Emric asked Millicent.

She also gave a slight shake of her head.

I looked at Millicent's wide-eyed, fearful expression and, with pity, thought I knew where much of the Lethen had been used. Fenella likely enjoyed wielding the most information and keeping her sister useless. I doubted if we would learn much more from Millicent.

"Where are your correspondence and contact lists?" Rush demanded.

Millicent said nothing, her lips clamped shut in a thin line. Rush extended her sword so that it was only a few inches from Millicent's nose.

"She might not be able to answer," I said quickly. "It looks like her sister dosed her with Lethen occasionally."

"That works its way out of the system." Rush's gaze was fixed on Millicent. Millicent's eyes grew even wider. "I suppose we could use your sister's stash of Verum to find out if you remember."

I bit my tongue. I'd let Rush scare Millicent with the thought, but wouldn't let her use the Verum on Millicent. I needed it.

It did not take more than the mere suggestion. "Fenella keeps her correspondence locked up in her desk. I rarely handle any direct communication." Millicent's voice trembled.

"Where's the key?"

"In her apron," Millicent answered promptly, eyeing the tin in my hands. Rush immediately left the room.

I looked at Millicent, feeling a bottleneck of questions forming inside me. The first one burst out. "Did Miss Tepsom know that you two gave me Verum?" Millicent shook her head. "Why not?" I persisted. Although I knew that it would have been obvious if Tepsom had known before last night, I still felt a rush of relief for my past schoolgirl-self.

"We weren't supposed to have any of those." She flapped a hand limply at the tin in my hands. "Warwick operations carefully collects them and controls their usage. But Fenella has always been fascinated and found ways to obtain some of her own. I don't know how she came by them!" Her voice quavered as she spoke.

Rush returned at that moment with a ring of keys. She strode over to the desk and began fitting them, one after another, into the small lock on the roll top. "Aha," she breathed, when one fit in and turned easily. She flung up the lid, and I hurried over to have a look. There were several neat stacks of letters and a thick black-leather book. I picked that up while Rush leafed through the letters.

"Interesting. And very incriminating. To both of you," Rush tutted, smirking at Millicent.

I flipped open the book and found, in the first several pages, name after name, with addresses and code names, as well as aliases. I didn't see Miss Tepsom until I reached the Ws, where Tepsom was listed as an alias under the name Warwick. The whole network was named for her family. Eston was in the book with no alias. I shot a glance at Emric, then swiftly looked down through the Ds, for Dantis, then scanned the rest of the aliases to make sure.

"Although you and your sister acted as agents, you're not in here," I let him know. "Neither am I, Miss Rush, nor anyone else from the school. No one who was unaware of the true cause is implicated, at least not here." I felt a weight lift from my shoulders. It might not absolve us from all responsibility in the eyes of the crown, but it could help.

"All right," Rush announced. "Let's just take it all." She scooped up the piles of letters, and I set the book on top of the biscuit tin.

"So, what do we do with these two?" Emric asked us as we stood by the door with our stacks of evidence.

I glanced at Rush. She looked indifferent.

"Knock this one out too?" she suggested.

"No need for that," I said, indicating the key ring dangling from Rush's hand.

"Oh, right. Leave her there, Theon, and let's go."

Emric moved back, lowering his sword. Millicent mutely stared at us with wild eyes as we left the room, shutting her in. I checked in on Fenella and found that her pulse was steady, but she was still out cold. Carefully, I closed up her pouch of Nemere and added it to the biscuit tin. I dared not touch the dusting of black powder that caked Fenella's open palm.

I felt a twitch of guilt as Rush locked both her and Millicent inside their respective rooms, then tossed the keys down the hall. We hurried out of the house, and Rush glanced at me in irritation as I hesitated on the doorstep, looking back.

"We can leave word with the town authorities that someone needs to check in with these ladies," Emric offered.

I agreed, and we followed Rush down the front steps.

"Do you two have horses?" she asked over her shoulder. "I came by coach."

"We couldn't get a coach today," I told her. "Our horses are at the ale house."

She glanced around. "We can take mine. It will be more efficient for carting this evidence, and I'm not about to go up the mountain on horseback."

Emric retrieved our satchel from his horse and gave the animal an apologetic pat. I hoped someone would take care of the abandoned horses sooner rather than later.

"Who's your coachman?" Emric inquired as Rush led us to a small, two-horse, half-open coach that waited across the street.

"I am."

Emric raised an eyebrow. "And how did you get–" He stopped himself. "Never mind." It seemed best not to ask questions. Rush hiked up her skirts and clambered onto the driver's bench.

Emric and I stood next to the coach and looked at each other in indecision.

"Are you sure you want to go back to the palace?" Emric lowered his voice. "I understand if you want to keep on with our original plan. We're returning empty-handed as far as a cure for Roland and Rubia. And I haven't given up on finding it for you, either." He spoke with conviction, but I could see the conflict in his eyes.

"We need to get this information to the palace right away," I answered, knowing full well that we could be facing arrest. I definitely was, but maybe Rush and Emric would be spared. They brought valuable evidence–might even be stopping a war–and neither had killed a member of the palace staff. "We aren't sure what sort of welcome Rosalie and your sister received, and this might be of use in clearing them of suspicion, at the very least."

"But you don't have to go," Emric said, knowing my thoughts. He glanced sideways at Miss Rush, and I knew what he was thinking. We couldn't trust her to bring the evidence before the king alone.

"We need to move," she interrupted from the driver's seat, narrowing her eyes at us. "Are you coming? I do think that time is of the essence," she said severely.

Emric looked at me. "Yes," I answered, and climbed into the coach.

"Here." Rush handed Emric the stack of letters after he climbed up after me.

He stowed them carefully in his satchel, along with the black book. I kept the tin of powders clutched tightly in my hands, ignoring his quizzical look when I declined to pack it.

Rush clicked her tongue at the horses and guided them expertly onto the street. I felt almost foolish about trusting her so completely, but there was such an honest sort of frankness in her allegiance to herself, that I didn't really worry she'd drive us off a cliff, or into sinister new territory. We all had something to potentially lose, but more to gain by returning to the castle—I hoped. I blinked away the image of the dead man that I had left on the mountain, and prayed I'd be forgiven. The weight of taking a life was heavy, but I could not pretend that I wished that man still at large.

My faith in Miss Rush was bolstered when she did, indeed, stop by the local office of authority and reported that the old spinster sisters needed to be checked on at some point that day. She played the convincing part of a concerned acquaintance, and we left with assurances that an officer would check in.

After that, just in case we had given the authorities reason to give chase, we blazed a trail out of town and over the open red road toward Mt. Vindeca.

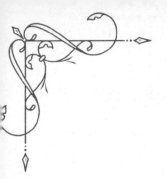

22

RUSH SEEMED TO VASTLY enjoy her role as our driver, shouting encouragement to the horses as we rattled along, and I was happy not to subject my still-aching legs to an even longer journey on horseback.

When we reached the crossroads, we took the road that headed north, rather than back toward Savinrue. The wind bit icily into our cheeks as we flew down the frozen red road for the next few hours. We took the northeast branch at another fork in the road (the other branch led seaward), and the mountain loomed nearer and nearer. The road grew rockier as we reached the foothills. Rush slowed the horses, and they picked their way carefully through the heathery path that the road had become. We turned to the west, travelling at the base of the mountain until we reached the white road that led directly up the mountain and to the palace.

My heart gave a lurch as we turned upward, and I gathered my cloak more closely around myself, keeping the tin tightly on my lap. The horses kicked up white dust, and I shut my eyes as it blew into our faces.

"I hope you don't feel pushed into returning to the palace." Emric leaned close to be heard.

I shook my head slightly. "Not at all. Rosalie, Rubia, and Vivian are up there too. I want to clear up our unintentional involvement in Warwick once and for all." I hoped I sounded more resolute than I felt. "I do wish we'd at least found a

Nemere antidote, though. If Roland and Rubia still need it." My voice faltered at the thought that they might sleep indefinitely because of me.

"Your fingers are blue," Emric observed, in lieu of empty reassurance. I looked down at my hands, which were stiffly clinging to the tin. I had lost feeling in my fingers hours ago. "Here." He stripped off his gloves and offered them to me. I took them gratefully, enjoying the warmth from his hand before it quickly faded.

My thoughts beat an anxious pattern, treading and retreading my fears, no sooner one dismissed than another replaced it. Would we be too late to stop Tepsom and Eston? Were our friends safe? Would I be arrested and charged with murder on sight?

The light was fading to a dusky grey when Rush pulled the horses over to a stream. Emric led the horses to the water while Rush and I drank. The water was icy and made me feel alert in every nerve of my body. The air was getting colder, but there was little snow under the cover of the trees that laced themselves together overhead. I knelt by the road and removed a glove, running my fingers over the cold, dry dust, wondering why it hadn't turned into frozen white mud.

Emric led the horses back onto the road, and we climbed into the coach again. While travelling by road in the coach, and dreading the destination with every clop of the horses' hooves, the journey seemed to take no time at all. Once we were within sight of the high iron gates that marked the entrance to the winding drive, Rush brought the coach off to the side of the road and we climbed out. Dusk had settled, and I trusted the oncoming darkness to hide our conveyance.

"So how do we go about this?" she asked briskly, tucking her wind-tangled hair back into a semblance of order.

Emric glanced at me. I gave a little nod. There was no point in trying to enter Shoncliffe by any means other than the way we left it.

"We know a way. It isn't far. It should keep us out of sight from the guards for as long as possible, and help our chances of getting in front of the king," he told her.

"Lead the way," she replied, and we followed Emric southward through the dense, ice-glazed trees and slippery inclines that surrounded the castle.

Finally, we located the outcropping that concealed the entrance to the secret passage. My toes were numb and my eyelashes were frozen. I hoped fervently that this marked the end of my career of prowling up and down the bitter mountainside.

We slid through the narrow space behind the boulder, into the passage, and moved quickly up the sloping tunnel. Once we reached the interior of the palace, we stopped to get our bearings.

"We should navigate these passages until we get as close as possible to whichever room the king is in," Emric said.

"I disagree," I countered quickly. I wouldn't admit it, but a breathless sort of panic had settled over me the moment we reached the stifling inner passage. "We don't know where to find the king, and we aren't going to get anywhere quickly by skulking about in the dark."

"Right. We need to get out of here and then get our royal audience," Miss Rush agreed. "I can make anyone tell me anything, so we'll find them quickly enough. Also," she remarked offhandedly, "I think we should pretend that I found you two and am bringing you in for bounty."

There was a pause. "But you're not doing that, correct?" Emric looked at her warily.

She snorted. "If I were, you'd both be unconscious from that old lady's powder supply and lying in the back of the carriage."

"You thought about it, then," he muttered.

"All right," I cut them off. "Let's find an exit."

We decided to go by way of the solar, as we knew we could

find it, and it was likely empty. It took us little time to find the stairs, and once at the top, we halted and listened intently. Confident that it was vacant, Emric tugged the door open and pushed past the tapestry. It was dim and cold inside, meager moonlight slanting through the wide windows. Miss Rush looked around with interest, but we did not linger.

We crossed the room and exited out the other side to the steep stone steps. Emric, descending the stairs with more speed than stealth, suddenly pulled up short and pushed his hands against the stone walls to keep us all from tumbling down the remaining stairs in a heap.

Miss Rush braced her hand against my back. "What's going on?" she hissed.

But the answer became evident. The stairs curved into the corridor, where a pair of guards, armed with heavy crossbows, were heading straight toward us. Emric looked like he was about to draw his sword, but pulled his cloak around to conceal it instead. I couldn't reach mine in the cramped stairwell, wedged as I was between Rush and Emric.

It was no good doubling back. I concealed the biscuit tin under my cloak as the guards approached. Emric stepped into the corridor and held his hands up in surrender. I followed him, but Miss Rush elbowed past me and marched boldly toward the oncoming guards.

"Direct us to the king," she demanded. "I bring vital information, concerning an attack on the kingdom, and I found these two lurking outside the palace. I believe they are wanted? The king will want to see them."

"He'll want to see you too, madam, as you don't appear to belong down the royal family's private corridor." The guard took hold of her as the other grabbed Emric, twisting his arms behind his back. The one who had spoken looked over at me.

"You. Walk in front where we can see you, and don't try anything. The lady was right—the king will definitely want to see you."

Miss Rush started to argue, but the guard tightened his grip. "Silence. Not a word from any of you."

They marched us down the corridor, barking directions to me and prodding my back with their crossbows as I blindly led the way, my heart racing. We made so many turns deeper into the center of the palace that I lost my bearings. Finally, it became evident that we were nearing our destination. A grand set of polished mahogany doors stood before us, and my memory of the palace's map suggested that this was the Great Hall, a grand chamber set directly in the center of the castle. The doors were flanked by four guards, and several maids hung around, clearly trying to hear what was happening inside.

The sentries opened the creaking doors to the Great Hall, and we stepped inside. The hall was a vast chamber of grey and white marble, and our entrance immediately echoed throughout the space. As we were in the center of the palace, there were no windows. A fire blazed in a long, cavernous fireplace on the far wall, and candles and lamps were lit at intervals around the room.

The guards marched us to the center of the hall, where a dais was erected, atop which was a vast, shining wood table piled with documents and lit candlesticks. At the head of the table sat King Arctus, with the queen next to him, and six or seven other men and women whose faces were tense and wary as we approached. I noticed with interest that Father Harrick, the frail monk whom we had met on our first visit to the monastery, sat to the right of the queen. There were guards at every corner of the room.

A small woman sat with her back to me, ramrod straight. I noticed the stained travelling cloak and tangle of blonde hair, and I realized with a shock that it was Rosalie. Her side of the table was otherwise empty, and there was a small, dark bottle sitting on the table in front of her.

"What is this?" thundered the voice of the king as we came

near. "Young lady," his eyes darted to Rosalie, "tell us if these three are trustworthy."

Rosalie turned to us, her face flushed and her eyes bright. "Cressida and Mr. Theon are trustworthy, Your Majesty. They are no traitors. I have less faith in the other." The king nodded to Emric's guard, who immediately dropped his hold and joined the other guard in restraining Miss Rush.

"I have vital information for you, Your Majesty," Miss Rush declared loudly, "which is more than enough to exonerate me of—"

"Silence. We will deal with you presently. Miss Montshire, have you any other information of value to offer?" Rosalie shook her head, and the king turned his attention to Emric and me.

"Well. You two seem to have gotten yourselves tangled up in quite the mess. I do not use this by force, but I don't suppose either of you are willing to undertake what your friend here offered?" He lifted a hand. "Miss Montshire has taken a potion of her own free will, in order to convince us of her honesty. The potion compels her to speak the truth."

I bit back a gasp and stared at Rosalie.

"Your Majesty, did she tell you yet that the monastery is in danger? Men need to be sent immediately to—"

The king interrupted Emric's urgent words. "She told us that information first thing, and a troop of my men has been sent to protect Rounelith and arrest the traitors. Do either of you two have any new information to offer? As I asked once already, are you willing to put your honesty to the ultimate test for your king?"

"We do have information for you," I answered promptly. "And I have been under the influence of Verum for half my life. Ask me what you like."

"Cressida!" Emric hissed.

I took a deep breath and looked steadily at the king. He stared at me, startled for a brief moment. Then, he raised his heavy brows.

"How am I to know that is true? Miss Montshire ingested the substance, verified to be legitimate by my personal chemist, and she did so in front of my council and myself. Why should I believe you?"

"Ask Miss Montshire," I suggested.

"I know this is true," Rosalie responded without question.

"Your Majesty," Emric cut in. "We have vital information for you about a threat to your kingdom, and evidence to support it. We have written proof of traitors from both Dernmont and Porleac plotting to gain control of the powerful substances that are mined from this land with the intention of starting a war. Two of the traitors and their own men are at the monastery now, in an attempt to find maps that lead to those substances. They will be ruthless."

A blend of fury, confusion, and disbelief played over the king's features. When he spoke, his voice had lowered to a timbre of dangerous calm. "I am not sure what exactly you think you're talking about in regard to these mines you speak of, but as I said, the trouble at the monastery is being attended to. And I have reason not only to mistrust the two of you, but to throw you in my dungeons." He pointed directly at Emric. "You, a member of our household, colluded with these young women to subject my own son, the royal prince, to the effects of not one, but *two* of these substances. What have you to say about that?" The king's eyes were as sharp as a hawk as they bore sharply into Emric.

"I believe you've likely already heard the truth of that situation from Miss Montshire, but I offer my sincere apology for Prince Roland's condition," Emric responded. "The Verum was a mistake, made by a young woman sadly deceived and misled by a traitor, and the Nemere, which he ingested willingly, was an act of protection from those who would exploit his condition to hurt the kingdom and the crown."

King Arctus glared at Emric, then shifted his attention to

me. "Do any of you three know anything about the murder of a palace groom?" he asked.

My chest constricted. "I killed him," I said, my voice barely able to push past a whisper.

"Your Majesty, he was attacking her—" Rosalie jumped to her feet, her voice clashing with Emric's, as his also rose in my defense.

"He was in the pay of a traitor and threatened her life, Your Maj—"

"Enough!" the king bellowed. "We will discover the truth of the matter." He stood and leaned across the table, his dark eyes focused on me. "After this *mistake* that has rendered my son sleeping like the dead for two days, why did you leave the palace?"

"To escape discovery and arrest, Your Majesty," I said. "And to find a cure."

"And did you?"

"I believe so," I said.

Emric uttered a surprised sound, and Rosalie stared at me. I approached the table cautiously and set the biscuit tin upon it.

"Is that it?"

"Not exactly. Your chemist may want to have a look. These are all powdered rock of Lethen, Nemere, and Verum. I don't know their potency, if they are diluted or not. I believe not."

"How on earth did you—never mind. We need a definite cure!" The king growled. "If you are indeed under the influence of Verum, then you are living proof that my son is in very grave danger. Suppose the sleep he's under doesn't wear off either?"

I thought of Rubia and Roland and swallowed nervously. I had better be right, or I was a murderer three times over.

King Arctus said crisply, "I will not discuss this point further at the moment, but the very fact that you had these substances in your possession is alarming, could even be considered treasonous. Do you or do you not have a cure?"

"I have a suspicion, that I am willing to test on myself," I answered, glancing at the handwritten scrap of paper in the tin. The king sat down slowly in his chair.

"Indeed? And what if, as I suggested, you are lying about your own condition? You could still be trying to poison my son."

"I'm not."

"She's not," Rosalie asserted. "But if it will ease your mind, test her cure on me as well. You know I am recently dosed, and you can monitor its effects on me before giving it to the prince. I trust Miss Hoth."

Queen Ceridwen stood suddenly, and the councilors around the table all sat up a bit straighter. The king looked up at her. "I am tired of this, Arctus," she said plainly. "You have reason to trust Miss Montshire, at least, and her suggestion is sound. Let us hear out Miss Hoth and test her cure on both young ladies." Her face was lined with worry, but her expression firm.

The king's face softened as he looked at his wife, and he took her hand. "Let it be as the queen desires," he said.

A white-haired gentleman that I vaguely recognized jumped to his feet, his velvet robes swinging around himself in the process.

"Your Majesty, as your court chemist, I must advise against wasting your time when war is possibly at your door. These substances are utterly unknown to me. That is no small thing, as a lifelong and, I dare to presume, well-trusted scholar of elemental properties. I, therefore, believe that this girl knows nothing about them, either, and has nothing to offer." He gestured my direction.

"Sit down, Creedling. You will be consulted." The king looked at me. "What do you have?"

"I believe, sir—" I struggled to breathe as it was difficult to explain quickly before my curse took over. Also, I knew exactly how ridiculous it sounded. "–that the rock of the mountain, the vindeca stone, has healing properties. Perhaps antidotal, when mixed with the appropriate substances. I propose that raw vindeca dust be combined with raw Verum to create an antidote."

I heard Rosalie's sharp intake of breath.

"Ha!" barked the chemist. "You take literally the poetry of the mountain, I see."

"And she is wise to do so," came a fragile, yet sonorous voice, as Father Harrick struggled to his feet. The queen took his arm in support.

"But sir," Rosalie said in a small, but clear voice, "the hot spring at Rounelith. If I am not mistaken, that is a well-documented source of wellness. The cloudiness of the water suggests–"

"Yes, yes!" Father Harrick's voice shook with enthusiasm. "The white dust mingles with the hot spring, well observed, young lady . . ."

"Don't get me started on your ramblings of alchemy–nonsense–"

"Creedling!" Queen Ceridwen warned.

"I have studied the lore of the mountain my entire life," Father Harrick declared. "But not only that, I have observed it working upon the weak and ailing. I know well what you think, my learned friend, and I hold your views in the highest respect. But the writings I've carefully collected are not all stories, and not recorded and carefully preserved for naught." The king shifted uncomfortably in his seat, but he did not interrupt the monk. "I recommend trying as the girl suggests. I have ancient texts I can present. My king, you know I believe it is time. I will say no more." He turned unsteadily toward the king, looking dangerously close to toppling. The queen helped him settle back into his seat. My eyes fell on a white brooch that he wore on the breast of his robes. I could not make out the shape, but

I highly suspected that it resembled a raven.

The king inclined his head. "Thank you, Father Harrick. Creedling?"

"Trust me. It's no medicine. It's a rock," was Mr. Creedling's flat response.

"Perhaps," I said nervously. "But I'm willing to try it." I held up one of Emric's gloves before the chemist could interrupt. "I know there's no shortage of vindeca dust, but I collected some on the way here." I poured out a small pile of the white dust onto the table.

The chemist looked at the pile and the glove in disgust. "Even if it did work in some capacity, the only way to test the necessary proportions, or know if anything else needs to be added, is to use a human subject. You, your friend—and anyone else the king commands."

"Don't be morbid, Creedling," Queen Ceridwen said severely. "I have strong faith in Mt. Vindeca and its Maker. What would be more fitting than if it indeed were a source of healing? I insist that you get your most trusted chemists to work on this proposal at once."

"Do it, Creedling," King Arctus barked.

The fellow backed away from the table with a small bow, and I went over to him and handed him the tin and the glove with the rest of the dust.

"I suggest that you try one part vindeca dust to one part Verum," I said.

With a scathing look in response, he took the tin and the glove and scurried from the room.

"I brought water from the spring for the prince—perhaps it would be of some use in this experiment?" Father Harrick asked, producing a leather flask from his belt.

"Thank you, Father Harrick. Would you be so kind as to accompany Mr. Creedling? That would be most helpful, and I do believe your presence and knowledge would be an asset," the queen replied. The king nodded to a guard to accompany the old monk in Creedling's wake.

King Arctus fixed his attention once more on us. "You claim to have evidence for me?"

Despite his dogged unwillingness to discuss the mines or the substances, the king took our evidence very seriously. Miss Rush was given a room and told not to leave the castle, although her collection of evidence seemed to be enough to convince the king to pardon her involvement in Tepsom's scheme. Emric, Rosalie, and I were directed to a small sitting room outside the Great Hall once our materials were presented in full, while the council continued its tireless conference.

Emric turned to Rosalie as soon as we were alone. "Is my sister safe?"

"Yes, she's lying low up in Vivian's room," Rosalie assured him.

Emric exhaled in relief. "I can't believe you offered to use the Verum to give a testimony," he said.

"It was the fastest way to get them to believe me and send a troop to the monastery. They'd already made us wait for hours before allowing an audience. I had retrieved the satchel on the way back, and the king seemed to have no difficulty believing the Verum would do what I said it would after Father Harrick inspected it. Although, you can probably picture the king's expression when I first brought it up." Rosalie was exhausted, but animated.

I hugged her. "You're a hero. I'm sorry for . . . everything. Every time I failed you, and our team." I blinked away tears as I released her. "Honestly, that was the cleverest idea, if a little overly sacrificial."

Rosalie shook her head and smiled. "None of us knew what we were doing. And you're going to cure us. I can't believe I hadn't thought of the mountain dust myself—I've been reading about the Rounelith hot springs since we visited, and they really are extraordinary, although few people seem to realize it. And antidotes are often one part poison anyway, so . . ." she yawned. "Well, it's very clever, but I'll leave the rest up to the chemists. Now, I'm going to take a nap until it's time to wake up and take my cure." She curled up on a settee by the empty fireplace and closed her eyes.

Emric and I sat on another settee, quiet for a long time.

"I really hope I'm right," I whispered after a while of waiting and wondering.

"I think it's brilliant," he said to me. "I hope it works. I have to admit, I am a bit worried about you testing it on yourself."

"There's no other way. They are in a hurry to cure the prince, and if it works for this, then it should work for the Nemere, right? And they can't exactly use an untested antidote on him. I want to be the first to try it. I just hope if it does something . . . bad . . . they catch it in me before testing it on Rosalie."

Emric was still not able to hide the anxiety in his eyes. He cleared his throat. "So, is now the time to ask you anything before I lose my chance at guaranteed honesty?" He quirked a smile.

I only hesitated for a moment. "Now's the time," I agreed, although my stomach knotted.

"I won't, though," he assured me. "Wait. Yes, I will. I have important questions. What is your favorite food?"

"Roasted salmon," I answered obediently.

"And I was so close to serving you the best you ever had in the woods yesterday . . ." Emric said regretfully.

I wrinkled my nose. "Not that close."

"You're right, not at all. All right—what is your favorite . . ."

Footsteps marched loudly down the corridor outside the sitting room. "Out of time," Emric said quickly. He bent his face close to mine, his eyes uncertain but blazing. "Last question. May I kiss you?"

A thrill ran through me. "Yes," I said without hesitation, as the footsteps drew nearer.

But Emric kissed me like he believed he had all the time in the world, and nothing could make him rush the moment. It was sweet and perfect.

A key scraped in the lock. Emric smiled brilliantly down at me. "I might be in love with you, Cressida. I definitely have faith in you. You're going to be cured and change everything for this kingdom." He put my polished vindeca stone into my palm as guards opened the sitting room door.

I smiled, tears pricking my eyes, and found I was unable to focus on the fear that should have arrived with the guards. Emric's eyes held mine even as the guards waited silently.

"I might be in love with you too," I whispered.

A grin broke over his face, and he lightly touched my cheek. Suppressing foolish smiles, we awoke Rosalie and followed our escort back into the Great Hall.

Creedling stood importantly to the left of the king, holding a thin vial in his hand.

"Sit, if you please." Queen Ceridwen indicated three chairs that had been pulled out. As I sat nervously, Emric gave me a confident smile.

"My chemists and I have consulted, along with Father Harrick, and we've put together what we believe to be the likeliest combination of Verum and vindeca dust." Creedling held up a hand. "Let me amend—I don't believe it likely to work at all. But we suspended that assumption and worked with the materials as if the vindeca dust did indeed hold incredible powers of healing, for the sake of doing our best work for our royal family."

Father Harrick nodded his approval, a smile creasing all his other wrinkles.

"Thank you, Creedling," said the queen. "How do you advise the concoction be administered to the subjects?"

"However they like. It would be best taken in a liquid."

"Tea," I said calmly. Verum had first been administered to me in an innocent-looking cup of tea. And it had certainly worked then.

The queen nodded as if this were perfectly reasonable. She slid her own steaming pot across the table to me, and one of the other ladies at the table gave me her own, unused cup. I looked with a strange peace, a disconnection from the creamy, fine-bone dish before me. I ought to have felt fear. The innocuous cup was much like the one pushed at me when I was eight. But I wasn't afraid. I had asked for this.

Creedling bustled around the table and tapped a teaspoonful of the powder into the cup, then poured a measure of tea over it. The steam that curled up was thick and silver white.

"You understand that you will not be the only one to test this before it gets to the prince, unless something of negative occurrence takes place?" The king asked, his voice kinder than I had yet heard it.

"Yes, Your Majesty."

"If it proves effective, let it be agreed that a full twenty-four hours will pass before we administer such a mixture to the prince at all, to make sure that no adverse effects arise," he said to the table. "Should this cure work, we will need to make a similar test using Nemere."

"I volunteer to be dosed and tested with Nemere and the proposed cure, Your Majesty," Emric announced clearly.

I was unsurprised, but suddenly much more nervous.

"Agreed. Well, get on with it, girl."

I lifted the cup without hesitation, put it to my lips, and drank the hot liquid as quickly as possible. There was no bitterness, no flavor other than tea whatsoever. I worried that I had been tricked by the chemist.

Then, a wave of darkness washed over me, followed by a wave of delirious light. I gripped the edge of the table and blinked several times, struggling to keep my eyes open. My vision cleared, and then I felt perfectly normal.

"Did it work?" the king barked.

"I don't know yet," I answered uncertainly, as the fuzzy feeling in my brain receded.

Rosalie looked straight at me. "Cressida, where do you keep all of your weapons hidden?" I stared at her, keeping my mouth shut, but bracing myself.

Nothing happened. *Nothing.*

"It worked?" Emric's voice was hopeful. He leaned toward me. "Cressida, how do you feel?"

"I don't think I have to answer that," I said slowly.

I felt radiant. I felt *right.*

"Next," King Arctus said, waving at Creedling.

Another cup was brought to Rosalie, and Creedling administered the powder to her tea. She drank, and I felt a shiver run through me and prayed that nothing would go wrong.

"Miss Montshire, do you still have to tell the truth?" the queen asked a moment later. Rosalie said nothing, and I held my breath. "Miss Montshire, what color is your hair?" the queen prompted patiently.

"Pink," Rosalie responded with a nervous giggle. The queen smiled and looked at her husband as Father Harrick unexpectedly raised a cheer that caught on and resounded around the table.

"It would seem that Miss Hoth's hunch was a good one. How extraordinary," remarked Queen Ceridwen.

"Yes, I agree." King Arctus smiled in hesitant relief. "We wait twenty-four hours, and during that time, you ladies will report the slightest throat tickle, do you understand?" We both nodded. "Now. Creedling. A similar antidote must be developed to counteract the effects of the Nemere. Mr. Theon has agreed to test it for us."

"Yes. And, sire," Emric interjected, "if it works, another young lady in the palace will have need of it."

King Arctus sent a glance of exasperation heavenward, then shook his head. "Very well. Creedling." The stunned chemist shook himself from his daze and hurried out of the room.

"I have the remains of the Nemere that the prince took, Your Highness." Emric reached into his cloak and pulled out the bottle that he had taken to give to Roland.

"Indeed. How did the prince administer this? Under his own volition, I hope?" he queried somewhat severely.

"Yes, sir. I explained the situation to him and he, er, took a swig."

"The boy has secrets, eh? Just as well he protected himself." He hailed a pair of guards. "Have a cot brought in," he instructed. "We don't want you sleeping on the floor in a heap, lad."

The guards returned several minutes later with a cushioned bench. Emric stretched out on it, raised the Nemere to me with a wink, and drank the remaining drops from the thin vial. It took longer than a knife-prick would have done, but after a moment, his eyes drooped closed, and he was breathing deeply. A cold fear threatened, but I pushed it away, determined to have my wits about me.

Emric lay motionless on the cot while the royal council read through the evidence we had brought to them, pointing out incriminating material that damned Tepsom, Eston, and a handful of other families known to the court. I kept an eye on the steady rise and fall of Emric's chest, as Rosalie and I sat listening inconspicuously. Most of the names listed were from Porleac, but the count of traitors to Dernmont was sobering. I noticed that the king steered the conversation away from any specific questions about the mines, and the members of the council soon stopped asking.

"I need an audience with the king of Porleac as soon as possible," King Arctus muttered, shifting the papers before him. "I am inclined to believe he is unaware of this attempted warmongering, but we need to be sure."

"Our peace with Porleac has been uneasy in the decade since Warwick first struck, Arctus," the queen observed. "We need to strengthen the currently fragile state of our relationship before this incident weakens it even further. I think Roland can help us with that." They lowered their voices further.

Rosalie and I glanced at each other.

"She's already on her way," Rosalie whispered to me.

"What?"

"Vivian did some digging and learned more than we did—Prince Roland is in love with a woman from Porleac. That's who Elin is. That's his secret. She's a member of the royal household. Vivian used the prince's own messenger bird to send a letter urging her to come immediately. Quite bold of her, but timely."

I gaped at Vivian's audacity.

"Anyway, that should help kingdom relations, if they were to marry," Rosalie added. "Prince Roland's parents will actually want it now."

A guard entered the room and went up to the table, bending to speak into the king's ear. The king nodded.

"The dungeons for the lot of them, for now. Search them for any weapons or suspicious substances." The guard departed, and the king bent to talk quietly to his wife.

The better part of the night passed before the chemist returned with his mixture. When he finally did, it looked just like the smoky bottle of Nemere, but with a pearlescent trail swirling through it. The chemist dipped a thin dagger into the shimmering liquid.

"Is that necessary, Creedling?" the queen asked.

"It is the most expedient way, madam."

"All right. But do not cause unnecessary harm."

"Of course, Your Majesty." Creedling knelt next to Emric.

I hurried over and watched as he pricked the side of Emric's neck with the blade. A fat bead of blood welled up. I held my breath, as Emric's chest grew still.

Then, with a gasp, he was awake, and relief washed over me. The king leapt to his feet, and the previously sleepy council began to applaud. Emric shook his head, blinking slowly, and looked around.

"How do you feel?" I asked anxiously.

"I don't think I have to answer that," he answered with a rather lazy wink.

Tears surprised my eyes, and I smiled at him through them. I gripped his hand and held it tight.

"Miss Hoth, I am astonished," Creedling said. I turned to the small, wide-eyed man in surprise. "I don't know how you knew, but your supposition about the properties of vindeca stone was astounding. This means enormous things for the furtherance of our research. Great things can be accomplished." He raised his voice. "Your Majesties, I propose a center of research be established in Miss Hoth's name, to discover how we can best utilize and maintain this miraculous stone."

I opened my mouth in shocked dismay, but King Arctus held up a hand, looking slightly amused. "An excellent suggestion, Creedling." The king stood. "Miss Hoth." I automatically dropped into a curtsy before looking nervously up at him.

"Your Majesty?"

"The groom you killed in self-defense was presumably working for Lord Eston?"

I swallowed and willed myself to keep still. "Yes, Your Majesty. Eston said as much, and the groom confessed to spying for someone." Out of the corner of my eye, I could see Rosalie nodding vigorously.

"Then based upon your witness and the evidence I find in

these documents, I've decided it to be the best course to clear you of any wrongdoing. Let it be so recorded and declared in the presence of my council, that you are innocent of any crime."

"Thank you, Your Majesty," I whispered as a lump rose immediately to my throat. I curtsied again.

"Now," the king said briskly. "If you all will excuse me, I have a monastery to visit and a dungeon full of traitors to intimidate. I want the three subjects monitored. We will awaken the prince tomorrow. Good night to you all, and frankly, good riddance."

He helped Queen Ceridwen to her feet, and they strode purposefully out of the hall together.

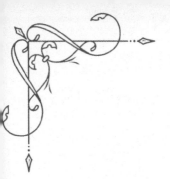

23

ROSALIE AND I WERE GIVEN

a chamber with two small beds in which to spend what remained of the night. Emric was in a nearby room on the same corridor. A couple of medics and a guard were placed outside our rooms, and the medics came in every hour to check our pulses and peer into our eyes and mouths. They didn't seem to know what they were looking for, but they performed the assignment earnestly. I slept deeply, then awoke to more prodding and checking. It carried on throughout the day, but late in the afternoon, Emric joined us in the sitting room that adjoined our chamber. Our meals were brought to us, and I found that I was thoroughly happy to relax and do nothing.

This was not to last, however. As dusk was settling, a knock sounded at the door and a pair of guards entered. Emric stood quickly.

"You're all summoned to the king's chambers for a hearing," one of the guards announced.

"A hearing for whom? Concerning what?" Emric's inquiry was sharp.

"A hearing for the traitors who invaded the monastery yesterday. The king has further business to attend to as well, and requires your presence."

I glanced at Rosalie and Emric, both looking as grim as I felt at this summons.

"Lead the way," Emric said shortly.

The guards led us through the palace, to a chamber that was near the Great Hall. I felt instantly self-conscious when we stepped inside. The chamber was small, round, and paneled in dark wood. It was silent as a tomb. The king sat at a vast desk of white stone opposite us, and his councilors, which numbered many more than we had seen yesterday, were seated around the room, stately in their heavy velvet robes. In the middle of the room stood Miss Tepsom and Lord Eston. Neither turned when we entered, but every other eye was on us for a brief moment.

"Sit, if you please," said the king. There were empty seats near the door, which we took immediately. We could see Tepsom and Eston in profile. Miss Tepsom's face was hard, her mouth a thin line. Eston's expression was one of mild surprise. The king addressed the traitors.

"You have been charged with crimes of conspiring against the crown and the kingdom of Dernmont. How do you plead?" King Arctus asked stonily.

Lord Eston gave a shallow bow. "First of all, Your Majesty, I would like to begin by stating that I have served your family loyally for years, and the very idea of treason has never entered my head. I understand you've been given correspondence which you consider evidence against me. But these are falsified documents, Your Majesty. I swear, by the name of Eston, a family who has proudly served as host to yours for so many summers, that I hold the crown in the highest of respect. Reverence, even."

I felt a curious tingling in my fingertips as Eston spoke, and I clasped my hands together on my lap, hoping that the king would not believe a word of those lies.

"You are aware, are you not, what the substance Verum can do, my lord Eston?" the king asked.

"I–I . . . believe its uses have never been put to so mean a task as questioning loyal subjects, Your Majesty," Eston said, his voice tight.

King Arctus smiled faintly. "Indeed? Well, we are re-examining its purposes and uses now that we appear to be in danger of having these substances used against us by a radical band of warmongering traitors. Eston, you may sit, if that is all you have to say in your own defense. The evidence against you is damning. Not only have we correspondence written in your own hand, and dating back many years that implicate you in this Warwick's aims, we have received several accounts, by trusted witnesses, of your attempts to stir up dissent in my court. You have gone as far as to cast doubt upon my own legitimacy, and the unfortunate state of my brother. My younger brother." The king's grey, bushy brows lowered so far as to knit together over the bridge of his nose.

"I–that is to say, these accounts are untrue–"

"Eston, I said you may sit," the king said firmly. A guard stepped forward and escorted Eston to a chair near the door.

"Now. What do you call yourself?" King Arctus asked Miss Tepsom.

"I am Lucretia Tepsom."

Immediately, my fingertips once more began to tingle, almost burn. I ignored them, listening tensely as Miss Tepsom continued to speak.

"I am the proprietress of a school of young ladies, two of whom have proven to be disastrous troublemakers. Your Majesty," Miss Tepsom's lips quirked up in cold amusement, "I'm afraid I am not at all surprised to find Miss Hoth and Miss Montshire in the middle of this story. I am guilty of no crime, but must apologize for allowing such misguided and intrigue-hungry girls access to your gracious court. I thought better of them." She turned her head deliberately and slid her eyes over Rosalie and me with contempt. I noticed with anxiety that some members of the council turned hard stares upon us as well.

"Please explain what you and Lord Eston were doing yesterday at Rounelith monastery with a score of my own men," King Arctus said sternly.

"I cannot explain the presence of your men, Your Majesty. Lord Eston and I—well, we have an understanding, you see. We have infrequent opportunities to be together, and he suggested that we meet at Rounelith. An innocent liaison, Your Majesty."

I glanced back at Eston, who stared firmly at the floor.

The king narrowed his eyes and spoke without mincing his words. "Miss Tepsom—or, should I say, Miss Warwick—I know who you are. I admit, I believed your organization to be completely dismantled as of a decade ago, when the last of its attempts to gain control of our mines was thwarted and your father was thrown into a Porleac prison. I wrongly believed that in unseating your leader and destroying all of the confiscated maps, you would be rendered unable to resume in this vein."

Miss Tepsom's face drained of color, but she said nothing. Eston had gone rigid.

"It was an oversight to lose track of all of Warwick's offspring," the king continued. "Your alias, and the name and purpose of your school, have been compromised, thanks to the collection of data from your own dwelling and one of your communication centers. Also, a list of your contacts has been apprehended. Although you have shown yourself unwilling to comply with our interrogation, you and Lord Eston will both be provided with counsel and a trial. Treason is punishable by death. Leniency will be considered if you agree to cooperate in our investigation into the further activities of your organization."

Miss Tepsom did not flinch, nor offer another word. A guard stepped forward and took her arm, and she and Eston were led, stone-faced, out of the chamber. I watched her as she passed, but she did not turn to look at either me or Rosalie again.

After the door clicked shut, the king gazed down at the surface of his gleaming desk for a long moment as his council waited in respectful stillness. I noticed, with some bewilderment, that Father Harrick sat a few seats away from the king and was beaming a joyous smile. The queen watched her husband, her expression one of patient serenity. Finally, the king looked up and cleared his throat.

"Most of you here today will be curious, no doubt, as to some of the charges laid before the two accused traitors I just questioned. You have heard references to mines and substances which you, presumably, know nothing about, and warmongering schemes pertaining to them." The king shifted infinitesimally and folded his hands on the desk. "There is a very good reason why these topics are a mystery to you. What I am about to tell you violates a treaty put in place several hundred years ago."

King Arctus cleared his throat and glanced over at Father Harrick, who nodded in encouragement. The entire council seemed to be holding its collective breath, members leaning forward in interest. I, too, waited in suspense for the king's next words.

"The two we just questioned are accused of having colluded with a radical, anti-Dernmont organization from Porleac, not affiliated with their royalty. They have murdered many Dernmont citizens in an effort to gain control of some very particular mines in our land, which are deeply hidden, well-protected, and highly secret. These mines contain substances, which, in the wrong hands, are very dangerous indeed." The line between his heavy brows deepened.

"I bear some responsibility for the disorder these mines have caused. About a decade ago, a series of murders occurred. Due to differences of circumstances, and in all ways seemingly unrelated, the general public did not notice anything amiss. But I was aware of their connection—the common factor of the mines on their lands. I was duped by a trusted advisor—I'll not speak his name, but a few of you will recall the man—who was aware of the mines and convinced me that upon the unfortunate deaths of some of their landowners which he, himself, had commissioned, the lands ought to be returned to the crown in order to provide the families some protection. His plan, no doubt, was to use his position to provide access to the object of his true allegiance—an operation known as Warwick, then headed by a very dangerous man indeed, whose daughter styles herself as 'Miss Tepsom.' My false advisor, and his operation, were thwarted by his own death, which took place under mysterious circumstances, conveniently after my own well-placed spies apprised me of his treachery.

"Warwick has been plotting ways to access the mines ever since, and fomenting rebellion in the meantime by putting it about that I've killed my own subjects in order to greedily reclaim their estates. Absurd." He snorted.

"Now, to the substances themselves. The treaty I spoke of—that is, the one I am violating at this moment—is called the Lementhe Treaty." The king smiled a bit wryly at the bemused expressions around his chamber. "Yes, lementhe—as in the traditional Evenfrost holiday drink. Perhaps I am not starting this right. Hundreds of years ago, Dernmont was well-known for the extraordinary properties that could be mined from our land. Legend even says that people traveled from great distances to experience healing from our mountain, and although there is little documentation on the veracity of that story, recent discoveries have proven it likely." His eyes flicked toward me for the barest instant before he continued, "The diversity of our people is owed to centuries of immigrants seeking healing or other results from the various elements, the most well-documented of these being called Verum, Lethen, and Nemere.

"Unfortunately, Dernmont's great appeal to some made her an enemy to others—namely, Porleac. As you know, Porleac has port access that we lack, and this put them in a position to make trade very difficult for Dernmont, as they attempted to gain from our land's good fortune by placing exorbitant taxes on harbor trade. Thus began a series of wars known as the

Dust Wars—so named originally because they began over taxes on powdered stone from our mines and, eventually, because these powders became the primary weapon used in battle."

I caught Emric's eye and saw the same excitement that I felt reflected in his expression. The weapons in the secret chamber, listed as outlawed in the scroll, were beginning to make sense. The room was completely silent as the council listened with rapt attention.

"In those days, Dernmont had alchemists of extraordinary prowess serving their royals, concocting various combinations of the substances in order to make more and more effective weapons. Nemere bulbs, when developed and wielded to the optimum effect, could wipe out scores of men at a time, sending them into a deep, wakeless sleep for which Porleac had no cure.

"One of these alchemists, armed with secrets of the highest caliber, turned against Dernmont, taking his knowledge and skills to the Porleacan king. Porleac had made a vital discovery, you see—a substance of their own, some sort of—"

"Mollusk shell!" Father Harrick piped up, enthusiasm written all over his ancient face.

King Arctus nodded courteously. "Thank you, Father, yes. A shell which, when ground to a powder and combined correctly with Nemere, was the deadliest weapon of all. Hundreds of Dernmontians were obliterated with one sling from a catapult, and the death toll became catastrophic. Dernmont alchemists eventually found their own way to duplicate the weapon, and with such ruthlessness, both kingdoms suffered grave losses. Finally, the reason for war having been swallowed up in the decades of bloody strife, a decision was reached. For the good of both kingdoms, the Dust Wars had to end. And so, we come to the Lementhe Treaty."

The king sighed heavily as his audience waited in captive silence.

"The first Evenfrost, a holiday of remembrance, memorializing those lost in the Dust Wars, was enacted alongside the treaty. The people were encouraged to put the messy wars firmly in the past, and to surrender and abandon all use of the various powders. It took many generations before the substances truly passed into legend, but finally, those legends all but disappeared. Only the most dedicated of scholars"—he nodded again to Father Harrick—"have managed to collect and preserve any evidence of this period in our kingdom's history. Otherwise, it is known as a cautionary tale to the crown and his heir alone, to pass on and protect the secret of the mines, and keep Dernmont from falling to such disaster again."

The king looked over at his wife, who nodded at him. Taking courage, he turned back to his council. "However, I have decided that we have had enough of such secrets, especially in light of the recent murders. Innocent landowners who knew no more than their neighbors, unless family history preserved the knowledge, have lost their lives because the secret of these mines never completely died out, particularly among those who would use it to harm Dernmont. As much as it pains me to betray the wishes of my father and forebearers, I believe that there must be a better way forward. It is time for Dernmont to know the truth."

Thus followed hours of councilors discussing their newfound knowledge. The king and Father Harrick answered as many questions as they were able, or were willing. It became clear to me, and likely to Emric as well, that King Arctus was either unaware, or had no intention of revealing a rather significant part of the story. If the scroll we read was to be believed, a kingdom-wide memory potion had been administered to the populace, and history had been rewritten at the time of the Lementhe Treaty. The people had not been encouraged to forget, they had been forced to do so.

Otherwise, he seemed determined to be transparent, and Father Harrick was downright eager to have the secret in the open. Long into the night, the king and his council discussed the matter of Dernmont's secret mines and plans for reintroducing knowledge of them to the kingdom. Their acceptance of our presence in the room baffled me, but I listened with awed attention. Finally, the council slowly began to disperse.

As we stood to surreptitiously slip out of the room, the king beckoned to us. "Please approach my desk, you three," he said, his voice tired but welcoming.

We stood before the smooth white desk, and I longed to reach out and touch it, certain that it was vindeca, cut from the mountain.

"How do you all feel?" he asked, looking us over. Dark shadows ringed his tired eyes.

"Fit, Your Majesty," Emric replied.

Rosalie and I nodded.

"Excellent. We are eager to use your antidote on my son," King Arctus said. "You have all been instrumental in uncovering a danger to our kingdom, and you have my heartfelt thanks. I understand that Miss Tepsom's schemes drew in some young women whose families were impacted by my own attempts to protect the mines and keep them a secret, as well as Warwick's treachery. The displacement of the families, and the secrecy, was intended for their own safety, as well as that of the mines. I see now that the pain of that ran deep, however, and I hope my explanation tonight is a start toward making amends."

He stood. "I propose a banquet be held in the honor of all of those families, during which I will offer my personal apology and attempt to make reparations." He paused, looking at each of us almost uncertainly, and I realized with shock that he was actually awaiting our approval on this idea.

"A thoughtful suggestion, Your Majesty," I said, and Rosalie and Emric concurred.

"Good. I cannot say yet what will become of the properties, as the mines are still dangerous locations, but something will be done. Until that banquet, at least—perhaps until the trial—will you all stay at my court? Your testimonies may be needed again."

We all nodded and murmured our agreement.

"That is all. You may return to your chambers until your monitoring period is over. You have my thanks." He smiled a genuine and warm smile, and I left the room with my head reeling.

Midmorning the next day, we were surprised when Vivian, Rubia, and Ambrosia arrived at our door, followed by two maids with heavily laden tea trays. I jumped up and hugged Vivian as Emric greeted his sister joyously.

Then, facing Rubia, I realized that I had no idea what to say to her. She looked well, but a little thin and pale. Her face was drawn into a frown.

"Rubia. Please have a seat," I said, indicating a chair by the fire. "Are you all right?"

"I'd be better if I hadn't been poisoned and then left for dead," she said flatly.

"Rubia, honestly." Vivian's chide was gentle. "We talked about this. I was with you the whole time, and Cressida found the antidote for you."

"No, she's right," I said, remorse prickling at me. "What I did was indefensible. I'm so sorry, Rubia. It was a terrible choice that I made in that moment. I can't tell you how relieved I am that you're all right. We could have used your skills when Miss Tepsom showed her true colors."

"I wouldn't have let her get to the monastery," Rubia said darkly, slanting her eyes up at me with a flash of her original mettle. "You know I'm technically a better fighter than you."

"I'd rather not put it to the test," I said, allowing a small smile.

"My brothers taught me," she said. A muscle pulled at the corner of her mouth, and my heart broke for her.

"They must have been the best of the best, then," I said softly.

She flashed a half-tormented, half-grateful grin for a moment and then looked away, scrubbing her eyes.

"Vivian, do you know if Roland is awake?" I asked as Rubia composed herself.

"We haven't heard yet. Medics came in and administered the antidote, and after monitoring Rubia for a bit, we were told we could visit you all."

"How did you find out about Roland's Porleacan lady?" Rosalie asked. "How did you know that sending for her was exactly what needed to happen?"

"I snooped around his room, that's all," Vivian said. "I was tired of not knowing anything, so I sneaked past snoozing guards and helped myself to a pile of love letters. Then I wrote to her and told her that Roland's life was at stake."

"Well, it's a good thing," Emric acknowledged. "His parents might not have approved the match before, but they'd give anything for it now. She's coming at the perfect time."

"I *am* a genius," Vivian proclaimed airily. "I also got Sylvie sacked after I caught her searching my room."

"On Eston's orders, no doubt," I said darkly. "He wanted the Verum." I hugged her again. "I'm so glad you weren't hurt!"

We sat down at the heaping tea table. Here with my friends, and the undercurrent of my curse gone, I felt warmer, more at home, and more myself than I had felt in years. Rubia quickly regained her spirit and asked innumerable questions about everything she missed. Halfway through our second pot of tea, someone tapped at the door. I realized that it had been a couple of hours since our medics had come to check on us. Emric opened the door, and in strode Prince Roland.

"Have room for one more?" he asked exuberantly, slapping Emric on the back.

We jumped up and curtsied.

"I can't tell you how thankful I am to all of you," Prince Roland said, smoothing his floppy hair and taking a seat. "I just got word that Elin is on her way, and my father is delighted. He's already read up on her family and says she's perfect. As if her family matters. I thought they'd never go for it because they've been pounding into my head for years that they wanted me marrying someone from here to endear us to our countrymen, or some such nonsense. I'm glad they think that peace with Porleac is more important now." He consumed three or four tea cakes while he spoke, and the feat was impressive enough to be distracting.

"Father has ideas for you lot, if you're interested. He's turning that sham school of Miss Tepsom's into a research center for the Verum and all the others, as well as the vindeca stone. He needs people willing to do some exploration, chart some decent maps, and collect specimens. The mountain's potential is untapped, and he believes that the caves on the far north side are worth exploring, as the stone there is reported to be as red as blood.

"And Miss Guildford," he turned to Vivian with a winning smile, "my father intends to start sending ambassadors to the royal court of Porleac as soon as possible and is hoping you will consider being our first. He's made the mistake of holding our closest neighbor at arm's length when, given our history and the threats from overseas, he would do better in strengthening the relationship."

We all sat in stunned silence while Roland rattled off his news and polished off our cakes. He looked up, suddenly aware of our expressions. "You're, of course, expected to give it some thought before you decide."

Vivian laughed in relief, and Emric looked at me, excitement dancing in his eyes.

"I could probably stand another journey with you," he said with a wink.

I felt my cheeks reddening, and Prince Roland threw back his head and hooted with laughter. We stayed at the table laughing and conversing until past sundown, although we thoroughly abandoned talk of everyone's futures. The present, for the first time, felt like the right place to be.

True to his word, the king held a banquet on behalf of all the families who had been displaced by his attempts to protect the mines and had lost family members to Warwick's schemes to gain control of them. It was strange, seeing many of my classmates, and putting our lessons of gentility into practice. Lessons that we had been taught by a traitor.

I felt the sting of rising tears as King Arcus offered his heartfelt apology, and wished as desperately as I ever had that my parents had not been among the victims. There were many tears also among the families gathered around the shining marble hall, but the crown's apology was graciously received.

"I suspected her all along, you know," said a silky-snide voice in my ear when the king had finished and the orchestra began an elegant piece.

I turned to see Marigold, resplendent in mauve and amethysts, standing at my elbow.

"Hello, Marigold. You suspected whom?" I asked innocently.

"Miss Tepsom, of course. I suspected her treachery. That's why I chose not to join the mission. I was her top pick, you know."

My fingertips began their strange tingling yet again, and I simply smiled at her in bemusement. I glanced over the couples gathering for the dance. Roland's engagement had been recently formalized, and his betrothed, Elin, proved to be a delight. She was diminutive and dusky, clad in yellow, and looked positively radiant with happiness as Roland swept her enthusiastically along the dance floor.

"Are you listening to me, Cressida?" Marigold asked impatiently.

"Oh yes," said Vivian, who sidled up next to me. "We do remember that you were a favorite of hers. This must be hard for you." She put a blue-gloved hand on Marigold's arm.

Marigold looked uncertain if she wished to accept the sympathy or not.

Vivian removed her hand and turned to me. "Emric's looking for you," she said sweetly, tilting her head toward the doorway.

I grinned at her, nodded pleasantly to Marigold, and sidestepped the growing number of swirling dancers on the marble floor. I nearly laughed as I caught Rubia's gimlet eye as Mr. Lupei spun her to the center of the floor, and one glance at her aggressive delight told me that she was fully recovered. My relief that my impulsive action hadn't harmed her permanently was perpetual.

Emric stood in the doorway, scanning the room. His skin glowed against his crisp white collar, and his eyes brightened when he saw me approach. I couldn't help but feel pretty in the crimson ball gown that I finally had a chance to wear. I was fully armed, in spite of no longer being an agent on a mission. It seemed a shame to waste the excellent wrist sheaths concealed in the draping sleeves.

Emric took my hand and, instead of proceeding to the dance floor, led me out of the vast, noisy hall. We didn't speak as we navigated the palace, and I was unsurprised when he headed up the narrow stairwell to the prince's solar. He did manage to surprise me, however, when he opened one of the large windows and climbed out, reaching back to help me follow.

We walked the cold, stone battlements that surrounded the outside of the prince's solar, looking out over miles of dark forest, silver rivers, and the winding, white mountain road.

"Have you had any . . . strange symptoms after taking the antidote for Nemere?" I asked him suddenly.

"Not yet. I mean, I don't much like the memory. It was isolated, rather like sinking sightlessly through a dark sort of mire. Not pure unconsciousness." He looked at me curiously. "Have you?"

"Maybe? I want to try something." I looked him in the eye. "Say something that's not true."

"All right. I think you look terrible tonight. A real, shocking mess." His eyes twinkled.

My fingertips began tingling again. So did my toes. I cleared my throat. "How about something unrelated to me? Something simple."

"Hmm. It's a lovely, sunny morning."

My fingertips tingled again. "I think I have a new . . . gift. I don't know what to call it." I looked at him uncertainly. "I can tell when someone is lying."

"That wasn't a particularly believable lie," Emric remarked with an eyebrow lifted in amusement.

"I know." I laughed. "But there are new symptoms that show up when someone lies to me."

Emric's eyes widened slightly. "Are they painful? Or dangerous?"

"No, nothing like before," I assured him quickly.

"Please don't tell anyone else," he said. "I mean, I would advise that you don't, even if it seems innocent. I don't want anyone trying to use you again for their own purposes."

I nodded, agreeing. It was a gift, perhaps, but possibly another sort of curse. A part of me yearned just to be normal for once. But at least this way, it would be much, much harder for anyone to take advantage of me ever again. We stood together in silence for a long time, Emric's arm around me, drawing me closer.

"Oh! I keep forgetting," he said suddenly. To my bewilderment, he turned and crawled back through the solar window. He was back before I had decided if I should follow or not. "Here."

He placed an old, faded shortbread tin into my hands. The only remaining tokens of my parents. Tears sprang to my eyes in an instant, and cooled on my lashes in the chilly wind.

"How did you get these?" I asked shakily. "We left them behind."

"I knew that guards would be sent to search for your false aunts, so I asked Roland to have a man retrieve them before the house was turned inside out. He agreed immediately, of course." Emric smiled down at me as I clutched the tin.

I hastily tried to wipe my tears.

Emric wrapped his arm around my shoulders again. "Have you thought over the king's suggestion? That we explore the mountain and help learn what there is to be discovered about it?"

"Yes," I said. "And I want to do it. I want to see more of this kingdom, and this mountain, and learn all its secrets."

"With me?" he asked.

"I guess so," I shrugged indifferently. Then I smiled and leaned against him, preferring to tell the truth. "Particularly with you."

He laughed then, and the rich, joyful notes were lifted by the swift breeze and carried away as he kissed me. We stayed on the battlements for a long time, looking over the mountain together.

THE END

ᴀCKNOWLEDGMENTS

For a book to come into existence, it takes a lot more than a little girl playing dress-up with her sister, dreaming up stories and pretending to be a writer. This girl wouldn't have had the courage to do more than pretend without the wisdom, enthusiasm, and loving support of some extremely special people. Heartfelt gratitude is owed to many, beginning with my husband.

Dan, thank you for your unconditional love, steadying words, and bear hugs. For working so hard, and then sending me to the library with my laptop and a latte. Thank you for being an ever-present, ever-patient listener and sounding board, a brilliant "ideas man," history and weaponry consultant, first editor, brainstorming buddy, plot disentangler, and an incredible cartographer! This book would not exist without you. Above all, thank you for being you and sharing this life with me. I love you.

To my children, thank you for bringing more love, laughter, and growth into my world than I thought possible. In my writing life, you watched me try and try again, and then celebrated with such genuine enthusiasm when my dream came true. You humble and delight me daily. I might work with words, but I'll never be able to find the ones that communicate just how much I love each of you.

To my parents, thank you for giving me a childhood that nurtured my imagination and love of reading. Thank you for being gentle, enthusiastic, and discerning readers and offering invaluable feedback when I put my unedited words into your hands. I love you.

To my siblings, thank you for making it so extremely hard for me to write from the perspective of a lonely character who is *not* surrounded by an incredible, goofy, loving family.

Jessica, thank you for always giving me an impressive example of a dedicated bookworm to look up to. Marissa, thank you for being my stalwart writing champion and first reader, a vital source of inspiration and brainstorming hilarity, and for all the love. Joseph, the fencing in this book makes sense because of you! You probably don't know how often your words of love, excitement, and support bolstered and uplifted me. Thank you. Leah, this story would have remained slumbering on my laptop if it weren't for you. Thank you for reawakening my spark to keep trying. For your emphatic support and enthusiasm, and a gazillion other reasons, you're kind of a big deal. Jeffrey, thank you for dropping off stacks of comic books for me to read when my head was overloaded with plot tangles, and for offering to read my book so many times. I know it's not your cup of tea, but the fact that you offered made me feel loved. To Audrey, Isaac, Joe, Lee, Sabrina, all of my precious nieces and nephews, and the rest of my extended family, I didn't know that familial love could expand so much, but you're living proof that there is no limit.

To friends that I am incredibly honored to know: Alexa, thank you for your godly example, loving encouragement, and astute advice. Joannah, thank you for many priceless years of passionate support, devoted friendship, and sushi dates. Lindsay, thank you for your perpetually generous encouragement, invaluable beta-reader prowess, and uplifting wisdom. This thank you is the abbreviated version. I thank Jesus for each of you!

To all of the wonderful people at Enclave Publishing, I am blown away by your warm welcome, professional expertise, and support. Steve Laube, thank you for your incredible vision of excellent and God-honoring storytelling, and for your wisdom, guidance, and collaborative generosity. From the bottom of my heart, thank you for taking a chance on my story. Lindsay Franklin, thank you for gracefully fielding endless questions and working tirelessly behind the scenes. Trissina Kear, I am thankful for your expert advice and brilliant marketing strategies. Lisa Laube, thank you for your thoroughness, direction, and gentle encouragement. Thank you to Emilie Haney for your beautiful and inspired cover design, and to Jamie Foley, for your exceptional work on interior, e-book, and ARC creation. Avily Jerome and Megan Gerig, your sharp eyes and proficiency are hugely appreciated. Stephen Smith, Lisa Smith, and everyone at Oasis Family Media, thank you for everything that you do. Nadine Brandes, Rachelle Nelson, Katherine Briggs, and Jasmine Fischer, thank you for your early readership and overwhelmingly positive example of gracious generosity. It means so much.

To the Enclave and *Truth Cursed* street teams, bookstagrammers, Facebookers, and readers who have cheered me on and helped me find my home as a debut author: Thank you for the inspiration and conversations, and for making me feel so welcome in the encouraging, world-brightening, bookish community of my dreams.

To the bats in the walls of my attic office: I am not thanking you for anything, you give me the creeps.

To you, reader: From the bottom of my heart, thank you for being here. You are a richly answered prayer.

And named last because words fail me, but truly first in everything: I thank my Creator and Heavenly Father. Every good gift comes from you. Yours is the only Truth, and it is good and beautiful. In the paraphrased words of J.R.R. Tolkien, thank you for making "everything sad come untrue."

ABOUT THE AUTHOR

Angie Dickinson is a lifelong lover of magical stories that point to hope and redemption. Growing up, she was obsessed with the romanticized lives of fictional writers such as Anne Shirley and Jo March, and the truth-laden wonder of imaginary worlds such as Narnia and Middle Earth. These influences planted the seed of a dream to create her own worlds and lovable characters one day.

She received a B.A. in English Literature and is now an author of young adult fantasy, living in the woods of Michigan with her heroic husband, their four children, a cat, and a startling number of books and swords.

Angie is saved by grace alone and is in awe of her Savior's unrestrained love. She is blessed by her big, boisterous family and is fond of Earl Grey tea, reading too late at night, and taking every opportunity to share her passion for fantasy and fairy tales.

IF YOU ENJOYED

TRUTH CURSED

YOU MIGHT LIKE THESE OTHER YA NOVELS:

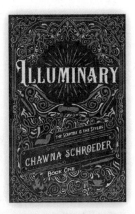